IDAHO!

The thirteenth thrilling novel in the saga of *WAGONS WEST*—true-to-life stories of high-spirited Americans who dared to leave safety behind as they pressed onward into the danger and excitement of vast, unexplored lands.

WAGONS WEST

IDAHO!

**A nation's destiny follows its boldest and bravest
into a majestic mountain land**

TOBY HOLT—

Riding at the head of peacekeeping Cavalry troops, this true
son of the West is determined to stem the tide of lawlessness
. . . even if he must fight to the death to do it.

CLARISSA HOLT—

The new first lady of Idaho finds her dreams of happiness
coming true at last . . . until an old nightmare returns.

ROB MARTIN—

Strong and handsome, he closes his eyes to one woman's
honest passion and falls into the darkness of another's wicked
desires.

PAMELA DRAKE—

An independent Englishwoman as good with a gun as she is
beautiful, she chooses to play a dangerous game of love.

EDWARD BLACKSTONE—
A dashing Englishman visiting America for the first time, his love for the West is equaled only by his love for a homeless young woman.

KALE SALTON—
A former courtesan, her lurid past is a barrier between her and the man she loves . . . a past she may have to repeat.

STALKING HORSE—
Loyal Indian companion of the late, famed Whip Holt, he forms a vital link between the white man's and the red man's worlds.

RUNNING BEAR—
Hot-headed young rebel of the Nez Percé Indians, his words urge his people to war; his hate demands death for his greatest enemy—Toby Holt!

CINDY HOLT AND HENRY BLAKE—
Young lovers separated by thousands of miles, their faithfulness will be tested by sweet, forbidden temptations.

WANG—
Huge, powerful hatchet man for a San Francisco tong, he yearns to avenge his honor by drenching the streets of Boise in the blood of the man who crossed him.

MURPHY—
A grizzled old miner whose best friends are a talking crow and a patient burro, he finds the gold he covets may be a deadly desire.

Bantam Books by Dana Fuller Ross
Ask your bookseller for the books you have missed

WAGONS WEST ★ THIRTEENTH IN A SERIES

IDAHO!

DANA FULLER ROSS

Created by the producers of
White Indian, Children of the Lion,
Saga of the Southwest,
and Haakon.

Chairman of the Board: Lyle Kenyon Engel

BANTAM BOOKS
TORONTO · NEW YORK · LONDON · SYDNEY · AUCKLAND

IDAHO!

A Bantam Book / published by arrangement with
Book Creations, Inc.

Bantam edition / August 1984

Produced by Book Creations, Inc.
Chairman of the Board: Lyle Kenyon Engel

ISBN 0-553-24256-3

Published simultaneously in the United States and Canada

PRINTED IN THE UNITED STATES OF AMERICA

H   0 9 8 7 6 5 4 3

★★ WAGONS WEST ★★

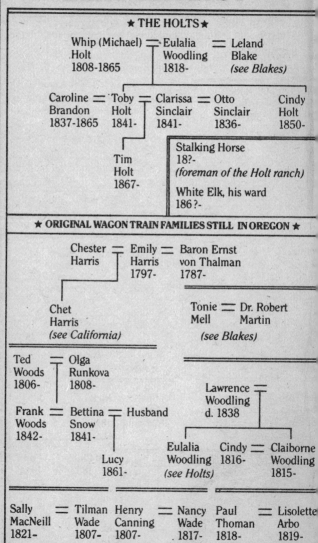

★ THE HOLTS ★

Whip (Michael) ⚊ Eulalia ⚊ Leland
Holt   Woodling   Blake
1808-1865   1818-   *(see Blakes)*

Caroline ⚊ Toby ⚊ Clarissa ⚊ Otto   Cindy
Brandon   Holt   Sinclair   Sinclair   Holt
1837-1865   1841-   1841-   1836-   1850-

Tim
Holt
1867-

Stalking Horse
18?-
(foreman of the Holt ranch)

White Elk, his ward
186?-

★ ORIGINAL WAGON TRAIN FAMILIES STILL IN OREGON ★

Chester ⚊ Emily ⚊ Baron Ernst
Harris   Harris   von Thalman
        1797-   1787-

Chet   Tonie ⚊ Dr. Robert
Harris   Mell   Martin
(see California)   *(see Blakes)*

Ted ⚊ Olga
Woods   Runkova
1806-   1808-   Lawrence ⚊
                        Woodling
Frank ⚊ Bettina ⚊ Husband   d. 1838
Woods   Snow
1842-   1841-

                 Eulalia   Cindy ⚊ Claiborne
                 Woodling   1816-   Woodling
     Lucy   *(see Holts)*   1815-
     1861-

Sally   ⚊ Tilman   Henry ⚊ Nancy   Paul   ⚊ Lisolette
MacNeill   Wade   Canning   Wade   Thoman   Arbo
1821-   1807-   1807-   1817-   1818-   1819-

★ ★ FAMILY TREE ★ ★

★ THE BLAKES, MARTINS, AND BRENTWOODS ★

Eualia
Woodling Holt
(see Holts)

= Leland
Blake
1804-

= Cathy
van Ayl
1814-1865

Sam
Brentwood
1797-

— Claudia
Humphries
1809-

Tonie = Dr. Robert
Mell   Martin
1814-   1798-

Rob   = Beth
Martin   Blake
1841-   1841-1869

Susanna = Andrew Jackson
Fulton   Brentwood
1837-   1839-

Hank Blake
(adopted)
1850-

Cathy
Martin
1869-

Samuel
Brentwood
1866-

★ LIVING IN IDAHO ★

Millicent   Jim
Randall   Randall
1845-   1843-

Edward
Blackstone
1840-

Pamela
Drake
1841-

Kale
Salton
1846-

cousins, from Baltimore   From England   From San Francisco

★ LIVING IN CALIFORNIA ★

Chet   = Clara Lou
Harris   Hadley
1822-   1823-

Wong = Wing
Ke   Mei-Lo
1809-   1835-

Heather   = Danny
MacGregor   Taylor
1828-   1823-

Melissa = Rick
Austin   Miller
1824-   1815-

Ted Woods
Taylor
1850-

Ginny (Virginia) = Hector
Dobbs   Mullins
1814-   1804-

Child
1853-

Child
1854-

Child
1849-

Child
1851-

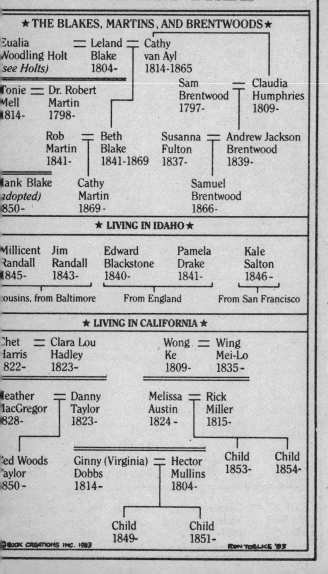

© BOOK CREATIONS INC. 1983   RON TOELKE '83

IDAHO!

I

By the late summer of 1869, people who lived within sight of the railroad tracks that now spanned America, from the cities on the Atlantic Seaboard to those on the Pacific Coast, had grown sufficiently accustomed to the trains rushing past that they no longer raced outside to watch them. These Americans now took it for granted that people or goods could cross the continent, not in three or four months as before, but in less than a week.

Certainly the curiosity of these people would have been aroused if they had realized that attached to the rear of one train making its way westward through the Rocky Mountains was a private railroad car. Such cars were as new as the transcontinental railroad itself and were reserved for the very well-to-do. This particular car was sumptuously furnished, with a bedroom at either end, two full baths, and a handsome sitting room, as well as its own dining room and kitchen. It was paneled with heavy, dark wood; there were glittering brass sconces on the walls; and thick, ruby-red carpeting imported from Persia covered the floors. A railroad porter was provided to make and serve the meals.

The car had been rented in New York for an indefinite period by Edward Blackstone, a debonair, polished young English gentleman, who had acquired it quietly, without fanfare. That was the way he liked to operate.

A lean and hard man, with dark hair and a pencil-thin mustache, Blackstone was quite wealthy. He had inherited a fortune, which he had multiplied several times by investing wisely and shrewdly. He was endowed with a quick, charismatic smile that caused men to like him and women to regard him as exceptionally handsome.

Always a realist, Edward had not rented the car to bolster a sense of self-importance but rather to become acquainted with the United States, where he had recently made some major investments. He found the railroad the fastest and most comfortable mode of travel and preferred renting a car for the sake of privacy. He was traveling now to Ogden, Utah, to pay a visit to his cousins, a Baltimore veteran of the Civil War, Jim Randall, and the dark-haired Millicent Randall, a flutist to whom music meant almost everything.

Accompanying Edward on the journey and occupying the second bedroom of the private car was his next-door neighbor in rural Sussex, Pamela Drake, an independent, free-spirited, and proud young woman. Most young ladies of the era would have scrupulously avoided traveling on such an intimate basis with a man for fear of compromising their reputations. But Pamela was indifferent to what people said about her.

Pamela, a beautiful young woman with wheat-blond hair,

shared Edward's restlessness and love of adventure. She was accompanying him on his journey because it provided her with a fresh sense of excitement and a life very different from the stultifying existence she led as daughter of a very wealthy and elderly industrialist who had retired to his lavish estate in the English countryside. She had been courted by any number of boring young English gentlemen, but her chief desire was to have fun, not to settle down with a man.

Actually, she and Edward had indulged in a brief affair several years earlier but had discovered that they had no sexual appeal for each other, although both of them were enormously attractive. Since that time, they had been content to enjoy a friendship that was far less personal.

Edward had completed his morning toilet and now sat in a horsehair-stuffed easy chair in his bedroom, looking out an oversized window at the magnificent panorama of Utah that unfolded before him. The sky overhead was a bright, dazzling blue, a color peculiar to the vast American West. In the distance, majestic, white-capped mountains rose to meet the sky, and nearby were endless, rolling hills. Here and there herds of wild horses or bison could be seen grazing, but there was no sign of human habitation in these endless acres.

Suddenly, for no discernible reason, the train began to move more slowly. Finally it ground to a jarring halt.

Flicking the lace cuffs that hung down over his hands, Edward adjusted the silk cravat at his throat, then stood and absently tightened the fringed tie of his velvet smoking jacket. Walking quickly to the bedchamber at the opposite end of the private car, he tapped politely at the door.

"Pamela," he called, "I'm going to find out why we've stopped. Do you want to come with me?"

3

"Of course!" she replied in her clear, English soprano. "I'll be with you in just a moment."

The door opened, and a smiling Pamela Drake emerged into the open. A critic would have said that her use of cosmetics was a trifle too lavish, that she used more rouge on her lips and cheeks and more kohl on her eyes than befitted a lady. Her dress of red and green silk fitted her a little too snugly, and its neckline was just a bit too low for good taste. Regardless, she radiated a clear, wholesome beauty.

As they walked together to the exit, Pamela asked, "Where are we?"

Edward chuckled. "As nearly as I can tell, my dear," he said, "we're in the middle of nowhere." He descended the train's steps, then turned and assisted her.

Pamela took his arm, and together they strolled up the track toward the front of the train. There, near the engine, they saw a knot of men conferring and recognized the train's passenger conductor. Talking with him and gesticulating wildly were several men in flannel shirts and heavy work pants, who carried long picks or shovels. They appeared to be laborers employed by the railroad line. As the couple drew nearer, it was plain to them that a heated altercation was in process.

"What seems to be the trouble, Mr. White?" Edward asked the conductor during a pause in the argument.

The man's voice shook with rage as he replied, "It's this work crew, Mr. Blackstone. They're supposed to be working for the railroad in the town of Ogden, but here they are, blackmailing us. They're demanding that we pay them a hundred dollars in cash, or they're threatening to tear up the line in front of the train and stop our journey right here and now."

"Oh, I say," Edward murmured. "Such conduct is strictly against the law, isn't it?"

The leader of the crew, a burly man with a barrel chest and hamlike hands, looked at the Englishman contemptuously. "Oh, I say," he declared, mimicking Edward's speech. "These naughty chaps are breaking the law, aren't they? I shall have to slap their wrists." Suddenly his tone changed, and his manner became menacing. "Go about your own business, mister, if you know what's good for you."

Edward's lips parted in a forced smile, revealing two rows of even, white teeth. But he made no move.

"Do something useful," the man snarled. "Take your doxy to bed and bounce her on the sheets, if you're able. If not, I'll take care of her myself as soon as I've settled my business with the engineer and conductor of this here train."

An ominous look crossed Edward's face. The wretch had insulted Pamela, which was going too far.

Enjoying himself, the other man addressed Pamela directly. "You look like you could tolerate some loving by a real man, honey."

Edward, his dark eyes fixed intently on the man, removed his smoking jacket and, after folding it with great care, handed it to Pamela. "I thank you for looking after this for me, my dear," he said, and then he removed his silk cravat, which he also folded and gave to her. As though he had all the time in the world at his disposal, he removed his gold cuff links, put them in his pocket, then carefully rolled up his sleeves above his elbows.

Watching him, the members of the work crew chuckled. But their laughter died in their throats when he suddenly whirled about, becoming a dynamo. His left fist abruptly lashed out, snapping the crew leader's head upward, and then his right crashed into the man's nose, causing it to bleed profusely. The man roared in pain and anger and then waddled forward, his movements bearlike as his arms flailed. Edward stepped nimbly inside his opponent's loose guard and struck two more blows, the first to the pit of his stomach, which doubled the man over, and the second to his chin, which straightened him again and caused him to lose his balance.

The bigger man was frantic, as well as furiously angry, and his arms were swinging wildly in roundhouse punches. Had one of his punches connected with Edward's chin, the fight would have ended then and there.

But the Englishman avoided the lethal blows and continued to pepper his foe with devastating punches of his own. Dancing effortlessly on the balls of his feet, he moved in and out, his fists flying so rapidly that it was impossible to follow them.

Blood began to trickle from a gash on the burly man's cheekbone, and one of his eyes became swollen shut. The man's blows became wilder but more feeble. It was clear that he was getting the worst of the confrontation.

Edward sensed precisely the right moment to end the fight. He moved in swiftly and launched a series of short, sharp jabs that rocked his opponent back and forth and finally sent him crashing to the ground, where he lay unconscious, blood streaming from his face.

Sighing gently, Edward took several backward steps, lowered his sleeves with meticulous care, and fastened them at his wrists with the gold cuff links. He took his clothing from

Pamela and smiled at her after donning his jacket and adjusting his cravat.

The woman returned his smile warmly. She showed no surprise over the development; she had obviously expected no other outcome of the fight.

Edward turned to the other line workers, who were staring at him openmouthed as he nudged their unconscious leader with the tip of one boot. "You may remove this person's body," he said, "and then please do clear the tracks. Mr. White, I would also appreciate your requesting the engineer to proceed. We're now behind schedule." Offering his arm to Pamela, he walked with her to the private car, helped her aboard, and then disappeared into it.

As was his custom, Ah-Sing, the Chinese man who for years had been the cook for Ralph Granger's ranch, had prepared a meal far too large for two people to eat. Granger, his former employer—from whose estate the cousins Millicent and Jim Randall had purchased the vast property—had always insisted on a variety of dishes. Ah-Sing had found it difficult to limit his meal preparations when the Randalls had purchased and taken charge of the ranch immediately after Granger's self-inflicted death nearly half a year earlier.

Standing in the doorway of the dining room, Millicent Randall looked with dismay at the platters and bowls of food that comprised the noon meal and absently tucked a wisp of dark hair into the mass at the crown of her neat head. She hated waste, and Ah-Sing's bounty disturbed her sense of propriety. Not that the food would really be wasted, of course; the ranch hands employed by her cousin, Jim, would be delighted to eat the roast beef, the browned potatoes, the four or five vegetables, and the enormous salad, not to mention the Chinese cook's generous dessert, which usually consisted of pie and ice cream. "Oh, dear," she murmured.

A suntanned Jim Randall, who wore a patch over one eye, had spent the morning riding the range and now, having washed up outside, came into the house for the noon meal. He heard his cousin sigh, and coming up behind her, he demanded jovially, "What's wrong, Millie?"

The woman sighed again. "Ah-Sing is just too much," she told him. "He insists on preparing meals for an army."

"The hired hands here eat better than the employees of any other ranch between Ogden and Salt Lake City," he replied, laughing.

Millicent stared at him indignantly. "It's no laughing matter!" she protested. "The expense—"

"Hang the expense," he told her. "Let's eat."

As Millicent took her place at the table opposite him, she knew she had no real cause for complaint. Never had she known anyone to adjust so well and so quickly to a completely new life, as Jim had. Instead of being a disgruntled, disabled veteran of the Civil War, living in idleness in their native Baltimore, Jim had become a self-confident, successful rancher, who, despite the loss of an eye, was proving to be good at his chosen vocation.

Jim began to carve the roast, while Millicent ladled potatoes and vegetables onto their plates and then served the salad. At that moment they heard the hoofbeats of an approaching horse, which halted near the hitching posts outside the front door. Millicent looked at her cousin and raised an eyebrow, but Jim shrugged and continued to carve the meat.

A few minutes later Ah-Sing came into the room, treading

softly in his felt-soled slippers. "Mr. Burns come to see you," he said.

The cousins looked at each other blankly.

"He work for Judge Brennan," Ah-Sing explained.

Jim Randall's face cleared. "Of course." U.S. Circuit Court Judge J.B. Brennan, who visited Ogden frequently, had a young law clerk named Burns. "Show him in, Ah-Sing."

Moments later the young law clerk came into the room, full of apologies for disturbing them at a meal. The cousins would not acknowledge his arrival as a disturbance, though, and Jim insisted he join them for dinner, which pleased Millicent, for less of the abundant meal would be going to waste.

They heaped the young law clerk's plate high, but their generosity seemed only to add to his discomfort. "I—I have some bad news, and I don't quite know how to break it to you," he said.

Jim nodded complacently as he skewered a choice bit of beef with his fork.

"Old Ralph Granger," Burns said uncomfortably, "killed himself too soon when he heard that his nephew was killed in that stagecoach ambush, because Paul Granger—the young fellow who graduated last spring from Yale College—turned up at the judge's office today, and he's very much alive."

Jim lowered his fork to his plate, the beef on it untouched. "You say that Paul Granger is alive?" he asked blankly.

"Yes, sir," Burns said. "It seems that young Granger's name was mistakenly put on the list of passengers, and of course after the Indians got through with their massacre of those on the stagecoach, there was no way to identify any of the bodies. No, the fact is young Granger was delayed back

East and came out on a later stage, and he showed up today. Now he wants to know what he has to do to get hold of this property, which his uncle left him under the terms of his will.''

Jim grasped the edge of the table with both hands, his knuckles white beneath his tan. "Paul Granger won't have to go to court for any property that's rightfully his," he said hoarsely. "All I want in return for this ranch is the money that we put into it, plus the extras we spent since we've acquired it."

The law clerk was greatly relieved. "Judge Brennan was sure you would feel that way," he said. "He told Granger that if ever there has been a gentleman in Utah, you're it, Mr. Randall!"

A scant two hours later the cousins were seated in the chambers of a sympathetic Judge Brennan. Jim Randall was grim-faced and tense, while Millicent succeeded only in showing utter bewilderment.

"Paul Granger," the judge said, "is every bit a gentleman, just as you are, Jim. I conveyed your offer to him, and he accepted it with thanks. Just let me know what he owes you for improvements and such, and he'll write you a bank check immediately from his uncle's estate, which I'll then validate as a trustee. Of course, the money you paid initially for the property will be refunded to you by the territory of Utah, which was administering Granger's estate."

Jim wearily took a sheet of paper from an inner pocket and unfolded it. "Here," he said, pointing, "is what we paid for the ranch, as you will have down in your own records. And here is what we laid out for the herds and for the improvement of the house. All we want is to get our money back.

10

Well," he added, looking sadly at Millicent, "there go our dreams."

"These figures are correct and fair," the judge replied. "I neither question nor dispute them in any way."

"I'd like to make one thing very clear, Your Honor," Jim said. "This has been a severe blow to us, as you well know, but Millicent and I are determined to buy another ranch, whether in this area or elsewhere in the West, we don't yet know. That will depend on what's available."

The judge nodded.

"Ah-Sing, the cook we inherited when we bought the ranch, wants to come with us wherever we go," Millicent blurted, "and I've promised him that no matter where we settle, he has a job."

"The same is true of the ranch hands," Jim added. "All of them came to us just before we rode into town for this meeting with you. They said they want to come with us, no matter where we may go, and foolishly or otherwise, I promised them that there would be places for them wherever we land."

"I'm not in the least surprised to find your employees showing you such loyalty," the judge said, "and I wish you well in whatever enterprise you may undertake. I'm quite certain that Paul Granger joins me in that wish."

Lights were burning in virtually every room of the large house at Fort Vancouver, Washington, the home of the commanding general of the Army of the West, Major General Leland Blake. He was scheduled to leave the next day for a visit to the Eastern Seaboard, where he would confer in Washington City with President Ulysses S. Grant and with the army chief of staff, General W. T. Sherman, before going on to the United States Military Academy at West Point to see his adopted son, Henry, who was a cadet there.

Two open wardrobe trunks stood in the center of the master bedroom, and gaping suitcases lay on every available piece of furniture. The dignified General Blake, whose uniforms and civilian clothes were already stashed away in a single, modest-sized case, shook his gray head and grinned as he looked at his busy wife, who was methodically checking items off a list as she packed them.

Dark-haired Eulalia Blake, widow of the fabled Whip Holt, was expending some of her seemingly inexhaustible energy as she prepared for the journey. Her husband, the only man on earth who dared to tease her when her mind was occupied, continued to smile at her. His great love for Eulalia was what sustained him now after the tragedies of losing his first wife, Cathy, and then their daughter, Beth.

"Just because we're going east by train doesn't mean we'll have an entire baggage car at our disposal," the general now said mildly.

"I'll need one evening dress for dinner at the White House," she said, flashing him a reproving look with her violet eyes, "another for our dinner with General and Mrs. Sherman, and a third for the reception at West Point that will follow the review in your honor. Plus one in reserve, in case any of the parties being given for us in New York City require formal dress."

"I'll be wearing the same dress uniform to all those occasions," he replied, one corner of his mouth raised in a teasing smile. "I don't see why you couldn't get along with just one evening dress."

Eulalia sighed in exasperation, looked at him, and suddenly began to laugh. "You may be able to maneuver a dozen divisions at a time brilliantly, General Blake," she said between giggles, "but in over a half-century of living, you've learned next to nothing about the dictates of fashion!"

The tall general accepted defeat gracefully. "It was just an observation," he murmured.

The bedroom door opened, and Eulalia's nineteen-year-old daughter, the pretty, vivacious Cindy Holt, burst into the room. Over one arm she carried an evening dress of peach-colored satin, and in the other she held a delicate gown of off-white lace. Cindy was to accompany the Blakes for this special trip east before resuming her studies at Oregon State College.

"Hello, Papa," she said, kissing Lee on the cheek. "You're home early tonight." Turning to her mother, she held up both dresses. "Which of these should I wear to the gala at West Point?"

"I see no need to decide that now," Eulalia replied, brushing a loose strand of sandy-colored hair from her daughter's face. "You have room for both of them in your trunk, so pack them, and when the time comes, we'll decide."

Not satisfied with her mother's answer, Cindy turned to the general. "Which do you think Hank will prefer, Papa?" she asked, holding up the two dresses for his inspection.

There was no need for Lee Blake to ponder long and hard. His adopted son, Cadet Henry Blake, formerly Hank Purcell, corresponded regularly with Cindy, in spite of the exceptionally busy life he led at the military academy. "If you really want to know, Cindy," he said quietly, a twinkle in his eyes,

"Hank will think you look perfectly lovely if you show up for the party wearing a burlap gunnysack."

Cindy did not appreciate his sense of humor. Turning beet red, she stamped her foot. "Really, Papa!" she said, and swept out of the room.

Eulalia paused in her packing long enough to smile and shake her head. "Cindy and Hank are in earnest about each other," she said. "Neither of them sees anything amusing in their relationship."

"So I gather," Lee replied, and sighed gently. "This enforced separation is good for both of them, I believe. If they continue to feel as they do now, we'll have a real family wedding on our hands when Hank is commissioned in another three years."

The ringing of the front door bell sounded up the stairs from the front hall.

"That must be Toby and Clarissa," Eulalia said, referring to her son and daughter-in-law. "I told you they're coming for supper tonight and bringing little Tim with them, didn't I?"

"Indeed you did, and I'm very pleased," he said, starting toward the bedroom door. "Their visit will save me a good deal of valuable time. I need to discuss some official business with Toby."

"In that case, send Clarissa up here. She can help me pack, and we'll keep my grandson out of your way while you and Toby attend to your official business."

He smiled, knowing she sought any excuse to visit privately with her small grandson.

One of the general's aides had admitted the Holts, who had gone into the living room.

With each passing year, Lee thought, Toby Holt's resemblance to his father, Whip Holt, became stronger. Whenever he saw his stepson, Lee was reminded of Eulalia's famed first husband, and of the horrible landslide in which Whip Holt had died. His own first spouse, Cathy, had perished in the same accident, and he and Whip's widow had been drawn together in their mutual grief. How fortunate he felt to have acquired such a wonderful family along with his attractive wife.

Lee had never seen the redheaded, statuesque Clarissa look happier, and he reflected that although the couple had recently suffered some severe marital problems, their troubles appeared to be past.

Their two-year-old son, Timothy, was usually unable to stand still for even a moment, but he obviously had been coached by his mother for this occasion. She whispered something to the child, and he immediately stiffened to attention and raised his right hand above his eye in a creditable version of a salute.

Lee gravely returned the salute, then swept the child off his feet and hugged him before kissing Clarissa and shaking hands with Toby. "You and your son are invited to our bedroom to help your mother-in-law finish her packing," he said to Clarissa. "I hope you can create some order out of the total chaos that exists up there."

Toby laughed and shook his head. "I doubt it," he said. "Our own house has been looking like it was attacked by an eggbeater ever since I got my new appointment."

Clarissa grimaced and playfully stuck out her tongue before she gathered her child in her arms and disappeared up the stairs.

Lee went to a sideboard and began to prepare drinks. "I

haven't seen you, Toby, since President Grant appointed you military governor of the Idaho Territory. Accept my congratulations.''

His stepson laughed ruefully. ''From what I've heard of the territory,'' he said, ''I'm not sure whether to accept congratulations or condolences. The presence of rebellious Indian tribes, together with the crooks and criminals attracted by the gold and silver mines, apparently has made Idaho a wild country.''

Lee handed Toby a drink, then sat opposite him in an easy chair. The stars on Lee Blake's shoulders gleamed in the light of the fire burning in the hearth. ''I must admit,'' he said, ''that you'll be wise to brace yourself for what lies ahead. An extremely difficult time awaits you, from what I've been told.''

''I've been studying the short history of Idaho,'' Toby replied, ''and I realize that I'm going to be inundated with troubles. Governor after governor has had difficulties, and because of them, few have held office for more than a year. Some have resigned because they've been unable to tolerate the primitive conditions. Others have been discharged by the federal government for graft and other crimes, and still others have simply disappeared. I presume they went off to seek their private fortunes, but they may have been killed by people whom they antagonized. Idaho is such a primitive country.''

''That it is,'' Lee replied. ''I've been ordered by the War Department to help you to the best of my ability. Specifically, I'm going to provide you with two full battalions and a number of half-battalions and independent companies—a total of fifteen hundred men in all.''

"That should certainly help," Toby said.

"The largest units," Lee continued, "will be commanded by lieutenant colonels, but you should have no problems with seniority."

Toby looked at him questioningly.

"As military governor, you'll hold the rank of full colonel, so the troops will be under your direct command."

Toby laughed uncomfortably and ran a hand through his sandy-colored hair. "I was mustered out of the service as a captain," he said, "and suddenly I'm going to be a colonel. That's quite a jump. I hope I can handle the responsibility."

"I'm sure you'll do well," his stepfather told him. "You'll be making most of your decisions in the political realm, and for military affairs I'd urge you to lean on your lieutenant colonels for advice. As regular army officers, they're experienced in Indian fighting and in mob control, and you know I'll stand behind you all the way in your dealings with the Indians."

Toby sighed. "I was flattered when President Grant gave me my appointment, but the more I learn about Idaho, the more I suspect that he's turned me loose in a hive of angry bees."

General Blake's boat and crew transported Toby and Clarissa Holt and their son across the broad, swift-moving Columbia River to the Oregon shore, where their own horses awaited them for the short ride to the extensive ranch that had once belonged to Toby's father. Toby held his sleeping son in one arm as he mounted his stallion and fell in beside his wife.

Clarissa was still aglow from the excitement of the evening. "Your mother," she said, "is so proud of you that she's ready to burst. Twice tonight she mentioned that at your age even your famous father didn't hold as responsible a post as you've been given. I must admit that I'm as proud of you as she is. But I don't know that I'll ever grow accustomed to being the first lady of Idaho.''

Toby smiled and said quietly, ''You wouldn't be quite so eager to see me in the governor's chair if you had heard the general and me discussing our future in Idaho. There's no rougher, more dangerous region anywhere in America. The Indians of the area are hostile. The white population includes large numbers of men with criminal records, who will automatically regard me as their number-one enemy. The territory is enormous, and though President Grant and General Blake have given me their full support, I still feel my authority is limited and that I'm being given too few federal troops to maintain order effectively.''

Clarissa shook her head. ''The worst danger we ever faced came to an end when Otto Sinclair disappeared down that cliff high in the mountains when you and he were fighting for your lives. Any other troubles we may face will be mild by comparison!''

Silently Toby reached out to Clarissa, who was riding beside him, and stroked her arm. Otto Sinclair had been her first husband, and she had suffered a terrible shock when he had appeared out of the blue years after the War Department had reported him killed in action in the Civil War. He had tried to blackmail her and had so frightened her that she had spent many months living in terror. Not until Sinclair had attacked Toby, instigating a fight that climaxed with the blackmailer's supposed falling to his death from a mountaintop, had Toby learned the truth about his resurrected predecessor.

After hearing of Sinclair's efforts to terrorize Clarissa, Toby had understood his wife's strange behavior of the months past, and the two of them had been able to restore to their marriage the trust and affection that had been lacking for so long.

The trio arrived home without incident, and Toby handed the sleeping boy down to Clarissa, who took him off to bed. After taking both horses to the stables and turning them over to one of the stable hands, Toby wandered into the kitchen. To his surprise he found his ranch foreman, Stalking Horse, waiting for him there.

The Indian was a Cherokee brave who had been the late Whip Holt's intimate friend and close companion on the long journey they had made together when they had guided the first wagon train across North America to Oregon. Stalking Horse had become the foreman on his friend's ranch when Whip had settled in Oregon, and the Indian had served faithfully for many years in that capacity. Now his hair was gray and his skin had become wrinkled, but he continued to stand straight and tall and spent many hours in the saddle every day.

Toby poured the foreman a glass of apple juice, his favorite beverage. Then the two men sat opposite each other at the kitchen table.

Toby knew it was highly unusual for the Cherokee to seek him out after ten at night, and he was consequently somewhat on edge. "Do you have a problem, Stalking Horse?" he asked.

"No, no problem!" the Indian assured him. "No trouble."

Toby's earliest memory was of Stalking Horse teaching him to ride, and he knew better than to try to force the older man to reveal his thoughts prematurely. He would have to be allowed to express himself in his own way and in his own good time.

"For many moons," the Cherokee finally said, "thoughts have crowded the mind of Stalking Horse. Now the son of Holt has been made the chief of all who live in the territory of Idaho, and much is changed. The thoughts of Stalking Horse have become clear."

Toby exerted his patience to the utmost. "It may be," he said, "that Stalking Horse wishes to share his thoughts with the son of his old friend."

"That is true," the Indian said, and stared silently into space.

Toby nodded and waited.

At last the old warrior stirred. "For many moons," he said, "Stalking Horse has supervised the work of the men who raise horses on the ranch of his blood brother, Holt. Many years have passed in this way. Others who work at the ranch have grown strong and wise, but they continue to take orders from Stalking Horse." He inhaled sharply. "Now Stalking Horse is sad. His spirit yearns to be wild and free in the wilderness that he knew and loved in his youth. He longs for the smells and sounds of the forest, for the taste of deer meat when it's cooked soon after a kill."

Toby became alarmed. "Are you saying you want to resign or retire?"

"No! Never!" the Cherokee exclaimed. "As long as there is life and breath in the body of Stalking Horse, he will continue to work for the son of Holt."

Toby felt greatly relieved. The older man had been so

much a part of his life that Toby knew he would be lost without him.

"Soon Toby will go to Idaho, where he will see snowcapped mountains always in the distance. He will find great mountain ranges and deep gorges. He will see swiftly flowing rivers and gentle streams. He will listen to the thunder of high falls and will look at broad, placid valleys and narrow ravines. He will see deep forests, fertile farmlands, and other lands suitable only for cows and for horses. He will also find parched deserts, where only prickly cacti grow. He will breathe the pure air of Idaho, one of the last great frontiers of America."

Toby saw Stalking Horse's eyes shine as he described the land he had not visited in many years. "You want to go there?" he asked.

The Indian nodded. "Soon you will leave for the Idaho country," he said. "After you have been there for a time, you will settle there, and you will establish your roots there. When you are settled, perhaps you will send for Stalking Horse and will allow him to roam as he pleases through the wilderness."

"I can think of nothing that will give me greater pleasure," Toby said, and each clasped the wrist of the other, Cherokee style, to bind and validate their agreement.

Visitors' hours were ending, the relatives and friends of patients leaving for their homes, and Portland Hospital, the only institution of its kind in the young state of Oregon, began to grow quiet for the night.

Suddenly the loud, insistent clanging of a patient's bell broke the silence, and the three nurses on duty exchanged weary glances.

"It's Mr. Thomas again," one of them said.

There was no need for further explanation; the other two knew precisely what she meant. The patient who called himself Lionel Thomas was a trial to the entire staff. Plentifully supplied with funds that he carried in a money belt around his middle, he was the sole occupant of a private room, where he was recuperating from broken ribs and severe bruises incurred, he said, from an accident when he was thrown from a wild horse and was nearly trampled to death. During the weeks he had spent in the hospital, no one had come to visit him, and he had received no mail. The nurses could well understand why.

When he was in an ugly mood, which was the better part of the time, Lionel Thomas cursed, shouted, and ranted at the staff, and nothing they did could please him. Then his mood would change, and he would become lascivious, an attitude the women of the hospital staff hated even more. Nurses were forced to flee from his room when he made passes, and several of them had had narrow escapes.

"I'll go to him before he awakens every sick person in the place," the chief nurse said primly. She started down the corridor, her starched white skirt crackling.

Otto Sinclair, a patient at the hospital under the assumed name of Thomas, continued to ring the bell furiously. It did nothing to assuage his feelings, but he knew it disconcerted the staff, and he took a perverse pleasure in knowing that they would be upset. He was growing increasingly impatient as the time for his discharge drew near, and he found he could relieve his feelings best by taking out his frustrations on those around him.

The chief nurse poked her head into his room. "I hear you,

Mr. Thomas," she said severely. "I'm sure that everyone else in the hospital is aware of your presence, too, and the fact that you're trying to summon someone."

He glared at the woman. "Damn your eyes, you bitch!" he shouted. "You're trying to starve me to death. It's been more than an hour since I reported that you forgot to bring me my dessert tonight. How do you expect me to regain my strength if you insist on starving me?" He scratched the new, full beard he was growing to help change his appearance.

The nurse surveyed him coolly. "Frankly, Mr. Thomas," she said, "I'd be infinitely relieved if you did starve to death. I'd be spared your abuse, and so would everyone else around here."

Sinclair was startled by her show of spirit, and he chuckled. "I like a wench with spirit," he told her. "Come over here, and I'll give you a reward you won't forget."

The woman made no move. "For your information, Mr. Thomas," she said frostily, "I have recommended to the staff of physicians that you be discharged from the hospital immediately as completely cured. I've seen you sneaking into the kitchen at odd hours for food, and I've watched you prancing about the corridors when you think no one is awake."

He glowered at the nurse, but she ignored him. Instead she picked up the hand bell from his bedside table and left the room.

Little by little Otto Sinclair's rage subsided. To hell with the nosy woman and her whole, useless staff. Perhaps it was just as well that the doctors were on the verge of discharging him. He was due to leave in any event; he knew that the time had come for him to seek his destiny elsewhere. His bones had mended, his bruises had vanished, and he was emerging into the world again as good as new.

Better than new, he thought, because once again he was presumed dead. All to the good. That made the task that awaited him that much easier.

Just that evening he had read an article in the Portland newspaper that had enabled him to complete his plans. Toby Holt, Clarissa's second husband, who had come within an inch of killing him in the mountains, had been appointed military governor of Idaho and was being escorted, along with his family, to his new post by the Twenty-ninth Battalion of the U.S. Infantry. Sinclair intended to dye his hair and beard and then enlist in the Twenty-ninth Battalion under his assumed name. He had achieved the rank of sergeant in the Civil War, so he had no doubt that he would act acceptable enough for the army to take him.

Once a member, he would await his chance, and then he would shoot down Toby Holt in cold blood. As a matter of fact, he would be using arms and ammunition supplied to him by the U.S. government, and he relished the irony.

After Holt was dead, he would change his hair to its natural color, shave off his beard, and reappear as himself. Then, after claiming Clarissa as his wife, he would inherit the fortune left to her by Holt, including the ranch property in Oregon, the lumbering property in Washington, and Holt's share of the gold mine he and his partner Rob Martin owned in Montana. No one would be able to dispute Sinclair's right to claim his legal wife's acquired property.

The thought of the good life that awaited him lulled Sinclair, and because of this, his last night in the hospital became bearable. He extinguished the oil lamp on his bedside table and fell into a dreamless sleep.

Wang, the three-hundred-pound hatchet man for a San Francisco tong, inspired terror just by appearing in public. He stood six feet, six inches tall, but in spite of his great bulk, he was not overweight. Most men could not compete with him in trials of strength, but Wang also possessed another advantage. As he went about his business—that of enforcing the will of the tong on the Chinese people of San Francisco—he was totally unscrupulous and would resort to any extreme in order to force his will on his victims.

Wherever Wang went in Chinatown, its inhabitants shook with fear. On this late summer morning, the owner of a noodle emporium and the proprietor of a curio shop cut short their friendly conversation and vanished into the dim recesses of their respective establishments when they caught a glimpse of the giant, moving mountainlike down the street. Three small boys playing a complex game with match sticks in the gutter stared at him in silent awe, and a young woman, having her fingernails painted in the window of a beauty parlor, hastily drew the bamboo blind.

Stark silence accompanied Wang on his walk, and after he had passed, a tremulous breath was drawn by those whom he had left unmolested.

If he was aware of the dubious honor that the frightened residents of Chinatown paid him, Wang gave no sign of it. He walked purposefully to the restaurant that served as headquarters for the wealthiest and most powerful tong in North America, and when he had disappeared into its inner recesses, life gradually returned to normal on the busy streets of Chinatown.

In spite of his great bulk, Wang climbed the steep stairs with agility and speed and walked quickly to a room at the rear of the second floor, where three frail, elderly Chinese men, all of them dressed in black, awaited him.

The hatchet man bowed respectfully before them, and his air of subservience was no pose. Not only did he have the traditional reverence of the Chinese toward their elders, but he also displayed additional homage in this particular case, for he knew he was dealing with the three leaders of the tong, men whose word was absolute law and who ruled the entire Chinese community of San Francisco.

They nodded complacently, accepting his obeisance as their due. "You asked for this meeting, Wang, and we are here," one of them said. "You may speak."

Wang stood erect before them and tugged at the hem of his simply cut tunic. "Revered fathers," Wang said, again bowing deeply, "I devote my life to doing your will. When you decree that the merchants of this community pay a tax into the coffers of the tong, it is I who make certain that each and every one of them complies. When you rule that an individual must as a punishment be whipped—or must lose an arm or a leg—it is I who inflict that punishment upon him."

He would have continued at length in the same vein, but one of the elders interrupted him. "We suffer no doubts regarding your loyalty or your devotion to the tong," the wizened old man said. "What is it you want?"

"The revered fathers," Wang continued, "will recall sending me to the territory of Utah to persuade our countrymen working on the railroad lines there to stop work and to otherwise hamper the building of the railroad. It is no secret that I suffered disgrace and humiliation when I was driven out of the territory by Toby Holt, who took my hatchet from me and threatened to kill me unless I departed from Utah at once."

The elders nodded, and although they were hard, unfeeling men, they looked at him sympathetically.

"I have hated Toby Holt with a terrible vehemence, and my soul has yearned for revenge against him. Now I have my opportunity. I have read in the newspapers that he has been appointed military governor of the Idaho Territory. There is no wilder or more lawless area in all of the United States. My opportunity for vengeance lies before me brightly, and I cannot afford to miss it. I crave the understanding of the revered fathers, and I beg you to grant me a leave of absence from my duties here so that I may follow Holt to Idaho and there dispose of him. Only when he lies dead at my feet will my honor be restored."

The old men looked at each other, seeming to exchange thoughts without speaking.

"The favor is granted to you, Wang," one of them said. "Take a leave of absence with our blessings, and do not return until your hands are red with the blood of Toby Holt."

"Take your time," another of the elderly men said, "and exercise patience. Do not make your presence known to this Holt until you are sure you will succeed in your goal of killing him."

Rob Martin sat in the comfortably furnished private compartment of the train that was taking him from San Francisco to Ogden, Utah, from which point he would take the stagecoach north to Boise. Rob was immersed in government studies about life in Idaho. For the first time since the tragic death of his wife, the former Beth Blake, he felt a surge of genuine anticipation. He had accepted the offer of his lifelong friend and business partner, Toby Holt, to serve as lieutenant governor of Idaho and was en route to the city of Boise to take up his duties there. Like Toby, he would face great challenges in his new position, and he looked forward to meeting them. A new and different chapter of his life was about to unfold.

The red-haired Rob glanced through the open door to the adjoining compartment and told himself, not for the first time, that he was most fortunate despite the loss of his wife. There, sleeping soundly in a crib, was his nine-month-old daughter, Cathy, and beside her, reading a book, was Kale Salton, his daughter's governess. An extraordinarily attractive and vivacious former courtesan, Kale had given up her profession in order to care for her friend Beth's baby. As Beth was dying, she had begged Kale to look after little Cathy, and Kale had agreed, accepting the charge as a sacred trust.

Rob was thoroughly familiar with Kale's background. In fact, at her instigation, they had slept together once when she had tried—with great success—to teach him a lesson about the meaning of fidelity in marriage. Now, looking at the charming woman, feeling pleased that she no longer used a lot of cosmetics or dressed garishly, he told himself he was very lucky. Nowhere could he have found a more devoted governess for his infant child.

There was one aspect of the situation that Rob did not know. Lacking worldly experience, he had no idea that Kale was motivated by more than her promise to Beth—that, in fact, she was head over heels in love with him.

Kale became conscious of Rob's gaze fixed on her, and raising her head, she smiled at him.

When he grinned back, she rose, went to him, and sat beside him on the plush-covered, horsehair-padded seat.

"Would you like to glance through these pamphlets?" He indicated the government publications.

Kale looked at them, then shook her head. "I'm afraid," she said with a self-deprecatory laugh, "that statistics about agricultural products and the tonnage produced by territorial mines aren't my idea of inspiring reading. I just hope," she continued, her voice becoming somber, "that I'll be accepted in Idaho."

"I'd like to know why anyone wouldn't accept you," he replied indignantly. "You're a wonderful woman, and I'll be the highest-ranking official in the territory, next to Toby."

"Let me remind you," she said softly, "of what just happened to me in San Francisco. I've never had a more unpleasant reception. I've reformed and given up my former profession, but you'd never know it from the way people acted there. I was accosted constantly, and a great many men were actually insulted when I sent them packing."

"Well, that's understandable to some extent," he said. "After all, you weren't unknown in San Francisco. You had attained celebrity status there—"

"You mean notoriety," she interrupted bitterly.

Rob shrugged. "Call it what you will. In any event, you were well known there."

"I hope that's the reason," she said dubiously. "I'm beginning to think that I must be carrying a badge announcing my past on my sleeve. No matter where I go, people seem to assume that I'm a prostitute."

"That's just your imagination at work," he assured her. "Once we get to Idaho, you'll find that nobody will know or care about your past."

"Oh, I hope you're right, Rob," she said earnestly, failing to realize, as did he, that her somewhat flamboyant and sophisticated manner called attention to her in the wrong ways. "I certainly don't want to influence baby Cathy adversely. Rather than have that happen, I'll resign my post as her governess and go my own way."

"You'll do no such thing," he replied with firm good humor. "My daughter depends on you, and so do I."

She wished his dependence on her was sufficiently great that he would ask her to marry him, but she was afraid that her past formed a barrier to any permanent attachment. Well, she simply could not worry about that now. She would have to live each day as it came and hope for the best. Smiling at him, she rose and returned to her own compartment, where she pretended to resume her reading. Actually, the words on the page swam before her, for her eyes had filled with tears.

II

Pamela Drake sat in the ornate, high-ceilinged dining room of the Ogden House and told herself that just from looking at Edward Blackstone and Jim Randall, one would know they were cousins. Both were dark, tall, and slender; both were endowed with an air of crisp competence; and both had magnetic personalities that made them instantly attractive to ladies.

By contrast, Millicent Randall looked as though she were not related to either of the men. Equally dark, she was so shy and retiring that she blended into the background and became virtually invisible. Her features were regular, but she wore no cosmetics to emphasize her large eyes or her full mouth. She was slender and probably had an attractive-enough figure, but one never would have guessed it from her high-necked, long-sleeved dark paisley dress, which made her look almost dowdy.

When they first sat down at the table and were getting acquainted, Millicent had spoken shyly of her love for music and her ability to play the flute, but since that time she had fallen silent as the others carried on a lively conversation.

"There you have the long and short of it," Jim Randall said, spreading his hands in a quick gesture. "When I woke up in the morning, I was the owner, along with Millicent, of a large Utah property, a prosperous ranch that had a solid present and an even more solid future. That afternoon we were homeless. Only because we have money were we able to rent a suite here at the Ogden House—or we wouldn't even have a roof over our heads!"

"Can't you fight for the property?" Pamela asked.

"The truth is," Jim admitted, "that the property doesn't rightfully belong to us. We only got it in the first place because of a tragic accident and an unfortunate misunderstanding. So we're right back where we started."

"Not exactly." Millicent unexpectedly entered the conversation. "We have another choice, it seems to me. We *could* go back to Baltimore."

"As far as I'm concerned, that's not a choice," Jim said emphatically. "The West wins, hands down! I don't quite understand how it's happened, but the West has crept into my blood. I think I'm speaking for Millicent, too, when I say that neither of us would ever be satisfied to live on the Eastern Seaboard again."

"I can certainly understand how you feel." Pamela looked at him and spoke slowly. "I must say I'm under the spell of this section of the country already. The scenery alone is breathtaking." She neglected to say that she was finding more than the scenery to admire as she continued to gaze at the dashing, distinguished-looking Jim Randall.

"I can think of so many things I find extraordinary about the American West," Edward said brightly, gesturing toward his plate with his fork. "The size of the beefsteak portions, for example. I can't possibly eat a steak this size."

"I asked for half a portion," Millicent said, "and even that's too large for me. Eventually you'll become accustomed to the ways of the West."

"Did you lose an appreciable sum of money when you lost your ranch?" Edward asked.

"Not at all." Jim was conscious of Pamela's candid scrutiny. "As a matter of fact, we didn't lose a penny. The nephew of the old man from whose estate we bought the property reimbursed us to the penny for the money that we sank into the ranch after we acquired it, and the territory of Utah refunded us the initial price."

"That's extraordinary," Edward murmured.

"That's the West," Jim replied. "Most people here are completely honest and aboveboard in all their dealings. That's one of the primary attractions of this part of the world."

Pamela seemed so absorbed by what he was saying that he found himself addressing his remarks primarily to her.

"Surely there's greed and dishonesty and chicanery here," she murmured.

"Of course!" Jim said. "But it's relatively easy to spot the dishonest people."

Edward seemed to be working out something in his mind. "What do you know about the Idaho Territory?" he inquired at last.

"Not much," Jim said, "other than the fact that a good

friend has been appointed military governor of it, and an even closer friend has become his lieutenant governor."

Millicent reddened at the reference to Rob Martin, but made no comment. The dark-haired woman had been strongly attracted to Rob from the first time they met, when he was still married, but she had tried to hide her feelings.

"I've been assured that the vocational opportunities in Idaho are as varied as the scenery," Edward said briskly. "There's an opportunity to invest in gold and silver mines. There's rich farmland for sale, and fertile pastures for grazing. And there's plenty of room for settlers. I've read in one of the recent government publications that there are approximately only fifteen thousand people in the entire territory now, and that about half that number live in or near Boise, the capital."

"You're very well informed," Jim said with a trace of amusement.

"I make it my business to be well informed when I'm thinking of investing money in an area," Edward replied. "Look here. You have no particular ties that are holding you in Utah, do you?"

Jim shook his head, and Millicent agreed with him.

"Come to Boise with Pam and me," Edward said. "We're going to be acquiring a large wagon to take us there, and we have more than enough room for you. We'd love to have you. If you take your time looking around—which is what I intend to do—who knows? You may find something that will be every bit as attractive as the property you just lost here in Utah."

"I'm willing," Millicent replied swiftly, looking at Jim for confirmation. "I don't see where we have anything to lose."

Jim knew that by accompanying Edward he would be prolonging his association with Pamela; therefore, the notion was doubly attractive. He didn't want to show an unseemly interest in the woman he assumed was his cousin's mistress, however, and so he replied casually, "We stand to lose nothing and perhaps to gain something. All right, we'll go with you."

"Good!" Edward said. "We'll begin making arrangements at once. I'll need to dispose of my private railroad car, but I'm certain I'll find someone to rent it who is as interested in traveling in style as I. Then I'll buy the wagon, and we can be on our way."

Toby and Clarissa Holt left Fort Vancouver, Washington, with their son, Tim, on the journey that would take them to Idaho. They would head east on the Oregon Trail that Toby's father, Whip Holt, had made famous more than three decades earlier when he had led the first wagon train across the North American continent from the Eastern Seaboard.

Conditions were far different now from what they had been for the earlier journey: There was a well-defined road, and they would pass through many towns. As military governor and first lady of Idaho, Toby and Clarissa would be escorted by two full battalions of troops, one of infantry and one of cavalry, twelve hundred men in all. The other three hundred of Toby's command were already in Idaho, awaiting his arrival.

Toby and Clarissa rode their own mounts, with Tim sharing his mother's saddle. They were surrounded at all times on the trail by a cordon of cavalry sharpshooters, who allowed no strangers to come near them.

All of their needs were anticipated, Clarissa noted with some wonder. An orderly heated water every evening for Tim's bath, and at night they slept in a real bed, carried in a horse-drawn cart and placed in a large tent that was erected for their privacy. Their meals were prepared by a mess sergeant assigned to them alone, but generally they invited the commanders of both battalions to supper.

The conditions of the journey were a far cry from those of the previous trips that Toby had made to Idaho over the years, first with his father and subsequently as a surveyor for the Northern Pacific Railroad with his good friend and partner, Rob Martin. But he didn't allow himself to be fooled by the comforts that he and his family enjoyed, nor did he delude himself about the protection that they were given. He knew that a grueling task awaited him in Idaho. He was responsible for establishing and enforcing the law over people who were sure to resent him—rugged, rough individuals, who would thwart him at every turn.

Not one of his predecessors as governor had been successful. Without exception they had been defeated by the primitive conditions of frontier living and the opposition they had repeatedly encountered. But he had accepted the challenge and was determined to succeed. His entire life, he now felt, had been nothing more than preparation for this supreme confrontation, and he was fully determined to emerge from the struggle as Idaho's master.

The Holts and their escorts climbed higher and higher into the mountains that cut off the Pacific Northwest from the rest of North America, and Toby was pleased from time to time to see parties of workmen busy laying tracks for the railroad that he and Rob had laid out. The day would soon come when the

Pacific Northwest, like San Francisco, would be linked by rail to the rest of the United States.

Late one morning, after riding up a winding trail that zigzagged perilously, Toby instinctively halted at a high pass in the mountains. Not a single cloud marred the serene blue of the sky, and the sun overhead was dazzling. At this height, however, there was a distinct hint of autumn in the air, a feeling that was lacking at lower altitudes.

Clarissa looked at her husband questioningly as she drew to a halt beside him, and the men of their personal escort were alert, not knowing what to expect next.

"There is Idaho," Toby said softly, the pride in his voice evident as he made a broad gesture with one hand.

The view he indicated, with snowcapped peaks rising in the background, was utterly breathtaking. Stretched out ahead was the most extraordinary topography in all of the United States. There were towering mountain ranges and dizzyingly deep gorges. They could make out swift-flowing rivers and gentler, meandering streams, as well as thundering, high falls. Here and there were deep forests that gave way to land suitable only for grazing, and finally deep, broad valleys that contained some of the most fertile soil in all of the United States.

Clarissa took in the panoramic landscape, then glanced at her husband, whose profile appeared as though it had been carved out of granite. Toby looked firm and unyielding, without appearing grim, and in his eyes there shone a light of anticipatory challenge. He was actually looking forward to a confrontation with any man or any problem that he might face in Idaho, Clarissa thought. There was no question about it: The Holt men were a breed apart.

As though conscious of her thoughts, Toby suddenly reached out and took their son from her. "Look yonder, Tim," he said, his voice quietly confident. "This is the land in which the President of the United States asked me to establish law and order. For your sake, Tim, for you and for your generation—born and as yet unborn—I'll do my damnedest to turn the tide of Idaho in the right direction."

He silently handed the child back to his mother and then called out to the captain commanding the immediate escort, "Let's be on our way, Captain. We have work to do, and we can't pause here all day to admire the scenery!"

That night they made camp high in the mountains. There was such an absence of flat land that it was necessary to prepare and serve their evening meal at a campfire set below the spot where their tent had been pitched. After supper Clarissa put Tim to bed, and then she and Toby sat in camp chairs outside the entrance to the tent. The night was overcast, with a layer of clouds obscuring the moon and stars. A stiff breeze brought a hint of the coming winter to the mountains.

The couple chatted for a time, but the weather was too chilly for them to sit outside without a campfire, so eventually they retired. Their bed, erected for them on the side of the tent, opposite their son's cot, was comfortable and warm, and they soon fell into a deep sleep.

At some time during the night, the clouds disappeared, the moon and stars emerged, and the night brightened considerably.

Clarissa awoke, and then as she started to rise from the bed, she saw the face of a man appearing in the upraised flap of the tent. In his arms he held a rifle that picked up the glint of the moonlight. Reacting instantly, instinctively, Clarissa threw herself across Toby's body in order to protect him and screamed at the top of her voice. Simultaneously the sharp crack of a rifle shot sounded and echoed through the mountains. The man's face disappeared from the tent opening, and pandemonium followed.

Toby, immediately wide awake, first assured himself that his wife and son were unharmed, and then he took charge of the search. A dozen officers and sentries were milling around the tent, and little Tim, wide awake, added to the confusion by bawling.

Toby's first thought was that the whole incident was the result of a bad dream Clarissa had had. But then he found a bullet hole in the top of the tent, about three feet from his head. There was no question that his wife had interrupted an intruder, who had fired wildly and then had managed to escape in the confusion that followed.

Colonel J.J. Kane, the commander of the infantry battalion whose unit had supplied the sentries, came to the tent and conferred privately with Toby at some length. They agreed that it would be wise to post a double guard. Toby would question his wife in private, after she grew calmer.

The mess sergeant provided warm, canned milk and cookies for Tim, who soon dozed off again, and gave his parents steaming mugs of coffee, which they drank gratefully.

Clarissa gradually grew calmer, but as she and Toby sipped their coffee, she remained visibly lost in thought and deeply upset. "You're going to think I'm mad," she said, "but I recognized the face that looked at me. I could see it in the moonlight. So help me, it was Otto Sinclair!"

"You're sure?" Toby demanded. "You aren't hallucinating?"

Clarissa was quietly firm. "Believe me, I know the face of

Otto Sinclair," she said. "He was fully bearded, but there was no mistaking his eyes. They were his, I'd swear it."

"Well," Toby said, "I've taken an oath to the effect that I saw him fall off a mountain ledge and tumble to his death below. I can't swear that I saw his body after he died, however. In fact, now that I think of it, I didn't watch him actually fall down the side of the cliff. So I suppose a boulder or a tree or some other obstacle could have broken his fall and made it possible for him to survive. I can't think of anything else that would account for his being alive today."

"All I know," she replied stubbornly, "is that it definitely was Otto. He had a rifle pointed directly at you, and I must have startled him and caused him to misfire."

"I'm grateful for that much," Toby said softly.

"Come to think of it," she said, her expression thoughtful, "he was wearing a uniform."

"What kind of uniform?" her husband demanded sharply.

She looked and sounded somewhat confused. "Why, an army uniform, of course. Like the soldiers on sentry duty were wearing."

"That's it!" Toby said, grasping her shoulders. "I think you've got the explanation." He hurried to the entrance and called to a sentry. "Ask Colonel Kane if he'll be good enough to return here for a few moments."

The battalion commander rejoined the couple, and Toby asked his wife to repeat what she had told him. Kane stroked his chin repeatedly during her brief recital.

"The whole sequence appears obvious to me," Toby said. "This fellow, Sinclair, who hates me for personal reasons, appears to have enlisted in your battalion, presumably under a false name. He managed to get himself assigned to sentry duty near our tent tonight, which explains his proximity, and when my wife upset him by screaming just as he was about to fire at me, he managed to escape in the confusion that followed.''

"You're probably right, Governor Holt," Colonel Kane said. "But there's one way to make certain. I'm going to take a battalion roll call—right now!"

Soon bugles blared, drums rolled, and the air was filled with shouts as units lined up for a head count. Then, a short time later, Colonel Kane returned to the Holts' tent, accompanied by a young officer.

"Allow me to present Captain Dawson, my battalion adjutant," he said. "Dawson, be good enough to relate your findings to Governor Holt."

The young officer saluted smartly. "Sir," he said, "we think we know who the culprit is. An enlisted man named Lionel Thomas is missing. He's disappeared, taking his rifle and his uniform with him."

"What do you know about him?" Toby asked.

"He was a new recruit who enlisted a few days before we left Fort Vancouver, Governor," the captain said. "His company commander was glad to have him because he was already familiar with military procedures."

Toby needed no one to remind him that Otto Sinclair had held the rank of sergeant when the War Department had reported him missing in action.

Clarissa interrupted the exchange. "Lionel Thomas," she said hesitantly, "was the name of Otto's mother's father—his maternal grandfather. I never met him, but Otto spent his whole boyhood with his grandfather, and I heard a great deal about him."

41

"That's all the proof we need," Toby said emphatically. "The rest is easy enough to deduce. Otto Sinclair somehow survived the incident in the Oregon mountains and enlisted under his grandfather's name, intending to shoot me at the first opportunity. He waited until he was assigned to sentry duty, and he regarded that as his chance. Fortunately, my wife woke up and interrupted him before he had the opportunity to kill me."

"Should we post a wanted notice for him, sir?" Colonel Kane asked.

"By all means," Toby replied. "Have it sent out to every military establishment and law enforcement body." He thought it strange that his first act as governor of Idaho should relate to his wife's first husband. He had no desire to alarm Clarissa unnecessarily, but he vowed silently to take every possible precaution until Sinclair was apprehended and sent to jail.

Boise was one of the first cities in the United States to benefit from active, coordinated urban planning. The governor's large, gracious mansion was located in the center of the community on Capitol Square. Directly across the street from the territorial capitol was a building housing the legislature, the offices of the governor, and the courts. The buildings of the business district were unusually large and substantial, many of them sturdily built of stone, as well as the more commonplace clapboard.

Main Street, the principal thoroughfare, was an exceptional ninety feet wide, and although the town had been built in an area lacking in vegetation, many trees had been planted to line not only Main Street but a great many of the town's subsidiary thoroughfares as well.

Fort Boise, the military headquarters and army barracks, was located at a spot where the Oregon Trail crossed over a road that led to the gold mines in the mountains. There were many farms in the area, and the town was the natural market center and bread basket for the entire territory. To be sure, since there were a number of mines in the vicinity, Boise also had its fair share of visiting miners.

Cattle and horses were raised on ranches scattered throughout the region, which was regarded as perfect for grazing, and so there were visiting ranchers in Boise at all times.

The community was not devoid of industry, either: There were two smelting plants where ore containing gold was refined, and a third smelter was devoted to the refining of silver. Boise boasted two schools and the only hospital that existed for hundreds of miles in any given direction.

In spite of its relatively advanced state, however, Boise was still very much a wild community of the classic American West. The more respectable elements deplored the presence of its numerous saloons, gambling halls, and bordellos, but they were powerless to rid the community of them, just as they could do nothing to curb the presence of the shifting population of miners, ranch hands, and other transients. The local sheriff had his hands full trying to maintain law and order in the town.

Something had just been done, however, to curb the excesses created by young warriors of the Shoshone and Nez Percé, who had been raiding and robbing the homes of ranchers and other settlers in the area. Both tribes had signed treaties with the United States and were living on reservations.

Even so, there were many hotheaded young braves who continued to go out on raids, and the peace was disturbed nightly by violent incidents.

Lieutenant Governor Rob Martin had just arrived in the town and had taken up residence in a house owned by the territorial government near Capitol Square. He, Kale Salton, and baby Cathy had settled into their new dwelling, and Rob had been fortunate enough to acquire the services of a competent housekeeper, Mrs. Carson.

Learning of the disturbances created by the young Indian braves, Rob did not wait for the arrival of Toby Holt to find a solution to the problem. He promptly issued an executive order, which was good for two weeks, stating that any roaming bands of Shoshone and Nez Percé warriors would be apprehended by the military and arrested. Those Indians who had legitimate business in Boise were forced to report to the lieutenant governor first before conducting their affairs. Admittedly this was a temporary solution to a problem with which Toby would be forced to grapple as soon as he took office. But for the moment, order was restored, and the violence in the outlying areas ceased.

Lying in the shadows of Capitol Square was Maloney's Saloon, one of the busiest and most popular establishments in town. Maloney, the proprietor, was celebrating the arrival of the new governor with a more elaborate than usual free lunch. In honor of the occasion, the menu for the day included hard-boiled eggs, fresh ham, and sliced leg of lamb.

Among those taking part in the festivities was a former habitué, Murphy, a small, bandy-legged miner perpetually in need of a shave, who spoke with a thick Irish brogue. He had vanished into the wilderness of Idaho two years earlier, and now, suddenly, he had reappeared out of nowhere, apparently well fixed for funds; presumably he had found gold or silver in the mountains.

Murphy was accompanied by two inseparable companions. One was Julia, a small burro with large, sad eyes and impeccable manners. Julia stood quietly outside the saloon, tied to a hitching post, patiently waiting for her master to come out.

Perched on Murphy's shoulder was Gilhooley, a black, talking crow, who measured a scant twelve inches from the top of his head to the tips of his tail feathers. Like his master, he spoke in a thick brogue.

"I'll thank ye kindly if ye'll give us room to breathe," Murphy said to the patrons who crowded around him and the bird curiously. " 'Tis only an old wives' tale that crows learn to talk if you split their tongues. I nursed Gilhooley here back to health when he was sufferin' from a broken wing, and we passed a whole winter in a cabin in the mountains with me teachin' him how to talk. Ain't that so, Gilhooley?" He muttered something unintelligible to the bird.

The crow fixed a beady eye on a customer who was crowding close. "Move along, me bucko," he ordered. "What do ye think this is, a free lunch counter?"

The patrons howled with laughter.

Murphy reached into a pocket of his tattered jacket, produced a packet of birdseed, and shook out several grains, which the crow proceeded to eat one by one from the palm of his hand. As Murphy subsequently explained to the proprietor of the saloon, he imported the seed all the way from San Francisco.

Gilhooley cocked his head to one side, looked at another

patron, and announced sweetly but firmly, "Ye've had your fun, and now yer time is up, me dear."

The gleeful crowd howled. Those in the know, which included most of the patrons, realized that the saying came from the girls at Sadie's Place, one of the more popular after-dark establishments in Boise.

When the crowd had become quiet again, Gilhooley surveyed the men and announced haughtily, "There's got to be gold in this here mountain."

His audience applauded heartily, and Murphy again rewarded him with several grains of birdseed.

"Top o' the mornin' to ye," Gilhooley declared.

The onlookers broke into spontaneous applause.

"I'll give you one hundred dollars in gold for that bird, Murphy," someone shouted.

Gilhooley replied on behalf of his master. "Go hang yourself on a crab apple tree," he declared.

The unruffled Murphy continued to put the crow through his repertory of sayings and doggerel verses. The recital was interrupted by the blaring of a military band, and the entire population of Maloney's Saloon rushed out into the street in order to catch a glimpse of the new military governor.

Leading the parade were a troop of cavalry and the military band, both of them stationed in Boise. They were followed by the twelve hundred men of the newly arrived battalions, and halfway through the line of march there was an open wagon, in which Clarissa Holt and her small son were riding.

Clarissa was wearing a broad-brimmed hat and a colorful dress with sunflowers on it. She was enjoying her new celebrity status, and she smiled and waved to the crowd. Timothy, too, was enjoying the excitement and bounced up and down so energetically that he was in danger of falling off the wagon.

Governor Toby Holt was not seated at the front of a wagon, nor was he dressed in the customary politician's uniform of stovepipe hat, black morning coat, and black striped trousers. He rode easily on his own spirited stallion, and he wore black pants tucked into his old boots, an open-throated shirt, and his battered, broad-brimmed Western hat. His two six-shooters hung from his belt, and laid across his pommel was his much-used rifle, which was kept in the best of condition.

Those in the crowd who had never heard of Toby and knew nothing about him agreed wholeheartedly with those who were more familiar with his background and history: The new governor obviously meant business. He was not just some fancy-pants politician with a smooth tongue. Certainly he was serving notice on the people of Idaho that he was a true son of the West and that he intended to tolerate no nonsense from those who refused to obey both the letter and the spirit of the law.

The Holts left the parade at the governor's mansion, and while Clarissa was shown through her new home by Kale Salton, who had taken responsibility for preparing the house for her, Toby made the short ride to his new office with Rob Martin, who brought him up to date on what had been done in the ten days since he and Kale had arrived in Boise.

"Here's a list," Rob said, "of the robberies and other crimes committed by the Indian nations prior to my temporary order, and here's a list of the reduced disturbances since that time."

Toby sat back for the first time in his new gubernatorial

chair. "Obviously," he said, "the younger warriors aren't satisfied with the terms of the present agreement with the United States. So I'd say one of my first orders of business will be to negotiate a new treaty."

"A new treaty and an essential firmness in dealing with the braves are imperative to maintaining peace," Rob told him.

"Has there been a lack of firmness?" Toby asked.

Rob shrugged. "The situation was rather touch and go until we took office."

"When am I being sworn in?" Toby demanded.

Rob glanced at his watch. "In about an hour," he said. "The territorial chief justice will be here then."

"Then there's no time like the present to get a few things done." Toby pulled a rope that sounded a bell in a secretary's outer office, and when the young man came into the room, the new governor introduced himself. "Be good enough to prepare executive order number two," Toby told him. "This is a directive to all battalion and independent unit commanders, United States Army, and all law enforcement officers in the territory. Copies are to be sent to the chiefs of the Nez Percé and the Shoshone at their reservations, and additional copies are to be posted in all public places in Idaho. This order amends and amplifies the order previously issued by Lieutenant Governor Martin, and it applies to all members of both Indian nations currently living in the territory. Every male Shoshone and Nez Percé between the ages of sixteen and sixty who leaves his reservation without a written permit signed personally by me or by Lieutenant Governor Martin is to be apprehended and, if necessary, returned forcibly to his reservation. That will put an end to the disturbances," he said to Rob. "At least until we can negotiate the new agreement.

It doesn't stop the ferment under the surface, of course, but that can't be helped.''

In the hour prior to his inauguration, Toby also requested the army commanders to supply adequate sentry details to guard him and his family until such time as Otto Sinclair was apprehended. Only then did he go to the balcony at the front of the mansion to take the oath of office from the territorial chief justice.

Immediately after the ceremony, he issued an informal call for all men who had dealt in any way with the Nez Percé or the Shoshone in recent years to come to the governor's mansion for a conference. He was determined to get to the bottom of the problem as rapidly as he could and to end the threat to the security of Idaho during this critical period in its growth.

After his inauguration Toby Holt set a blistering pace for himself. First he conferred individually with each of the sixteen members of the territorial legislature. Then he and a half-troop of cavalry that had been assigned to escort him launched a whirlwind tour of Idaho, visiting every district and covering as much ground as possible before the coming snows of winter made travel to remote places more difficult.

Everywhere he went he spoke at length with farmers and ranchers, finding out what they did and didn't like about what the federal government was doing for them and gaining their views on what needed to be done. Going straight to every Indian reservation in Idaho, he talked with the chieftains of the Nez Percé and the Shoshone, particularly about their grievances against the United States. He conferred with gold and silver miners at their mines and talked with smelters about their problems. He spoke knowingly and at length with both producers and consumers about the benefits that Idaho would enjoy from the expansion of railroads, and he talked in secret with the commanders of army posts about problems of security.

He spent several crowded weeks on the road, and his head was filled with facts he had acquired. This information spilled over into several notebooks.

In his travels Toby gleaned a great deal of valuable information that he had not yet had time to put into practical use. First and foremost was news to the effect that the government's troubles with the Indians were being inspired by a hotheaded young rebel named Running Bear, a senior warrior of the Nez Percé. Resolutely ignoring the treaties signed with the United States by the elders of his nation, Running Bear had gone from reservation to reservation to harangue the young braves and to insist they join him in his fight against the United States government. The only way the Indian nations could achieve true independence, he swore, was to fight the white usurpers and drive them and their government from the territory.

Even though Running Bear's ideas were unrealistic, considering the numbers and strength of the white opponents, he was a skilled orator, and his message had been taken to heart by enough young warriors to create serious problems for the residents of Idaho.

Toby was convinced that a meeting of minds would be achieved only in a face-to-face confrontation. His own record, as that of his father before him, indicated that he not only was on friendly terms with the Indian nations but also had their best interests at heart. Thus, he enjoyed their respect.

But Running Bear, for reasons of his own, refused to consent to a meeting with the newly appointed governor of the territory and continued to spread his poison.

Somewhat frustrated by his inability to arrange a meeting with Running Bear, Toby at last decided that the time had come for him to return to Boise and put the knowledge he had gleaned on many subjects to good use. He and the twenty-five men of his cavalry escort were traveling through the highlands of Idaho at the time that he reached his decision, and early the following morning they changed directions and headed toward home.

They had spent only a short time in the saddle when Toby saw a strange sight. In the distance he caught a glimpse of a farmer driving a wagon pulled by two large workhorses across the open countryside. Sitting in the vehicle were a woman, presumably the man's wife, and a half-dozen small children. The man was urging his team of horses to greater and still greater speeds, while the woman kept looking over her shoulder and peering at something in the distance.

Soon the reason for the couple's agitation became clear. Toby saw they were being pursued by a dozen warriors whose presence on small, swift ponies marked them as Nez Percé. The wagon bounced and jolted as it crossed the rough ground, and as Toby watched, he was horrified to see a little girl thrown from her place in the wagon onto the ground.

The child rose groggily to her feet and appeared to be unhurt. But there was no way to retrieve her, and the wagon continued to put distance between itself and the girl. In the meantime the Indian warriors were gaining on her.

Instead of ordering his small cavalry escort to rescue the little girl, Toby decided to perform the deed himself. He spurred his stallion forward, and none of the troopers' geldings could match the pace of the great beast.

The stallion thundered toward the child, and Toby felt a measure of relief when he realized that he was going to win the race with the Indians to reach the little girl first. Timing his move perfectly, he leaned low in the saddle, scooped up the child in one arm, and then, placing her firmly in front of him, he drew his pistols and wheeled to meet the onrushing Nez Percé.

Both of his pistols blazed, then fired a second time. The Indians were still too far to be within range of his firearms, and his shots had the desired effect: The warriors swerved away from their target to remain out of his pistols' range. Toby was relieved that he wasn't required to use his rifle and kill a number of the braves.

The cavalry unit now bore down on the Indians, quickly surrounding them and forcing them to surrender.

Toby slowed his stallion to a walk and headed in the direction of the wagon, which was now careening across the fields toward him. He dismounted, and when the wagon finally arrived, he handed the child to her mother, soothing the girl with a few quiet words.

The father wiped a film of perspiration from his forehead. "That was the fanciest ridin' I ever seen, mister," he said. "Not that I can ever repay you, but who are you? I'm in your debt forever."

"Anyone would have done what I did," Toby told him. "The name is Holt."

The man's wife peered at him sharply. "Mr. Toby Holt?" she asked.

He nodded.

"Governor Holt of Idaho?" The father seemed awestruck.

"I reckon I am," Toby said in considerable embarrassment, and extricating himself, he hastily joined the cavalrymen, who had succeeded in disarming the Nez Percé.

At Toby's order the weapons of the dumbfounded braves were returned to them.

The subchief, who was the leader of the band, began to make a long, self-justifying speech in which he claimed that he and his companions had meant no harm to the little girl.

Toby cut him short. Mounting his stallion again, he stared at the warriors, his eyes hard, his manner unyielding. "You are acquainted with the brave known as Running Bear," he said harshly in their language, and made the statement sound like an accusation.

The Nez Percé nodded affirmatively.

"You have heeded the voice of Running Bear," he continued in the same accusing tone. "You have engraved his words of insurrection and violence upon your hearts. You have branded as your enemy all who swear allegiance to the United States. You will kill and destroy them if you can, you will ruin their property, steal their livestock, and take unto yourselves all that belongs to them."

Thumping his own chest once, Toby jabbed a forefinger at the braves and declared, "Listen to the words of him who has become the sachem of all who live in Idaho. Listen to the words of him who represents the great white father who lives in Washington. Tell your wise men and your sages and your war chiefs and your medicine men that it is Toby Holt who speaks. Tell your elders, who remember the past, that it is the son of Whip Holt who speaks. Like my father before me, I have long been the friend of the Nez Percé and of the

Shoshone. I have proved my friendship in countless ways. I have proved it once again within recent minutes by restoring your arms to you when you would have used them to kill an innocent child. My heart overflows with kindness to those to whom I bear friendship.''

The warriors nodded, evidently taking his words with great seriousness. Their attitude was formed in part because of his fluent command of their own tongue.

''But those who reject my friendship and proclaim themselves my enemies will be treated as my enemies,'' he continued. ''To them I will show no kindness, no friendship, no mercy. Those who hate me, I will hate. Those who would destroy me, I will first destroy. Those who would expel me from Idaho, I will send fleeing in terror. Let my words be repeated to Running Bear. Let him ponder them well. Then let him decide whether he seeks my friendship or my enmity.''

He pointed toward the snowcapped mountains that, as always, formed a background in the territory. ''Go at once!'' he commanded. ''Go before I change my mind and have your souls removed from your bodies.''

The Indians turned and raced off, their ponies' hoofs clattering on the hard-packed soil as they fled.

Toby's manner changed. Grinning amiably, he rode to the wagon and, reaching over, stroked the head of the little girl. The child had recovered from her fright and, no longer weeping, was now playing happily with her brothers and sisters.

''It well may be,'' he said thoughtfully to the child's parents, who had taken in every detail of his confrontation with the Indians, even though they had not understood a word of what he had said to them, ''that your daughter will be instrumental in establishing a real peace in the territory. Perhaps this incident involving her will be the key to an understanding with Running Bear."

The band of young warriors rode hard, trying the stamina of their mounts to the utmost. After spending many hours in the saddle, they finally arrived at a remote town of the Nez Percé. This was the community where their leader, Running Bear, had established his temporary headquarters, and they went directly to him.

Two of their number acted as spokesmen, and others in the group intervened from time to time to add remarks of their own. So, in one way and another, the full text of Toby Holt's message was repeated to the young rebel chieftain.

Compact and stocky, Running Bear sat stolidly on the ground, his arms folded, an unlighted pipe clenched in his teeth as he listened to the recital of his subordinates. His dark face looked darker still as he listened, but otherwise he showed no emotion. Then, when his subordinates finished speaking, he deliberately removed the pipe from his mouth and spat onto the ground.

"It is to be regretted," he said, "that the warriors of the United States intervened before you had a chance to kill the girl child of the settlers. Perhaps the parents would have become so discouraged that they would have fled from Idaho and returned to their former home."

Suddenly he drew his tomahawk from his belt and flourished it over his head. "Are you stupid?" he shouted fiercely. "Are you so blind that you accept the promises of Holt, who is employed by your enemies? Are you women that you fear the arms and skills of the warriors of America?'' He rose to his feet, and his manner became majestic.

The braves drooped and listened respectfully to every word.

"For seven long years," Running Bear said, "I attended the schools of America. There I learned their language and much about their treacherous ways. By the time I grew to manhood, I had lost my fear of them, and today I still fear them not. No matter what they promise or what they threaten, I will not rest until I have driven these intruders from our land for all time. I invite all Nez Percé and all Shoshone who think of themselves as men to join me in my crusade and rid our sacred soil of the trespassers for all time."

Carried away by his rhetoric, the warriors shouted in approval. Drawing their tomahawks, they waved them threateningly.

Edward Blackstone and Pamela Drake engaged the largest suite at the Boise Inn, the leading hostelry of the territorial capital, and soon became the talk of the town. Those who were inclined to mimic Edward because of his upper-class English drawl, his fastidious manners, or his impeccable manner of dress, were soon dissuaded and wisely minded their own business.

"So help me," Murphy reported to his colleagues at Maloney's Saloon, "the limey is a dead shot. There he was, big as life, practicin' with a pair of six-shooters on targets that he'd put up in the yard back o' the Boise Inn. While I stood watchin', he emptied both pistols and hit the target, with every shot neat as ye please. Then he turned to me real polite-like and wanted to know if I had business with him. I skedaddled out o' there as fast as me legs would move."

"Sure, and if you'd had wings, Murphy, like Gilhooley there," Maloney said, nodding toward the black crow, "you'd of flown like a bird to get away from the gent'man."

Pamela Drake called attention to herself because her cosmetics and clothes were too garish for the unsophisticated ways of Boise. Men who attempted to engage her in intimate conversation soon learned, however, to avoid her as though she were a carrier of the bubonic plague. Pamela habitually carried a small reticule attached to a girdlelike belt, and the more persistent males soon discovered, to their sorrow, that it contained a tiny pistol, no more than five inches long. Pamela appeared determined to use the little weapon unless her would-be admirers transferred their attentions elsewhere, which, upon seeing the weapon, all of them were eager to do.

Tales of her skills with firearms circulated widely in Boise: "I saw her at target practice with the Englishman back of the Boise Inn this afternoon," one story went, "and you could take my word for it. She's an expert shot. She had a target the size of your fist, and by the time she was through shootin', it had as many holes as the lace cover on the easy chair in Madam Suzanne's fancy-house parlor!"

Although most residents of Boise continued to regard Edward and Pamela warily, the English couple won rapid acceptance with the Holts and their friends. When Toby encountered the Randall cousins in town shortly after he returned from his tour, he invited them to bring Edward and Pamela to the governor's mansion for dinner. Soon after that, Rob Martin and Kale Salton extended a dinner invitation of their own to the Randalls and to the English visitors.

Millicent Randall was delighted, accepting the invitation with alacrity because she had long been secretly in love with

Rob, and in recent months, with his wife no longer on the scene, she felt she might have a chance to win his attentions. With the loss of their Utah property, Millicent felt that her life had become transient and aimless, and she was vesting all her hopes in the love of a good, gentle man like Rob.

Millicent was so shy and retiring that Rob, who had known of her feelings for him when they had lived in Utah, believed she was totally uninterested in him now. Kale was aware of Millicent's interest in him, however, but did not think the plain, unaggressive young woman was in any way a rival to her.

Edward and Pamela joined the Randall cousins for dinner at the lieutenant governor's house, and the party sipped apéritifs before dinner in a parlor that commanded a view of the mountains in the distance.

Jim Randall had once proposed to Kale Salton, and though she had turned him down, he still had a high regard for this independent, self-assured young woman. It was delightful to see her again, and he was now eager to share some good news with the entire group. "Wish us luck!" he said ebulliently.

He increasingly intrigued Pamela. "Don't tell me," she said, "that you've put money into the gold mine that Edward invested in today."

"No, I know nothing whatsoever about mines and mining," Jim said, "but I do know ranches, and I know a bargain when I see one. I've sunk a small fortune of Millicent's and of mine into a ranch this afternoon."

"Where is it?" Rob Martin asked.

"I bought three hundred and fifty acres of prime grazing land, due south of the Boise town line. The main house lies on a little road that comes off Abe Lincoln Road, and there's a sturdy ranch house and several useful outbuildings.''

"I know the property," Rob said. "The previous owner couldn't keep up payments until his herd matured, and so it reverted to the bank.''

"I paid cash for it," Jim said proudly. "The property is ours now, free and clear.''

This was news to Millicent, who had given free rein to Jim to find them a new home.

Jim realized his cousin needed some cheering up, and he tried to rouse her. "I telegraphed Ah-Sing immediately after I closed the deal this afternoon, and I asked him to come up here as soon as he can. I also telegraphed our former ranch hands in Utah, offering them positions here, as I promised them I would. Within a few days we should be in full operation at the new ranch.''

Pamela regarded him with open admiration. "I must say, you waste no time," she told him.

Jim exchanged a quiet grin with Edward. "It's an old family trait," he told her.

"Make sure, Jim," Rob said, "that you register your purchase at the office of the secretary of state. Also, post your men around your property to ward off intruders.''

Kale wrinkled her nose in distaste. "Is that really necessary?''

"You just bet it is," Rob replied emphatically.

"The territory," Jim added, "is not only being harassed by rebellious young Indians, but it's also filled with light-fingered men—unsuccessful miners and petty crooks and drifters—who aren't above stealing a cow or a horse or any other domesticated animal if they think they can get away with it. The new administration hasn't been in office long enough to establish a strict code of law and order yet."

"Just give us a little time," Rob said confidently, "and the whole territory will be as safe as the parlors of your own houses."

"How do you intend to accomplish that?" a wide-eyed Pamela asked.

Kale felt a stab of jealousy and wondered if the English-woman's interest in the subject was genuine or if she was just attempting conversation with Rob.

Rob took her question at face value. "Toby—Governor Holt—" he said, "was discussing the problem with me just today. As you probably know, we've begun to crack down on the rebellious Indians by demanding that they stay on their reservations and having army troops enforce that order. Now as to the other troublemakers in the territory, we can put a stop to their activities by enlisting every respectable, able-bodied citizen of Idaho into a militia and authorizing him to search out and arrest every burglar and robber. This would unfortunately turn the entire territory into an armed camp, and grave injustices would be done to innocent people in the name of justice. This leaves us with another solution: We get tougher with the criminals we now catch."

"How do you do that?" Pamela persisted.

"It's quite simple, really," Rob replied. "We persuade the courts to hang every thief who is condemned, instead of sending the guilty men off to prison for terms of a few years each. After a few thieves have dangled from the ends of ropes, you'd be surprised how the urge to take property that belongs to others leaves someone."

"I should think," Pamela said, "that such crude, violent forms of justice would only cause crude and violent crimes."

"The American frontier," Rob said, "has been moving westward from the Atlantic Ocean to the Pacific in fits and starts since the seventeenth century. And in all that time violence has been the curse of the frontier, blunting the benefits of civilization. The best elements in our society, the good and strong and brave, have always been attracted to frontier living. Unfortunately, so have the worst elements—the unscrupulous, the dishonest, those who use chicanery rather than honest, hard labor to get by. There's been an ongoing running battle between the bad and good on the American frontier for more than two hundred years now. And the good have learned that the only sure way to beat the bad is to adopt their own tactics and beat them at their own game."

"Dinner is ready," Kale said, seeing the housekeeper's signal and bringing an abrupt end to Rob's speech. The interruption relieved her greatly. Rob seemed to be returning the interest of the Englishwoman with far too much enthusiasm.

The dinner, although simple, reflected Kale's sophistication. The meal was composed of cold, smoked mountain trout, rack of lamb served with potatoes and vegetables, and was followed by a green salad. Instead of dessert, they were served a variety of cheeses that Kale stocked in her larder, having ordered them sent from a shop in San Francisco that she had long patronized.

Pamela began to realize that the California woman was more subtle and sensitive than she seemed to be at first glance. As for Millicent, she recognized Kale's assumption of the role of mistress of Rob's house and quietly despaired of ever having an opportunity to develop a relationship with him.

The men were unaware of these delicate nuances of feeling among the three women. Rob Martin and Jim Randall had become friends in Utah and were now taking advantage of their proximity to expand and cultivate that friendship. Edward, being Jim's cousin and a socially presentable man, was highly acceptable to the lieutenant governor.

After dinner the men stayed behind at the table for drinks of rum sweetened with honey, while the women adjourned to the parlor. Pamela had the definite feeling that life was becoming more exciting. She liked Jim Randall enormously and was aware of his keen, growing interest in her. As for Lieutenant Governor Rob Martin, Pamela was delighted at the heightened sense of jealous competition that she had aroused in Kale Salton. Knowing nothing of Kale's background as the intimate friend of Rob's late wife, the Englishwoman assumed that Kale was his mistress. Therefore, it would give her great pleasure to challenge Kale on her own ground and try to win Rob away from her. The future held great promise.

Clarissa Holt had been greatly relieved when her husband returned safely to Boise from his extensive tour of the territory. She had tried to extract a promise from him that he would remain in the capital until such time as Otto Sinclair was apprehended, but Toby laughed at her fears. He was taking sensible precautions, he told her; beyond that, he dismissed Sinclair from his mind.

His duties as governor required that he be very social, and he and Clarissa not only gave a number of dinner parties but also began to accept invitations. One that he did not regard as a formal event was an invitation to visit the new ranch of his friends Jim and Millicent Randall. Ever since they had moved to the same region, he had hoped Clarissa would become friendly with the Randalls, and this invitation—to Sunday dinner, at which little Tim was also included—seemed like a perfect opportunity.

Ah-Sing, happily ensconced in the Randall kitchen, once again proved that he was an inspired chef. His oxtail soup was extraordinary, his roast beef done to perfection, and the Yorkshire pudding he served with it had been made with buttermilk, which gave it a distinct, piquant flavor. For dessert he served cherry pie with his homemade ice cream, and little Tim proved his mettle by eating two helpings.

Jim was anxious to show his newly acquired property to the governor, so after dinner they saddled their horses and set out on a ride to see some of the ranch. They left the ladies to become better acquainted in the parlor, and Tim was put to bed for a nap in an upstairs bedroom.

As the two horsemen made their way across the rolling hills, the high grasses now turning brown with the arrival of autumn, Jim revealed that all of the hands whom he had employed in Utah had responded to his call and were again working for him.

Toby, interested in everything he saw, asked a number of questions, including how much land was needed to sustain a single steer. Somewhat to his surprise, Jim had the answer readily available and rattled on with great confidence as to herd management.

After they had been riding for over an hour, Toby felt moved to observe, "You know, Jim, for a city dweller from the East, you've taken to ranching like a duck takes to water."

"It's strange," Jim admitted, "but when I was mustered out of the Union Army, I felt totally lost. Particularly with only one eye. I had inherited a fair sum of money, but I was far too restless to reinvest it and spend the rest of my days idly living off the interest. I knew I had to do something more challenging with the rest of my life."

Listening as they made their way past a small grove of apple trees, Toby nodded.

"I have always been fascinated by the West," Jim continued, "and I've read everything about it I could get my hands on, especially about men like your father and Kit Carson. Well, I came here out of a sense of curiosity, also as a favor to Cousin Millicent, who as you know was looking for her missing fiancé at the time. But a strange thing happened to me. The moment I hit ranch country, I felt I had come home. The routines of ranch life have somehow felt familiar to me from the start, and I've become quite comfortable with the economics of ranching."

"It strikes me," Toby said, chuckling, "that you're a natural-born rancher, and that's all to the good. Idaho has a real need for men like you. The territory has unlimited potential, but it's going to require hard labor and sacrifices as well as facing serious dangers to achieve our goals for Idaho. It's going to take time and patience to solve the problems facing the territory, but if everyone hereabouts had your talent and your enthusiasm, there is no doubt in my mind about the eventual outcome."

While the men continued their tour, Clarissa sat with her hostess in the parlor of the ranch house. For a time Millicent's conversation was tentative, her manner reticent, but eventually she began to respond to Clarissa's natural warmth. She found herself revealing confidences to the sympathetic Clarissa.

"For many years," she said shyly, "music was the most important thing in my life—the only thing, really. I earned a master's degree at the conservatory in Baltimore, and I was well on my way to a doctorate when I came West with Jim. I suppose you might say I'm a professional flutist. You see, not only did I give a great many concerts but I also compose for the flute, and several of my pieces have already become standards. For a long time I was quite proud of my record and my standing."

Clarissa thought she detected something troubling in the other young woman's words. "But you don't have that pride any longer?" she asked.

Millicent shook her head. "I was exposed to the grandeur of the elements for the first time in my life when Jim and I came West," she said. "Just look around us! The high, snow-covered peaks in the distance; the endless sky; the rolling hills that stretch out to the horizon; the rivers that pound and thunder and flow with such speed and energy. Everything I see makes me dizzy. Most of all, it makes me realize the puniness of mankind and the inadequacies of people in the face of nature. So—suddenly—music is no longer enough. There is a terrible void in my life that it no longer fills."

"I see." Clarissa nodded thoughtfully.

"I've tried to tell myself not to be so shortsighted and silly," Millicent went on. "The grandeur of the West has been here for ages and will be here long after I live and die. I'm in no position to harness its power, and nothing I can do can change or influence it. I'd be far better off if I continued to devote myself to music. But I don't listen to such sensible self-advice anymore. Even the very best of music seems somewhat frivolous to me now."

"I think I know what you mean," Clarissa said, "but don't denigrate the importance of music, my dear. It has a great significance, not only to you, but to the people who've enjoyed your concerts and to those who play and listen to your compositions."

"You're very kind, Clarissa," Millicent said, "but I'm afraid I can't delude myself any longer. Music seems to be inconsequential now. It no longer fills my needs."

Later that day, when the Holts were riding back to the governor's mansion in Boise, surrounded by the cavalry escort that now accompanied them everywhere, Clarissa related to her husband the conversation she had had with Millicent. "I feel dreadfully sorry for her," she said, "but there seems to be nothing that I can do to help. There's nothing anyone can do."

"What do you suppose has happened to her?" Toby asked.

"Reading between the lines and judging from what she didn't say," Clarissa replied, "I suspect she's in love."

"Let me be the last to argue with your feminine intuition," Toby said, grinning. "Do you know or can you guess the identity of the lucky man?"

"If my guess is right," Clarissa replied, "he's not so lucky, and neither is Millicent."

Toby lifted an eyebrow.

"Based on a few isolated remarks that she let drop from time to time, I think she imagines herself enamored of Rob Martin."

"Oh, no!" Toby exclaimed.

"Oh, yes," Clarissa said. "That's why music has lost its meaning for her and life has gone flat."

"Beth's death is far too recent for Rob to even think in terms of falling in love with someone else. Besides, when he does, I believe that Kale Salton will have the inside track to his emotions—if she wants them."

"She does, I assure you," his wife said complacently. "Haven't you noticed how Kale bristles when Pamela Drake starts to flirt with Rob? And Pamela knows good and well how Kale feels about him."

"Then what's going to come of all this?" he asked in bewilderment, shaking his head.

"From Millicent's point of view, absolutely nothing," Clarissa said flatly. "That's her problem. She sees herself in love with a man who doesn't know it and who wouldn't care if he did. She regards her situation as hopeless."

Toby was becoming confused. "Is it really hopeless?"

"My crystal ball becomes cloudy whenever human emotions are involved," she said, and smiled. "All we can do is wait and see."

III

"Have you ever noticed," Millicent asked her cousin one morning over a breakfast of flapjacks and syrup, "a rust-colored mare who hangs around the outskirts of the ranch?"

Jim Randall nodded. "She has a young colt, no more than six months old, that follows her everywhere. He's her same color."

"That's the one," Millicent replied eagerly. "I find it very strange. Whenever I'm going somewhere or coming home, the mare, followed by her colt, appears out of the wilderness and seems to be on the verge of coming up to me. But the moment I even turn toward her, she gallops off into the wilderness again."

"That's just the experience I've had with her," Jim said.

"How do you account for it?"

Jim shrugged. "As a guess, purely a guess, I'd say that she

once belonged to somebody and was domesticated. Then she was set free, or broke free, or somehow regained a wild status that she's had ever since. I'd say she yearns to be with humans again but is afraid to take the plunge."

Millicent uttered a faint sigh. "We'll never know, I guess," she said, pouring them more coffee.

After breakfast she announced that she was going into Boise, where she intended to buy some yarn, thread, and other sewing supplies. "I'll be back in time for noon dinner," she said.

"All right. Just be sure you take your rifle with you," Jim told her.

"Must I?" she asked in a forlorn voice. "You know how I hate firearms."

Jim tried to conceal his sense of exasperation. "You're not in Baltimore or Washington or New York now," he said. "You're living in the wilds of Idaho. I've taught you to shoot, and you handle a gun well. So there's no need to be bashful about it. In fact, to go unarmed is to behave in a foolhardy manner. There are too many unsavory characters in the territory for a lady to go about unprotected."

She accepted his edict and loaded her rifle, shuddering with distaste before setting out on her journey. The autumn day was cool and the air crisp and clear as she started on her ride. She walked her horse as far as the fence that marked the boundary line of the ranch, intending to increase her pace once she reached the open road beyond it. As she rode through the gate, however, she caught a glimpse in the distance of the rust-colored mare.

The mare advanced slowly, hesitantly, inching with infinite caution closer to the woman. The ungainly, long-legged colt frolicked behind the mother, oblivious to any danger and enjoying itself for the sheer pleasure of the moment.

Hastily deciding that her errands could wait, Millicent moved with equal caution toward the two wild horses. Perhaps the mare would gain sufficient confidence in her that she would be able to approach it and make friends without difficulty. She drew nearer, then nearer still.

All at once the mare panicked, realizing that the human being was perilously close, and she bolted toward the rock-strewn canyon behind it. The colt hesitated for a moment, then took off after its mother, making surprisingly good time in spite of its age.

Millicent watched the pair descend the tricky slope to the base of the canyon. She could have pursued them, she knew, because the area into which the two wild horses were heading was a blind section, cut off completely, with no means of escape. But she reasoned that she had other business to attend to and reluctantly turned back to the road to resume her journey. Someday when she had both time and opportunity, she thought, she would do her best to make friends with the mare and with its colt. Patting her mount by way of consolation, she continued on her journey into Boise.

Once in the city, Millicent went about her errands with her customary efficiency and dispatch. She was surprised by the number of people who greeted her on the street and in shops. Although she and her cousin had been living in the area only a short time, they were already well known, and the friendliness of the people in Boise was heartwarming. But lacking the courage to respond in kind, Millicent only nodded and gave them shy smiles.

At last she finished her errands and started the ride toward home. A glance at the watch that was hanging on a chain from her neck assured her she would be at the ranch in ample time for noon dinner.

She made good time on her homeward journey, and when she came to the dead-end canyon where the rust-colored mare and colt had taken refuge, she glanced at it idly to see if the wild horses were still in sight. Suddenly she froze, and her heart missed a beat.

Backing toward the steep cliff wall that marked the end of the canyon was the colt, cowering but unable to escape in any other direction. In front of the colt was its mother, back also to the wall, rearing on hind legs and lashing out furiously with her front legs as she neighed and snorted.

Facing the pair, pacing from side to side as it tried to sneak past the flashing hoofs of the mare in order to get at the colt, was a tawny, long-tailed mountain lion, a sleek beast the size of a very large dog. Snarling and displaying great cunning, the lion edged closer, then backed away from the mare's hoofs, all the while maneuvering mother and child closer toward the base of the cliff wall, from which there was no outlet. Its intentions were clear to the horrified young woman: Craftily taking its time, the beast was maneuvering the two horses into position for the final kill. It would get the mother out of the way, then attack the colt and devour it.

Millicent realized that by the time she summoned help from the ranch, it would probably be too late to save the horses. All that would remain of the mare's colt would be its mutilated carcass. She could depend on no one but herself.

Controlling a wild tremor that shook her, she forced her frightened mount down into the canyon. Taking from the saddle sling her rifle—an old-fashioned, single-shot model—

she was sorry now that she had not carried any extra ammunition with her. There was one shot in the loaded weapon, which, she had reasoned at the time, would be sufficient for her needs. She knew that she was engaging in a most hazardous enterprise: She had to make her single shot good, or she would be placing her mount and herself in as grave jeopardy as the mare and colt.

The lion looked back across its shoulder and became aware of the slowly approaching horse and rider. But it remained intent on its immediate task of killing the colt and once again devoted its full attention to that end.

When Millicent reached a point about one hundred feet down the slope from the lion, her mount suddenly balked and could not be persuaded to advance any closer. Ignoring the young woman's spurs in its flanks, it stubbornly stood very still.

Millicent, who had never in her life fired a shot in anger, knew that the time was at hand for her to act swiftly and decisively. It was essential that she act quickly, before the lion turned on her and her horse. Grasping the rifle so tightly that her knuckles whitened, she raised the weapon to her shoulder.

She felt a sense of utter panic and wanted to drop the rifle and flee as rapidly as her horse would carry her. She knew, however, that her conscience would give her no rest if she deserted the mare and colt. Although the air was very cool, a film of perspiration spread across her forehead, and several drops stung her eyes. She could feel still more sweat trickling slowly down her spine.

She knew it was necessary to calm herself, that she could

not possibly fire her rifle with accuracy in her present state. But how could she become tranquil when the lives of innocent animals were at stake?

Suddenly, inexplicably, the notes of a Bach sonata flashed through her mind, and all at once she heard the soothing, pastoral tune. The familiar music encouraged her, lifted her spirits, and soothed her as nothing else on earth could. In some way that she could not understand, the entire sonata took only a few seconds to play. By the time it was finished, her hands were calm, her mind was at peace, and she was tranquil, ready for any test.

The mountain lion crept still closer to the hysterical mare.

Millicent knew she had to act immediately. "Now!" she whispered, and remembering all that her cousin had taught her, she raised her rifle, settled the butt in the hollow of her shoulder, and peered down the length of the barrel, sighting the head of the lion. Then, when she pulled the trigger, she squeezed it gently rather than jerking it, and the shot echoed and reechoed through the canyon.

Afraid to look, Millicent forced herself to peer at the scene ahead and felt a quick surge of relief, mingled with elation, when she saw the mountain lion stretched on the ground, moving feebly, blood gushing from a wound that she had inflicted.

Lacking ammunition, she could not fire a second shot to put the animal out of its misery, but that proved unnecessary. The mountain lion suddenly ceased all movement. It was clearly dead.

One last chore remained for Millicent to perform: She was determined to make friends with the mare and her colt.

Slowly, scarcely daring to breathe now, she spurred forward and approached the skittish pair. She had them cornered, just as the mountain lion had cornered them, but her motive was benevolent. To prevent the mare from rearing and attempting an escape, Millicent knew she would have to lasso the animal. Strictly for her own amusement, Millicent had been learning from the ranch hands how to handle lariats, never dreaming that she would ever put her new knowledge to use. But all at once, her rifle shot having been so effective, she felt a surge of confidence, and swinging the rope above her head in a widening circle, she released the loop at the right moment and watched with great satisfaction as it dropped over the head of the mare, closing around her head and neck.

Gently drawing the loop shut, Millicent anticipated that the mare would try to break away, but the animal surprised her by being docile and cooperative. As the loop became smaller and the line became taut, the horse, her fear having dissipated, trotted closer to the woman and her mount. Apparently the killing of the mountain lion had given the horse a sense of trust for Millicent that had been missing previously.

Marveling at what she had achieved, Millicent started back toward the ranch. The mare followed close behind, never letting the line grow taut. Meanwhile, the colt, saved from the marauding designs of the mountain lion, frolicked unconcernedly as it followed its mother into benign captivity.

Millicent and her strange entourage created a sensation when they arrived at the ranch and made their way up the dusty road to the house. Jim and the hired hands stared at her, and even Ah-Sing came from the kitchen to view the spectacle. After Millicent told them about the attack, two of the hands rode off and returned a short time later with the carcass of the dead mountain lion.

"We'll have the head and skin made into a rug for you," Jim told his cousin. "In that way you'll have a memento of this occasion for many years to come."

"Thank you," Millicent replied. She did not give voice to her thought that she much preferred a living memento. She walked toward the heretofore skittish mare, who nuzzled her hand and looked at her, huge brown eyes gleaming.

Jim was sensitive to the rapport that existed between the woman and the horse. "Transfer my cousin's saddle to her new mare," he said to one of the hands. "She's going to ride her at once."

Millicent looked at him questioningly.

"Right now," Jim explained, "while her gratitude to you is fresh in her mind—or whatever it is that she may feel—is the time for you to ride her, and she'll be broken in forever."

Millicent quickly agreed.

Two of the hands were holding the mare with difficulty, while two others struggled to put a saddle on her; but as soon as Millicent approached, the animal stood still.

Ah-Sing came up behind Millicent and slipped her an apple, which she offered to the horse, who ate it happily, and that gesture cemented their friendship. The mare stood still while the woman mounted and then took off at a slight sign of pressure from Millicent's knees. Soon they were cantering down the narrow, dusty main road of the ranch, the young colt following crazily and kicking up its heels.

Three-quarters of an hour later Ah-Sing rang the dinner gong outside the kitchen door repeatedly before a breathless and joyful Millicent Randall appeared.

Her eyes were shining when she arrived at the dinner table a few minutes later. "I'm glad to see that Ah-Sing has cooked a roast for this noon," she said. "I'm ravenous!"

Jim, who was already carving the meat, smiled but made no comment.

"As recently as last night and this morning," she said as she took her seat, "I was wondering whether I should let you buy out my share of the ranch and go back to Baltimore."

"What would you do back East?" he asked, not looking up from his carving.

"Well," she said tentatively, "I was thinking of getting my doctorate in music at the conservatory and then devoting myself to composing for a number of years."

"It seems to me," he said mildly, as he served their roast and added potatoes and vegetables to her plate, "that that would be a rather sterile existence."

"Very sterile," Millicent said, speaking more forcefully than she had done in the months that she and her cousin had been traveling. "I'm better acclimated to this part of the world than I dreamed would be possible," she continued proudly, "and I'm sure that Lady and I will continue to learn a great deal from each other."

Jim raised an eyebrow. "Lady?" he inquired.

"My new mare," she said. "I've already instructed the hands that no one else is to ride her—ever! She and I have a great deal to learn from each other."

Toby Holt and Rob Martin sat in the governor's office and waded through requests for various building projects. These documents had been submitted by the legislators representing the territory's districts, and those projects that met with Toby's approval would be forwarded to Washington for consideration by the federal government. For years each legislator had included his own special, pet projects in the list, and the man in the governor's chair had approved them automatically, considering them to be the political prerogative of members of the legislature.

All that was changed now. Toby had explained to the legislators when he met with them before his tour of the territory that he would consider each project on the basis of its own merit; only those that he deemed worthy would be forwarded to Washington.

He and Rob waded through each document to determine whether it was worth the expenditure of federal funds, and they rejected far more than they passed along. The work was dull and time-consuming but was necessary for the proper functioning of an honest administration. Toby and Rob went at their labors doggedly, considering each project and then approving it or reluctantly rejecting it. They knew full well that each time they turned down a territorial legislator, they were creating opposition to the executive branch of the government, but neither man cared. Toby had issued a warning on his first day in office that he intended to be scrupulously honest in his dealings, and he meant to keep his word.

They were interrupted by a tap at the door, and one of the governor's secretaries entered. "The captain in charge of an infantry patrol that has just returned to town wants to see you on a matter of great urgency, sir."

"What does he want?"

The secretary became even more agitated. "I think, sir, I'd

better let the head of the patrol explain this to you in his own way. If you don't mind, sir," he added apologetically.

"Show him in," Toby replied. "Stay where you are, Rob. This is our day for headaches; you may as well share another one with me."

An infantry captain came into the office, wearing a somewhat stained field uniform. Reluctantly following him was a small Indian boy of about eight or nine years. The child was wearing a shirt embroidered with dyed porcupine quills, marking him as a Shoshone. He glared at Toby and Rob, then stared down at the floor, his face impassive.

"The colonel's compliments, sir," the captain said, saluting. "He apologizes to you for involving you in this matter, but it's beyond his capacity to handle, and he says that no one but the governor can deal with it."

"Sit down, Captain " Toby told him. "Who is your young friend?"

"He's the problem, sir," the officer replied gloomily. "My unit picked him up one day on a scouting patrol. He was alone and was starving to death, so we fed him and brought him back to life, so to speak. And now, blast it, we seem to be stuck with him." He turned to the child. "Don't just stand there gaping at us, boy," he said. "Sit down!"

The child made no move.

Toby addressed the child fluently in the language of the Shoshone. "One grows weary if one stands for too long a time," he said gently. "Sit down in the chair there, why don't you?"

The boy was startled to hear a white man speaking in the Shoshone tongue with the ease of a warrior. Looking stunned, he lowered himself gingerly into the chair.

Toby spoke to him again. "What is your age?" he asked. "How many summers have you?"

The child looked confused. "I don't know," he replied. "My mother told me, but I cannot remember her words. It is either eight summers or nine, I'm not sure which."

"It doesn't matter," Toby said lightly. "Where is your father?"

The child raised his head. "I do not remember my father well," he said. "He was a fine, proud warrior of the Shoshone and was killed in battle with the Nez Percé in the last war that we had with them."

"That was five years ago," Toby replied, as Rob nodded in agreement. "It's no wonder you can't recall him very well. You were very young when he was killed. And what of your mother?"

"When the present moon, which is now full, was new," the boy said, his voice quivering, "I traveled with my mother from our old home to go to a new home. I do not know where that home was to be; I only know that she was taking me there. A terrible flood rose up and roared through the valley. My mother dragged me to higher ground, but she stumbled and was drowned." He blinked back the tears that forced their way into his eyes. "Since that time I have been alone. I wandered for many days, but I had no weapons and could shoot no game. I lived on a few wild berries and roots until the warriors who carry thundersticks, the warriors who are the enemies of my people, found me. They gave me food to eat, and they brought me to this place as their captive."

Toby eyed him in silence for a long moment. "What is your name?"

"I am called White Elk."

"Hear the words that I speak to you, White Elk," Toby told him solemnly, "and heed them well. Take them into your heart and do not forget them. I am the sachem of all who wear the blue uniform of the United States and of all who live in the town and on the farms and the ranches, and I say to you that White Elk has no enemies among our people. My people are his people, and he is welcome in our midst for all time."

White Elk regarded him dubiously.

Toby tugged a bellpull that summoned a secretary, and when the door opened almost at once, he said, "Go to my home, if you please, and fetch a container of milk for our young guest here. While you're about it, you might ask Mrs. Holt if we could have a couple of the chocolate cookies that were made for Tim today."

The secretary vanished at once.

Toby turned to the young infantry officer who had not understood a word of Toby's conversation with White Elk. "Captain," he said, "you've done your duty, and I accept responsibility for this orphan. Thank your colonel for me and tell him to dismiss the problem from his mind. The whole matter is no longer the concern of the battalion. It has become my exclusive responsibility."

"Yes, sir." The officer jumped to his feet, saluted, and appeared glad to escape.

Rob Martin looked quizzically at his old friend. "So you've accepted responsibility for the boy, have you?"

Toby nodded thoughtfully. "Yes," he said. "I don't know what might happen to him if I were to just let him go."

"I was prepared to jump in and offer my assistance, but you beat me to it," Rob said with a grin. "As it is, I'd like to share the responsibility with you."

"The financial cost is negligible, at least for the present," Toby said. "As for the rest of it, you don't want to impose too heavy a burden on Kale, who already has your daughter to take care of. You leave the problem to Clarissa and me, and if we're not able to handle it, we'll call on you at once for some help."

"Please do," Rob said. "I meant my offer."

"I know you did," Toby replied, "and I'm grateful for it."

The secretary returned with a container of milk and a bag containing several large, chocolate-covered cookies. He produced two of these and poured out a glass of milk.

White Elk took a small sip of the milk and found it to his liking. Then he nibbled one of the unfamiliar cookies, his eyes brightened, and he proceeded to devour both the treats.

The business of the executive branch of the government of Idaho came to a complete halt while the small Indian child consumed his snack.

Toby prolonged the hiatus by taking White Elk to his house and turning the boy over to Clarissa, who accepted him into the family without question. Returning to his office, the governor resumed work with his lieutenant governor.

Rob Martin made no further mention of the boy until they finished their work after night had fallen. Then he asked, "What are you going to do with the child?"

"I assume we have no real choice in the matter and we'll

have to keep him," Toby replied. "I've had no chance to discuss the matter with Clarissa, but at first glance she seems willing enough, and as for my son, he'll have to acclimate himself to having a big brother around the place."

"I can see one problem growing out of all this," Rob said thoughtfully. "A good many settlers are certain to resent the fact that their governor has taken a Shoshone into his household."

"I'm glad you mentioned that," Toby replied forcefully. "I hope that we'll serve as something of an example to the people of Idaho. There won't be any lasting peace with the Indians in this territory until we learn to live together in friendship and harmony. That's the only permanent solution to what we call the Indian problem, and if anybody in the territory doesn't like what I'm doing, let him come to me with his objections. I'll set him straight fast enough!"

Later that evening, Clarissa Holt heard her husband's analysis of the situation and agreed wholeheartedly that it was necessary to make the Shoshone boy a part of the family. Any fears the couple entertained about White Elk and their son getting along were dispelled the next day when the two boys played together harmoniously. Displaying the natural resilience of children, White Elk seemed to have forgotten his earlier distress and began to teach Tim the rudiments of the Shoshone language. Tim, in return, did the same, attempting to instruct the Indian in the speaking of a few English words.

During the next several days, however, White Elk displayed what his hosts could only regard as a refusal to adjust. He dutifully ate the meals placed before him and did not object to going to bed when he was told. But he remained sullen and withdrawn in the presence of adults, never addressing them, never smiling, and never playing in their presence. Not even Toby, speaking the child's own language, could persuade him to do any more now than reply in abrupt monosyllables.

One evening Edward Blackstone, who had invested in the new Northern Pacific transcontinental railroad line currently under construction and also had put a large sum of money into the building of a new hotel in Boise, came to the governor's mansion with Pamela Drake for dinner. As usual, Pamela politely asked to see Tim, so Clarissa took her off to her son's playroom while the men remained behind and discussed business.

White Elk, who had been playing happily with Tim, withdrew and became surly the moment the two women entered the room. The child could not be cajoled by Clarissa or Pamela into smiling or into talking.

As they returned to the parlor, Clarissa said, "I have an idea that I know what's ailing him. He spent all of his young life being taught that we're the enemy. He's been taught an exaggerated version of our faults and failings, just as we in turn are guilty of giving our children the same exaggerated views of Indians."

Toby and Edward were drawn into the conversation. "Clarissa is right," Toby said. "White Elk is the victim of the lies and false propaganda that have been pumped into him practically since birth. I refuse to worry about him, however. I'm convinced that if we're patient and resolutely ignore his sullen moods, he'll outgrow them and learn to accept us for what we are."

"What a dreadfully unhappy period for the little boy!" Pamela said, somewhat surprised by the intensity of her feelings for the orphan child.

"I'm afraid you're quite right," Clarissa told her, "but there's nothing we can do about it. Children must learn by experience—and that experience is often quite painful for them."

"It needn't be painful," Pamela said, and was silent for a moment. "Would you agree to let me have White Elk?" she asked a trifle breathlessly, her eyes wide and her appeal almost irresistible. "I'm not asking you to give him to me permanently. Just for a time so I can help him make the transition until he becomes accustomed to our kind of civilization."

"Don't be too impulsive, Pam," Edward said quietly. "Don't bite off more than you're able to digest."

"I swear to you, Edward, I am being neither impulsive nor thoughtless," Pamela said firmly. "I came with you to America because I, too, was curious about the West. You've found an outlet for your own restlessness. You're investing funds in various enterprises and becoming involved in the development of Idaho. While you examine properties and go to meetings, I do literally nothing. I fritter away the hours on useless shopping, and even that is terribly limited. I've been seeking some outlet for myself, some way to become more deeply involved in the life of Idaho, and this is my chance. I can devote myself completely to White Elk. I'm prepared to give him so much love and devotion that he'll soon forget the horrid lies he was taught about the Idaho settlers!"

Looking at the attractive, somewhat flashy woman, Clarissa

realized Pamela meant every word she was saying. Obviously her own surface analysis of Pamela had been mistaken. There was more depth and more substance to the woman's character than she had given her credit for possessing.

Troubled by Pamela's suggestion, Toby looked at his wife for guidance. Clarissa nodded slowly, and although she made no comment, her attitude was clear to him. She saw nothing to be lost by trying Pamela's suggestion and seeing if her love could break through the barriers of hate that White Elk had erected.

Toby, however, continued to be troubled. "I have another solution in mind that I'm not prepared to discuss openly as yet," he said, "but I see no reason why we should refrain from trying out your suggestion, Pamela. I'm willing to relinquish White Elk into your temporary custody. But if his attitude does not show a very marked improvement within a few weeks, I will need to try another approach."

Pamela accepted his terms immediately without further discussion.

So it happened that White Elk transferred his domicile to the suite shared by Pamela and Edward in the hotel the following morning. Toby believed in dealing honestly with the child and explained the situation to him: He was going to live for a while with a lady who was anxious to have him and to shower care on him.

White Elk did not protest, accepting his altered situation with remarkable docility. But his expression remained wooden and unchanged, and he showed neither pleasure nor displeasure at the change in his living arrangements.

Toby kept his reservations about the situation to himself

until that evening when he and Clarissa were at dinner. Then he finally spoke freely. "I'm sure you remember my telling you that Stalking Horse made a request of me before we left Oregon," he said. "He very much wanted to come to Idaho for a final taste of frontier living. I sent for him today. I thought it unwise to ask him to come here until I had some specific mission that he could perform, and I've found that mission for him now."

"What is that?" Clarissa asked.

"It may be," Toby said, "that Stalking Horse is better equipped than anyone to solve the dilemma of White Elk."

Clarissa's face cleared, and she smiled. "Of course! Why didn't I think of Stalking Horse? He's wise and he's kind, and he'll know just what to do with the poor child."

Stalking Horse responded to Toby's summons with the alacrity of an old firehorse who hears the sound of alarm bells for the first time in years. Taking with him a bedroll, a few necessary cooking utensils, his bow, a rifle, two six-guns, as well as extra ammunition, he mounted his stallion and set out at once for the journey across the mountains. When he arrived in Boise, his eyes gleamed brightly, and he actually looked rested after his arduous journey.

Assigning him quarters in the governor's mansion and inviting him to eat as many meals as he wished with the Holt family, Toby told his old friend to take some time to become acquainted with Boise. So the old Cherokee deliberately set out on some short exploratory trips.

After spending more than a generation at the ranch in Oregon, Stalking Horse dressed like a rancher in work pants and boots, an open-throated shirt topped with an unbuttoned leather vest, and a wide-brimmed hat. Most important, he carried a brace of six-shooters on his belt.

Although most residents of Boise were not inclined toward friendliness with either the Nez Percé or the Shoshone, they treated the Cherokee with respectful attention. Not only was Stalking Horse the better part of a foot taller than the warriors of the Western tribes, but his rancher's attire, combined with his virtually flawless English, marked him as being unlike the Indians with whom the Idaho settlers were having so many problems. What was more, the six-shooters that Stalking Horse carried, combined with the air that he exuded of knowing how to use the guns, guaranteed him a cordial reception everywhere.

One of the last places in town that Stalking Horse visited was Maloney's Saloon. He wandered into the place on his second afternoon in Boise and was immediately struck by the friendly, cheerful atmosphere. A small wood fire was burning in the hearth, taking the chill off the air, and Stalking Horse went directly to the bar, where he ordered himself the only drink that he ever had, a glass of apple juice. As he raised his mug to his lips and sipped the contents, a black crow standing on a nearby perch spoke mournfully in a thick Irish brogue.

"Where's Murphy?" the bird asked, hopping back and forth on its perch. "Where's Murphy?"

Startled, Stalking Horse laughed aloud. "Who or what is that?" he asked the proprietor. "And who is Murphy?"

"He's a talkin' crow named Gilhooley," Maloney answered, gesturing toward the bird. "Murphy is his best friend, an old miner who taught him to speak in a cabin up in the mountains."

"Where's Murphy?" Gilhooley demanded dolefully.

"The old man went into the mountains on an errand," Maloney explained, "and he said he had to get up there before the snow started to fall. I suspect that he has a mine up there somewhere and he doesn't want to reveal the whereabouts to anybody. In any case, he left the bird here for safekeepin'." He took a small handful of birdseed and dropped it into a tiny cup at one end of the perch.

Gilhooley eyed the birdseed sadly but made no attempt to eat. "Where's Murphy?" he asked again.

Maloney sighed. "This here is the damnedest reaction I've ever seen. Gilhooley hasn't taken a grain of birdseed in days, and although he usually chatters his head off, all he does now is ask for Murphy. So help me, if anything has happened to the old man, it wouldn't surprise me if this bird starves himself to death."

Stalking Horse had seen much that was strange in the course of his long life, but he had never encountered anything as odd as Gilhooley.

Night was falling, and the saloon began to fill up with patrons who had finished their day's work. Maloney put out several platters of cold meats and hard-boiled eggs, and as each new arrival came into the establishment, he was greeted by a mournful Gilhooley, who again and again inquired after the whereabouts of his dear friend.

A number of the customers were acquainted with the crow and tried to persuade the bird to eat and to say something else, but Gilhooley would have none of it. Refusing to be cajoled, he did nothing but repeat his dirgelike question.

Stalking Horse marveled at the bird. As nearly as he could

discern, Gilhooley's grief for the missing miner was genuine, and his sorrow had virtually incapacitated him. Slowly sipping his juice, the Cherokee stood silently and shook his head. If he had not been witnessing the phenomenon with his own eyes, he would have refused to believe it.

Suddenly two patrons near the door began to shout. "He's here! Murphy is here!"

The old man tied his faithful burro, Julia, outside, then entered slowly and made his way toward the bar. His boots were covered with dust, and when he removed his dilapidated hat and slapped it against one leg, a cloud of dust emerged from it. He had not shaved in many days, and he looked utterly exhausted.

"In the name of Saint Michael," he croaked, "be merciful to an old codger, Maloney, and give me a wee drop of whiskey before I drop dead of thirst."

While the bartender obliged him, a dozen voices chimed in to bring Murphy up to date, and they related the saga of his talking crow, one after another picking up the refrain. Gilhooley was almost forgotten in the excitement. Only Stalking Horse was conscious of the bird, and while the Cherokee watched surreptitiously, Gilhooley began to eat, picking up grain after grain of birdseed and popping it into his beak with such rapidity that his head bobbed up and down like an automaton.

Murphy's equilibrium was restored by the consumption of two shots of whiskey, and at last he wandered over to the perch, where the crow, still eating, paid no attention whatever to him.

"So, Gilhooley, m'lad," Murphy said, "ye missed me somethin' fierce, did ye? Wouldn't eat and wouldn't drink and wouldn't sleep the whole time I was gone."

Gilhooley slowly raised his head and fixed a pair of shiny button eyes on the old miner. He hopped onto his shoulder as Murphy pushed his way through the crowd at the bar. Then on the street they joined the sad-eyed little burro, whom Murphy unhitched from the rail and led away.

Stalking Horse shook his head. If what he had just witnessed was any criterion, Idaho was the strangest portion of the entire United States.

White Elk was convinced that he was the unhappiest Indian in all the world. The woman with whom he lived and who insisted that he call her "Pamela" meant well enough, but she appeared too stupid and insensitive to realize that she was smothering him with her unwanted affections and that he loathed every aspect of his day-to-day living. He hated being forced to wear the attire of an Idaho settler instead of the honest clothing of the Shoshone that he had worn all of his life. He hated being forced to accompany Pamela into the hotel dining room, where he tucked a napkin into his shirt and observed the table manners of the settlers. He felt like retching when he was served the rich foods of the settlers, instead of the simple broiled meats and parched corn of his own people. He found it difficult to sleep in the settlers' soft beds that were equipped with down-filled mattresses, and most of all, he hated being expected to speak English and to demonstrate the white man's manners that he was being taught.

Blissfully unaware of the boy's feelings, Pamela continued to lavish her love upon him. Aware that her custody was only temporary, she began a campaign to enlist the support of others to help her keep White Elk.

Edward Blackstone, long experienced in Pamela's methods, refused to have anything to do with her scheme. She invited Jim and Millicent Randall to noon dinner and not only won their sympathy but actually persuaded Millicent to let White Elk ride her mare, Lady. With that the Randall cousins were won over to her cause.

The experiment proved so successful that Pamela tried to repeat it with Rob Martin, but of course she had to invite Kale Salton to dinner as well. Pamela made such an obvious bid for Rob's support that she won in addition Kale's opposition to the move, assuring herself of Kale's lasting enmity— although she had no idea that she was sowing seeds of destruction for herself.

As for White Elk, he remained unaware of such maneuvers and manipulations. Instead he dreamed about the feel of buckskin next to his skin, the smell of a wood fire, and the taste of freshly killed meat roasted over it. He longed for a night that he could spend in the open, wrapped only in his blanket as he lay on the ground; he despised the regimen of civilization imposed on him by the woman he was obliged to call Pamela.

One day, after a dinner of beef that had been spoiled by overcooking, White Elk had returned with Pamela to her hotel suite. Still hungry at the end of the meal, he had gorged on ice cream as a way of appeasing his still-raging appetite. Now, comfortably full at last, he was trying to reconcile himself to the inevitable English lesson to which she would subject him.

The tutoring session was barely under way when a tap sounded at the front door. Pamela answered the summons, then conversed for a long time with someone in the outer hall.

When she returned to the parlor, she was followed by a very tall man in typical rancher's attire. To the boy's astonishment, he was a full-blooded Indian, and because his hair was gray, White Elk knew he deserved immediate respect. Therefore, the boy jumped at once to his feet and extended his left arm as far as he could reach it, holding it palm upward in the traditional sign of Indian greeting.

The man studied him at length, wise eyes probing and searching, his immobile face revealing nothing of his inner feelings. At last he elected to speak. "So you are White Elk," he said in the boy's native tongue. "You are the boy whose destiny, that of becoming a Shoshone warrior, has been changed, and who will now become the adopted son of the chief sachem of the Idaho Territory."

"I am White Elk," the boy said, but admitted no more.

Stalking Horse did not raise his voice, and his expression remained unchanged, but there was a cutting edge to his words that made the child cringe. "Are you so lacking in gratitude that you would refuse the food and shelter of him who saved you from starvation and death in the wilderness?" he demanded. "Are you so burdened with false pride that you lack the grace to express your thanks to him who has rescued you from degradation and slow death? Would you prefer that he left your body as a feast for the vultures, who come and eat the flesh of those who have departed from this life?"

White Elk hung his head. "I did not mean to offend you, O Venerable One."

Pamela gazed first at the elderly Indian, then at the small

boy. She had no idea what they were saying, but it was obvious to her that the man was blasting the child, who was displaying the greatest possible chagrin.

"I have suffered an insult within an inch of my life," Stalking Horse said fiercely, and only someone who knew him well could have realized that he was acting. "The father of Governor Holt was my closest friend and my blood brother," he declared. "His skin was white, but eleven Indian nations voted him full membership. As to his son, I have known him all his life. It was I who taught him to ride a horse. It was I who first introduced him to the mysteries of the wilderness. He is as close to me as though he were my own kin, my own son. Now White Elk in his ignorance has rejected the help of the best friend the Indian nations have in all of North America."

"I crave the pardon of him whose hair is gray," the miserable boy said.

Deciding he had been punished enough, the Cherokee said, "I am called Stalking Horse and have been so called for more than six times ten summers. You may call me by that name also."

"Thank you, Stalking Horse." White Elk was humbly grateful for the small crumb of a favor from the old man.

Stalking Horse turned now to the young woman, and addressing her in English, he said, "Governor Holt has suggested that I take the boy into the wilderness with me for two weeks, and there we will see whether we are compatible with each other or whether he is as surly with me as he is with you. In all fairness, I mention this first to you, before I broach the subject to him."

Pamela hesitated. She had already been told by the Cherokee that he was the foreman of the Holt ranch in Oregon and had been a close associate of the governor's renowned father, as well as an intimate friend of Governor Holt's. She was afraid she was fighting a losing battle and that Stalking Horse ultimately would gain custody of White Elk, but her English sense of fair play demanded that she give him every opportunity that she herself had had. Raising her chin, she said bravely, "Do what you think is best for the boy, and if he finds contentment with you, that is more than enough to satisfy me."

"So be it," Stalking Horse said, and bowed to her in appreciation. Then he turned to the boy and asked, "Would it interest White Elk to come with me for a fortnight in the wilderness?"

The little boy was ecstatic. "Would it interest me?" he shouted. "I would rather make such a journey than do anything else in all the world."

All at once he remembered his manners and pulled himself together with a great effort. Folding his arms across his chest, he inclined his head slightly. "It would give me great joy," he said, "to go with Stalking Horse into the wilderness."

Stalking Horse knew that his attitude, at first stern and then suddenly relenting, had had its desired effect. "Does White Elk have suitable clothes for wilderness travel?" he asked.

The boy's heart hammered hard against his rib cage, but he managed to speak sedately. "I have one pair of moccasins, one pair of buckskin trousers, and one buckskin shirt, the clothes I was wearing when the soldiers of Idaho found me and captured me."

"They did not capture you," Stalking Horse said, quickly

rebuking him. "They saved your life. However, we will speak of this and of many other things when we leave the civilization of the settlers behind us. Change into your wilderness clothing and come with me."

The boy tried hard to maintain his dignity, but his efforts failed. He bolted from the room, returning in record time wearing his own clothes, which he had been forced to put aside on the day that he had first arrived in Boise.

"Do not neglect to express your gratitude to her who gave you such a comfortable and splendid sanctuary," Stalking Horse said, prodding him gently.

The child turned to Pamela. He had hated his life with Pamela Drake and had convinced himself that he hated her as well. But at this moment of parting, he felt sad that he was giving up his intimate relationship with her. He knew that he would miss her, that there would always be a special place for her in his heart. "Thank you," he said, struggling to express himself in English. "You—very good—to White Elk." Words failed him, and giving in to his impulse, which he rarely did, he threw his arms around her neck and kissed her.

Pamela returned the hug and kiss with a ferocity that matched his. Her eyes were unashamedly wet, and White Elk brushed a tear from his cheek.

Stalking Horse averted his face so they would not feel disgraced by the knowledge that he saw them weep.

As White Elk followed the elderly Cherokee out of the hotel suite and into the streets of Boise, he felt a reaction that he pondered for a long time without finding an adequate answer. Not until years passed and he neared adulthood would the truth of his relationship with the white woman dawn on him.

*   *   *

Stalking Horse made an indelible impression on White Elk during the two weeks they spent together in the wilderness. Never had the young boy encountered any brave so adept in the ways of the wild, so resourceful, so inventive, so skilled.

Stalking Horse took with him two horses to carry their supplies, which included rifles, ammunition, and blankets. He also carried his bow and arrow. He brought no food or cooking utensils along, for he intended to bring down what they ate and cook it Indian-style over their fire.

The first lesson that the boy learned was how to track animals and humans and how to avoid being tracked in return. He had learned the basic concepts from braves before, but White Elk had no idea that the art was so complex, its methods so numerous.

They ate exclusively off the land, and White Elk was taught the rudiments of how to hunt game, large and small, with bow and arrow and with firearms. He was also taught the rudiments of fishing, and equally important, how to cook meat and fish and how to prepare it for use at a later date. He was given lessons in how to dress the skins of animals that they had slain and, in brief, was instructed in the basics of survival, obtaining food, shelter, and clothing.

He was taught so much that his head spun, but what impressed him most of all was that Stalking Horse made each function appear simple and easy to perform. Only when White Elk tried to emulate him did he discover that the various tasks were far more difficult and complicated than they seemed.

At no time in the boy's short life had any man lavished such care and attention on him. White Elk rapidly developed a case of hero worship and took every word that his mentor spoke completely to heart.

One day White Elk was shown an impressive sample of Stalking Horse's expertise. They were walking on high ground in the hills of the territory, an area of short grass suitable only for pastures and strewn with heavy boulders. Stalking Horse was delivering one of his customary lectures when suddenly he broke off. Dropping to one knee, he pressed his ear against the ground, nodded, and then motioned his young charge to a place behind a heavy boulder, where he quickly joined the boy. Putting a finger to his lips to indicate the need for silence, he unslung his rifle, made certain it was loaded, and then waited, totally at ease and in command of the situation.

After a considerable wait, four mounted warriors appeared, all of them heavily armed, all wearing war paint that identified them as Nez Percé braves. They were following tracks left by Stalking Horse and White Elk and were having their fair share of difficulty in interpreting which way the pair had gone.

The quartet reached a point about one hundred and fifty paces from the boulder behind which the man and boy were concealed. One of their number dismounted and inspected the grass closely there to see which way the strands were bent.

Stalking Horse decided they had come close enough. He had no idea whether these braves were friendly or unfriendly, and he had no intention of finding out. Raising his rifle to his shoulder, Stalking Horse squinted down the length of his barrel.

To the consternation of the young boy, he appeared to be aiming at the brave who was kneeling on the ground. Demonstrating no concern, the elderly Cherokee squeezed his trigger, and the crack of his rifle sounded loud and clear on the autumn air.

To the utter astonishment of White Elk, who peered around the corner of the boulder, the bullet had struck an ornamental feather that rose straight into the air from the Nez Percé's scalp lock. Now the feather was neatly cut in half.

Seeing what had happened to their comrade, the other braves hastily decided to absent themselves from the scene. Without waiting for him, they turned their mounts around and cantered off in the direction from which they had come. The unfortunate brave on the ground reached up to his head, felt his severed feather, and decided to join his companions. Mounting his horse in panic, he followed them as rapidly as he could ride.

White Elk could contain himself no longer and whooped in sheer glee. The sober expression on Stalking Horse's face remained unchanged, however. "What is the lesson to be learned from this incident?" he demanded.

White Elk could not stop giggling. "I—I don't know."

"We were badly outnumbered by the braves," the Cherokee explained patiently. "We knew they were searching the countryside for us, but we had no way of knowing whether their intentions toward us were friendly or hostile. There was nothing to be gained by waiting and finding out in a direct confrontation with them. Therefore, we faced a difficult problem. How could we best discourage them without causing them personal harm or injury? The sight line to the eagle feather worn in the scalp lock of the brave who dismounted was without obstacle. By destroying the feather, I killed their desire to overtake us.''

"But—but weren't you taking a great risk?'' the boy demanded breathlessly. "The eagle feather extended upward only inches from the warrior's scalp lock, and if you had missed your target, you could have killed him.''

Stalking Horse smiled and patted the stock of his rifle. "There are occasions in one's life,'' he said, "when one is required to have confidence in the abilities that one has worked so hard to learn. With such confidence all things are possible. Without it—I do not like to think of the consequences.''

Looking up at him in awe, White Elk was convinced that no feat was beyond the capacity of this remarkable old Cherokee.

At last the two-week sojourn in the wilderness came to an end, and Stalking Horse returned to Boise with the boy. They went straight to the governor's office, where they presented themselves to a secretary.

Toby Holt did not admit them to his presence immediately. First he insisted on sending word to Pamela Drake, requesting that she come to his office at once. A short time later the trio was ushered into Governor Holt's office together.

Toby was immediately struck by the appearance of Stalking Horse and White Elk. The boy was radiant, his expression ecstatic. For his part, the Cherokee had shed years from his age in the two weeks they had been gone.

Toby motioned the child to stand closer to his desk, and when he spoke, he addressed him first in English and then repeated his question in the tongue of the Shoshone so that both the boy and Pamela would know what was being said. "Did you enjoy your trip into the wilderness?" he asked.

White Elk nodded with such joyous ferocity that his head seemed to bob up and down.

Toby looked to Stalking Horse for corroboration. The elderly Cherokee replied first in English, then in the language of the Shoshone, to make sure that White Elk also understood what was being said. "We wasted no time in the wilderness," he said. "It requires many years of hard work to transform a man-child into a warrior who is a credit to his people. Those lessons have been properly started."

"Did White Elk enjoy the excursion?" Toby persisted.

Stalking Horse shrugged. "So he has indicated," he replied impassively.

Toby motioned the boy to a chair. "What is your wish, White Elk?" he asked. "With whom do you want to live?"

The little boy answered unhesitatingly. "I like the lady very much," he said. "She has been kind and good to me, as you have. But Stalking Horse is my own kind, and if he would consent to take me under his roof, act as my instructor, and become a grandfather to me, I would gladly do his bidding in all things and obey his will."

Toby was not surprised by the reply and thought he knew Stalking Horse sufficiently well to anticipate from the gleam he saw in the old man's eyes just what he would say.

But the Cherokee surprised him. "I am willing to take White Elk under my roof and to be like his grandfather," he said. "But he will grow to adulthood in a world far different from the world that I knew. When I was young, it was essential that a warrior learned, above all else, how to survive in the wilderness. If he knew that, nothing else was required of him. But life today is far more complicated than it was in my youth. Settlers have moved into areas where only Indians lived and into other places in the wilds where no one resided. Today a warrior must know how to live with his neighbors, the settlers, if he is to be happy and if he is to survive. He must learn, even as I learned, to accommodate, to compromise, and to be a good neighbor."

Toby was struck anew by the old man's wisdom.

"Therefore I say this to White Elk." Stalking Horse turned and addressed the boy. "I will gladly take you under my roof and be like a grandfather to you. I will teach you all that I know about the wilderness, about weapons and how to use them. But that is not enough. You have a great need, also, for all that the lady known as Pamela Drake can teach you. If you are to survive and prosper in the world of today and the world that will exist when you grow to manhood tomorrow, you must become her pupil, as well as mine. You must open your heart and your mind to all that she can teach you, and you must absorb her lessons as eagerly as you take to mine."

As Toby translated for her, Pamela was deeply affected by the Cherokee's words and smiled tremulously. Stalking Horse had found a perfect solution to a problem that had loomed as insoluble.

"What do you say, White Elk, to the suggestion proposed by Stalking Horse?" Toby asked.

The boy smiled steadily. "I will happily abide by the decision of my grandfather."

When White Elk's response had been translated, Pamela sprang from her seat, went to him, and hugged him.

So it was amicably arranged that White Elk would spend a part of each year with Stalking Horse and the remainder of the year with Pamela. No time limits were set for either, but it was agreed that each would keep him long enough to imbue him with the virtues of the civilizations that his two mentors represented.

As Toby commented that night to Clarissa, "You'll have ample opportunity to see this new arrangement in action. Stalking Horse and the boy are going to spend the winter here, with both Stalking Horse and Pamela teaching him. When the spring comes, it'll be decided whether he'll begin his portion of the year with Stalking Horse back in Oregon or whether he'll stay in Idaho in Pamela's custody."

"It strikes me," Clarissa said, "that whomever he goes with first, White Elk is going to get the best of two worlds."

"That's precisely what's going to happen," her husband replied. "He's an exceptionally fortunate boy."

IV

Most residents of Boise no longer regarded Edward Black-stone as a foreigner. He had been present for the ground-breaking ceremonies for the new hotel being constructed in town, and it had been accepted without comment that he was part owner of the hostelry.

A short time later he had set out with two companions for the Lost River Range, in the mountains almost due east of Boise, to inspect the mining property in which he had invested. When he returned after being trapped in the mountains for a week by the autumn season's first snowfall, he and Pamela Drake once more became familiar sights as they rode daily through Boise.

To be sure, he and Pamela had their idiosyncrasies. Not the least of these was their insistence on using flat English-style saddles instead of the U-shaped saddles that were used in the West. Pamela was subjected to even more criticism than

Edward because she rode sidesaddle, as befitting a lady in England. Since she invariably carried a small, high-powered rifle when she rode, jokes about her alleged prowess, or lack of it when riding sidesaddle, became legion.

Edward and Pamela demonstrated their good-natured sportsmanship by making no objection when they were the butts of humor, and they let people say what they would. "We can ride with the best of them," Edward said, "and we're fair enough shots, so let them laugh."

A rodeo was held that autumn, and ranchers and hands from properties as distant as two hundred miles entered the contests. Prizes were given for various feats of skill, and the largest sum was to be awarded for a shooting contest to be held on horseback when cantering. Not only did Governor Toby Holt offer an auxiliary prize equal to the purse being presented to the winner, but he also added to the excitement of the occasion by personally entering his name as a competitor.

His act inspired Edward Blackstone to participate in the shooting contest, too, and interest in the event was aroused to a fever pitch. Wagers were placed on many contestants. Edward was a relatively unknown quantity, however, and he remained a long shot.

Seats made of planks had been constructed at one end of the field for the distinguished guests, who included Governor and Mrs. Holt and their young son, as well as Lieutenant Governor Martin, his baby daughter, and Kale Salton.

The entire morning was taken up with races, branding and roping contests, and other trials of skill. Most people had brought picnic hampers with them. They ate their noon meals in the open and then returned to their places for the afternoon's events.

First among these was one of the highlights of the rodeo, the shooting contest, and Toby Holt excused himself, mounted his horse, and went off to join the other contestants. The managers of the rodeo wanted Toby to begin the contest, but he insisted on being given no special treatment and drew for his place, as did everyone else. As it happened, he was awarded the next-to-last position, while Edward drew eleventh position out of thirty-one.

The rules, the chairman of the judges' committee explained to the entrants, were simple. Six targets were located within a one-hundred-yard range on one side of the field, and a horseman was expected to cover the distance of one hundred yards in no more than two minutes, firing at each of the targets with one of his six-shooters. Then he was to reverse himself and on his return down the field, fire at six other targets located on the opposite side, which would require the use of the other six-shooter. Only one shot was to be fired at each target, which was a circle approximately the size of a baseball, drawn on a sheet of white cardboard and painted a bright orange color.

No excuses would be tolerated, and each contestant would be judged exclusively on his score. Anyone who took longer than the required time would be disqualified, as would any contestant who drew his mount to a halt during the period in which he was expected to fire.

The contestants clustered together and listened as the rules were explained again, this time to the audience. Toby and Edward found themselves sitting their mounts adjacent to each other.

"I wish you the best of good fortune," Toby said as they shook hands.

"The same to you, Governor!" Edward replied heartily.

The person who had drawn for first position was called forward. The crowd became quiet, and the contest was under way. Watching closely, Toby knew he had nothing to fear from the first contestant, a ranch hand who hit four targets out of a possible twelve.

By the time Edward Blackstone moved into the starting position, the highest score yet had been achieved by a sergeant of the cavalry battalion, who had scored six out of the possible twelve. A wave of good-natured jeering greeted Edward as he cantered onto the field in his English saddle. The laughter soon died away, however, and became respectful silence. And by the time Edward completed his ride up the field, then down again, the audience was cheering. The chief judge announced that he had achieved a score of nine strikes.

Contestant after contestant tried in vain to break his record, but with one exception, a ranch hand who hit eight targets, none came close. By the time that Toby moved into the waiting position, most people in the crowd were conceding the victory to the Englishman.

The announcement that the next contestant would be Governor Holt brought forth an excited spattering of applause.

Toby quickly increased his stallion's speed to a canter, and then he amazed the spectators by adopting an extraordinary technique. Rather than emptying one six-shooter before drawing the other, the governor drew both his pistols simultaneously and subjected the targets to a cross fire, shooting at those targets on his right with the pistol he carried in his left hand, and those on the left with the pistol he carried in his right hand. As the spectators watched the governor execute his unique method, a deathly quiet settled over the assemblage.

Reaching the end of the course, Toby scarcely slackened his stallion's speed as he grabbed the reins, wheeled the animal around, and trotted back to the spectators. Pandemonium broke loose in the enthusiastic audience, and Clarissa had a difficult time in controlling Tim, who jumped up and down on his plank seat screaming, "Papa won! Papa won!"

It was scarcely necessary for the chief judge to announce the results: Governor Holt had achieved a remarkable record, hitting all twelve targets in only half the allotted time. The efforts of the final contestant were anticlimactic, and the judges scarcely found it necessary to consult each other before it was announced that Governor Holt was the unqualified winner of the contest. Toby had demonstrated conclusively to his excited, thrilled audience that he was equal to his fabled father in marksmanship and that he took second place to no one in Idaho.

Thunderous applause greeted the governor as he rode into the arena and removed his broad-brimmed hat. Then he raised one hand, and when the crowd had grown quiet, he made a simple announcement. "Seeing as how I offered a purse equal to the first prize being offered today," he said, "I disqualify myself from first place. I offer the prize instead to Edward Blackstone, who achieved a better than respectable nine out of twelve."

Removing his own hat, Edward laughingly declined to accept the money. He had entered the contest for the sheer sport of it, he said, and he had satisfied himself that, in spite of his English saddle, he was as good a shot as anyone in the territory "excepting Governor Holt, whom no mere mortal could hope to beat."

The prize finally was awarded to the third place winner, the ranch hand who had racked up a score of eight targets.

From that day onward, Toby was treated with even greater awe as a marksman without a peer, and Edward no longer had to listen to laughter when he appeared on his English saddle.

Edward Blackstone was invited to the ranch of his cousins, Millicent and Jim Randall, for Sunday dinner, and Pamela Drake was included in the invitation. Edward, who appreciated Ah-Sing's efforts in the kitchen, accepted with alacrity, and Pamela was delighted to attend for reasons of her own. She was flattered by Jim Randall's obvious interest in her. Although he presented her with far less of a challenge than did Rob Martin—who never went anywhere without Kale Salton at his side—she appreciated the attention that Jim showed her.

The couple left for the Randalls' ranch just as the churches of Boise were discharging their Sunday morning worshipers, and the streets were crowded with pedestrians. Because Edward had proved his worth at the rodeo, people now ignored his English saddle. But Pamela still called attention to herself by riding sidesaddle, and pedestrians smiled broadly at the sight of her. Still, no one dared to comment. Edward was far too good a shot, and Pamela was carrying a rifle in a sling suspended from her saddle.

The sky overhead was blustery and gray, and there was more than a hint of an approaching storm in the air, so Edward started out at a gallop. Pamela kept up with him easily. They were both enjoying the outing.

When they left Boise behind them, Edward shifted to a

canter, and Pamela instantly adjusted her speed to his. It was no wonder that they had maintained such a close friendship for so many years. They had an instinctive understanding of each other and responded instantly to subtle shifts and changes.

Suddenly Pamela saw Edward reach for the fine, new-model repeating rifle that he had brought from England and carried in a shoulder sling behind him. Quickly drawing her own rifle and making sure that it was loaded and cocked, she looked around. In the distance she saw a group of horsemen heading toward a small ranch house owned by some middle-aged neighbors of the Randalls, and as Edward turned toward them, he realized that they were Indians.

"They're Nez Percé," Edward told her, "and they appear to be looking for trouble. I'm in favor of accommodating them. What do you say?"

"Lead on, old boy," she replied cheerfully. "A spot of exercise before dinner should put an edge on our appetites."

As they drew closer to the group, Pamela counted eight braves in the party, all of them mounted on swift-moving ponies and all of them carrying large, cumbersome rifles. The warrior in the lead called out something over his shoulder, and the entire party changed direction. Forming a single, horizontal line, they began to advance across open country toward the English couple.

"How convenient," Edward said cheerfully. "They're intending to meet us, which saves us the trouble of chasing after them. I daresay we can keep them busy enough so they'll forget about attacking that ranch house. Are you ready for them, Pam?"

"As ready as I'll ever be," she told him, seemingly unconcerned about the prospect of a battle with an enemy who outnumbered them by four to one.

"See here," Edward said, a hint of urgency in his voice. "Instead of meeting the blighters head-on, we will sweep across their front from left to right, and then from right to left, in the manner we used during the rodeo shooting contest. If you get my meaning."

"Most assuredly," she said. "You lead, and I'll follow."

"We'll stay on the move," he told her. "Keep in mind that a moving target is much harder to hit than one that stands still. Try to make every shot count. We hold a decided advantage, you know."

"No, I didn't know," she said lightly. She saw the Nez Percé drawing nearer, their dark faces streaked with war paint, which gave them a ferocious look. They were still not within close enough range to open fire, however.

"Those rifles they carry are one step removed from ancient blunderbusses and belong in a museum," Edward said. "They're devilishly difficult to load, and harder still to fire. Certainly they're no match for the accuracy of our weapons."

"How comforting," she said wryly. "You have no idea how you encourage a lady with your dulcet words, Edward."

His smile was reassuring. Then it faded, and his voice became urgent. "Break to your left and canter as far as the big rock on the road over there. Then wheel about, tightly now, mind you, and follow me in a dash in the other direction. Those savages won't have any idea what we're doing and will no doubt keep coming right at us. Hold your fire until you're sure you can hit a target, and then fire as though you were being pursued by devils. Do you have all that?"

"Righto," she replied steadily.

"Ready, steady—go!" His mount broke suddenly to the left.

Copying his move precisely, Pamela's mare also veered sharply to the left.

Edward spurred forward. As he swept past the line of oncoming braves, who were still too far away to open fire with their old-fashioned rifles, he raised his own rifle and, with a single shot, picked one of the warriors off. The man slumped and fell to the ground.

Pamela, engaging in the same maneuver, emulated Edward, and even though she was riding sidesaddle, she raised her rifle to her shoulder, fired, and managed to wound a Nez Percé.

By the time they reached the end of the line, Edward was gratified to see that the advance of the horsemen had slowed appreciably. Both he and Pamela quickly ejected the spent shells in their rifles and slid home new bullets. Then Edward reversed his maneuver, with Pamela again directly behind him. He now raced the other way, and again his marksmanship paid dividends. He brought down a second brave.

Pamela was obliged to twist around in her saddle in order to get off another shot, but again she succeeded in wounding one of the Nez Percé.

The surviving warriors had suffered enough and were interested only in saving their own skins. They turned with one accord and beat a hasty retreat, leaving their dead behind them. The two wounded braves followed at a slower pace.

Edward sat his mount in silence, watching the horses of the two dead warriors chasing after the column of braves. "We'll be right on time at the Randalls' for dinner," he said.

Pamela was equally casual. "Good," she replied. "It's so rude to be tardy when one is invited to a meal."

As they resumed their journey, leaving the bodies of the two warriors whom Edward had shot sprawled on the ground, he turned to Pamela, and there was a note of genuine admiration in his voice as he said, "You've lost none of your skill with firearms, I see. That's all to the good."

"It's fortunate," she replied cheerfully. "One can't be too careful these days." Ejecting the used shell from her rifle, she proceeded to slide another bullet home so that it would be ready for use should she find it necessary to fire again.

The government of Idaho faced still another crisis.

During the previous few years, the population had been stable, and immigration had dropped to within reasonable bounds ever since gold and silver had last been discovered and orderly mining had been introduced. To be sure, there was the occasional light-fingered drifter or miner that Jim Randall and Rob Martin had talked about, who might try to steal a cow or a horse. Now, however, the discovery of a mother lode of gold in the Bitterroot Range northeast of Boise set off a stampede from all parts of the United States. Experienced miners and eager amateurs from every walk of life poured into the territory, as did criminals and others who preyed on the unwary.

Because the troops of United States infantry and cavalry were urgently needed in the outlying areas to subdue the rebellious Indian braves led by Running Bear, there was a severe shortage of law enforcement officials elsewhere, leaving the way clear for miners and criminals to wreak havoc.

"Trouble is brewing everywhere," Governor Toby Holt

remarked to his lieutenant governor, "and we're suffering a severe shortage of manpower to keep both the Indians and miners in line."

Toby applied to the Army of the West for reinforcements, and when none could be spared, he sent an urgent appeal to Washington City by telegram. President Grant replied at once, promising help but indicating that aid would not be forthcoming for several months. First it would be necessary to train the additional troops needed.

Toby, consequently, faced a critical, dangerous situation during the winter months ahead. Each day brought reports to the governor's office of violence, murders, and riots in the vicinity of the newly found mines in the Bitterroot Range.

To protect his citizens and restore at least a measure of lawful order to the territory, he was therefore forced to resort to extreme lengths.

His first act was to transfer more than fifty percent of the federal troops in the territory from duty near the reservations to the scenes of disturbance. This move promptly restored a rule of law to the rebellious mining districts, but it left the territory woefully short of manpower to protect farmers, ranchers, and townspeople from Indian uprisings.

Toby found it impossible to leave the capital during the emergencies, so he dispatched Rob Martin as his deputy to the towns of the Nez Percé and the Shoshone. Speaking their languages and long familiar with their ways, Rob was an excellent choice as an emissary to plead with the sachems, elders, and medicine men of the two nations to uphold the treaty that had existed for several years.

Rob's assignment kept him out of town for weeks on end, and Toby spent eighteen to twenty hours a day at his desk receiving reports and shifting his forces to meet changes in the situation. Toby's schedule created difficulties for Clarissa, but she adjusted with good humor and coped as best she could, changing meal hours almost daily so that she could at least eat dinner with her husband. Toby appreciated her efforts but was too busy to express his gratitude appropriately.

The individual who suffered more than anyone else during the emergency, however, was Kale Salton. Ever since she had first come to Idaho, she had felt like a fish out of water. She was convinced that she was accepted in Boise's polite circles only because of Rob's standing in the community, and that if she were there alone, she would be snubbed royally. She had made no friends in Boise, and there were women in the town who obviously disliked her because of their own interest in Rob. Pamela Drake, she was convinced, truly hated her, and she knew that Millicent Randall, who was too naive to keep her feelings to herself, was not at all fond of her.

Complicating her situation was the reception she endured whenever she left the house that Rob had rented. Men inevitably spoke to her on the streets and tried to pick her up, making rude comments about what they would like to do with her. Even Madam Suzanne, the blowzy blond proprietor of Boise's most notorious bordello, invariably greeted her with a broad smile and some cheerful remarks whenever their paths happened to cross, even going so far as to offer her employment as her "star girl." It was sad, but it seemed Kale's reputation preceded her wherever she went.

Mrs. Carson, the hired housekeeper, was very efficient, and Rob had also employed a cook. Thus, Kale had no responsibilities in cleaning the house or in preparing meals. Her only duty was to tend to little Cathy. She loved the child but spent so much time alone—thanks to the discomfort she experienced with the ladies of Boise—that she felt she had been relegated to the role of a nursemaid.

Clarissa Holt was her one friend, but Clarissa now led an extraordinarily busy life. Not only did she have to discharge her functions as first lady of the territory, but she also had to take care of her house, raise and care for her son, and somehow adjust her schedule from one day to the next to fit that of her husband. Consequently, Kale saw her only infrequently.

Now that Rob was away, Kale was miserable, and the longer the period of her loneliness was extended, the more miserable she became. Loving Rob, she had no interest in any other man, and the idea of developing a relationship with someone else was unthinkable. Because of her feelings for Rob, Kale had exaggerated the interest that Rob had displayed in Pamela and consequently developed a hatred for the other woman, who certainly made no secret of her attempts to win Rob's attentions.

Rob returned a day earlier than he had anticipated from his latest visit to the various towns of the Indians, and going to the governor's office even before stopping off at home, he reported in full to Toby on the results of his talks. He appeared to have succeeded in his attempts to convince the leaders of the Shoshone to honor their treaties, but he was under no false illusions concerning the Nez Percé. That nation was particularly volatile, and its young warriors could erupt in an uprising at any time. Rob was not convinced that he could prevent such a development, but he intended to return to the Nez Percé towns to continue his appeal for peace.

Toby reluctantly agreed to this but urged his old friend to spend several days at home in Boise before he once again set out into the wilderness. The effects of Rob's long days of hard labor were taking their toll, and by the time he left Toby's office, he was dragging his feet.

Mounting his gelding, he left the governor's office building and started for home. The short ride took him past the Boise Inn, and as he approached the entrance, he heard the voice of a woman behind him calling his name. Turning in his saddle, he saw Pamela Drake approaching on foot, obviously pleased to encounter him.

Removing his hat, he grinned at her. He was oblivious that her style of dress and makeup were reminiscent of the bold manner of adornment that Kale had once used—and that this was one of the reasons he liked Pamela.

"What a nice surprise!" Pamela said. "I had no idea that you were back in town."

"As a matter of fact, I've just arrived and was on my way home," Rob replied.

"I'd be terribly remiss if I didn't offer you a drink," Pamela said. "Do come into my suite and let me give you something to celebrate your return."

He tried to protest without sounding ungracious, saying that he was tired and wanted only to go home, but Pamela rode roughshod over his objections. She insisted that she lead his horse into the corral maintained by the hotel and then took Rob's arm as she guided him through the lobby.

Edward Blackstone was sitting in a card room at the far side of the lobby, engaged in his latest enthusiasm, a game of stud poker. Through the open door he caught a glimpse of Pamela and the weary Rob, and he smiled cynically to himself. Pam was digging her long, manicured talons into the fellow, there was no question about that.

Chatting easily and glibly, and expertly flirting with Rob as she talked, Pamela led him to the lavish, ground-floor suite that she shared with Edward. Not until Rob sank wearily into the cushions piled on a divan did he have the opportunity to express himself. "You'll be doing me no favor if you give me whiskey," he said. "I'm so tired that I'm afraid one drink would knock me flat."

"I certainly understand," she replied sympathetically. "Suppose I open a bottle of the wine that Edward and I brought with us? That's very mild by comparison."

"I think I can tolerate a little wine," he replied.

She removed the cork from a bottle and poured each of them a generous glass. "Tell me about your trip into the wilderness," Pamela suggested, handing him his glass, then sitting close beside him on the divan.

His work had been his sole occupation for days, and he was tired of thinking about it to the exclusion of everything else. He shrugged indifferently. "I went to a number of native communities on the reservations and held endless discussions with the tribal leaders."

"Were you in any danger?" Pamela leaned toward him, her green eyes wide, her lips parted, as she placed a protective, concerned hand on his arm.

"I didn't think about it much, one way or the other. But I suppose, now that you mention it, there was a slight element of risk involved."

"Really?" She made the single word sound like a deeply concerned exclamation, rather than a question.

"Well, the actual danger to my person was very slight," Rob said self-deprecatingly. "It so happens that I speak the languages of the Nez Percé and the Shoshone fluently, and that fact, combined with my rank, prevented me from suffering any personal harm. Even the hotheaded young warriors, who are spoiling for an all-out war, would think twice before laying a hand on the lieutenant governor of the territory. They know that if they should harm a single hair on my head, federal troops will sweep in and burn their entire community to the ground in no time."

"You're too modest," Pamela said. "If you ask me, you showed tremendous courage."

"Nothing of the sort," he protested, more or less truthfully. All the same, he enjoyed having this exceptionally attractive woman making such a fuss over him.

"Here's to your very special brand of courage," Pamela said, and drained her glass.

Lightly cajoling and prodding, she finally persuaded him to finish his own wine and then refilled both glasses.

He glanced out the window at the sky, from which daylight was slowly fading. "I really can't stay too long," he said. "I've got to get home."

"Of course you do," Pamela agreed quickly, sympathetically. "I know how eager you must be to see your little girl again." She deliberately chose not to mention that he might feel some desire to see Kale Salton, also.

Rob looked at her anxiously. "Do you happen to know if Cathy is well?"

"I saw her just yesterday," Pamela said emphatically, "and she's just fine! And you know, young White Elk visits me daily and is making excellent progress learning English and civilized ways. I shall miss him if he decides to go back to Oregon with Stalking Horse next spring."

Rob sighed, absently drained his second glass of wine, and

relaxed against the cushions. Pamela quickly refilled his glass again, then sat beside him. She looked up at him, her red lips parted, her huge eyes warm and inviting.

Neither then nor at any later time was Rob quite sure how it happened, but the next thing he knew, his hands were on Pamela's shoulders, and he was kissing her.

Her lips parted slowly to accept his kiss, and her arms wound around his neck. His hands moved from her shoulders to her back, and he pulled her close. The warmth and softness of her flesh made his body go rigid. He inhaled sharply, and the scent of Pamela's perfume intoxicated him further, causing his passion to grow and his reason to dissolve.

They embraced tightly as they continued to kiss. Gradually, inevitably, both of them became aroused, and their breathing became labored as their hands started to seek out more of each other's bodies.

Pamela was flushed with the desire this man had kindled within her. She had always found Rob attractive, but her yearning for him now surprised her. It was more compelling, more burning, than anything she had experienced before, driving her to abandon all propriety.

Suddenly Rob let his arms fall to his sides, and seeming to exert the greatest possible willpower, he drew back. "I'm sorry," he muttered hoarsely. "I shouldn't have done that. I—I'm just so tired I can scarcely control myself."

Pamela concealed her chagrin at Rob's abrupt rejection. Had they continued their embrace for another minute or two, she was certain their relationship would have developed quite naturally into a full-fledged affair. She wasted no time on regrets, however, telling herself that Rob surely would not be able to put her out of his mind and that the next time they met, it would be relatively easy to pick up where they had left off. "The fault is mine," she murmured, clinging to him.

"Not at all," he replied gallantly, rising to his feet. "I take full blame, full responsibility."

"Don't even think in such terms," Pamela said to him, smoothing her dress as she stood. Then in a somewhat constrained tone, she said, "I'll show you to the door."

"I call you," Edward Blackstone said, laying down his cards face up and exhaling a stream of blue smoke from his long, thin cigar.

He lost the hand, the fifth in succession, but he no longer cared. He had a far more serious matter on his mind now than stud poker. Lieutenant Governor Martin was spending an uncommonly long time in the suite, and knowing Pamela and her ways with a man who interested her, the Englishman was very much concerned.

She had not yet learned that in America—unlike the high society she had left behind in London—it was dangerous to play with someone's affections, particularly here in the West, where romance, like everything else, was a simple, straightforward matter.

Cashing in his few remaining chips, Edward thanked the other participants and left the game. Something had to be done before Pamela created trouble for herself—and for others.

He knew better than to admonish her outright, realizing that to spite him she would only redouble her flirtation with Lieutenant Governor Martin. Instead he had to seek some other way of handling the problem. Only one way occurred to him, and so he donned his new leather, sheepskin-lined jacket and had his gelding saddled.

Without further ado, he rode to the house of the lieutenant governor. To his infinite relief, Kale Salton came to the door herself.

"I'm afraid Rob is still out of town," she said, shivering from the cold wind the open door allowed into the house. "I don't expect him until tomorrow."

"If you can spare me a few minutes," he said, removing his broad-brimmed hat, "I've come to see you, not Rob."

"Of course," she said, though suspicion lurked behind her eyes as she stood aside to admit him.

Edward followed her into the parlor, where a wood fire was burning in the hearth. She sat down, then gestured to a chair opposite her.

Instead he stood with his back to the fire, his feet planted wide apart. "If I were in England right now," he said, "to get my point across I'd engage in a verbal fencing match, complete with countless subtle hints. I hate that kind of talk, though, and I much prefer the American way, which is blunt, straightforward, and to the point. May I be blunt with you?"

"By all means," Kale said, folding her hands in her lap and looking up at him, obviously puzzled as to his intention.

"I don't know the nature of your relationship with Lieutenant Governor Martin, and frankly it's none of my business."

The startled Kale could feel color rising in her cheeks. His words were totally unexpected.

"I do know—strictly from my own observations, mind you, because I've been curious—that you're very much in love with Martin and you have a strong interest in him, a proprietary interest, shall we say."

"I won't argue with you," the stunned Kale said, "and I certainly won't deny anything that you've said so far. What—"

"Hear me out," he said, cutting short her question. "I'm here strictly because I've known Pamela Drake for many years, ever since she was a small child, and I'm familiar with her ways and her moods. She has set her cap for Rob Martin."

Kale stiffened. "That doesn't surprise me."

"Wait!" Edward interrupted. "Let me finish. I don't necessarily say that Pamela has marriage in mind. She's looking for an emotional conquest, rather than a husband, if my meaning is clear to you."

"Very clear," Kale said venomously.

"May I smoke? Thank you." He took a long, thin cigar from his breast pocket, lighted it with a large sulfur match, and then threw the match into the fire. "Pamela can be a wonderful woman, but she is also capable of great mischief," he said. "She collects men the way some people collect trophies."

"Why are you telling me all this?" Kale demanded, a sharp edge to her voice.

"Quite simply," Edward said, "I'm trying to avoid unneeded complications for Pam. I'm endeavoring to keep her out of trouble."

"Why do you tell me all this the day before Rob is expected to return from the wilderness?" Kale demanded. "Do you imagine—"

"I imagine nothing," he interjected sharply. "Lieutenant Governor Martin may not be expected in town until tomorrow, but he's already in Boise. At this very moment he's being entertained by Pamela Drake in her suite at the Boise Inn."

Kale stared at him hard and had to control a feeling of

nysteria that swept over her. "Are you quite certain?" she asked, rising.

Edward said suavely, "My physician assures me that I have perfect eyesight. I saw them a little over an hour ago, walking together through the lobby of the hotel. Putting two and two together and adding to it what I know of Pamela Drake, I'd say that Lieutenant Governor Martin was very tired and that Pamela either persuaded him or inveigled him, use whichever word you prefer, into going with her."

"Are you suggesting," she demanded breathlessly, "that they've gone to bed together?"

"Not necessarily," Edward said lightly. "That all depends on the gentleman and how far he's willing to go—or can be persuaded to go. As far as Pam is concerned, she'll do everything to encourage him, and the more thoroughly he gets involved, the better she'll like it."

"I see." Kale walked slowly to the fireplace and then looked up at him. "I can't thank you enough for this information, Edward," she said formally.

He clicked his heels and bowed. "I won't go so far as to say that the pleasure is mine," he replied. "On the contrary, this has been a thoroughly unpleasant experience, but if I've saved Rob Martin from making an utter fool of himself over a woman who delights in collecting the scalps of fools, then I've done him and you a service. I just ask you not to be too severe in your judgment of Mr. Martin. I've known men who are far more worldly and far more experienced sexually than he who have behaved in an even more abominable manner over Pamela."

"I'll keep that in mind, sir." Kale walked the Englishman to the door, and her attitude was the essence of dignity as she extended her right hand. "I'm deeply in your debt, sir, and I assure you I won't forget this favor you've done me."

"Then I did the right thing by coming to you," he said. "I hoped I was right."

"We shall meet again in the near future," Kale assured him as she shook hands with him, "and by that time, I believe the situation will have righted itself and will be under strict control."

"Then this visit certainly has not been made in vain," he said, and bowed sharply before taking his departure.

After he had gone, Kale returned to the parlor and sat staring absentmindedly into the fire. Her mind was in a turmoil, but one by one she sorted out her problems, deciding upon a course of action, and by the time that Rob finally arrived home, she had achieved a remarkable inner serenity.

Rob was tired when he came into the house. He embraced Kale, and it was not accidental that when he kissed her, his lips found only her cheek, as she had averted her face at the last possible moment. She detected the smell of wine on his breath, and even worse, she was aware of the faint but elusive musky scent of expensive perfume that clung to him.

As they mounted the stairs together on their way to the nursery, Kale listened in silence as he explained that he had come home a day earlier than he had expected and had already reported in detail on his journey to Toby Holt. Kale was disturbed by his omission of his stop at the hotel, but she refrained from mentioning it or her visit from Edward Blackstone.

Baby Cathy occupied their joint attention for a time and smoothed the awkwardness of their reunion. Then, as they descended the staircase together, Kale noted that Rob was very nervous and that he also was incapable of meeting her direct gaze. This, she decided, was all to the good. Rob had no reason, legal or personal, to be loyal or faithful to her, and she was pleased that he was suffering guilt because of what he had done with Pamela. Studying him surreptitiously, Kale concluded that he and the Englishwoman had not gone to bed. It had been her experience that a man inadvertently relaxed after lovemaking, and Rob was too tense, his nerves too taut, for him to have bedded Pamela. She was greatly relieved by that realization, but in no way did it alter the situation in which she found herself.

Kale agreed quickly—almost too quickly, actually—when Rob said that he intended to take a nap for about an hour before they ate dinner. "That's fine with me," she said. "I have an errand to run." Offering no explanation, she went off to her room.

A quick glance in her mirror told her that her attire was all wrong for the scene she had in mind. She should be wearing her most sultry, glamorous gown; instead she was wearing an open-throated man's shirt, mannish trousers, knee-high boots, into which she had tucked her pant legs. No matter. She touched up her lip rouge and her eye makeup, then shrugged into her short, sheepskin coat and went out into the dusk.

The groom in the stable hitched up a team of two horses to the light carriage, and Kale drove swiftly through the chilly air to the Boise Inn, not pausing to determine whether what she was doing was right or wrong or to plot out what she intended to say.

Arriving in a very short time, she left her carriage in the corral, and still grasping the horsewhip that had been resting in its accustomed place on the buckboard, she stalked into the hotel and headed straight for the suite of Pamela Drake and Edward Blackstone. Scarcely cognizant of what she was doing, she rapped forcefully on the door with the handle of the whip.

Pamela blinked in amazement when she opened the door and the auburn-haired woman brushed past her and stalked into the living room. "Won't you come in," Pamela asked dryly.

"I'm already in," Kale replied flatly.

Pamela noted at once that Kale's eyes glistened and that color ran high in her face.

"You and I," Kale said, speaking quietly but with a steely tone of voice, "need to come to an understanding, or someone is going to be hurt very badly—specifically, you."

Refusing to be intimidated, Pamela drew herself up haughtily. "I beg your pardon!"

"And well you might," Kale told her, not yielding an inch. Kale planted her feet apart, hooked her thumbs in her belt, and rocked back and forth on her boots, her whip tucked under one arm. "I know your type," she said. "I've been familiar with it for a long time. You're a man stealer. You're not interested in marriage or even in a betrothal. You collect notches on your bedpost the way an Indian brave collects scalps. You're satisfied only if you can trap a man into falling in love with you. You're quite happy to have him follow you around like a little puppy, whom you can order about and amuse yourself with when he jumps to obey your slightest whim."

There was enough truth to the charge that it struck home, and Pamela did not quite know how to reply. She refused to dignify the statement by denying it, yet at the same time she knew she couldn't quite square a denial with her own conscience.

"I know I speak the truth. You see, I recognize you for what you are," Kale continued with a faint smile, "because I was once the same way. That was before I met Rob and my whole life changed. I won't bore you with details, other than to say his late wife was my best friend and I promised her on her deathbed that I would take care of her baby daughter. I don't intend to abdicate that responsibility, not to you and not to anyone, not even temporarily."

Pamela was regaining her poise. "I'm afraid you have a mistaken premise," she said icily. "You assume that I have an interest in Rob Martin, when actually I have none."

Grasping the handle of the whip, Kale suddenly cracked it, and the loud retort sounded like a pistol shot. "Don't lie to me!" she shouted, her voice becoming ugly. "I won't tolerate it." With a great effort she calmed herself and became more reasonable. "I'm not trying to embarrass you," she said, "or force you to embarrass yourself. What has happened in the past, I'm willing to forget. But let me make it very clear to you that you've now been warned. You'll approach Rob only at your peril. If you want to stay healthy, you'll treat him as a casual acquaintance. You'll keep your hands off him, and you'll do nothing to encourage him to lay hands on you. You and I know that you're in control of the situation, and you had better understand that I hold you strictly responsible for anything that may happen. Do I make myself clear?"

"Painfully so," Pamela replied, trying to gather together her shattered dignity.

"Good!" Kale replied, again cracking the whip to emphasize her words. ''Heed my warning, and you'll be unmolested. Forget or defy me in this, and I'll horsewhip you through the streets of Boise, and I'll drive you out of the territory. If you don't believe I can do it—try me!'' Spinning on her heel, she stalked out of the suite and slammed the door behind her.

Edward, who had heard every word from the next room, smiled to himself as the sound of the door slamming reverberated through the suite.

V

For the first time in her life, Pamela Drake heeded the advice of another person. She took to heart what Kale Salton had said to her and wisely decided to give Rob Martin a wide berth. Edward Blackstone silently approved when, instead of going to the lieutenant governor's house to call on him after his return from another trip to the interior of Idaho, she elected instead to ride out to the Randall ranch.

Edward, who acted as her escort, knew Pamela's ego had been bruised and that she was in need of balm. He also knew that his cousin Jim Randall was ready and willing to provide it in large quantities.

Jim, making no attempt to conceal his delight at Pamela's presence, and realizing by now that she was not his cousin's mistress, took the rest of the day off and invited her on a tour of the ranch. Edward, who had previously made such a tour, found a convenient excuse to stay behind with Millicent, with whom he said he wanted to discuss family matters.

Jim and Pamela set out at once, with Pamela riding sidesaddle, as usual. As they rode, Jim pointed out aspects of the property that he thought would interest her. She knew nothing about operating a ranch and raising cattle, but he was so eager to explain to her in detail the ways that his business functioned that she found herself listening with genuine interest. She was surprised by his knowledge of ranching and was flattered by his eagerness to impart all that he knew about it to her.

Deeply impressed, Pamela nodded soberly. "You seem to love the life you lead here," she said.

Jim took a deep breath. "Have you ever wondered," he asked, with just a hint of diffidence in his voice, "whether you would like living on a ranch?"

She immediately recognized his motive for asking. It was based on his love for her and was intended as a preliminary to an eventual proposal of marriage. There had been a time when she would have strung him along, teased him, and kept him on tenterhooks for the sake of gratifying her ego. But the session with Kale Salton had taught her more of a lesson than she knew. She pondered Jim's question and then answered it as honestly and as forthrightly as she could. "Until recently," she began, "the idea of living on a ranch never crossed my mind. It's such a far cry from any form of life in England. But since I've been here in Boise and have seen the way people around me are living, the thought has entered my mind."

"And?" he prompted.

"Quite honestly, Jim," she told him, "I can't answer your question. It would all depend on the circumstances. For instance, if I were asked if I intended to invest in a ranch and then live on the property and try to protect my investment, the answer would be a loud and resounding no. I just couldn't imagine that kind of an existence under such circumstances. On the other hand, if I were to fall in love with a man and were to consent to marry him, I could live quite happily with him on a ranch for my whole life." She looked at him and smiled a trifle apologetically. "I'm sorry, but that's the best answer that I can give you."

He beamed at her. "That's good enough for me," he told her.

Jim was tempted to propose marriage to her on the spot but wisely resisted the urge. He was making far better progress with her than he had anticipated, and it was wiser not to press his luck than to open the door to a possible rejection. He would be prudent to wait, he decided, until he was sure that she would accept him when he asked her to marry him.

Pamela was surprised by Jim's reticence. She had assumed that he would propose to her at once, and his failure to respond as she had anticipated indicated that there was far more substance to Jim than she had initially recognized. Every time she saw him, she was impressed anew by his manly self-control. She realized she could not afford to play her customary games with him because she didn't want to risk losing him. Whether she wanted a permanent association with him was a question she was not yet prepared to answer, and for the time being, she was at loose ends.

Ah-Sing acted on his own authority and prepared an elaborate meal for the guests, so Pamela and Edward were obliged to stay at the ranch for an early supper. When they finally headed back to Boise, Edward glanced at Pamela obliquely and saw that she was quite restless. Wanting to offer her relief from her obviously troubled feelings, he said, "When we get back to Boise, suppose we go out on the town."

Pamela turned to Edward and smiled gratefully. She realized that he had no way of knowing she was disturbed because of her unresolved relationship with Jim Randall and the unpredictability of her future with him. Ordinarily she was used to being in control, to having things work out the way she wanted, but on this occasion, her entire relationship with Jim was still up in the air.

Edward's recipe for relaxation sounded like what she needed. Nevertheless she was somewhat bewildered. "Where do you suggest we go?" she asked. "Boise isn't London, nor for that matter is it Chicago or Saint Louis."

"I've heard recently," he replied, "that the best place to spend an evening is in Davenport's Saloon. There are always one or two card games in progress, and it's one of the few places in town where a lady is welcome after dark."

"By all means," Pamela said enthusiastically, "let's try it."

Davenport's was a large, spacious establishment with a bar that ran the length of the main room. It was so long that three bartenders were needed behind it to accommodate customers. Most of the patrons were men, and they either stood at the bar or sat at small tables, where demurely dressed waitresses served them. One of the novelties of the place was that the females who worked there were not prostitutes; on the contrary, they were encouraged to behave properly, and any woman customer who came into the place intending to proposition a man was invited to leave.

Dan Davenport, the proprietor, was pleased to have customers of the quality of Pamela and Edward patronizing his saloon, and he went to them at once, sat with them, and insisted on buying them a drink. A swarthy man, whose black hair was parted in the middle, he dressed habitually in black, which emphasized his darkness. There were customers who swore they had never seen him smile; those same customers would have been astonished had they watched him fawning over Pamela.

For her part, Pamela flirted with him brazenly as a way of obtaining relief from the restraint she had shown in dealing with Jim. No matter how bold she became, however, Davenport answered her in kind, and eventually Edward Blackstone began to feel uncomfortable.

He wanted to warn Pamela that a wise woman would not flirt with a man of Davenport's character unless she was serious about him—which Pamela obviously was not. But it would be a complete waste of time, he knew from past experience, to say anything of the sort to her in her present mood. Whenever she became restless, Pamela was inclined to be indifferent to personal danger and to react angrily to advice meant for her own good. If Edward said anything to her now, she would be sure to do just the contrary in order to show him that she was in charge of her own destiny. Consequently, he gritted his teeth and tried to ignore the spectacle of watching her as she went out of her way to be charming and sweet to Davenport, whom Edward considered far beneath her socially.

After some time, one of Davenport's underlings, acting in response to a hidden signal, approached the table and tried to persuade Edward to participate in a game of poker. Edward refused, but the man insisted, and it took some minutes to be rid of him.

Davenport, meanwhile, took advantage of the disturbance he had created to ask Pamela privately if she would stay on with him and have a drink with him after Edward departed. He would see her safely back to the Boise Inn, he told her. The invitation suited her mood, and she accepted in high glee.

As soon as Edward had rid himself of the persistent card player, he turned to Pamela. Slightly annoyed but not showing it, he said, "I think we'd best be on our way."

She patted him lightly on the arm. "You go by yourself, darling."

"But—"

"Dan has promised to see me back to the inn, which is terribly sweet of him," she said, giving Edward no chance to interrupt or protest. "I'm not in the least tired, and I'm enjoying myself immensely, so I think I'll stay on here for a time."

Edward knew she was telling him politely, in her own way, to go off by himself and to leave her to her own devices. Again he realized that if he tried to make an issue of the matter, she would create a scene and would tell him to go about his own business and leave her to manage hers. Ordinarily Pamela was quite sensible, but on the rare occasions when she dug in her heels and became stubborn, she could create an awful scene.

He wanted to warn her that Davenport was an oily character whom she couldn't trust, but his hands were tied. He could only hope that in the event an unpleasant situation should arise, she would be able to take care of herself.

Rising, he kissed her lightly behind one ear, bowed to Davenport, and walked off, his right hand resting lightly on the butt of a six-shooter as a subtle warning to anyone who saw him that Pamela was not to be molested.

Davenport was elated that Pamela had managed to get rid of Edward Blackstone so easily. Only one goal was on the saloonkeeper's mind, and he felt increasingly certain that he would achieve it before the night ended. He promptly ordered another drink, a potent mixture of brandy and whiskey. He was further encouraged when Pamela sipped it calmly. He had no idea that she had often been accused of having a hollow leg, that she could drink liquor almost indefinitely without feeling or showing any ill effects.

Chatting lightly with Pamela while she sipped her drink, Davenport fumbled beneath the table, found one of her knees, and began to caress it. Showing no surprise, Pamela promptly tugged her skirt high above her knees. Davenport was delighted. This was going to be a far easier conquest than he had dared to hope, and his right hand began to slide up her thigh.

The proprietor did not know it, but while sipping her drink with one hand, Pamela had reached down with the other and plucked an ultrasharp, double-edged knife from its resting place against her thigh, where it was held by a garter that she wore well above one knee. Now, smiling faintly as Davenport's hand continued up her leg, she brought the blade above the table and plunged it into the wood less than an inch from Davenport's left hand, which rested on the tabletop near his drink.

His other hand froze on her thigh.

Pamela smiled sweetly and looked him straight in the eye. "If you'll examine the knife carefully," she said in dulcet tones, "you'll find it's a splendid blade, made of the finest Sheffield steel. The next time I use it, it will be driven into flesh, not into wood." She paused and let the information sink in.

The color drained from Davenport's face, and he looked for a moment as though he were about to faint.

Calmly tugging the knife from the table, Pamela examined it, then proceeded to polish it on his sleeve before returning it to its resting place in her garter. Pulling her skirt down to its normal length, she gathered her belongings and rose to her feet. "I'll bid you good night, Dan," she said. "Never mind taking me home. I'll see myself back to the inn. I can manage quite well by myself, thank you." She calmly walked out of the saloon.

Davenport's fury was enormous, but within moments he managed to regain his equilibrium. "Petrie!" he called.

One of his henchmen, a short, slender man, with a weasellike face, hurriedly joined him.

"Follow that woman," Davenport growled angrily, jerking a thumb in the direction of the departing Pamela. "Stay close enough to her that you don't lose her, but whatever happens, don't let her see you. She's dangerous! Stick with her as long as it's necessary."

"Necessary for what?" Petrie asked blankly.

"I want you to learn what you can about her," Davenport replied. "Find out where her hotel room is, what she does at night. There may very well come a time when I will, ah, take measures to persuade her to come to my saloon for a prolonged stay."

The man's face cleared, and he darted out.

Petrie followed his employer's instructions to the letter, but unfortunately for him he was unaccustomed to the fine art of surveillance, and Pamela soon became aware that he was tailing her. Therefore, instead of riding directly to the Boise Inn, she stopped first at the governor's mansion, ostensibly to pay a call on White Elk. Actually, she was sure the child was already in bed, sound asleep, but the visit gave her an excuse to talk to Stalking Horse, with whom she engaged in a brief, intense conversation.

The Cherokee listened for a time, then nodded emphatically and spoke briefly.

Pamela returned to her waiting mare and mounted it, while Stalking Horse went to the stables behind the mansion. In a matter of minutes, he reappeared, carrying a burlap sack in which he had placed a bulky object. He handed the sack to Pamela, who thanked him for it and tied it to the saddlehorn, then quickly resumed her ride back to the inn.

Petrie once again fell in behind her, following her on his horse.

When she reached the hotel, she carried the sack, with some difficulty, to her ground-floor suite. After depositing it in her bedchamber, to which there was a private entrance off the hall, she hastened to join Edward Blackstone in the sitting room.

He looked up with relief when he saw her. "Well," he said, "you decided to end your stupid little adventure rather quickly, I see."

"Please don't lecture me, Edward," she said. "I do believe I've learned something of a lesson tonight, and I promise you I'll behave hereafter."

"That's good," he replied grimly.

Glancing casually at a small mirror on the wall, Pamela

glimpsed the reflection of a dark shape hovering outside the window behind her. The man who had been shadowing her ever since she had left Davenport's Saloon still had her under observation, and, she decided, that was all to the good.

Suddenly, a cracking sound, followed by a rustling noise, came from outside the window. It sounded as though someone had stepped on a brittle, fallen branch. Hearing the sound, Edward promptly snatched one of his six-shooters from the belt that was hanging on a hallstand, and opening the window, he climbed out into the dark yard beyond it.

Pamela, completely unruffled and in no way surprised by the disturbance, sat in a chair and calmly waited for him. She was certain that the man who had followed her had been responsible for making the noise.

After a brief time, Edward climbed back into the room through the open window. "I couldn't find anybody," he said, "but that doesn't mean much. Somebody stepped on a dead branch out there—I found the branch—but whoever was responsible has vanished, which isn't too difficult a feat on a dark night like this."

Pamela said nothing.

"We may be in for a spot of trouble," he told her. "If you think you hear anyone, don't hesitate to call me."

As she started toward her bedroom, Edward extinguished the lamps in the sitting room and then retired to his room.

Once alone, Pamela took off her shoes, then returned again to the parlor, dragging the heavy burlap sack after her. She busied herself with the contents of the sack for several minutes and then went to the window that Edward had closed behind him and opened it a few inches. She was making it as easy as she could for the man who had been on her trail.

After returning to her own chamber, she undressed quickly, donned her nightclothes, and extinguished the oil lamp after climbing into bed. The quiet that enveloped the inn was typical of Boise at night. No one stirred, no one was abroad, no one was awake. The silence was deep, all-encompassing.

Suddenly a long, terrified scream shattered the peace.

Behaving as though she had expected just such a development, Pamela arose quickly, donned a negligee, and lighted her oil lamp. She calmly left her room, and as she opened the door to the parlor, Edward, a silk dressing gown thrown over his pajamas, entered from the other side. He also carried a lighted lamp, but in his other hand he held a cocked pistol.

In the middle of the room, a man was sprawled helplessly on the floor. His left leg was caught in an ugly bear trap, the huge, unrelenting claws of which were biting deep into his flesh.

"Please, please!" Petrie begged, tears and perspiration mingling on his face. "Get this thing off me. I can't stand the pain. Please!"

Edward looked thoroughly bewildered. A heavy pounding sounded at the door, and Pamela opened it to admit the manager of the Boise Inn and two of his security men. All three were in night attire, and all were carrying loaded rifles. They, too, gaped at the unfortunate prisoner.

"Fetch the sheriff," Edward commanded, regaining his poise, and one of the security guards immediately went off.

Edward pointed an accusing finger at the writhing Petrie.

"Talk!" he directed. "Or that gadget can stay on your leg long enough to cripple you for life!"

The agonized Petrie jerked a thumb in the direction of Pamela. "Damn Davenport," he gasped, "told me to follow this here woman, and that's what I was doin'. I didn't mean no harm to her or to nobody."

Edward glanced at Pamela, then looked harder at her. Something indefinable in her attitude indicated that she knew more about the matter than she had revealed. "What's this all about, Pam?"

She refrained from looking at the pain-stricken man. "It's all quite simple," she said. "When I left Davenport's Saloon, I became conscious that I was being followed by this chap. So I went to the governor's mansion and borrowed a bear trap from Stalking Horse, who was delighted to lend it to me once he discovered my purpose. When I returned to the hotel, I knew I was still being watched, and after we had said good night, I returned to this room and deliberately set the bear trap. It seems we've caught quite a prize."

"Please," Petrie begged. "Take this thing off me before I faint."

"You admit, then, that Dan Davenport ordered you to spy on Miss Drake?"

"Yes," the man replied. "I'll confess to that, I'll confess to anything, but open up this awful contraption!"

Edward bent down and pried the ugly jaws apart sufficiently to extricate Petrie's bloody leg.

Pamela felt a stab of pity for the unfortunate wretch and poured him a shot glass of whiskey, which she handed him. He downed it in a single gulp, but his leg hurt him so much that he still could not stand on it.

The manager of the inn probed and poked the leg; he was none too gentle, and every time he touched it, Petrie winced. "You're in luck, bud," the manager said roughly. "You have no broken bones. Once your flesh heals, you ought to be as good as new again."

Before Petrie could reply, the sheriff arrived, and everyone started talking to him simultaneously. He raised a hand for silence and finally gleaned the full story from Pamela and Edward. At last he turned to the unfortunate Petrie. "Do you admit these charges against you?"

"I didn't do nothin' wrong," Petrie wailed. "I just did what Davenport told me, and I didn't break no law."

"The hell, you say!" the sheriff retorted. "You're guilty of breaking and entering." He snapped a pair of handcuffs onto the man's wrists and started to lead him away. "I'll report to you first thing in the morning," the law enforcement officer said to Edward and Pamela as he led the man away.

Soon the couple were once more alone. Pamela patted the bear trap and shuddered. "A most useful little toy," she said. "I'll return this to Stalking Horse tomorrow."

"I should have known better than to worry about you," Edward told her. "You're about as helpless as a hooded cobra."

As a result of the activities that had kept them up until the small hours of the morning, Pamela slept much later than usual the next morning, as did Edward. Consequently, they were the last patrons for breakfast in the hotel dining room.

They were just starting to eat when the sheriff came in search of them. "I've been having hell's own time getting anything useful from Petrie," he told them.

"You mean he won't talk?" Edward inquired.

The sheriff shook his head. "That's not the trouble. The bear trap that the lady here set for him was a great persuader, and he'll tell us anything and everything we want to know, and a heap more, besides. We have him nailed dead to rights on breaking and entering your suite, but that's about the end of it. As for his following Miss Drake on the orders of that damned Davenport, well, Davenport denies the whole thing."

Pamela offered him a seat, and he gratefully accepted it and ordered coffee. "The basic problem we face," he said as he took a sip of his coffee, "is that Petrie is just a small fry and has no say in what happens and what doesn't. Davenport is something else, again. He's one of the most notorious criminals in the whole territory, and we've been after him for years without being able to pin a blasted thing on him. We just can't get him."

Edward nodded affirmatively. He knew how elusive criminals of Davenport's nature could be.

"Sometimes a customer of his will come to my office with the complaint that he's been cheated at cards, but he can't prove it, and in a court of law, it's his word against Davenport's. Occasionally there is a beating at the saloon, but the victim has a terrible time identifying the men who attacked him. Every now and again someone is shot and killed there, but I never have been able to pin down the identity of the killer. Everybody who works in the place swears it was a total stranger who fired the fatal shot and then promptly disappeared. We know they're lying, and the judges know they're lying, but there's not a blamed thing that anyone can really do about it. You can't go running around a territory as wild as Idaho and start arresting people for murder on vague or hearsay evidence."

"You sound discouraging, sheriff," Edward commented.

"That's exactly how I mean to sound, Mr. Blackstone," the law enforcement officer replied. "I'd give six months of my life to be able to nail Dan Davenport to the wall, but I haven't had a chance to catch him redhanded. The experience that you and Miss Drake had last night is simply the latest in a long line of frustrating incidents." He stood, hitched up his gun belt, and added before strolling off, "I just thought I'd let you know how things stand."

When they were alone again, Pamela said nothing as she sipped her coffee, and Edward was equally silent as he continued to eat. Only after he had consumed the last of the hash brown potatoes that had been served with his bacon and eggs, did he lean back thoughtfully in his chair. "It appears to me," he said, speaking more to himself than to Pamela, "that I am obliged to teach Mr. Dan Davenport a lesson myself."

"Oh, dear," she replied, deeply concerned. "Must you?"

"I'm afraid," he said, "that I have no choice. The man is a criminal, a menace to society. If he'd ordered you killed last night instead of just followed, that would have been the end of you. I hope you realize that."

She recalled what had happened and shuddered as she told him what she had done with her knife.

Edward listened carefully, nodding gravely from time to time. "Every word you speak," he said when she was finished, "adds certainty to my conviction that I shall need to attend to the man myself."

After having returned to their suite, Edward dressed with

meticulous care for the adventure that lay ahead. Then he wandered into the sitting room and began to load a strange little pistol, which was no more than five or six inches in length and had no trigger guard. It had two barrels, one of which fired when the trigger was pulled halfway, while the other discharged when the trigger was pulled the rest of the way.

Pamela came into the room while he was finishing loading the weapon, and she realized Edward meant business. "I see you're taking the derringer," she said calmly.

"I think it's by far the best insurance policy that I own," he replied, and removing his coat, he slid the weapon into a special harness that fitted over his right arm. Then donning the coat, he experimented. When he shook his hand slightly, the derringer dropped into it, ready for instant use. To be safe, he repeated the process. Then, with the weapon concealed beneath his coat sleeve, he donned his high, stovepipe hat, threw his lightweight cape over his shoulders, and tucked his swagger stick under one arm. "I'll join you in time for dinner," he said. "When I return, I daresay that Boise will be a safer and healthier town in which to live."

"Do be careful, Edward," she told him. "Just remember that you're not facing some amateur now. You're dealing with a professional criminal."

"I shall keep that thought in the forefront of my mind, my dear," he assured her, and saluting her with the swagger stick, he wandered out into the street.

Since the air was crisp and clear, he decided to walk the few blocks to Davenport's Saloon and was invigorated by the exercise. When he arrived, he stood inside the entrance for a few moments in order to acclimate his eyesight to the relative darkness. He was surprised to discover that although it was not yet noon, the saloon was already doing a brisk business.

Dan Davenport stood in the shadows at the far end of the long bar and frowned when he saw Edward enter. The proprietor had already learned what had befallen Petrie the previous night, and he suffered no false illusions regarding the significance of Edward's appearance there that day. His presence meant serious trouble. Davenport was determined to strike first.

He caught the eye of one of his dealers, who was engaged in a card game, and the man left the table and came to him at once.

"Don't look now," Davenport said, "but there's a dude in a top hat and a cape who has just come in. I want you to involve him in a friendly game of cards, but don't be in a rush about it. I don't want him to suspect a setup of any kind. After you've got him involved in a game, start an argument with him. The louder and more violent it is, the better it will be."

"Sure, boss." The man nodded and wandered back to the card game.

Davenport looked around his domain and then snapped his fingers twice. A dark, intense young gunslinger, with two six-shooters hanging from his belt, materialized at his side.

Davenport muttered to the man, "Do you see that dude in a stovepipe just inside the entrance?"

The young gunslinger nodded. "I see him, Dan."

"Ace is going to strike up a conversation with him," Davenport said, "and is going to invite him to play a friendly game of cards. Stay inconspicuous, but I want you to keep watch on him. Eventually Ace is going to pick a quarrel with him. Let them both get good and hot under the collar, and then I want you to pick off the dude before he has a chance to draw. You remember the exhibition he put on at the rodeo? Well, he's a pretty fair shot, and we don't want to give him a chance to exercise his shooting arm.''

"I got you," the gunman replied. "You want me to wing him in the shoulder or the arm enough to spoil his aim, huh?"

Davenport shook his head. His face hardened, and his voice sounded brutally cold. "No," he said. "Drill him, and waste no time about it. Kill him with one shot, if you can."

The gunslinger whistled under his breath. "No wonder you want me to remain inconspicuous. Don't worry, Boss. If I've got to drill a customer, I'm gonna be blame near invisible."

Edward had spotted Davenport moments after he had entered the saloon but had given the proprietor no indication that he had seen him. He now strolled slowly to the bar and ordered himself a whiskey, which he mixed with a substantial quantity of water. A number of the patrons, quietly egged on by Davenport, made fun of the newcomer, commenting on his hat, his cape, and the lace cuffs of his sleeves, but Edward remained oblivious to their gibes.

An elderly, ragged miner, who looked completely out of place in the gathering, created something of a stir when he wandered over to the free-lunch counter, which stood at a right angle to the bar, made a sandwich, and began to eat it ravenously.

Davenport was outraged. "You!" he shouted. "Keep your grubby mitts the hell off my food. The only people who are entitled to eat free lunch around here are those who pay for a drink.''

The old man dropped the sandwich he had made for himself and backed away from the bar.

Edward, who had scarcely touched his own drink, ordered another shot of whiskey and paid for it promptly when it was placed in front of him. He beckoned to the old man and said, "This is for you," as the ragged old codger's eyes widened.

The man, his hand trembling, started to reach for the glass.

"If I were you," Edward suggested in a kindly tone, "I'd let the drink wait a few minutes while I put some food into my stomach."

"Ye heard what Davenport told me, didn't ye?" the old man asked anxiously. "I ain't allowed to eat because I ain't a payin' customer."

"Ah, but you are," Edward told him brightly. "Your entire situation is altered, old boy. The drink that now sits before you has been purchased with hard cash. That means that you are now a paying customer and are therefore entitled to free lunch. I urge you to help yourself."

The old man's eyes lighted, and he mumbled, "God bless ye," before tottering back to the free lunch counter and beginning to gorge himself.

The proprietor was helpless and could only glare at the old man and at Edward in turn while the patrons who lined the bar laughed heartily, enjoying a joke at Davenport's expense.

Meanwhile, the dealer named Ace to whom the owner had given instructions had become embroiled in a disagreement with two card players—judging from their appearances, a salesman and a farmer. The attention of almost everyone at the bar was drawn to their table.

"I called you, gents, and that's the end of it," Ace said emphatically. "One of you has a pair of tens and the other a pair of kings. But I got both of you beat with three eights, and that's that."

"Not so fast, Ace," the farmer protested. "We turned up our cards, which is right and fair, but we ain't seen your three eights yet. Where are they?"

"I got 'em right here," Ace said, his voice ugly as he tapped three cards lying on the table before him.

"Sure," the salesman declared, "but you got 'em face down. Turn 'em up so's we can *see* you got three eights."

"That's right," the farmer added indignantly. "Since when do we have to take your word for it? Prove to us that you have three eights in your hand!"

Ace reached for one of the six-shooters in his belt and drew it swiftly. "Are you gents callin' me a liar?" he demanded. "For your sakes, I hope not! When I say I got three eights in my hand, I got 'em, and I don't have to show 'em to nobody. Is that clear? I got 'em."

The two players found themselves staring, in turn, into the muzzle of the six-shooter. As nearly as they—and the majority of the onlookers in the place—could judge, the dealer was in dead earnest and intended to use the pistol if they persisted in their argument. They hastened to assure him that they accepted his word. Snorting in contempt and with false indignation, Ace raked in their money. The crestfallen salesman and farmer had no recourse but to beat a hasty retreat from the saloon.

Scooping the money into his pocket, Ace looked up, and it

was no accident that he happened to catch the eye of Edward Blackstone, standing nearby at the bar. The dealer grinned at him. "Care for a friendly little game?" he asked, "or is the brand of draw poker we play hereabouts a mite too strong and fast for your tastes?"

Edward appeared to consider the question as he sipped his drink. "Now that you mention it," he replied, his voice casual, "I think a game of draw poker is just what I need." Carrying his drink with him, he strolled to the table.

The attention of virtually everyone in the establishment was drawn to him and to Ace. After a hand was dealt to him, Edward discarded two cards and drew two others to replace them. Ace, who raised Edward's initial bet, drew only one card and then proceeded to raise the betting still higher. The onlookers were impressed when they saw a sizable sum of money resting on the table.

Puffing lightly on his cigar, Edward doubled the bet. Ace matched him and decided the time had come to end the game. "I have three aces," he said.

Edward flicked a glance at him and turned his cards face up. "I'm inclined to doubt your assertion," he said. "You'll note that I have a pair of aces."

The dealer saw that both his opponent's hands were resting on the top of the table, and he knew, therefore, that the Englishman was at a distinct disadvantage. "So what?" he demanded roughly.

Edward remained reasonable and calm. "There are a total of four aces in any one deck of cards," he said. "As you and anyone else who cares to examine the hand may see for himself, two of those aces are right here in my hand.

Consequently, I am inclined to doubt your claim that you hold three aces in yours.''

The dealer's bluff had been called. His only recourse was to resort to a threat of violence, and as he reached for his pistol, he demanded, ''Are you calling me a liar?''

Edward Blackstone knew he had no time to lose. ''I am,'' he replied flatly, shaking his wrist. His derringer slid down into his hand, and as the dealer raised his pistol, Edward pulled the trigger halfway, sending a bullet into Ace's heart. The dealer pitched forward, and his head crashed on the table.

Out of the corner of one eye Edward could see the young gunslinger, drawing a pistol in the shadows on the far side of the room. Not wasting as much as a split second, he wheeled, aimed, and pulled the trigger of the derringer the rest of the way. The man crumpled to the floor, a bullet lodged in his head.

The derringer now was empty, but Edward decided on impulse to attempt a monumental bluff. Reasonably certain that no one in the saloon had ever before seen a derringer and that everyone in the place assumed that the gun was a six-shooter, he determined to act accordingly. ''If anyone else cares to continue the argument,'' he said, sweeping the room with the little pistol, ''be good enough to step forward, and I'll be glad to oblige you right now.''

No one moved.

''This money is mine,'' he declared, sweeping the silver off the table and dropping it into his pocket. ''I won it fairly—and honestly.'' Still holding the derringer, he strolled to the door and then turned. ''I don't see Dan Davenport anywhere,'' he said, ''but I'm sure he's within the sound of my voice. Let this be a lesson and a warning to you, Davenport. You'll use no more terror tactics in Boise, and you'll treat your patrons honestly hereafter, or you'll meet the same fate that your dealer and your private gunslinger faced.'' Tipping his hat politely, he tucked his swagger stick under his free arm and strolled out into the street.

Exactly as he had intended, he was going to be on time for his dinner engagement with Pamela.

Meanwhile, sitting in a dark corner of the saloon, a giant of a man dressed entirely in black had quietly watched the violent encounter between Edward Blackstone and Davenport's men. Wang, the hatchet man from San Francisco, had arrived in Boise a few weeks earlier. He had taken a room in a rundown boardinghouse that catered to the Chinese who came to the area, and he was gradually learning whatever he could about the territory's military governor, Toby Holt. The bloodshed in the saloon just now, Wang was convinced, would be nothing compared to what it would be when he made good his vow to take the life of Holt.

Wang kept mostly to himself, making only occasional forays into town and keeping himself inconspicuous in the dark recesses of Davenport's large saloon, where there were any number of strangers and disreputable-looking men. But by carefully watching everything that took place in the town and by speaking with some of the other Chinese in his boardinghouse, Wang had managed to learn a great deal. He knew where the military governor and his family lived, he knew the grounds surrounding their dwelling place and the positions of the men guarding it. All he needed to do was exercise patience and then, one day, his hatchet would put an end to Toby Holt.

*   *   *

The long, gray line of uniformed young men swept down the parade ground of the United States Military Academy at West Point, overlooking the Hudson River, as the corps of cadets passed in review. The cadets marched with the precision for which they were noted, and when they passed the reviewing stand, they saluted smartly.

Standing to the right of the superintendent of the academy, taking the salute, was the guest of honor, the commander of the Army of the West, Major General Leland Blake.

Himself a proud alumnus of the academy, Lee Blake stood as ramrod straight as any cadet as he meticulously returned the salutes.

Directly behind him, in a section of bleachers reserved for the families of cadets and friends, stood his wife and stepdaughter, who had accompanied him to the East Coast. Cindy Holt, looking beautiful in her stylish fur coat and hat, stood very still, anxiously scanning row after row of cadets. Suddenly she reached out and grasped her mother's arm so tightly that her fingernails dug into flesh. "Look, Mama," she murmured in ecstasy, "there's Hank!"

Eulalia Blake winced. "Yes, I see him, dear," she replied with relative calm.

Cadet Henry Blake, the recently adopted son of the Blakes, was now a noncommissioned officer of the corps. He turned toward the reviewing stand as he saluted his adoptive father.

Cindy had to curb a strong desire to jump up and down in excited glee. "He sees us, Mama!" she whispered fiercely. "I'm sure he sees us."

Eulalia could detect no hint of recognition in her adopted

154

son's eyes. It was impossible to know from his unchanging expression that he had seen anyone except the general, but she refused to spoil Cindy's pleasure. "Of course, dear," she replied.

After the parade ended, the cadets were presented individually to General Blake, an informal ceremony that nevertheless lasted for more than two hours. Hank, by prearrangement, was the last member of the corps to be presented.

"Cadet Henry Blake, third classman," the brigade adjutant said crisply.

Hank stepped forward and saluted sharply. "Sir," he said, "you don't know how pleased I am to see you."

Lee returned the salute with a flourish. "Hello, son," he replied, and they shook hands with a warmth that told everyone within eyesight of the closeness of their relationship.

Hank turned, saw Eulalia, and embracing her swiftly, kissed her. "Hello, Mother," he said.

Her hands on his shoulders and her arms outstretched, she gazed up at him proudly. He towered above her by more than a head. "I'm so glad to see you again, Hank."

Then Hank looked directly at Cindy, who had been waiting patiently for a sign of recognition from him. For a long moment both of them stood rooted to the ground, finding it impossible to move. Finally Hank regained a measure of mobility, and putting his hands lightly on the girl's shoulders, he planted a firm but shy kiss on her cheek. Cindy's face turned a fiery red; Hank, too, blushed deeply.

At last Cindy found her voice. "Hi, Hank," she said breathlessly.

Hank had imagined this moment many times during the year and two months he had spent as a student at the academy.

However, he was conscious now of the proximity of General and Mrs. Blake, not to mention the army brigadier, who was the superintendent of the academy, and the full colonel who was the commandant of cadets. So all he could manage was a miserable, "Hi, Cindy."

When he and Cindy accompanied the Blakes to the hotel on the academy grounds for Sunday dinner, they walked side by side, but they were so self-conscious that they took great care not to touch, and both were so frozen that it was impossible for them to speak. Not until noon dinner was served and they began to eat did the two young people start to thaw.

Eulalia was quick to note the drastic change in Hank's table manners due to his training at the academy. Instead of slouching in his chair, he sat very straight at the table, holding his elbows close to his sides, and his manners were impeccable. That did not prevent him, however, from consuming vast quantities of food.

General Blake put the cadet at ease by talking to him first about his studies, then about various athletic competitions at the academy. The general had learned earlier from the academy's superintendent that Hank was the star of the rifle team and that the coach of the boxing team believed that he held great promise in the lightweight division. Hank, however, tended to downplay these achievements during his discussion with the general.

"I suppose," Lee said, "it's too soon for you to have decided which branch of service you intend to apply for after you've graduated."

"No, sir," Hank replied firmly. "My mind is already

made up. I'm going to apply for a commission in the cavalry."

Lee raised an eyebrow. "Why the cavalry?" he asked.

"Because that was your branch, sir," Hank replied.

Lee looked a trifle distressed. "I don't want you just copying me, son," he said. "Your career will flourish best if you enter the branch of service for which you're best suited."

Eulalia put a detaining hand on her husband's arm. "If he wants to join the cavalry, let him do what he wishes," she said quietly.

Her husband immediately saw the wisdom of her remark and subsided.

At last Hank turned to Cindy. "Dad told me you intend to go to New York City for a few days to visit an army post there. When do you leave?"

"We leave by train immediately after supper tonight," she replied.

He looked at her anxiously. "But you'll be back in time for the dance on Saturday, I hope?"

"I wouldn't miss it for the world," she replied, and her tone was so fervent that it thrilled him.

That afternoon Eulalia tactfully saw to it that the young people had an opportunity to spend some time alone. "You and I," she told Lee, "are scheduled to visit the superintendent and his wife at their house. Hank, do you suppose you could show Cindy around the grounds and meet us back here later for supper?"

"I can think of nothing I'd like better, Mother," Hank replied sincerely.

Eulalia and Lee watched the young couple move off. "They

look so natural together," she murmured, "and both of them are growing up so fast."

"Do you think they're serious?" he asked.

"Serious?" She laughed. "They're totally, wholeheartedly in earnest, as only people of their age can be in earnest when they've fallen in love for the first time in their lives."

"Fortunately," Lee said, "there's a natural brake on their emotions. Academy regulations won't permit them to marry until Hank has graduated and won his commission."

"The time will pass far more rapidly than either of us realizes," Eulalia said wistfully.

Continuing to watch them, Lee said thoughtfully, "I just hope they don't change their minds in the course of the next two and a half years. They seem so right for each other, and I can't think of a marriage for either of them that would give me as much satisfaction."

"I don't think you need have any cause for concern on that score, Lee," Eulalia said emphatically. "If I know Cindy and Hank, they're tremendously loyal people, and I can't imagine either of them changing an opinion!"

The young couple turned a corner, and as they passed from the sight of their parents onto a well-trodden path that led through a wooded copse, they instinctively moved somewhat closer together. Displaying great dignity, Cindy reached up and took Hank's arm. He crooked his elbow and held her hand close to his side.

"I suppose," she said, "that the dance on Saturday evening will be typical of academy social affairs."

Sensing the underlying question she was asking, Hank formed his reply carefully. "I've been told that this and a ball held at the end of May are the two biggest and most important social events of the year. But I really wouldn't know. This will be the first dance I'll have attended since I got here."

"Really?" Cindy feigned surprise. "I thought that all cadets were required to attend all dances."

"Oh, no," he said. "Attendance is strictly voluntary."

"Why haven't you gone?" she demanded bluntly.

He looked at her steadily. "I've had a very good reason," he said. "There's been no one I've cared to take."

Her heart beat faster, but her voice remained calm. "I've been informed," she said, "that there are hundreds of attractive girls in New York and Philadelphia who would give almost anything to be invited to a West Point dance."

Hank glared, and succeeded in looking mildly ferocious. "It may be that you're right," he said. "However, it so happens that I have no interest at all in any girl from New York, Philadelphia, Boston, Baltimore, or Washington City, to mention only a few places on the Eastern Seaboard. I'm interested in only one girl, and she happens to live on the post at Fort Vancouver, Washington. If she lived closer to the academy, I would automatically invite her to every dance and every other social function to which young ladies are allowed. I hope," he concluded firmly, "that my point is clearly understood!"

She was triumphant but was so. breathless that her reply sounded timid. "I—I understand."

Like the cavalry officer he intended to become, Hank quickly assumed the offensive. "I suppose," he said, "that you've become enormously popular at home."

She actually managed to inject an element of surprise into her reply. "Not at all," she said. "Oh, I've been invited to my fair share of picnics and dances and the like by young lieutenants at the post and by some of the boys at my school. But I dropped a discreet hint here and there, and the suitors have lost heart.''

"What do you mean by a discreet hint?'' Hank asked.

Males, Cindy decided, were sometimes annoyingly obtuse. "I've made it plain to everyone,'' she said, "that I'm interested only in a cadet at the U. S. Military Academy. That has served to discourage all potential suitors.''

He had to curb a desire to shout for joy. "What do Mother and Father say to that?'' he asked. "They must disapprove, because you lead too lonely an existence.''

"So far they haven't said anything,'' she said slowly, "and I'm not at all lonely. When I'm home from school, I help Mama when she and Papa have to entertain visiting generals and senators and other important people, and up until recently I was having dinner with Toby and Clarissa at the ranch a couple of nights a week. Of course, they're in Idaho now, so I won't be able to visit them when we return to Oregon. But I'm as satisfied with my existence as I could possibly be, considering that the one boy I care about is thousands of miles away.''

He glanced at her, then shook his head. "Why is it, I wonder,'' he mused, "that you and I fence and talk around the subject of—of our future without ever meeting it head-on?''

"I don't really know,'' Cindy confessed, beginning to giggle.

He laughed, too, and they stopped short on the path. All at once they looked at each other, and their laughter died away. With one accord they embraced, then kissed hungrily.

When they finally drew apart, staring at each other, Hank

said huskily, "You have no idea how long I've wanted to do that, or how much."

"I've wanted it, too," Cindy murmured, "so I can imagine."

He drew in his breath. "Will you wait for me?" he asked, suddenly unsure of himself.

"Of course!" She didn't know whether to laugh or cry.

"What do you suppose," he asked tentatively, "the folks will say?"

Her smile was soothing, her tone convincing. "Oh, they'll be delighted," she replied. "They won't be in the least surprised. They've been expecting something like this for some time."

Hank's grin was uncertain. "You don't suppose they'll object on the grounds that I'm not good enough for you?"

"Not good enough? Ha! Mama thinks you're just wonderful. As for Papa, you can do no wrong in his eyes. Why, just the other night when we had dinner at the house of the army chief of staff, Papa was boasting to General Sherman about you, telling him about your academic record and your athletic prowess and your military standing in your class, and so on. He was so proud I thought he was going to burst."

"He really talked to General Sherman about me?" Hank was incredulous.

"General Sherman made it plain that if you can keep up your record here for the next two and a half years, he'll have a special assignment for you when you're commissioned. I didn't know what he was talking about, but Papa understood him well enough and was enormously pleased. But don't you dare mention it to him. I don't believe he intends for you to know as yet."

"Your news," he said, "makes me much more sure of

myself. I guess I'll have to speak to the folks about us before the reception tonight. It will be my last chance to see them alone before the dance. They've been asked to chaperon it.''

"I know," Cindy said. "They're looking forward to it. May I come with you when you speak to them tonight?''

"By all means. I like the idea of our doing things together.''

"So do I."

Again he hesitated. "You don't think they'll object on the grounds that I'm your adoptive brother?''

"Hardly," she said firmly. "We're related legally—technically—but since there's no blood relationship between us, there's no reason for them to object.'' She sighed happily. "We'll ask Papa to make an announcement to the press, and I'll go back to Oregon formally engaged to you. I like the sound of that—very much!''

VI

By early winter, the tempo of Indian attacks against Idaho settlers had increased dramatically. The already thinly spread army troops were managing to keep troublesome miners and riffraff in line, but they were hard-pressed to do anything about the increasing number of Indian attacks.

One chilly night a vicious assault was conducted against a ranch in central Idaho. The corral and another outbuilding were burned to the ground. The rancher, his wife, and sons were routed, and their home was gutted. When morning came, the distraught family discovered their cattle and horses had vanished, but they knew better than to search for them. By then the livestock would be scattered and driven into hidden canyons known only to the Indians.

Less than twenty-four hours later, two farmhouses in the southern part of the territory were attacked, and this time the marauders were more violent, killing and scalping the farmers and their families before setting fire to their homes and property.

Each day fresh reports were received in Boise, and the news grew continually worse. No ranch or farm in the territory was safe. The braves were growing increasingly bold, even attacking schoolhouses and burning down churches.

At first the exact identity of the marauders was unknown. According to all reports, they vanished into the night as swiftly as they appeared. Gradually they became bolder, however, allowing themselves occasionally to be seen. Without exception, they were young, and without exception, they wore the distinctive war paint of the Nez Percé.

The Idaho authorities were certain that Running Bear was responsible. The Shoshone braves, it seemed, were taking no part in these latest raids, thanks no doubt to the control exerted by the Shoshone chiefs and the efforts of Rob Martin to get them to honor their treaties with the United States. So Lieutenant Governor Rob Martin confined his visits solely to the towns of the Nez Percé, demanding that the attacks be halted immediately.

Everywhere he met the same response. The sachem and the subchiefs of the Nez Percé all told him that they had lost control over their young braves, who had become dedicated followers of the inflammatory Running Bear. These warriors were indifferent to the fact that their actions blatantly broke the treaties their nations had signed with the United States. They had only one goal in mind and didn't care how they achieved it: They were determined to drive all settlers out of Idaho.

After Rob had returned and made a full report of his findings, Governor Toby Holt called a meeting of the battalions' lieutenant colonels and the commanders of all of the army's independent units in Idaho, as well as the leaders of the legislature and several prominent businessmen, including Edward Blackstone. To this assemblage Rob Martin repeated his entire story. Toby then asked for comments and opinions.

Lieutenant Colonel O.E. Fairweather, a great bear of a man, lumbered to his feet. He was upset and made no attempt to hide his anger. "These Indian braves," he said, "are committing outrageous, unwarranted depredations against our people—American citizens. I say we launch an all-out campaign against the devils and kill as many of them as we can find. Then the rest of them will run scared from the territory!"

There was a smattering of enthusiastic applause, and then Colonel J.J. Kane, commander of an infantry battalion, asked for recognition. "I'm in total agreement with my colleague, Colonel Fairweather," he said. "By this time, the troop reinforcements that have been promised us by the War Department must be ready to join us. I suggest that the governor send a telegram to Washington urging the dispatch of those troops at the first possible moment and that we delay our counterattack until they arrive. I want to ensure that we have sufficient troops to smash the rebellious Indians permanently and drive them out of Idaho completely."

As the colonel resumed his seat, the men attending the conference applauded even more vigorously.

Toby looked at the two regular army officers. "Gentlemen," he said, "what you are recommending, in essence, is all-out war against the Nez Percé. What you fail to take into consideration is that only a part of the entire Indian nation is engaging in this campaign against us. The senior warriors are not participating in or condoning these attacks, nor are any of the older Indians, not to mention that their women and children have no part in the campaign against us, either.''

"What you say is quite true, Governor,'' Colonel Kane interrupted, "but all the same—''

"One moment, Colonel.'' Toby held up a restraining hand. "Let me also point out to those of you who may have forgotten that the Nez Percé are a very extensive nation. The better part of the tribe lives in Washington, not in Idaho, and that faction has been quiet since their extensive rebellion a few years ago was put down. The Nez Percé nation also extends into Montana, and there, too, they are currently being quite peaceful.

"Let me point out to you that your proposal would automatically put us at war not only with the Nez Percé from Idaho but also with those in Washington and Montana. In order to engage in such a war and to be assured of victory, I estimate that the Army of the West would need to be doubled, at the very least, and from my knowledge of both Washington and Montana, as well as of Idaho, I would say that two to four years, at the minimum, would be required to defeat the Nez Percé. I don't believe that General Blake's forces are prepared for such a campaign, nor do I think that President Grant and his administration would look with favor on such a war. Before engaging in it, I would feel obliged to explain the situation in detail to Washington and to obtain the personal approval of President Grant.''

He made complete sense, but his words put a damper on the gathering, and the participants looked at each other blankly.

"But we've got to do something, Governor,'' the speaker

of the territorial house of representatives said. "What do you suggest?"

"I know the Nez Percé, just as they know me. They are a proud, courageous people who will fight to their last drop of blood if they're backed into a corner, and I hate the thought of additional, needless bloodshed. The only solution I can see is for me to ride into the mountains alone and have a face-to-face confrontation with the renegades. I once asked Running Bear for such a meeting; he refused me at that time. Now I don't intend to ask, I will insist. Only if I see him myself can I convince him that his tactics are all wrong and that they will only lead to his people's demise. My name will gain me some measure of respect from Running Bear. I've encountered other stubborn Indians in my day and have made them see the light of reason, so I'm reasonably sure I can convince Running Bear to change his tactics, too."

A long silence followed Toby's statement, and Colonel Kane was the first to break it. "You can't do this thing, Governor," he said emphatically. "You'd be sacrificing your own life for nothing. It would be a purposeless suicide."

Heads nodded, and voices rumbled with assent.

Even Rob Martin disagreed with his old friend's plan. "With all due respect, Toby," he said, "you're wrong. You surely won't be able to win the agreement of all of the Nez Percé rebels. And the Shoshone, when they learn of it, will interpret your move as a definite sign of weakness, and they'll join in the rebellion. Your chances of staying alive would be very slim."

Everyone present agreed with him. Toby knew it would be useless to attempt to persuade his colleagues to go along with his plan in their present mood, even though he himself was convinced that it would be the only effective means of ensuring that Running Bear and his followers would terminate their campaign and would resume the peace. Therefore, he concluded the meeting on a tentative, indecisive note, and those attending the session agreed to meet again in forty-eight hours to discuss the problem at greater length. But whether or not Toby would be able to persuade them at that time, he was determined to go ahead with his plan.

After the meeting ended, Toby went in search of Clarissa and found her in their living quarters. The day was cold but clear, and he suggested that they stroll in the gardens of the governor's mansion to give him an opportunity to clear his mind.

Tim appeared, hugging a huge ball. "Can I come, too?" he asked.

"Of course, son. Go get your heavy coat and your hat and mittens," his father told him. After they were appropriately clothed, all three adjourned to the extensive gardens behind the mansion.

There Tim amused himself by throwing the ball and then chasing after it and retrieving it, sometimes finding it necessary to dive into snowdrifts in order to locate it.

Toby and Clarissa found a cleared bench in a sheltered area that was surrounded by thick bushes, and they sat there enjoying the warmth of the sun. He began to talk to her about the meeting.

Clarissa listened intently. When he was done, she said, "I know very little about Indians and their ways, but it seems to me that your colleagues are right. You'd be taking a terrible risk if you went alone into the mountains to see this Running Bear."

Toby idly watched his small son scramble into the thick bushes directly ahead as he chased after his ball. Sighing patiently, Toby began to explain in full detail to Clarissa the necessity for his going alone into the mountains to meet Running Bear.

All at once Clarissa stared openmouthed at something straight ahead; her eyes bulged in horror, and she gasped, raising a hand to her face.

Toby followed the direction of her gaze and froze for an instant when he saw the six-and-a-half foot, three-hundred-pound Chinese giant emerging from the bushes. Grinning evilly, the man had Timothy in one arm, using him as a shield. In his other hand, he carried his weapon—a gleaming hatchet. Toby recognized him immediately as Wang, the hatchet man for the San Francisco tong.

To Timothy's eternal credit, he behaved like a Holt in the emergency. Although he was badly frightened, he neither cried out nor made any move that would obstruct his father's attempts to help him.

Recovering his wits instantly, Toby drew one of his six-shooters. "Don't make a sound," he whispered to Clarissa. "I don't want Tim to get hysterical."

When Clarissa grasped his intent, she was even more concerned than she had been. She knew he was intending to fire his pistol at the giant, who was holding Tim before his face and chest. Toby would have to hit Wang above the nose or below the waist, and if their little boy moved, the results of the shot would be catastrophic.

His feet planted apart, Toby raised the six-shooter to shoulder level, and grasping it with both hands, he pulled the trigger, just as Wang raised his hatchet, preparing to throw.

Never had it been necessary for Toby to fire so accurately, and never had he responded better to an emergency. His bullet drilled the hatchet man between the eyes, and the Chinese giant died and sank slowly to the ground.

Tim Holt sprang free and raced to his mother. Not until she had her arms around him holding him tightly did he give in to his feelings and burst into tears.

A dozen heavily armed sentries were milling about the scene within moments. An apologetic young lieutenant, the officer in charge of the detail, offered a lame explanation to Toby. "I'm sorry, Governor," he said, "but a couple of the boys had to put out a fire in their sector, and they left their posts unguarded for a couple of minutes. I can see now that this big brute must have started the fire in order to create a diversion so he could sneak onto the property."

"There's no harm done, Lieutenant. Everything has turned out nicely." Toby hoisted his son onto his shoulder and held him there, putting his free arm around Clarissa. Carrying Tim in this manner, he led his shaking wife into the house.

As the completely unnerved young woman began to regain her equilibrium, her husband explained the identity of the hatchet man and told her in detail why Wang had regarded him as a mortal enemy.

"I see," she said at last. "You appear to make enemies as well as friends wherever you go." She paused and looked at Toby. "Now I'm more opposed than ever to your plan of going off into the mountains alone to meet the Nez Percé rebel leader."

Toby shook his head but kept his own counsel. As in the case of Otto Sinclair's attack, the dramatic incident that had just occurred demonstrated, in his mind, more emphatically than anything he could say, that he was well able to look after himself—and others—in an emergency. He had nothing to fear from a journey into the mountains to meet Running Bear, but he had no intention of arguing about the matter with Clarissa, particularly now while she was still suffering from the traumatic shock of seeing the giant holding Tim as a hostage. The biggest consolation they could both take would be that at least Wang was dead and that Otto Sinclair had not been heard from in a very long time. To be safe, Toby would be sure the governor's mansion continued to be guarded twenty-four hours a day. In the meantime, he was more determined than ever to proceed with his plan.

Traveling in twos and threes, the subsachems, the war chiefs, and the medicine men of the Nez Percé nation left their towns and villages in Washington, Idaho, and Montana, and made their way to the remote highlands of the Bitterroot Range in northeastern Idaho.

There, they were made welcome by Serpent's Tooth, the grand sachem of the Nez Percé, and when they had all gathered, they went into a conclave.

The information they had received from a spy in Boise was disturbing. He had told them that Governor Holt had summoned military and civilian leaders to a conference, which had lasted for half a day with no man willing to discuss what had gone on behind closed doors. It was generally understood that another meeting would be held shortly, and the Indians assumed that plans were being made for a major campaign against them.

Seated cross-legged in the sacred cave high in the mountains, the leaders passed a long pipe from hand to hand as they listened to the words of their grand sachem. "It is with a heavy heart, my brothers," Serpent's Tooth declared, "that I am forced to share with you my conviction that the armies of the United States are planning to wage a terrible and devastating war on us and our people. Their regiments of trained troops, horsemen and foot soldiers alike, will launch attacks on us wherever Nez Percé are to be found. They thirst for vengeance against us, and they will not be satisfied until the Nez Percé have been totally destroyed, our homes in ashes, our warriors and elders killed, our women and children scattered throughout the United States."

A retired grand sachem, Moose Antlers, shook his head in sorrow. "I cannot blame the settlers for their hatred," he said. "If I were one, I, too, would loathe the Nez Percé with all my heart. The hair on my head now is white, before that it was gray, and for many years before that, it was black. In all that time I have never seen such outrages committed by the warriors of our nation against people with whom we are supposed to be at peace."

"The words that Moose Antlers speaks are true," Serpent's Tooth declared. "And the blame belongs to only one man—Running Bear. You and I know this, and we must seek ways to curb him and end his excesses. That is the purpose of the meeting to which I have called you."

A grizzled war chief took his turn puffing on the pipe and then said gravely, "It is necessary that he be curbed by any means. If we were to catch him and hold him as a prisoner, that would be justified; if we were to find him and send his spirit to his fathers, that would be justified. He cannot and must not be allowed to incite our young braves to join in these senseless, meaningless raids any longer."

"All of us are agreed, I think, that Running Bear must be halted," Serpent's Tooth said flatly. "Are there any in our midst who take an opposing stand?"

His question was met with absolute silence.

"So be it," he said. "I have asked Running Bear to join us here tomorrow to plead his case before us and to hear our judgment. We will welcome him when he comes, but we will do what we must to see that he calls off his campaign."

The following day, shortly after noon, Running Bear arrived at the rendezvous. The leaders of the nation had taken it for granted that he would be accompanied by an escort of at least fifty of his more ardent followers, and when he arrived alone, they had to admire his bravery.

Serpent's Tooth immediately summoned the group to another parley in the sacred cave, and Running Bear was invited to attend. The grand sachem spoke first and outlined the indictment against the young warrior, whose actions were threatening the Nez Percé with extermination. He was followed by several elders and medicine men, who discussed the moral and ethical aspects of the situation, stressing that there was no justification for an attack against helpless settlers, particularly when the Nez Percé had signed peace treaties with the United States.

The final speakers were several war chiefs of the tribe, who emphasized in specific detail that the Nez Percé were incapable of winning a war against the United States. The Indian nation was small and poorly armed by comparison with the United States, which had millions of citizens and great arsenals at its disposal. The results of such a war would be certain catastrophe for the Nez Percé.

At last Serpent's Tooth called on Running Bear to reply to his critics.

The young warrior stood. He was short, squat, and quietly defiant. Looking slowly around the cave, the flaring torches lighting him and his hearers, he began his address on a mild conversational note. "The Nez Percé," he said, "are a proud and ancient people. Patiently, slowly, they have carved an empire for themselves that extends from the Pacific Ocean across what the white man now calls Washington, Idaho, and Montana. They have defeated other tribes that have laid claim to the land and have beaten off many enemies who have tried to take their empire from them.

"Most recently the Nez Percé have been at war with a new and different enemy, the United States, a nation with unlimited resources and manpower that rises into the millions. The Nez Percé fought bravely and well in that campaign but ultimately were overwhelmed and were forced to capitulate. They signed a treaty with the Americans that was unlike any previous peace they had known.

"Instead of seizing the spoils of war all for themselves, the Americans proposed that they and the Nez Percé live jointly on the land. This was a new experience for the Indian nation. But the younger braves smarted under the humiliation of being confined to reservations and not being able to roam and hunt wherever they liked. Therefore, Running Bear has consented to lead them in a new drive, the goal of which is the complete routing of American forces and American citizens from the sacred soil of the Nez Percé.

"This goal," the young brave insisted, "is not a dream, impossible to achieve. It is an end that can and will be attained because the Nez Percé have learned much about their enemy during the recent war that they have lost.

"Most important, they have discovered that Americans are vulnerable. They are an impatient people, and when they face a prolonged military campaign, during which they suffer steady, heavy losses, they become discouraged and are willing to settle on almost any terms.

"Therefore," the Indian warrior continued triumphantly, "Running Bear and his followers are employing a simple strategy. We are striking a blow against the enemy, then retreating swiftly and disappearing into the mountains. We will continue to employ that method even when the Americans assign many, many troops to fight against us. The Nez Percé," he concluded, "have the infinite patience that the Americans lack. Therefore, the Nez Percé are sure to emerge victorious from the war."

Running Bear ended his address on a personal note. "Running Bear has been warned by his followers not to go alone to the meeting with his elders, but to take a strong bodyguard with him. He has refused because all Nez Percé are brothers, and Running Bear feels certain that they will never raise a hand against a fellow member of the tribe. If Running Bear should be mistaken, however, what becomes of him no longer matters. Running Bear has sown the seeds of dissension and rebellion well, and they are now growing into sturdy, independent plants. Therefore, even if Running Bear should disappear permanently from the scene, the war will go on." He sat down, and those in the cave were silent.

Serpent's Tooth asked if anyone cared to comment, and when no remarks were forthcoming, Running Bear was excused and told to report back to the assemblage in an hour.

After he had gone, the grand sachem drew on a freshly lighted pipe and then exhaled the smoke in a thin stream. "Running Bear is clever," he declared. "He speaks with great conviction and with much guile. His words can convince almost anyone that his cause is right and just."

"He has convinced me," one gray-haired war chief declared. "I was opposed to him and to the young braves before, but now, if they wish it, I will gladly lead them into battle against the forces of the United States."

Several of his colleagues grunted in assent; the group was split.

Serpent's Tooth was in despair. "I have lost the first and most important of battles, that for the support of the leaders of our people. How many of you now support the position taken by the young?"

A number of the subsachems, the war chiefs, and the medicine men rose silently to their feet. The vote was overwhelming. Out of twenty-three men present at the parley, fourteen were ready to back Running Bear.

"So be it," the grand sachem declared sadly. "The violent strategy of Running Bear will continue; the war against the Americans will go on. Those of you who wish to go with the young warriors may regard yourselves free to do so. Those who would stand aside are under no obligation to join. As for me, I will not preside over the fall and total destruction of the Nez Percé nation. Therefore, I resign my post as grand sachem here and now, and I ask the gods to have pity on our people in the terrible struggle that lies ahead for us all."

* * *

IDAHO!

Establishing certain routines, Toby Holt had discovered, was essential to the efficient performance of his duties. Therefore, he devoted himself at breakfast to the reading of official telegrams received during the night and to the reading of reports from the various military districts of the territory. He also glanced through the night-watch reports of the army battalions and of the Boise constabulary. Only when he had finished looking through these various documents was he ready for conversation.

Clarissa Holt waited patiently, and when her husband finally glanced across the breakfast table at her, she handed him his cup of steaming black coffee. "What's the bad news today?" she asked.

Toby shrugged and looked at her soberly. "There's nothing in the overnight reports, but that doesn't signify much," he told her. "And Nez Percé attacks that have been directed against outlying ranches and farms aren't usually reported until much later in the day."

"Aren't you being pessimistic, dear?" she asked. "Are you so certain that there were attacks again last night?"

Toby nodded, then sipped his coffee. "Unfortunately," he said, "the Nez Percé have stepped up their activities to the point where scarcely a night passes without an attack against a ranch or a farm somewhere in Idaho."

Clarissa had not realized the situation was that serious. "Oh, dear," she said.

They remained silent while a housemaid entered with the governor's breakfast of two pan-fried mountain trout and fried potatoes.

When they were alone again, Toby nibbled at his food as he resumed their conversation. "What I find confusing," he said, "is that the senior members of the Nez Percé society—those who were responsible for making and signing the peace treaty with us—are satisfied with the quality of life under the treaty and make no objection to it. All the trouble is being caused by the younger element. According to Rob's report, the elders appear to have lost control of the young warriors."

Clarissa took a swallow of her coffee. "I was under the impression that every aspect of their society is governed by their elders."

"That's normally the case," he replied, "but it doesn't seem to apply in this instance. Now, perhaps, you can see why I'm so anxious to go off on a visit to seek out Running Bear and judge the situation for myself."

She sighed, looking weary as she placed her coffee cup on the table. "I've been hoping against hope," she said faintly, "that you'd give up that wild scheme of yours."

"It isn't so wild," Toby said, a trace belligerently. "In fact, it makes darn good sense. In the absence of anything better, I see no reason not to make the trip."

"Toby, you know I try not to be critical and not to interfere in your business," Clarissa said, "but since your personal safety is directly involved, this happens to be my business, too."

He tried to exercise patience, but his voice was harsher than he had intended it to be. "You should have learned from the incident with the hatchet man from the San Francisco tong—and with Otto Sinclair—" he said, "I'm capable of looking after myself."

"Your behavior in both cases was magnificent, Toby," she said, "and you acted in a manner that upholds the reputation of the Holt name. You did what not one man in a thousand is capable of doing.''

He grinned at her but did not speak.

''I know you're going to claim that you have the Holt luck, just as your father did. That may be, but let me point out to you rather reluctantly that your father's luck ran out when he and Mrs. Blake were killed in that rockslide in the mountains.''

Toby's grin faded away.

''Only the Lord in His wisdom knows how many hatchet men for how many tongs are skulking around the territory waiting to drive their hatchets into you! In case you've forgotten, Otto Sinclair is still at large. He failed in his last attempt to kill you, but you can be certain that he's going to try again and will keep trying until he either succeeds or is killed. And the young braves of the Nez Percé openly regard you as their enemy. For all I know, so do the Shoshone. So, too, do any number of prison inmates who owe their incarcerations to you. You're the natural target for everyone in Idaho who is disgruntled, for everyone who has a chip on his shoulder. Yet you remain so convinced that you lead a magic life that you actually propose to go into the mountains unattended to meet with the renegade Nez Percé, and you fool yourself into thinking that nothing untoward is going to happen to you. Maybe it isn't; maybe the Holt luck will hold one more time. But if it doesn't, I'm going to be a widow, and your son will grow to manhood never remembering his father!''

She was so incensed, so overwrought, that Toby didn't have the heart to persuade her further. Instead he rose from his place at the table, walked to her chair, and bending down, kissed her tenderly. ''All I can do is to ask you to trust me,'' he said. ''Believe me, I'm not going on this trip for pleasure or for my vanity. But I owe it to the people of the United States, and especially to the people of Idaho, to solve this problem with as little bloodshed as possible, and if I fail or if I'm injured or killed while making the attempt, at least I will have tried. I'm doing what I must, Clarissa, and I beg you, don't stand in my path and try to stop me. You can't, and I have enough trouble ahead without having to worry about us. Believe me, Clarissa, I love you, and I love Tim, and I'll move heaven and earth in order to come back to you safely and in one piece!''

Maloney's Saloon was filled with regular customers, and as usual, they were enjoying the incessant chatter of Gilhooley, the talking crow. Among those present was Stalking Horse, who dropped in almost daily for a glass of apple juice because he was fascinated by the bird. Accompanying him this evening was White Elk, who waited outside the saloon and shyly petted Julia, the burro, who was hitched to a rail.

Inside, there was a lull behind the bar, all the patrons having been served. Murphy, the old miner, left his normal place beside Gilhooley's perch and approached Maloney. "I'd like a private word with ye," he muttered.

Maloney, who was washing and drying glasses, moved a few feet away from a group of patrons and then looked across the bar at the old man. "What's on your mind, Murphy?"

Murphy took a long swallow of his drink, and the sigh that followed seemed to rise from his toes. " 'Tis a sad day for me, Maloney,'' he said, "but I find it needful to be goin' out of town again on a wee errand that needs doin'.''

"Where be you bound?" Maloney demanded.

Again Murphy sighed deeply. "I can't reveal me destination to a livin' soul, not even to ye, the best friend I've got in all the world," he replied. "But I've come to ye to ask ye if ye'd do me a great favor, once again."

"Let me guess," the proprietor said. "You want me to keep your talkin' crow safe and snug here for you, feed him his birdseed and water every day, and in general look after him until you come back."

"Ye guessed it!" Murphy cried in delight. "And I'm obliged to ye from the bottom of me soul. I knew I could count on ye."

"Not so fast," Maloney said, polishing a glass, then holding it up to the light to make sure it sparkled. "The last time you left him here, you were late—horribly late—in gettin' back to Boise. The poor bird drooped and carried on so mournful-like that I was sure his heart would break. He touched no food or water for days, and, well, I was afraid he'd drop dead on my hands! Wishin' you all the luck in the world, my friend, but I don't care to go through such an experience again."

"I blame ye not," Murphy said, "and I assure ye that they'll be no repetition this time. I'll attend to me business and return pronto. Quick as an elf leapin' into a jar of whiskey."

And so the issue was settled. Maloney agreed with reluctance to take the bird "for a few days, and not one minute longer," and Murphy went off immediately on his burro, leaving town as night was falling. It was assumed by most of his fellow patrons that he had gone off into the mountains to look after his secret mining interest there.

In the week that followed, Stalking Horse and White Elk sojourned into the wilderness for another intense training session, which they were in the habit of doing every month. White Elk was learning rapidly the art of tracking animals, of moving silently through the forest, of cooking game and cleaning animal skins. When they returned to Boise, White Elk was the proud possessor of numerous skins of beaver, muskrat, and mink that he had cleverly set traps for with cages Stalking Horse had shown him how to make.

Not until a few days after their return did they make the time to stop in at Maloney's bar, and when they did, they found a dejected Gilhooley hunched down on his perch, uttering a familiar complaint.

"Where's Murphy?" the crow asked mournfully. "Where's Murphy?"

Maloney sighed and shook his head. "My heart bleeds for the poor little critter," he said to Stalking Horse. "Murphy's been gone for more than a week, and Gilhooley here won't last much longer. He's behavin' exactly like he did the last time that blame Murphy disappeared. From first thing in the mornin' until I close the doors at night, the bird keeps askin' for his mate. Not another word does he speak, and he takes no nourishment—not a single birdseed or a drop of water."

White Elk, full of compassion for the despondent bird, walked over to Gilhooley and tried to entice him into a recital of his stock sayings. The bird would not be cajoled, however, and it kept repeating its mournful refrain, "Where's Murphy? Where's Murphy?"

Several of the patrons were gathered at the far end of the bar, holding a discussion in low tones, their expressions serious. When Gilhooley began repeating the question again, two of the number disengaged themselves from the party and approached the Cherokee.

"Excuse me," a middle-aged man, apparently the spokes-man, said, "but you've been comin' here for some time now. You must've heard Gilhooley speak when Murphy's around. He's got quite a gift of gab!"

Stalking Horse nodded.

"Well, Murphy's left Gilhooley for over a week now, and the poor bird just won't respond to anybody else. It's just like what happened before when Murphy left him, only this time it's worse," the man said. "From mornin' till night he cries out for Murphy, and it's gettin' on our nerves—we're about ready to jump out of our skins, in fact! We can't take out our feelings on Gilhooley, sad ole bird, but we need a mite of peace and quiet when we come in here to drink. So we're gonna try something else. We're formin' a posse that will go out and search for Murphy. When we find him—and find him we will—we'll drag him back here by the scruff of the neck, and that'll end Gilhooley's caterwaulin' once and for all."

Stalking Horse now understood why he was being con-sulted about the posse. "If you wish," he volunteered, "I'll be glad to join in the search with you."

The two men seemed to relax, and their faces beamed their appreciation. "We sure would appreciate it, sir," one of them said.

The two men returned to their friends after buying Stalking Horse a glass of apple juice. The other men in their party were noticeably relieved when they were told the good news.

So it happened that Stalking Horse, accompanied by White Elk, joined the other patrons of Maloney's Saloon in their search for Murphy that afternoon. One of the men recalled that Murphy had set out toward the east of Boise, so the entire party went in that direction, spreading out as they rode.

Stalking Horse mounted his stallion, then hoisted White Elk up behind him. The boy was wildly enthusiastic about being included in the search, but the old Cherokee was calm and methodical.

Stalking Horse and White Elk rode swiftly for more than an hour, outdistancing the other searchers. Occasionally the Cherokee indicated a clump of bushes or a small burro's footprint in the snow, but he spoke very little—until all at once he pointed. "There, I think," he said, "is Julia." He rode quickly across the hills toward the burro, and when he dismounted, he lifted White Elk to the ground.

The boy raced to the small animal, and Stalking Horse was not far behind. "Julia is not wearing her saddlebags, Stalking Horse," the boy cried, "and I do not see the man Murphy anywhere."

"No," Stalking Horse agreed. "He is not in sight."

White Elk patted the burro, and to the boy's great delight, Julia gently nuzzled his face and neck, rubbing up against him. He was carrying two apples in his pockets, and these he offered, one at a time, to Julia.

Careful not to hurt the child's hand, the burro nibbled at them gently, consuming both apples, including the cores. Her meal finished, she rubbed her head against White Elk.

Stalking Horse smiled at the boy. "I see that Julia has found a new friend," he said. He refrained from mentioning another observation, that he was certain the burro was lonely and craved human companionship, which she had been missing for a time.

White Elk threw his arms around the burro's neck and hugged her. "She is my good friend," he said. "I like her very much, too."

"If you wish to make your friendship permanent," Stalking Horse said solemnly, "I suggest that you ride her." He lifted the boy into the air and placed him on the bare back of the burro. Julia looked back over her shoulder at White Elk, brayed once in seeming approval, and pranced beside Stalking Horse's stallion when the Cherokee had again mounted.

Stalking Horse, convinced that Murphy was not in the vicinity, went in search of the rest of the posse and found them after a very short time. When the men saw Julia, they became optimistic about finding her owner, but their enthusiasm faded after Stalking Horse spoke to them outside White Elk's hearing.

"I fear for Murphy's safety," he said. "His burro was wandering across open country without her saddlebags, and she was hungry. When White Elk fed her two apples, she devoured them. Murphy does not starve his animals—he would first go without food himself. That is why I believe he is in trouble. I urge you to spread out on both sides of the road and to continue to search slowly and carefully for him."

Following his advice, the posse promptly resumed their search, with some riding to the left of the dirt road and others to the right of it. Stalking Horse slowed his pace to match theirs, and Julia jogged along near him, happy to be carrying the little boy whom she had adopted as her friend.

After an intensive examination of the frozen, snow-covered terrain for more than an hour, one of the men on the outside left flank suddenly yelled out. Stalking Horse ordered White Elk to stay where he was and immediately joined the group that was forming around the man who had cried out.

Lying on the ground, half hidden by a snowbank, was Murphy, his sightless eyes staring up vacantly at the sky.

Stalking Horse dismounted and dropped to one knee in order to examine the body. "He fought hard," he told the hushed onlookers, "but he faced too many enemies. They stabbed him to death." He pointed to a number of wounds over which frozen crusts of blood had formed.

"The motive for killing Murphy was robbery," Stalking Horse announced, pointing to several severed thongs dangling from the dead man's belt. "His purse was cut away." He studied the old miner's body for a time and then reached down to tug off the left boot, which protruded at a strange angle. After several hard pulls, it came off, and the Cherokee turned it upside down. Two large yellow nuggets rolled onto the ground.

The onlookers gasped.

Stalking Horse reached for the two nuggets and held them in the palm of one hand. "Murphy must have found a rich vein in his secret mine. No wonder he was robbed." Rising to his feet, he held out the nuggets. "Will someone take charge of these, please?"

The man who had organized the hunt took possession of them. "We'll use these," he said, "to give Murphy a funeral that he would be proud of."

The saddened members of the search party returned to Boise, going first to a funeral parlor to deposit Murphy's body and then to Maloney's Saloon, where they made elaborate plans for Murphy's funeral, scheduled for noon the following day.

Gilhooley sat silently on his perch during the discussion. Not once did he ask, "Where's Murphy?" He seemed to understand that his master was not going to return. The patrons found Gilhooley's silence more disturbing than his constant questioning had been.

The following morning Maloney opened his saloon long enough for those planning to attend the funeral to have a drink of whiskey before proceeding on their sad errand. As he crossed the floor of the establishment, he noted that Gilhooley's perch was empty. Looking down, he saw the bird lying unmoving on the floor, silent in death. The talking crow, having sensed his master's passing, had apparently lost the will to live himself.

When the others planning to attend Murphy's funeral arrived at the saloon, they swiftly reached a unanimous decision: Gilhooley would accompany his master to the grave. Two of the mourners quickly fashioned a tiny coffin and tenderly placed the bird in it.

After the funeral service was conducted, Gilhooley was buried in a tiny plot adjacent to Murphy's, and a small stone marker was erected at the head of the grave. It bore a simple legend: *A Loyal Friend*.

VII

White Elk had spent all his young life learning to suppress and conceal his emotions. His first teacher had been his mother, and she had been succeeded by Stalking Horse, who was even more determined that the boy learn conduct befitting an Indian brave.

On this day, White Elk attended a meeting about a matter so vitally important to him that all he had ever learned about self-control was brought into play. Standing in the executive office of Governor Toby Holt, the boy's body was rigid, his fists clenched tightly, his jaw clamped shut. Only by exerting the greatest willpower was he able to abstain from trembling violently.

Toby leaned back in his swivel chair, pressed his fingertips together, and tried to put the child at ease by smiling at him.

Stalking Horse, who sat nearby, also tried to encourage the

boy. "White Elk," he said, "may tell Governor Holt what is on his mind."

White Elk tried to speak but was so fraught with anxiety that he was incapable of getting the words out.

Toby looked at his foreman and raised an eyebrow.

"He has been this way for the past two days," Stalking Horse explained. "He expressed the wish to see you, so I brought him here to your office."

White Elk made a supreme effort to explain his anxious state. "It's . . . it's Julia!" he finally blurted.

Toby looked confused, but Stalking Horse understood. "Julia," he said to the governor, "is a burro that belonged to the old miner, Murphy, who was killed recently. No one has claimed her—" Stalking Horse started to say.

"I have!" White Elk interrupted, tears now making his eyes shine. "I have claimed her, and she has claimed me, too."

Stalking Horse smiled at White Elk and then turned to Toby. "For many years," he said, "I have been in the business of raising horses. From time to time through those years I have seen a man and a horse form a rare bond of friendship. Each seems to know what the other feels and thinks. Such a relationship is not common, but it does happen. I believe it has happened in the case of this boy and this burro."

"My father had that relationship with his stallion," Toby said softly, looking down at his hands. Then he roused himself. "Where is the burro now?"

"For two days she has been in a stall in the governor's stables," White Elk said, eagerness and apprehension warring within him. "Please—she is a very small burro and does not eat much oats or many apples. I will work in the stables to earn the money to pay for her keep and her food. I will—''

Toby silenced the child with a sharp wave of his hand. ''Who has cared for the burro during those two days?''

''I have,'' White Elk responded.

''Have you groomed her?''

''Yes, sir.'' The boy's left temple throbbed. ''I groom her every day.''

''Do you exercise her?''

''I do.'' White Elk was almost reduced to tears. ''I take good care of Julia. She is my friend. I alone am responsible for her. She will let no one but me ride her, and so it is my duty to exercise and to groom her. It is also my greatest pleasure.''

Toby found it difficult to keep from smiling at the boy's earnestness. ''What are your plans for the animal?''

''Stalking Horse says I may go with him to your ranch in Oregon when he leaves in the spring. There are many stables there, he says.'' White Elk paused, as if unsure of how to continue. ''Will you—may I bring Julia to Oregon? I will spend all my time caring for her, just as I do here.''

''But remember our agreement that you will also spend part of the year with Miss Drake. What will you do with Julia during the period you spend with her?'' Toby asked.

The little boy looked defiant. ''My heart tells me that she will not keep Julia from me. She will find a place for my burro in the stable of the inn. If Pamela will not do this, I will not go with her; I will stay with Stalking Horse.''

''I am quite sure that won't be necessary,'' Toby said firmly. Then he gave Stalking Horse a questioning look.

The Cherokee turned to White Elk. "What made White Elk think that Governor Holt and Stalking Horse would not agree to the keeping of the burro?"

"The ways of adults can be very strange," the child said.

"Let me end your suspense, White Elk," Toby said. "Unless Stalking Horse has objections I know nothing about, I know of no reason why you can't keep the burro."

"You may keep Julia," Stalking Horse said flatly.

The little boy was so happy he jumped up and down in joy. "I will work very hard in the stables," he promised. "I will—"

"You will do no such thing," Toby told him after exchanging a corroborating glance with Stalking Horse. "You will spend your time learning all that is good about the ways of the Indian, and all that is good about the ways of the settlers. When you become an adult yourself, you will serve as a bridge between our peoples."

The overwhelmed child stammered his thanks, then wanted to know if he could go to the burro at once, as it was time for her daily ride.

"Go ahead," Stalking Horse said, rising to his feet, and the boy raced out of the room.

"Sit down again, Stalking Horse," Toby said. "I have another matter to discuss with you."

The old Cherokee sank into his chair.

"I'm sure you've heard of the troubles we've been having with the Nez Percé," Toby said, and went on to bring the Cherokee up to date about the raids on ranches and farms by bands of young warriors.

Stalking Horse nodded. "There are braves who refuse to

learn that those who oppose the United States and her people will perish.''

Toby went on to tell him how he had resisted the demands of military and civilian leaders for a full-scale war against the Indians. Instead, he explained, he was seeking a personal confrontation with Running Bear, the leader of the rebellion.

Stalking Horse digested his words in silence, and finally he nodded. "Toby," he said, "has the wisdom that was given to his father. That which you propose is the best and most certain method of restoring a true peace to Idaho."

"There is only one major problem with my idea," Toby said, and smiled painfully. "Clarissa is opposed to my going alone into the wilderness on this mission. She fears for my safety. She's afraid that Sinclair, her first husband, is lying in wait and—along with any number of my enemies—will try to kill me when I least expect it. I have been unable to persuade her to listen to reason. Ordinarily, I would do what I think best, and go off into the mountains by myself without hesitation. But Clarissa has suffered too much for my sake, and I feel that it's wrong for me to leave her in an unhappy state."

"Toby is fortunate," the old Cherokee declared, "to have found such a squaw. She is a good wife and a good mother."

"She is, indeed," Toby said, "and I have been seeking some means to ease her mind. Would you be willing to travel into the wilderness with me? It could be that Clarissa would accept my mission if you were to accompany me."

"I will go with you," the Indian said.

There was no need for further discussion; all that remained was for Toby to obtain Clarissa's approval. He found an opportune moment soon after he had finished work for the day and joined his wife and small son in their living quarters.

"I believe that I've solved our problem," he told her, and he went on to explain that Stalking Horse would accompany him on his journey to see Running Bear.

Clarissa had hoped against hope that Toby would drop the idea of carrying out his project, but upon second thought she realized that she should have known better. A Holt never dropped an idea that he regarded as good; he persisted until he found some way to make it work. She sighed and tried to reconcile herself to the situation.

"Stalking Horse spent years roaming with my father through the West," Toby said. "They went from territory to territory under the most frightful conditions. They endured the worst of winter weather in the Rockies; they met and fought renegade Indians, bandits, and outlaws of every sort. And they led a whole wagon train of tenderfeet across the entire North American continent to Oregon. Stalking Horse will be an invaluable help to me on this relatively short journey."

The idea of Stalking Horse accompanying him was so natural, so right, that Clarissa no longer had any choice but to acquiesce gracefully.

"If you wouldn't mind," Toby said, "White Elk will remain here in your charge while Stalking Horse comes with me. I think the boy will be happier living here where Stalking Horse also is our guest. He will continue to visit Pamela for his lessons, of course, but the chief burden of looking after him will be on you."

"I'll be glad to look after White Elk," she said. "He's a dear little boy, and he'll be no burden to me, I can assure you." She raised her head and met her husband's gaze squarely. "Go on your mission, darling. I have done everything in my power to stop you, but I couldn't do it. I truly hope that you succeed as you intend to succeed, and may God go with you.''

Only when the many responsibilities of Toby Holt's office fell on Rob Martin's shoulders did the lieutenant governor fully appreciate the duties of his superior. For the duration of Toby's journey into the wilderness with Stalking Horse, the title and duties of acting governor fell on Rob, who had to work several hours longer each day in order to keep up with the paperwork.

One of his functions was the final validation of land claims, and he was surprised and pleased when Edward Blackstone came to him late one morning to have his claim to a gold mine validated. Rob grinned across his desk at his visitor as he looked through the claim.

"Congratulations," he said. "I've had some good reports on mine number two-thirty-one. Apparently you and your partners have hit a bonanza.''

Edward grinned at him in turn. "I put up a substantial sum for my twenty percent interest in the mine," he said, "but it's going to work out beautifully. If the present estimates are correct, I should be getting a several-hundred-percent return on my original investment.''

"I have no doubt of it," Rob said as he marked down the claim number in a large ledger and stamped Edward's document with the official seal of the territory. Then with a flourish he wrote his own name in the space provided for validation.

"Your financial interests in Idaho are certainly proliferating,''

Rob remarked as he leaned back in his chair. "As I understand it, you have a finger in a variety of pies these days."

"Well," Edward said, "I believe in the American West, and I think its development is crucial to the future of this country. I'd be foolish if I didn't demonstrate my faith by investing in ventures that seem bound to pay off."

As they arose and shook hands, Edward said impulsively, "Look here, if you have nothing better to do, why not join me at the inn for noon dinner? I'd like to celebrate, you know. It isn't every day that I make such a profit on my investment."

Rob was delighted to accept the invitation.

"Suppose we meet in the dining room in a half hour?" Edward said, consulting his pocket watch. "Does that give you enough time to finish up here?"

"Ample time," Rob assured him. "I'll be there. Thanks very much."

When he walked into the dining room of the inn thirty minutes later, Rob saw that Pamela Drake was seated with Edward. She appeared to be rather pleased with herself, while Edward glowered at her.

Looking very attractive in a green wool dress that set off her eyes, Pamela smiled radiantly at Rob as he approached their table. The fact that she had not heard anything more from Jim Randall dismayed her and contributed to her sense of restlessness—and recklessness. Deciding to ignore the earlier warnings of Kale Salton that the Englishwoman should leave Rob strictly alone, she no longer had any intention of avoiding him.

Edward continued to glare at her, looking up at Rob only when he reached for a chair. "I'm terribly sorry," he said, "but when Pamela learned you were coming to dinner, she insisted on joining us. She's been clinging to me like a leech ever since!"

Rob proved equal to the occasion. "That's perfectly all right," he said to Edward. Then turning to Pamela, he said, "As a matter of fact, I'm delighted to see you."

"I'm glad to see you, too," she replied, beaming at him provocatively and placing a hand on his arm. "Pay no attention to Edward. He's nothing but an old grouch."

Not responding to her gibe, Edward ordered drinks of whiskey for Rob and himself and reluctantly requested a glass of dry sherry for Pamela.

Conversation was somewhat inhibited due to Pamela's presence. Edward had hoped to discuss finances with the lieutenant governor, who struck him as knowledgeable in such matters. He did make an effort to do so when their drinks arrived, but he was conscious of Pamela's total lack of interest as she studied her fingernails and flirted coyly with Rob.

By the time the waiter appeared with their appetizers, Edward was becoming distinctly annoyed, and when the waiter handed the Englishman a folded note after serving their food, Edward read it quickly and rose to his feet. "I hope you'll pardon me for a short time," he explained, "but I'm afraid that I have a business caller in the lobby who can't be put off. I'll get rid of him as quickly as I can, but if it takes me a while, I apologize in advance." He bowed and walked quickly out of the dining room into the adjoining lobby.

Pamela sighed gently and leaned toward Rob. "Isn't this convenient?" She beamed at him, her green eyes sparkling mischievously.

He felt distinctly uncomfortable. "Yes, it's—it's very nice," he muttered.

She lifted her glass to him and deliberately waited until he raised his own in return. Then, clinking her glass against his, she said softly, "To you and me."

Rob found her intimacy disturbing but would have been less than a gentleman to have questioned it, so he smiled at her steadily and raised his own glass to his lips when she drank.

Neither of them knew it, but as they drank to Pamela's toast, appearing comfortably intimate, they were the objects of intense scrutiny. Someone was peering at them through the partially frosted window of the restaurant. Suzanne, the owner of the fanciest bordello in Boise, a place whose notoriety extended as far as San Francisco, had glanced in idly a moment before, wondering if she should stop in for dinner. Her business was slow, as it always was at this time of day, and she felt that she might kill an hour or two, perhaps find some lone male diners who could be clients for her establishment.

When she had seen Pamela Drake flirting with Rob Martin and had watched him grin at her in return, Suzanne's heart had jumped. This was a big break.

Through friends who were "in the business" in San Francisco, Suzanne had long since learned of Kale Salton's presence in Boise and knew her entire background. Again and again the Boise madam had gone to Kale hoping to entice her to work in her establishment, promising the voluptuous woman the leading role. She felt sure that with a woman of Kale's beauty, experience, and notoriety as her star, business at the bordello would be sure to double. But Kale had shown no interest in any proposition and had dealt brusquely with Suzanne, refusing even to listen to her.

Now, however, Suzanne had evidence that was sure to persuade Kale, and she fully intended to make the best use of it.

Without hesitation, Suzanne hurried the short distance down the street to the lieutenant governor's residence. Climbing the front steps quickly, she knocked forcefully at the heavy door. As luck would have it, Kale Salton herself answered the knock.

The instant that Kale recognized the blond-haired woman who stood on the stoop in a fur hat and coat, she tried to close the door.

But Suzanne was too fast for her and had already placed a foot in the opening. "Listen to me, Kale," the madam said in her husky voice. "All I ask is that you listen to me! While you loll around here doing nothing, Lieutenant Governor Martin is busy making a fool of you, having a tête-à-tête dinner with Pamela Drake at the Boise Inn."

Her words sank in, and Kale opened the door. "You lie," she said succinctly.

"I have no reason to tell you anything but the truth," Suzanne replied self-righteously. "If you don't believe me, just come with me now. You'll see for yourself whether or not I'm telling the truth."

Her anger thoroughly aroused, Kale went inside to inform the housekeeper she would return shortly and to look after the baby in the meantime. Then throwing on a coat, she joined the blowsy older woman on the street. "If this is one of your tricks . . ." Kale began.

Suzanne sniffed and regarded her haughtily. "You'll soon

discover that I have no need to resort to trickery," she replied in an icy voice.

They made their way to the Boise Inn, the self-confident Suzanne in the lead, followed by the angry and disturbed Kale. When they arrived, they walked to where the inn's restaurant was located, and Suzanne gestured grandly toward the window through which she had seen Pamela and Rob. "Don't believe me?" she asked, mockingly. "Look for yourself, sweetie. Maybe you'll believe your own eyes."

Luck had turned against Rob Martin. He and Pamela were still seated at the table by themselves, Edward not yet having completed his business with his visitor. By now they had finished their meals, and after clearing the table, their waiter had brought them snifters of brandy, which Edward had ordered for them from the lobby.

As Kale watched in shocked disbelief, Pamela, smiling intimately at Rob, put her hand on his arm, withdrew it, and raised her drink to him. He clinked glasses with her, and from where Kale stood, they appeared to be gazing into each other's eyes.

Kale had seen more than enough. The fact that Pamela Drake was once again sinking her talons into Rob, despite being warned, was a great source of anger to Kale, but this she should have expected. Women like Pamela had no scruples, no morals. No, what made Kale seethe was Rob's behavior. After all the sacrifices she had made for him in order to care for his baby daughter—giving up her way of life to adopt a whole new life-style and moving from San Francisco to this comparatively backwoods town—she found herself being ignored and pushed aside. And he was not even man enough to admit that he preferred the Englishwoman to her. He lacked even the courtesy of telling her about this private dinner engagement with Pamela, leaving Kale to be humiliated by finding out for herself under unpleasant circumstances.

White-faced and furious, Kale glared at Suzanne, whose doughy face reflected her triumph. "Don't just stand there looking at me like a mooning cow!" Kale said angrily. "Let's go someplace where we can talk."

Suzanne felt certain that she had won her gamble, but she was taking no chances and led the younger woman down the street to the bordello without further comment. Scarcely noticing her surroundings, Kale stormed into the parlor after her.

Secretly rejoicing, Suzanne took her guest's coat and then sent a maid to fetch her a strong drink of whiskey. She also took the precaution of ordering that they not be disturbed.

"Look around," Suzanne said proudly, gesturing grandly toward all corners of the room, "and tell me what you think."

Her eyes narrowing, Kale walked around the parlor, inspecting it with infinite care, then examining the sumptuous bar directly behind it. Finally she looked at the huge bedchamber at the rear of the main floor.

"Not bad," she commented as they returned to the sitting room. "Not bad at all."

Suzanne laughed abruptly. "What did you expect," she demanded, "moose antlers over the hearth and cows grazing beside the grand piano? Not on your life! Every piece of furniture in this suite has been brought here by rail and wagon. I challenge you to name one establishment in San Francisco that is more attractive and has more class!"

"I can't," Kale agreed, and absently sipped the drink that the maid brought her. "It looks quite—expensive."

"It is," Suzanne assured her flatly.

"Do you mean to say that you can charge San Francisco prices?" Kale asked.

Suzanne's frizzy blond hair bobbed from side to side as she shook her head no. "Not with my present personnel," she admitted, and then took the plunge. "But the current prices will hardly apply to you. You could command any figure you want."

Kale smiled reflectively. "As much as fifty dollars an hour?"

In spite of her determination to win over the auburn-haired woman, Suzanne was visibly taken aback. "Fifty an hour is an awful lot of money," she hedged.

Kale's voice was hard. "That's been my fee for years, and I've never yet been forced to take less."

Afraid that an acknowledged star performer would slip from her grasp, Suzanne hastened to reassure her. "I'm sure you could get it," she said. "In fact, you could get any figure you want. There are enough well-to-do miners and ranchers in Idaho for you to have all the business you want—and to take your pick as well."

Kale's luminous eyes narrowed. "What percentage of the fee do you usually take?"

Hesitating for only a fraction of a second, Suzanne replied, "I customarily split fifty-fifty with my girls."

The younger woman looked at her incredulously. "Give you twenty-five an hour? Ridiculous!" she snapped, setting her drink on a taboret. "I'll open my own house and operate it myself, first. I'll give you a flat ten dollars an hour, and you'll take care of all expenses. That's my only offer. Take it or leave it."

"I'll take it," Suzanne replied instantly. "When can you start?"

"Tomorrow," Kale said, and then changed her mind. "No . . . I see no point in waiting that long. If you have an adequate supply of gowns, negligees, and the like, I'll start whenever it suits you."

"I'll show you the whole supply," Suzanne said eagerly, "and you can take whatever you please."

"Good!" Kale recklessly drained her glass.

Suzanne found it difficult to conceal her elation. Soon her establishment would become known as the finest bordello between San Francisco and Saint Louis. Nevertheless, she was feeling somewhat apprehensive, wanting to make certain that she had covered all ground and that there would be no slips ahead.

"What about Lieutenant Governor Martin?" she asked.

Kale smoldered. Rob's disregard for her feelings made tears well up in her eyes, and she dug her long fingernails into the palms of her hands. She wanted to hurt him as much as he had hurt her, yet the thought of abandoning little Cathy—and breaking her promise to Beth—made Kale hesitate. In her dreams she had envisioned the three of them living as a true family, with Rob and her married and sharing the joys of domestic life. Then the thought of him clinking glasses with Pamela Drake shattered the image, leaving a surge of anger in its place. "What about him?" she retorted. "As far as I'm concerned, Lieutenant Governor Martin may go straight to the devil!"

Edward Blackstone returned to the table in time to join Rob and Pamela for coffee, and then Rob, thanking his host, took his leave and returned to his office, unaware of Kale's fateful decision.

He was uncommonly busy for the remainder of the afternoon, dealing with the unfamiliar routines of Governor Holt's work, and it was dark by the time he finished for the day. Dismissing his secretaries, he extinguished the lamps in his office, donned his greatcoat and fur-lined hat, and walked the short distance from the government building to his own house. Winter was in full season in Idaho, and Rob thought it odd that one could always tolerate a greater degree of cold in the mountains than one could in the valleys because the air was so much drier. He was tired after his long, arduous day, and as his boots squeaked on the well-packed snow, he was looking forward to a quiet drink and a hot dinner before the warm fire in the dining room.

The house was strangely silent and dark when he arrived home, and when he called to Kale, there was no answer. He walked through the house and located Mrs. Carson, the housekeeper, in the kitchen conferring with the cook, and she followed him into the living room. Miss Salton had gone out some hours ago, she informed Rob.

"But you don't know where she is?" Rob asked the woman in bewilderment as he poured himself a drink.

"Yes, sir," Mrs. Carson answered, and then hesitated. "That is, a blond lady wearing a fur hat and coat came to the door some time ago, and she and Miss Salton talked for a spell. Miss Salton seemed very upset, and then they went off together right after that."

He shook his head, unable to decipher where Kale had gone or with whom.

"I saw to it that little Cathy wasn't neglected none," Mrs.

Carson said righteously. "I gave her a bath, and I fed her supper just like Miss Salton would of done."

Rob thanked her and asked her to send in the head of his security detail.

When the young officer in charge of the security of the lieutenant governor's house came into the room and saluted, he found Rob standing before the hearth, staring uneasily at the logs burning there. "You wanted to see me, sir?"

"Yes," Rob replied, still looking at the fire. "I wonder if you might know of Miss Salton's whereabouts."

"Yes, sir, I do," the lieutenant replied, and fell silent.

Rob turned to him slowly and was surprised to see that the young man was beet red and deeply embarrassed. "Well?" he demanded somewhat testily.

The young lieutenant's voice was faint and hesitant. "I had dinner at the officers' mess this noon, sir," he said, "and I was just on my way to work when I happened to pass a place known as Madam Suzanne's. You—you might have heard of the place, I imagine."

Rob nodded. "I know of it," he said.

"Well, sir, there was a blond woman—I think it was this Madame Suzanne—who was just arriving there, and . . . and Miss Salton was with her. They went into the house together."

Rob peered hard at him. "You're sure it was Miss Salton who was with this woman?" he demanded incredulously. "You're sure it was she whom you recognized—or thought you recognized?"

"I'm in charge of protecting her and the baby every afternoon," the lieutenant replied, sounding aggrieved, "so I guess I sure ought to know Miss Salton when I see her!"

Dismissing the officer abruptly, Rob rang for Mrs. Carson.

"I'm afraid that something urgent has come up," he said. "It will be impossible for me to go up to the nursery to play with the baby this evening. I don't expect to be too long, but you might tell the cook to hold supper only for a reasonable length of time for me. If I'm more than half an hour late for it, I won't be eating here."

He hurried to the front hall, where he took the precaution of buckling on a belt with two six-shooters holstered on it. Then he donned his fur-lined hat, put on his short sheepskin coat, and pulled on a pair of old, supple gloves as he left the house. In too much of a hurry to wait for a horse to be saddled, he walked the few blocks to Suzanne's bordello, muttering to himself as he stalked down the frozen street. The few pedestrians whom he encountered took one look at his scowling face and prudently got out of his path.

After bounding up the front steps of Suzanne's establishment, he pounded so hard on the door that he nearly battered it down. The maid who immediately answered his summons assumed that he was drunk, and so she tried to cajole him by smiling at him conspiratorially. "Welcome, sir, welcome," she said with pretended gaiety. "Step inside out of the cold."

Rob followed her to the ornate parlor, where he opened his warm coat but did not remove either it or his hat.

"The bar is right back yonder," the maid told him. "Help yourself to a drink, and madam will be with you in a few minutes."

Moments later Suzanne swept into the parlor, her long skirt trailing after her. Her eyes widened when she recognized Rob, but instinct told her to pretend not to know him. "Good evening, sir," she called. "I hope you had a drink and that you're ready now to talk a little business."

Rob was in no mood for pretense. "Where is she?" he demanded.

Suzanne feigned innocence. "I'm afraid I don't know what you're talking about, sir," she replied.

"Either you tell me where she is and lead me to her right now, or I'll tear this joint of yours apart room by room," Rob thundered.

Carrying out her self-assigned role to perfection, Suzanne pretended to be indignant. "I don't know who you think you are," she said haughtily, "but I run a respectable, clean house, and you have no right to come bullying your way in here and threatening me. If you want a girl, all well and good; if you don't, get out, or I'll call the constabulary and have you thrown out!"

Rob hooked his thumbs in his gun belt and stepped closer to the woman. "Where is she?" he repeated. His voice held the threat of violence. "Where is Kale Salton?"

Suzanne knew men well enough to realize that she could maintain her pose no longer. Martin obviously meant what he said and would indeed cause damage to her establishment unless she complied with him. "Oh!" she cried. "You're here to see Kale! Why on earth didn't you say so? I think it's just amazing that word has already spread that she's here. You'll be her very first customer."

"Where is she?" he growled.

"Not so fast, sir," she replied. "Kale has her fee, and she doesn't come cheap. I'll require fifty dollars in advance for one hour with her."

It took all of Rob's willpower to prevent him from smashing the woman's head against the wall. He realized that he had to play the game in Suzanne's way, or he would be creating a first-class scandal. If he gave vent to his anger, she would call in the constables, and the incident would soon be the principal topic of conversation throughout Boise.

Silently, reluctantly, he reached into his hip pocket for his wallet and counted out fifty dollars.

Hastily taking the money from him, Suzanne told herself that she would savor her victory later. At the moment, she wanted only to be rid of this powerful official, and so she made the least amount of fuss possible. "Come with me, if you please," she said, and led him down a corridor behind the bar. Walking to a large oak door, she tapped lightly on it, stood aside, and discreetly took her leave.

"Come in," called a sweet voice. Rob recognized it as Kale's.

He opened the door and found himself in the entrance of a large bedchamber dominated by an oversize four-poster bed. On the far side of the room seated before a dressing table was Kale, applying rouge to a face that already was heavy with cosmetics. She was wearing a short, filmy black negligee, which revealed far more than it concealed of her superb figure.

The lighting in the chamber was romantically dim, and the musky scent of perfume was heavy in the air. Rob broke the sensuous spell by slamming the door shut behind him. "What the hell's going on here?" he demanded harshly.

Kale stiffened at the sound of his voice but, recovering swiftly, continued to apply her makeup. She seemed very busy and made no response.

Entering the room, he repeated the question.

Kale rose slowly and turned to face him. "I am minding my own business, sir," she replied quietly, "and I advise you to do the same. If it's necessary, I will summon assistance and have you removed."

"I'm not leaving," he told her, "until we have this thing out in the open, and anyone who tries to *remove* me, as you put it, is going to suffer some broken bones."

She had no doubt that he meant every word.

"What's more," he said, and his voice revealed his indignation, "I've paid Suzanne fifty dollars for the questionable privilege of this interview with you, and I damn well intend to get my money's worth."

Kale fought back a desire to roar with laughter, afraid that in his present mood he might strike her.

"Say what you have to say, then, and have done with it," she told him, facing him.

Her filmy attire made her look more ravishingly beautiful than ever before, and Rob found his anger dissipating. "I—I demand to know what in the devil you're doing," he said.

"I'm not obliged," she told him with spirit, "to respond to any demands that you may make on me. Besides, it should be rather obvious—I'm going back to work. I need to earn a living, and I'm doing the one thing that I know I can be paid well for."

"Any man who tries to go to bed with you will have to answer to me." He patted his six-shooters ominously.

Kale glared at him, her kohl-lined eyes enormous. She was perilously close to losing her temper. "How dare you dictate to me?" she demanded angrily. "Who do you think you are that you have the right to tell me what I may or may not do and how I should live my life? I am a free woman, and I can do whatever I damn well please—whenever I damn well please to do it!"

Rob took refuge in a glacial approach. "Naturally," he replied stiffly, "I assumed—"

"Your trouble," Kale raged, "is that you assumed too much! You assumed that because I promised Beth I'd look after her baby you could take advantage of me and ignore me as you pleased. You assumed that because I developed a genuine love for little Cathy you could trample over me and pay no attention to my rights or my feelings."

She had put him on the defensive, and he was annoyed. "I don't know what in the devil you are talking about," he said irritably.

"You don't? Well, listen good and maybe you'll learn." His words had infuriated Kale. "I've had all of the disadvantages of being a wife and none of the advantages. I've not only taken care of your daughter—which it just so happens I've enjoyed doing because I love her—but I've supervised the operations of your household, acted as your hostess, and for all practical purposes I've let the whole damn world assume that I've been living with you. I've had no social life of my own—no man in his right mind would ask me to go out with him. I have been forced to sit idly, with my hands folded in my lap in a ladylike manner, while you traipse around with other women and do as you please with them! You've been free to make eyes at Pamela Drake and to wine her and dine her, and you've expected me to accept your conduct and say nothing about it. Well, I refuse."

Rob tried in vain to interrupt, but she gave him no opportunity. "If you can see Pamela," she concluded, her voice rising to a pitch just below a scream, "then I can do what I damn well please with any man who happens to catch my fancy!"

Kale paused to catch her breath and noted, to her astonishment, that Rob no longer appeared angry. On the contrary, his expression was positively genial as he rocked back and forth on the heels of his high boots.

"You've outlined your way of seeing things very clearly," Rob told her, "and I'm grateful to you for it. In fact, you've done a great deal to clear the air. I don't expect you to believe this, but my relationship with Pamela Drake is completely innocent. I don't particularly care for the woman—I never have, and I never will. But that's all beside the point. You see, you've opened my eyes to my true feelings for you, and for that I'm very grateful."

Kale was truly bewildered by his change of attitude. "What do you mean?"

"You were right to become upset with me," he said, a new note of humility creeping into his voice. "I was taking you for granted, and I was taking advantage of you. I wasn't doing either deliberately, mind you. I guess I was blind to the fact that I love you. I—I just didn't quite realize it."

Kale stared at him in stunned surprise. "What's that you just said?" she asked.

He replied patiently. "In the first place, I love you."

"I did hear you correctly," she said with a soft cry. "Whatever may follow—in the second place, or whatever—doesn't really matter."

Their eyes met and held, and their mutual world suddenly righted itself.

Rob took a half step toward Kale, intending to embrace and kiss her, but suddenly he stopped himself. "No," he said loudly, "I'll be damned if this is the appropriate place to

211

propose marriage.'' He grinned at her. ''Let's get out of here. Let's go home!''

Her eagerness matched his. Hurrying to a nearby wardrobe, she threw her shoes, undergarments, and other attire into a bundle, then hastily donned her heavy coat and shoes and quickly tied a scarf around her long, flowing hair.

Not another word was said as Rob put an arm around Kale's shoulders, picked up her bundle, and walked with her up the corridor.

Business in the bordello had increased, and chattering couples filled the bar and the parlor. But all conversation ceased as the patrons stared in mute surprise at Lieutenant Governor Martin and a young woman, obviously a prostitute from her overuse of cosmetics, hugging her coat closely around her.

A dismayed Suzanne hurried forward, intending to intercept the couple, hoping that what she was seeing was untrue.

Rob, grinning in a self-satisfied manner, halted her with one remark: ''Keep the change.''

In the street passersby paused to stare at the sight of the lieutenant governor and his shivering, glamorous companion, who were laughing uproariously as they hurried home. When they reached Rob's house, the couple went straight to the nursery, where little Cathy was fortunately not yet asleep. Soon the sounds of loud laughter and wild whoops reached the far corners of the house.

Mrs. Carson and the cook, standing together in the kitchen, had known that something out of the ordinary was taking place, and the unorthodox sounds from the nursery proved it. They exchanged disapproving glances, and the cook muttered, ''If they ain't careful, they're going to spoil that baby so bad that she's never going to go to sleep!''

Still more surprises were in store for the two women, however. After the sounds of hilarity had emanated from the nursery for half an hour, the commotion died away, and all was quiet for a time. Then Lieutenant Governor Martin and the usually circumspect Miss Salton appeared in the dining room.

He was carrying her to the table, and her arms were entwined around his neck. Furthermore, Mrs. Carson reported to the cook, they were kissing passionately as they moved into the room, and their eyes were closed. It was a wonder they didn't smash into the furniture!

The curious cook served them their soup and hurried back to the kitchen to breathlessly describe the scene in the dining room. "Would you believe it?" she said to Mrs. Carson. "Miss Salton is wearing nothing but a flimsy black nightgown sort of thing that doesn't even cover her up decent! She's half naked in it, but she's sitting there brazen as you please, as though she was fully dressed. And that's not all. She and Governor Martin are holding hands across the table and looking into each other's eyes so hard that I swear they didn't even know I gave them their soup!"

One more shock awaited the hired help. Discussing it the following day, they decided that in view of all that had preceded it, it was inevitable. Governor Martin and Miss Salton, who had always been models of propriety, spent the night together in Lieutenant Governor Martin's bedchamber and did not emerge until late the following morning.

The business of the territory was postponed that morning. The acting governor and Miss Salton, who in the words of Mrs. Carson "looked radiant as a bride," took their time at breakfast with the baby. Then, taking Cathy with them, the couple left the house without leaving any word of their destination. Only by spying on them from an upstairs window did the housekeeper know that they went a short distance up Main Street to Art Russell's jewelry store, the best emporium in Boise. When they emerged from the store sometime later, Rob was grinning quietly and Kale looked deliriously happy.

Once on the street, they immediately encountered Millicent Randall. "Look!" Kale cried, and pulling off her left glove held her hand up to the startled young woman for inspection. On her ring finger a large diamond glittered impressively.

"You're the first to know," Rob said. "Kale and I are betrothed."

"My congratulations to both of you," Millicent replied, praying that her deep disappointment at Rob's engagement did not show. "I hope you will be very happy; I know you will."

"Thank you," a beaming Kale said, clinging to Rob's arm. "You and Jim are invited to the wedding, of course. We have yet to settle details, but we'll let you know." They parted company with Millicent after exchanging a few more words, and the euphoric couple returned home, the baby happily accompanying them.

Millicent completed her errands in a daze. She returned to the stable where she had left Lady and, mounting her mare, started to ride back to the Randall ranch.

She hugged her secret hurt to her, her one consolation being that no living being knew of her pain and humiliation. Not once had she ever hinted to anyone that she was secretly in love with Rob Martin, and now she was relieved beyond measure that she had been so prudent. It was only natural, she told herself bitterly, that a man as good-looking and as dashing as Rob should fall in love with a woman like Kale Salton. She was lovely, charming, and would make him a perfect hostess for the active social life he was expected to lead because of his position. Furthermore, Millicent told herself that Kale had an abundance of a quality in which she herself was sadly lacking—sex appeal. She could never arouse sexual feelings in a man. Rob no doubt thought of her as a pleasant and somewhat inconsequential young woman—and perhaps as an accomplished musician, as well—if he thought of her at all.

Her problem, Millicent reflected as she continued toward the ranch, went far beyond Rob Martin. Never had she known a man to give her as much as a second glance just because she was female. She had certainly attracted attention because of her musical talent, and occasionally because of her wealth, but not once had her gender alone caused any man to take notice. Even her now-deceased fiancé, who was the cause of her coming West in the first place, had proposed to her, she knew, because it would be a good marriage, not because of any love or passion on his part.

It did no good to feel sorry for herself, Millicent knew, but she could not help it. She had always been resilient and brave, able to rise above any circumstances. But now the circumstances and disappointments were simply too much for her, and she allowed herself to wallow in self-pity. She reached out occasionally and patted Lady on the neck or on the flanks, but otherwise she was in something of a daze as she rode out to the ranch.

At dinner she told Jim the news about Rob and Kale and then lapsed into silence. Jim was so lost in his own reaction to the news that he did not notice that his cousin was less

215

communicative than usual. He was vastly relieved to hear that Rob and Kale were going to be married, for he had been afraid that Rob was a source of competition for Pamela Drake's attentions. Jim couldn't stand the possibility that Pamela would reject him for Rob, and it was for that reason he had avoided her. Well, he could breathe more easily now that Rob was not going to offer him competition for Pamela's hand.

As he thought about it, he came to realize that having only one eye had caused him to be feeling inadequate and defensive where Pamela was concerned. Frequently he found himself thinking that she found him somehow lacking as a man because of his injury. Now he decided it was time for him to put aside these feelings and to behave with the boldness that had always been part of his character. He was the equal of any other man who was interested in Pamela, and it was high time he behaved like it!

Having made up his mind, he felt infinitely relieved and anxious to put his new resolve to the test. Still unaware of Millicent's depression, he rose from his chair, told her he had business to tend to in town, and went to his bedchamber, where he removed a small object from the box in which he kept his personal jewelry. After depositing the object in his jacket pocket, he went out to the barn to saddle his horse.

Arriving at the Boise Inn, Jim left his horse in the corral and went straight to the suite occupied by Pamela and Edward. To his relief, Pamela was there alone.

When she opened the door, Pamela was startled to see Jim, who she thought was snubbing her. She also felt enormously pleased he was there, even happy. Lately, it had seemed she had no control whatever over her feelings and what was happening to her. She had been feeling particularly dejected that day, having learned from one of the waiters at the inn at noon dinner that Lieutenant Governor Martin and his child's governess, Kale Salton, were betrothed. As usual, news traveled swiftly in a small community like Boise.

Ever since she had fallen in love with her tutor when she was sixteen years old, only to be callously rebuffed by him, Pamela had taken care never to allow that emotional process to begin again. Not that she had refrained from seeing men who interested her—quite the contrary. In fact, she had gone to bed rather indiscriminately with many of them, Edward Blackstone being one. But never again had she let her emotional guard down, and she had not been surprised to discover that these sexual experiences left her virtually unmarked.

The news of Rob Martin's engagement had hauled her up short, however, and had caused her to realize she was wasting her time. She was only in her mid-twenties; nevertheless, she had nothing to show for the experiences she had had along the way, and she was no closer now to settling down than she had ever been.

She had to admit to herself now that, in all honesty, she was relieved that Rob was engaged to marry someone else. To be sure, he was an attractive man, but being the wife of a government official and military man did not appeal to Pamela. Had the relationship followed her customary pattern, she knew she would have inveigled him into having an affair; then he would have proposed marriage, and she would have rejected it, chalking up another victim, and that would have been the end of it. As matters stood now, she could hold up her head knowing she had hurt no one, and at the same time she could realize that Rob had found a woman who was his equal. Pamela remembered with a little smile the day Kale threatened her with a horsewhip.

At this moment Pamela was prepared to enjoy Jim Randall's company. Knowing he was conscientious about earning a living on his ranch, she was even more surprised to see him at this hour on a midweek day, but she hoped that he would be instrumental in helping her to be rid of the sense of depression that threatened to ruin the day.

She offered him a drink, which he refused, and when she tried flirting, he failed to respond. Feeling therefore unsure of his reason for calling on her, she decided to allow him to take the initiative.

He began to talk about his ranch, and Pamela's mind wandered, but ultimately it occurred to her that he was discussing his financial situation—the sums he had invested in the ranch, his expenses, and the annual profits he could reasonably expect to earn. When he went on, doggedly, to tell her his net worth, the size of his bank accounts in the West and in Baltimore, and about various properties that he still owned in the East, the startling thought came to her that he was actually proposing marriage.

Still not concentrating on his words, Pamela let her mind race. Yes! Marriage to Jim—who would undoubtedly have more time for her than Rob Martin—was the obvious answer to her problems. She had landed in a thicket of prickly trouble by toying with the lieutenant governor, and only his betrothal to Kale Salton had saved her. If she rejected Jim's proposal, she would repeat all her past follies and would continue to lead a life of no consequence.

Until that moment she had relied totally on Edward Blackstone for her protection, but she knew it was unfair to him to count on him permanently. Someday he would fall in love himself and would be married, and then she would be completely on her own. She would be wise, very wise, to encourage Jim Randall and become his wife.

Jim continued to outline his finances, projecting what they could be in the future, and Pamela encouraged him now with a warm, steady smile. She knew her strategy was effective when she sensed his growing confidence as he continued his recital.

There was no need for him to go on and on, Pamela decided. Having made up her mind to accept him, she found the plodding preliminaries nearly unbearable. Putting a hand lightly on his arm to stop his flow of speech, she smiled tenderly at him, and meeting his raptured gaze, she said softly, "Jim, there's no need for you to go on. I accept. I can think of nothing that would make me happier or prouder than to become your wife."

There was a moment of electric silence, and then he gathered her in his arms and kissed her.

Returning his kiss with all of the skills at her disposal, Pamela was pleasantly surprised to discover that he was making her breathless, that her pulse was racing. His masculinity was far more commanding than she had anticipated, and she realized that he was still holding his passions in check.

Nestling comfortably in his arms, with one hand gently pressing the back of his head as they kissed, Pamela knew she had made an excellent deal for herself. Jim had ample funds to support her in the style to which she was accustomed, and his virility was sufficiently overpowering to keep her from straying.

VIII

It was a terribly cold winter in the high mountains of the Bitterroot Range, but Toby Holt and his elderly Indian companion traveled without difficulty, both of them dressed warmly in buckskins, boots, and blanket coats and both gifted with a sixth sense that told them where snows were too deep, where hidden crevices and other pitfalls might lie. They had left their horses with the nearest rancher in the area, who lived in the shadows of the mountain range, and now they were proceeding on foot, climbing steadily since early morning. As noon approached, they slowed their pace as they came to a windswept field in which the snow was only ankle deep. At the far end of the field overlooking a precipice stood a longhorned ram staring out across the vast expanse of space. The animal was very still, his silhouette etched against the dull gray sky beyond.

Stalking Horse indicated in pantomime that he was deferring to his companion the opportunity to fire the first shot.

Toby signaled his thanks and started to raise his rifle to his shoulder, but the old Cherokee stopped him by raising his arm. Then, grinning broadly, he reached for the bow and arrow he carried on his back and offered them to his young friend.

Toby understood that he was being challenged. He had been taught the use of firearms by his father, but he had learned to use a bow and arrow with Stalking Horse as his teacher. He hadn't been much older than his small son when he had started his lessons, and they had continued for many years until he had become as proficient as any brave in the shooting of an arrow. Now the Cherokee was demanding that he prove he had not lost the proficiency he had attained so long ago.

Toby took the bow, tested it, and then notched the arrow into it. Although he had used only firearms for many years, he instinctively assumed a natural stance, and he felt at ease as he pulled the bowstring taut and stared down the shaft of the arrow at the unmoving target. There was a faint twang as he released the bowstring. The arrow sped toward the ram and knocked the animal to the ground. The pair ran forward and quickly butchered the carcass. Then, building a fire from the little dry wood they could find, they roasted and ate their fill of the meat. While they were eating, they collected larger branches and began the long process of smoking the rest of the meat for future use. After they were done, Stalking Horse lighted his short pipe and stared out across the frozen waste.

"I wonder when we will come to the hiding place of the Nez Percé," he said, still gazing into the distance.

Toby shrugged and replied, "Who can say? It was reported to me only that Running Bear made his headquarters high in the Bitterroot Range. We might find clues this very day that will lead us to him, or we may spend many days searching the snowfields in vain before we encounter some sign that will take us to his lair."

Needing time to smoke their meat, they established camp for the night, and after eating supper, they almost completely smothered their fire so their presence would not be detected while they slept. Then they retired away from the smoking coals, their rifles close at hand.

At dawn they awoke and ate a breakfast of a few strips of the smoked meat, removing the balance from the coals in order to cool. Then they broke camp, packing up their smoked meat and heading on their way, first conducting a routine search of the vicinity for any sign of intruders who might have come into the area during the night.

Toby carefully scoured the ground as far as a mile from their camp. Stalking Horse was making a similar study about fifty yards away from Toby. Their sense of rapport was so great that although the Cherokee did not call out to him, Toby raised his head and looked sharply at the Indian. He knew instantly from the tension he could see in the old warrior's neck and shoulders that he had found something. Toby joined his companion promptly.

Saying nothing, Stalking Horse merely pointed. Following the direction of his finger, Toby saw what he meant. There, directly ahead, were many footprints in the snow. Leaning forward to examine one of the prints, he discerned the outline of a small moccasin.

It did not take much imagination to guess that a party of

Nez Percé had come through the area during the night. The Nez Percé were a short, small people and therefore had smaller feet than either the Cherokee or the settlers. Obviously the Indians had not been aware that Toby and Stalking Horse had also been in the vicinity, and they had continued on their way, their tracks heading farther up into the mountains.

Stalking Horse grinned broadly, and Toby smiled at him in return. Both were satisfied, although they didn't bother to exchange any words on the subject. These tracks were no doubt those of a party of Indians led by Running Bear himself. Now, if the two men could follow the footprints, they would come to the secret hideout of the Nez Percé rebels.

Clarissa Holt sat with her feet tucked beneath her on the couch in front of the open hearth in the second-floor sitting room of the governor's house. She was engrossed in Mark Twain's new book, *The Innocents Abroad*, which was about the author's travels in Europe and the Holy Land, and was conscious of nothing else but the crackling of the fire. When her eyes began to grow weary, she put down her book, yawned, and sat gazing into the fire.

She hated being unoccupied, having time to think, because then she was inclined to worry about Toby, and that, she knew, was foolish. She had heard nothing from her husband since he had gone off into the wilderness with Stalking Horse a week earlier, but that was no cause for concern. He was as cut off from civilization and its means of relaying messages as he would have been on the moon. To be sure, she was fretting unnecessarily about him. Not only was he fully competent at wilderness survival—able to take care of himself as few men could—but he was accompanied by Stalking Horse, whose wilderness exploits with Toby's late father were legendary.

Clarissa suddenly realized that she was chilly. Seeing that she had let the fire diminish considerably, she rose, stretched, and pulled the tie of her bathrobe more tightly around her waist. Picking up a poker, she stirred the fire and added another log. It was several minutes before the flames were again leaping high enough to satisfy her. Just as she was about to return to the couch, she heard a noise through the closed door of the adjoining bedroom, where her small son slept.

"Oh, dear," she murmured aloud. "I hope Tim isn't awake." It would be most unusual if the little boy woke up. Ordinarily he was a sound sleeper, who went to bed after supper and slept straight through until morning.

Some second sight, perhaps, caused Clarissa to retain her grasp on the fireplace poker as she opened the bedroom door and suddenly stopped short. On the far side of the room in front of an open window stood a man armed with a six-shooter—a man she instantly recognized as Otto Sinclair, her first husband.

Her free hand flew to her throat. "What—what are you doing here?" she demanded breathlessly.

He favored her with a sour, crooked grin and slowly walked toward her as he spoke. "I've stalked you and the governor of Idaho long enough," he said in a rasping voice. "I've watched this house from afar for God knows how long now, studying the guards' routines, just waiting for my chance. And now I have it. The guards change duty every night just at this time. So here I am. What's the matter, Clarissa, sweetie? Aren't you glad to see me?''

Sinclair was only three yards from where Clarissa stood in the doorway. Afraid for her son and herself, she backed into the sitting room, hoping to draw Sinclair with her.

''What—what do you want?'' she said. She was so frightened that she was afraid she might faint.

Sinclair's grin broadened. ''First off,'' he said, following her into the room, ''I aim to do in his excellency, Toby Holt. He has that big ranch in Oregon that earns him a kettle of money every year. Then he's got those lumber interests in Washington—and he's half-owner of a gold mine in Montana to boot. Add it all up, Clarissa, sweetie, and he's worth a heap of money. And since you're still legally married to me, that money will become mine when I kill Holt.''

Apparently he did not realize that Toby was out of town; Clarissa momentarily breathed a trifle more easily. ''You're mad, Otto,'' she hissed. ''Only a crazy man would think he could get away with this.''

Sinclair's laugh indeed sounded like that of a man who had gone insane. ''Next,'' he said, indicating the room behind him where Tim lay sleeping, ''I've got to get rid of that brat of yours. See, I can't leave him alive to foul up my inheritance. If I'm going to get all of it—and I mean every last penny—I can't have somebody else's brat hanging around and laying a claim to his share.''

The mere thought that he might harm her child so infuriated Clarissa that the fear drained out of her. ''I warn you, Otto,'' she said in a low tone, a hysterical note creeping into her voice, ''you harm my baby at your peril!'' Her grip tightened on the handle of the metal poker.

"Come to think of it," he said, "I'll take care of the kid first, seeing how he's handy. This isn't the way I planned it exactly, but his old man's turn will come next." He turned around, took a single step toward the bedroom, and started to raise the pistol, obviously intending to fire it.

Her last vestige of fear gone, Clarissa became enraged. Otto Sinclair had caused her untold misery during the years of their marriage, and his sudden appearance out of the blue when he had been declared dead by the War Department had so upset her that she had inadvertently jeopardized her marriage with Toby, and it had been saved only by extraordinary efforts. Now this madman was threatening not only to murder Toby but to kill her small son, whom she loved more than life itself.

Clarissa went berserk. Her baby's life was in danger, and that was all she needed to know. Lifting the heavy iron poker above her head, she lashed out at Sinclair with all her might, her eyes closing as she struck at him from behind.

The blow was so unexpected, so out of character for Clarissa, that Otto Sinclair had not anticipated her action, and the thick metal rod struck him on the top of the head and sent him staggering across the room into a table.

Recklessly ignoring her own safety, Clarissa pursued Sinclair to where he unsteadily stood. Before he could fully recover from her first blow and raise his pistol, she struck him again with the poker, this blow landing on his forehead and causing him to bleed severely. The sight of blood ordinarily would have made her ill, but that night it merely aroused her animosity that much more. Still grasping the handle of the poker with both hands, she swung it back and forth in a wide arc, each time delivering a sound blow that caused Sinclair to reel.

She gave him no respite, showed him no mercy. Again and again she pounded him with the poker until his pistol clattered to the floor, and he followed it, slumping and lying helplessly in a heap against the dresser.

Still Clarissa did not stop. She continued to beat at Otto Sinclair, putting more strength into each blow than she knew she had, and not caring what might happen to her in the process. All she knew was that she had to destroy this creature who had threatened her family.

Suddenly Major John Talbot, the chief of the governor's security detail, burst into the room, followed by a dozen of his elite cavalrymen who were on sentry duty. They took in the situation at a glance, and then Major Talbot went to Clarissa and forcibly tried to take the bloody weapon from her.

"Let go of the poker, Mrs. Holt," he told her repeatedly. "The intruder is dead. You can stop now."

At last his words penetrated Clarissa's consciousness, and she loosened her grip on the poker. Staring down at the puffy, bloody face of Otto Sinclair, battered almost beyond recognition, she didn't know whether to laugh or cry and did both simultaneously.

"Is your little boy all right?" Major Talbot asked her urgently.

Wrenching her gaze from Sinclair, Clarissa ran to her son's room and saw to her surprise and relief that he was still sleeping peacefully, unaffected by the commotion around him. "Yes, thank God," she whispered, and her tears began to flow even more freely as she closed the window, the lock of which Sinclair had broken when he made his entry.

The officer signaled to his men, who swiftly removed Sinclair's body along with his pistol and the instrument that had killed him. Then Major Talbot led Clarissa to the couch, gently seated her, and after handing her a clean handkerchief, poured her a drink of brandy.

After a time she recovered sufficiently to stop sobbing. Meanwhile, Major Talbot had left the room briefly to confer with one of his men.

"I owe you my sincere apologies, Mrs. Holt," Major Talbot told her as he came back into the room, "along with the apologies of the entire security detail. We have no idea how the intruder managed to avoid all of us and enter this building. My adjutant tells me that he's been recognized as the army deserter who tried to kill you and the governor when you were first traveling to Idaho. Perhaps he was familiar enough with our routines to sidestep our patrols."

Clarissa sipped her brandy and was conscious of the liquor burning as it slid down her throat.

"Be that as it may, please accept my heartiest congratulations, Mrs. Holt. You've proved yourself a heroine of the first order. I'm sure your actions will be an inspiration to our entire battalion." He stood, saluted smartly, and withdrew.

Alone again, Clarissa gradually became calmer. She reviewed again the incredible events of the past half hour. So much had occurred in such a short period of time, she reflected. She could not get over the fact that she had actually killed another human being, that she had bludgeoned Sinclair to death. However, she did not regret having performed the shocking deed any more than she was sorry that Otto was dead. She felt only infinite relief that he no longer represented a threat to her husband and her son, and for that relief she was quietly grateful to God.

Brooding and bitter, Dan Davenport was spending a great deal of time in the small office at the back of his saloon. The members of his staff had grown accustomed to his withdrawals, but those who knew why he was so despondent kept the facts to themselves. Davenport believed he had lost face in his dealings with Edward Blackstone and Pamela Drake, that they had made a mockery of his boast that "nobody ever got the best of me." The vindictive streak in his nature demanded retribution, and gradually a scheme formed in his mind. Sitting in his office day after day, he revised and refined his plan until it was foolproof.

Only when he was satisfied with his scheme was his good nature restored, and then he began to act like his old self, drinking with cronies in the saloon and keeping an eye on his lucrative gambling operations.

The only miscalculation in his plan was his failure to account for Jim Randall, for he knew nothing of Jim's betrothal to Pamela until shortly before he put his plan into effect. By then he was so anxious to obtain revenge that he hastily revised his scheme to include Jim, and he hoped for the best.

Jim arrived in town on the appointed day to keep an engagement with Pamela for noon dinner. He was concerned over Millicent's long silences and tendency to brood, which had become much more pronounced recently. He hoped that Pamela could offer him some sound advice on the best way to handle the problem.

Arriving promptly at the agreed upon time, Jim was surprised to find that Pamela was not awaiting him in her suite. So he went to the desk of the inn to ask after her whereabouts. The clerk excused himself for a moment, then returned with a strange message. "Miss Drake," he said, "will meet Mr. Randall at Dan Davenport's place."

Jim was confused. "Did Miss Drake write that message herself?"

The clerk shrugged and handed him the slip of paper on which the words were scrawled.

Jim was not familiar enough with Pamela's handwriting to know whether or not she had penned the message herself. He folded the note, put it in his pocket, and went in search of Edward Blackstone, whom he found in the dining room awaiting the arrival of two attorneys, with whom he was to have a business dinner. Jim sat down, explained his predicament, and showed him the message.

Edward frowned as he studied the sheet of paper. "I'm damned if this is Pam's handwriting," he said. "I find it very odd, to say the least."

"Exactly," Jim replied. "Why would she go to Davenport's place, of all the establishments that one could go to in this town?"

"That's a splendid question," Edward replied energetically, "and there's only one way to answer it. That is, to find out for ourselves." Excusing himself for a few moments, he wrote a note to his friends, saying he would be late for their appointment, and then he paid a brief visit to his suite. "All set," he said, as he rejoined Jim in the lobby.

They walked quickly to Davenport's Saloon, and when they arrived, Edward asked the bartenders for Pamela Drake.

When the men rewarded him with blank stares, Jim asked for Davenport and was told they could find him in the back.

The proprietor was not hard to find. He was standing outside his small office leaning against a newel post at the bottom of a narrow flight of stairs that led to the floor above. He grinned when he saw them, and there was a mocking note of cordiality in his voice as he called, "Morning, gents."

Jim Randall disliked the saloonkeeper on sight. "There was a message for me at the inn," he said quickly, "to the effect that Miss Pamela Drake would meet me here this noon. Do you happen to know whether there's any truth to the message?"

Davenport seemed to find the remark vastly amusing, and he chuckled at length. "Matter of fact," he finally drawled, "there's a lot of truth in that message."

"Was it written by Miss Drake?" Jim demanded.

The saloonkeeper laughed even more loudly and appeared to be gloating. "It don't much matter who wrote the message, does it? All that counts is whether it's true or not. One thing that's true, absolutely true," he went on with conviction, "is that she's here all right. I'd be willing to bet that she's expecting both of you to show up for her."

Jim lost patience with the gloating man. "Where in the name of all that's holy is she, Davenport?" he demanded.

The black-haired saloonkeeper held the upper hand, knew it, and relished his situation. "That information," he said, "is worth a lot of money, to be paid cash on the barrelhead, which I happen to know that you two gents can easily afford."

They stared at him, trying to make sense out of his remarks.

"Let's say," Davenport told them with a lilt in his voice, "that I've taken possession of Miss Drake. Yes, that's a good phrase. I like the sound of it. Now I've taken a lot of time and trouble to take possession of her; I've had to find out where she lived, when she came and went. Then I had to arrange to get her off alone where we wouldn't be seen and then, ah, give her a little tap on the head so I could take her without any fuss. Well, that's a lot of work, and in order to come out even—or maybe a little bit ahead of the game—I need to be paid. Give me cash for her, and I'll hand her over to you almost as good as new, without hardly a hair on her head being harmed."

"How do I know you're telling the truth?" Jim asked sharply.

"You don't," Davenport replied softly. "You just have to take my word as a gentleman on it."

Jim looked as though he was ready to become violent. Edward, however, who had taken no active part in the conversation, was leaning against the far wall studying Davenport coolly and taking in the overall situation. The saloonkeeper, he noticed, stood in front of the stairs with his feet planted apart and his hands resting on the butts of his six-shooters. In fact, he appeared to be guarding the staircase.

For his companion's benefit Edward frowned slightly as he nodded in Davenport's direction.

As Jim studied the saloonkeeper, Edward's meaning dawned on him. Davenport did appear to be standing guard over the staircase. Jim began to inch toward the man, intending to bolt up the stairs, knocking him aside if necessary. Pamela was most likely somewhere on the second floor.

"Go ahead," Edward said. "I'll cover you."

Jim had no idea how his cousin intended to do that, but he nevertheless had complete faith in Edward's word. Brushing past Davenport, he mounted the steps two at a time, paying no attention to what was going on behind him. Even though he was vulnerable to a shot from the rear, he concentrated his complete attention on reaching the second floor landing.

Davenport started to draw his six-shooters and turned toward Edward. Evidently he intended to dispose of the Englishman first and then shoot down the figure hurrying up the stairs.

But Edward beat him to the draw. Flicking his wrist, his derringer dropped from his sleeve into his hand. He aimed it and squeezed the trigger halfway. His shot was true, penetrating Davenport's heart.

Davenport, already dead, slid to the floor, and Edward leaped over his body and hastily followed Jim up the stairs. The pair paused at the landing and then heard the strident sounds of Pamela's voice raised in anger, emanating from a room at the far end of the corridor. They ran to it, broke down the latch, and flung the door open. Neither would ever forget the extraordinary sight that greeted their eyes.

In the center of the room stood Pamela Drake. In both hands she grasped the hilt of a long, wicked-looking cutlass, which had been used as a wall decoration and which she had pulled down, no doubt to the astonishment of the guards, who hadn't known what kind of woman they were dealing with. Now she was menacing the two burly guards, who were cowering in a corner, and to the amazement of Edward and Jim she was threatening first to emasculate the two guards and then to kill them. Edward looked down at his derringer and began to laugh.

The guards, relieved beyond measure, were glad to surrender to Edward.

Jim went straight to Pamela, and the cutlass clattered to the floor. She looked as though she were on the verge of swooning as he took her in his arms.

Edward was amused by what he believed was her masquerade of helplessness, but Jim was completely taken in by her attitude. In due time, Edward reflected, Jim would realize that his bride was about as helpless as a mountain lion on the prowl.

The deputy sheriffs were summoned and promptly took charge of the prisoners, removed Davenport's body from the premises, and took depositions from the cousins and Pamela, who seemed to be none the worse for her experience.

Jim, deeply concerned about Pamela's welfare, decided to take her out to the ranch for dinner and a rest, and Edward went back alone to the Boise Inn to keep his engagement with his attorneys. Once he had arrived and joined his associates, Edward apologized to them for his tardiness, and as he explained the reason for it, he began to laugh.

The senior partner of the firm shook his head. "You're amazing, Edward," he said. "You always seem to land in the thick of trouble. Whenever there's a shooting or anything untoward happens, you're always in the middle of it."

"That's true," his partner added. "You have an uncanny ability to make things happen."

Edward shrugged innocently. "I don't deliberately get involved in violence, you know."

The older attorney chuckled. "I hate to think that you habitually go about your business with a derringer concealed up your sleeve."

Edward grinned as he replied, "Let's just say that I have a habit of preparing myself for emergencies, which do pop up rather frequently, it seems. And that reminds me—with Davenport no longer among the living, I assume that his gambling establishment soon will be put up for sale."

"I'm quite sure it will," the senior partner said. "We'll probably hear from someone who's interested in buying it as word of Davenport's death spreads."

Edward raised an eyebrow. " '*We'll*' hear?" he said.

The attorneys exchanged a quick glance. "I thought you knew," the senior partner told him. "We represent Davenport's estate. Even people engaged in shady businesses need attorneys to protect their legal interests, and we have no objection to such customers provided their money is good."

Edward smiled broadly as he struck the tip of a wooden match with his thumbnail and then lighted a long, thin cigar with it. "This is most convenient," he said, puffing at the cigar. "I want to buy Davenport's place."

The lawyers stared at him. "Don't tell me you're planning on operating a gambling house," the younger partner declared. "You have enough interests that you don't have to demean yourself by getting into that sleazy a business."

Edward laughed heartily. "Don't worry," he said. "I have no intention of becoming another Dan Davenport. I'm thinking of closing down the place, remodeling the interior, and opening a large, first-rate restaurant. As things stand right now, there's no place in town where people can get a good meal except at my new hotel or the inn, and the population of the town has grown to the point where there's little doubt in my mind that Boise can support another first-class eating house."

"That's all very true," the senior partner replied. "But won't it take up too much of your time? It isn't like your other investments, where you put money in and let others do the work for you."

"Why can't it be? I have no intention of running such a place myself, you see," Edward said, grinning. "You're right that operating a restaurant is a full-time activity. What I intend to do is set up my cousin, Millicent Randall, and put her into business."

The attorneys looked relieved.

"Not that she knows anything about restaurants," he continued. "She'll have to learn from scratch, but she's an exceptionally bright woman, and I'm sure she'll learn quickly."

"You're certainly being generous to your cousin," the younger attorney commented.

"Well, Millicent seems to be rather upset lately," Edward explained in a confidential tone of voice. "She isn't aware that I know it, but she's suffering from a little affair of the heart. I think I've been around long enough to detect these things. Thus, I thought it would be helpful, most helpful, if she had something to keep her occupied to the point where she'll be too busy to think of anything else."

The attorneys were impressed. "Never fear, Edward," the senior partner said, "we'll get the place for you on the best of all possible terms. I think it's a wonderful thing that you're doing for your cousin."

When Cindy Holt and Hank Blake told her father of their engagement, the general gave a succinct and adamant response to his stepdaughter and his adopted son. "Your mother and I are not the least bit surprised to hear of your desire to be married once Hank has graduated from the academy. We've seen this coming for some time. However, we don't approve of your announcing the betrothal just yet. For one thing, it's customary for the engagement of an academy cadet to be made public when he becomes a first-classman—a senior. In addition, we don't think it's wise for you young people to cut off your social ties with everyone else when you're separated by the entire North American continent. Therefore, you'll wait another year and a half before you make your engagement public.''

Cindy would have argued the matter with him, but Hank—extremely conscious of the stars on his adoptive father's shoulders—abruptly said, ''Yes, sir!'' and that ended the subject.

When the Blakes and Cindy had ended their visit to the East, Hank had not expected complications in his arrangement with Cindy. Although he planned to tell no one of their engagement, he would nevertheless act the part of a betrothed man and not participate in the social events that were given by the academy. Instead, he reasoned, he would concentrate on his studies. But a month after Cindy had returned to her home at Fort Vancouver and then gone back to school, a problem arose.

Hank's roommate and close friend at the academy, Dave King, had come to him with a seemingly simple request. His girlfriend, Joyce Snyder, was traveling up from New York that coming weekend. ''The problem is,'' Dave said, ''her parents will let her come only if her sister Alice comes with her. Could I persuade you to help me out and to act as Alice's escort for the weekend?''

Hank hesitated. He was reluctant to accept without Cindy's approval, but there was no way he could get in touch with her by the weekend unless he sent her a telegram, and that would be blowing the situation up out of proportion.

Dave misunderstood his reluctance to accept. "It's true enough," he said, "that Alice has appeared as a singer and dancer in a couple of musical shows in New York, and as you may know from the last time she was up here, she smokes cigarettes, but I don't think she's really all that fast. Even if she is," he added, "you don't have to have that much to do with her. It's just that she needs an escort, and you're the handiest. If you like, I'll be glad to write a letter of explanation to your girl back home."

Hank's pride was touched. "That won't be necessary," he said. "I don't need Cindy's approval. I'll do it."

And so it happened that he had a social engagement that kept him tied up through the whole weekend. On Friday night, he and Dave met the sisters at the hotel for supper, and Hank was privately dismayed as he took Alice Snyder's measure. Her makeup and dress were flamboyant, marking her as very different from the usual academy visitors, and she looked like the New York actress that she was. Her elaborately coiffed hair was an almost whitish blond, obviously not its natural color, and her brown eyes had lost any softness because of the hard-edged line of kohl that encircled them.

She called further attention to herself by smoking several cigarettes, and Hank was truly horrified when she ordered a drink of whiskey and water after dinner. She was the only woman he had encountered in his life who drank hard liquor, but apparently she thought nothing of it and downed it without any ill effects.

At noon on Saturday, the sisters were invited to dinner at the academy mess hall. Joyce, as usual, was inconspicuous in her attire. Her sister, however, was elaborately made up, and her dress was more suitable for wearing to a big city night spot than to midday dinner at the military academy. Faculty members and fellow cadets who knew something of Hank's involvement with Cindy jumped to the conclusion that he had arranged to spend the weekend with Alice in order to have a sexual liaison with her. Hank was well aware of their assumption but knew he could not clarify the matter without further jeopardizing his standing as a gentleman. He was embarrassed, but he was also determined to see the weekend through to its conclusion.

After the noon dinner on Saturday, Dave and Joyce led the other couple in a walk along the high palisades that stretched out beside the Hudson River. The view was breathtaking, and it was customary for the cadets and their girls to walk there to kiss in private.

Aware of this, Hank set a slow pace for his walk with Alice, and they lagged far behind the other couple. He had deliberately chosen to do this so that Dave and his girl could exchange intimacies in private if they wished to do so.

But Alice, who was clinging to his arm, misunderstood his motives and assumed that he was seeking to be alone with her. She looked up at him provocatively, her kohl-laden eyes wide, her rouge-reddened lips soft and inviting.

Never before had Hank suffered such acute discomfort. He glanced at the attractive girl who was walking close to him, and he realized that not only had she misunderstood his reason for putting so much distance between them and the other couple, but she was his for the taking. She would go as far as he wanted.

His problem was that he wanted nothing to do with her. He was in love with Cindy, and the idea of being intimate with another girl was repellent to him. But he was too inexperienced in his dealings with the opposite sex to know how to handle Alice.

She nestled close to him, shivering slightly. "Put your arm around me," she commanded. "It's cold out here."

He was miserable, but there seemed to be no polite way to refuse, and so he obeyed.

Alice could feel the rigidity of the muscles in his arm, the tautness in his shoulder and body. Her laugh was like a gentle caress. "There's no need to be afraid of me," she murmured. "I won't bite you."

Hank's misery became more acute. "I know," he muttered.

Alice took charge, thinking him merely bashful and inept. She turned him toward her, slid her arms around his neck, and moved her face very close to his. "Kiss me," she whispered.

Half-frozen, Hank could not determine how to say no, and finally, he leaned over and bestowed a quick peck on her cheek.

Alice was vastly amused. This cadet was so painfully shy and unyielding that she decided, strictly for her own entertainment, to break down his resistance and compel him to give in to her charms. Her lips insistently sought his, and she took his lower lip between her teeth and caressed it with her tongue. Then her mouth opened, and her tongue darted in and out as it explored.

Hank could not help but become aroused. In spite of his resolve, he was a young and virile male, and he felt his self-control slipping. Grasping the girl, he pulled her closer and took the initiative, kissing her with increasing savagery.

This is more like it, Alice thought exultantly. Now he was treating her as she liked and deserved to be treated, and she responded to his lovemaking in full measure.

Hank was dimly aware that he and the supple, sensuous woman in his arms were reaching the danger point. If they continued in this fashion, they would be forced to go to her room at the hotel and fulfill their desires. There seemed to be no alternative.

Certainly Alice sought none. Her femininity had aroused this fresh-faced cadet, transforming him from a rigid statue into a responsive man with strong passions.

Hank realized that he needed to regain control of himself. The alternative was to lose himself to Alice, to engage in sex with her, and then to regret his disloyalty to Cindy for the rest of his days. It also occurred to him that it would be a waste of time to offer Alice a logical explanation of the stand he was trying so hard to maintain. He had already learned that she was not interested in reason and that she was determined to have her own way with him, no matter what else might happen. But it was up to him to stop their lovemaking from going any further.

Taking charge, he held her at arm's length while he regained his breath. Then, settling his uniform cap firmly on his head, he grasped her arm and silently led her back to the hotel.

Alice went with him willingly. She interpreted his firmness

as a sign of his intention of bedding her, and she was curious as to the kind of lover he would make.

Hank stood red-faced and silent behind her while she obtained her room key from the desk clerk, and then he marched as though on parade as he followed her to the room that she and her sister occupied. She unlocked the door. He came into the room after her, and she closed it. Then he helped her off with her coat.

"Will you light a fire, darling?" she murmured. "I got positively chilled outdoors."

Hank obediently placed several handfuls of kindling in the hearth, then laid a small split log across the andirons. After he had built a good, roaring fire, he turned around. He was stunned to discover that Alice had changed from the dress she had worn to dinner into a soft, filmy negligee. He stared at her in horror.

She smiled, tossed her long mane of blond hair, and started to move closer to him. "Surely," she said, "you're not going to keep wearing your greatcoat. I think it's warm enough in here now for you to take it off." She reached for the coat and managed to undo one of the buttons.

Hank hastily took a backward step, knowing that he had to tell her the truth now or again become aroused. "I'm sorry," he said stiffly, "but you and I seem to misunderstand each other."

"What is there to misunderstand?" she asked huskily, her seductive eyes fixed on his. "You want me and I want you, and that's all that matters!"

"I—I've got a girl," he blurted.

She accepted his unexpected announcement calmly. "Where

is the lucky young lady now?'' she asked, not moving away from him.

It was becoming somewhat easier for Hank to talk, however. ''She's at school,'' he replied, ''at Oregon State College.''

Alice's peal of relieved laughter seemed to fill the room. ''Oh, well,'' she said with a careless shrug. ''She's three thousand miles away, and what she doesn't know won't hurt her. You and I are here, right now, and we want each other. What could be plainer than that?'' She raised her hands to his chest, waiting for his embrace.

Hank continued to stand erect, his right arm at his side, his left arm cradling his uniform cap in the manner approved for academy cadets. She was so determined that he realized he would have to deal with her accordingly. ''I'm sorry,'' he said firmly, ''but I'm afraid my conscience would permit no such indulgence on my part.''

She looked at him as though he had struck her across the face. ''I can't believe what I'm hearing,'' she said. ''I can't believe any man would refuse what I'm offering you!''

Hank remained unyielding, but courtesy demanded that he soften his harsh rebuff of the young woman. ''Your beauty,'' he said, ''has only complicated the situation. I can't deny that you're very lovely and very desirable. I'm probably a damned fool to turn my back to you, but I can't help but be the way I am. No matter how I may want you—and I assure you, I do want you—I'd be unfaithful to my pledge to someone else. And if I don't have my honor intact, I'm of no use to my country or to myself as an officer in the army.''

The tension in the room was thick. Alice stared at him in utter disbelief as she digested his words. Suddenly, however, she shrugged and laughed. ''You're extraordinary, Hank,'' she said, "and you'll probably be a general by the time you retire. Your girl is lucky—very lucky—to have someone like you."

The crisis was ended, and he grinned at her. "You're all right, too, Alice," he said. "I hope you will someday find happiness with the right man."

She shrugged. "What do you say we go down to the lobby? There are some comfortable-looking chairs and sofas there, and we can get cups of hot chocolate."

"That sounds good to me," he replied, rejoicing inwardly because he had conquered his physical desires and kept his honor intact.

IX

The trail, sometimes barely visible, at other times clearly defined, led Toby Holt and Stalking Horse higher and higher into the Bitterroot Range of the Rocky Mountains. They climbed past timberline, making their way along narrow, snow-covered ledges. They were so intent on following the tracks of the Indians who had come into the vicinity of their camp that they paid scant heed to anything else and therefore had no time for fear.

Soon they came to a section in which their narrow path became a ledge, and directly above them was an outcropping covering the route they were taking. A drop of several thousand feet bordered the outer rim of the ledge.

They made their way cautiously in single file with Toby in the lead. Both of them realized that one false step could plunge them to certain death on the rocks directly below.

All at once Toby heard a faint rumbling noise in the

distance, high above him. He halted, listening intently, standing absolutely still on the perilous cliff. Stalking Horse also halted, listening and then nodding. The noise grew steadily in volume until it became a sustained, roaring sound that resembled no other on earth. There was no need for conversation between them; both recognized the sound immediately as one of the most dangerous of phenomena in the mountains—a rockslide. The last time Toby had heard and seen one was the terrible occasion when his father, Whip Holt, and General Blake's first wife, Cathy, had been killed. The memory of that horrible day filled him with sadness, but he was forced to put it out of his mind; he and Stalking Horse were faced with the immediate problem of staying alive.

Scores of rocks of all sizes thundered down the slope above the two men, pouring over the edge of the overhang above them and raining down the precipice beside them, only inches from where they stood. Toby and Stalking Horse could do nothing to protect themselves. As long as the roof of the overhang held firm, they were relatively safe. Should it crumble, however, the rocks would tumble straight down from above, and the two men would be crushed within seconds.

The rockslide was so severe that it was impossible for Toby and Stalking Horse to see more than a few inches in front of them. The world around them became very dark, and they stood still, scarcely daring to breathe, pressing against the cliff behind them.

After an eternity of anxious waiting, the thunder of falling rocks gradually subsided, ultimately dying away. Taking no chances, Toby and Stalking Horse stayed where they were for another quarter of an hour, knowing that beyond their current position, the ledge was unprotected from above, and they could be killed by a second rockslide.

At last, when they were sure that the mountain had ceased its rain of rocks, the two men set out. The ledge soon spread out to become a path, about twelve feet wide, and the going promised to become easier. But Toby quickly discovered that any hope of traveling more rapidly was futile. The rockslide had spewed enough pebbles, rocks, and small boulders in this area that walking was difficult. Also, he sadly realized, it was no longer possible to see any moccasin prints. While he and the Cherokee paused to consider this new dilemma, Stalking Horse raised his head and sniffed the air suspiciously.

"Snow," he said distinctly in his own tongue.

Toby had to admit that his companion was right. He, too, now caught the unmistakable odor that appeared in the air just prior to a snowstorm, and he also noticed that the clouded sky had darkened considerably and the wind increased to an angry howl.

They knew that they would be forced to brave the storm that soon would envelop them. They looked around the area where they stood but saw no sign of shelter anywhere. At best there were a few large boulders, deposited on the plateau by the rockslide.

With one accord, they made their way to the largest of the boulders and took up squatting positions on the side opposite that from which the wind was blowing. Swiftly they undressed, rubbed themselves with animal fat they had saved from the ram they had killed, and then slowly dressed again. By covering their skin with the fat, they had availed themselves of the best possible protection against the cold. Then, removing their blankets from the packs they carried on their backs, they spread the blankets over their heads and shoulders to protect themselves further from the cold.

While they attended to these simple preparations, the wind increased its velocity, bringing with it a biting cold. It was impossible for Toby and Stalking Horse to make a fire, as almost no wood or kindling was available above timberline, and they would be wasting precious energy if they went in search of it.

The snowfall started slowly, with only a few tiny flakes occasionally flying through the air. But as Toby peered up at the sky overhead, he frowned and pulled his blanket tighter. He and Stalking Horse both knew that they were in for a heavy snowfall.

Little by little, the snow increased in intensity, the individual flakes becoming as large as a man's thumbnail. The two men had difficulty seeing in front of them as they huddled against the boulder and awaited the heavier winds that they knew were coming.

Soon the wind picked up power, speed, and intensity, and began to blow great clouds of snow in huge, whirling gusts, some of which swept around the protected bulk of the boulder as though vindictively seeking out the two men huddled there for shelter. It was early afternoon, but the sky grew black.

Toby and Stalking Horse occasionally stood, swung their arms, and stomped their feet, brushing snow from their heads and shoulders. So far they did not feel the cold, but they knew that in a situation such as this, the initial effects were unimportant; it was the long-term haul that counted.

The blizzard seemed endless, and snow fell so rapidly that some of the smaller boulders soon were completely hidden. Toby, who had been caught in only a handful of snowstorms, was impressed by the quantity of the fall. He could understand now why the mountain men of the generations that had preceded him took special care to seek shelter whenever a major snowstorm threatened.

The icy winds whipped across the heights with such force that neither Toby nor Stalking Horse dared to face it, but instead turned their backs to it and hunched their shoulders. Their blankets covered their ears and mouths, but from time to time they touched the tips of their noses to assure themselves they still had feeling there and were not freezing, and similarly they tested their fingers and toes.

The storm raged on for hours. The accumulation of snow was staggering. It was so high that it came to the tops of Toby's knees.

Late in the evening the blizzard halted as suddenly as it had started. The wind died away, the sky cleared, and every star in the heavens appeared overhead. A three-quarter moon came out, its reflection on the snow a dazzling blue-white, and the view was breathtaking. A mantle of pure white covered the mountains in every direction as far as the eye could see.

Toby and Stalking Horse had little need to converse. The pair were sufficiently seasoned that they put first things first, opening the pouch of smoked ram's meat and consuming part of it along with several handfuls of parched corn. For liquid, they ate snow, letting it melt in their mouths.

Only after their hunger was satisfied did they examine their situation. "It strikes me," Toby said, "that we're stuck right where we are. Until this snow either melts or blows away, it's far too dangerous for us to press any farther into the mountains, much less to double back to where we came from."

Stalking Horse was in agreement with him. "We stay here," he replied firmly.

Their need for shelter was their next consideration, and Toby remembered what his father had told him about his handling of a similar situation in the Colorado Rockies many years earlier. Essentially, his system was to use the materials at hand—in that particular instance, snow. So Toby and Stalking Horse built out of the snow a little shelter, with an entrance just big enough for them to crawl in and out. Toby's father and other early American mountain men had survived by building themselves similar snow houses.

He and Stalking Horse, revitalized by the food they had consumed, worked so hard making their little house that both of them were perspiring under their warm wraps by the time they completed their task. When they crawled inside, they were astonished to discover that it was actually warm enough for them to remove their scarves and mittens and still be comfortable. The temperature hovered around the freezing point, but they were completely cut off from any wind, and they found the interior livable. Rolled up in their blankets, they dropped off to sleep, enjoying a full night's rest.

In the morning they ate a breakfast of smoked meat and parched corn. Their meals were monotonous, but at least there was sufficient food for them to eat their fill, and for that much they were grateful.

The sun was hot, the winds were brisk, and forty-eight hours after the storm had ended, the snows were beginning to melt and to blow away. By noon of the following day they could make out patches of rocky flooring underfoot.

Toby questioned the wisdom of staying where they were any longer. "I think we ought to be on our way," he said, "before another blizzard comes along and traps us here even longer. This is the season for snowstorms."

Stalking Horse peered at the sky, then spoke from the vantage point of his vastly greater experience. "I think we stay until tomorrow," he said. "We take the chance that no more snow will come down before then. By tomorrow the mountains will be clear enough so we can go on in safety."

The following morning they broke camp and resumed their journey but proceeded with caution. At noon they dipped below timberline and took advantage of the proximity of trees to gather wood for a fire, having decided that they should advertise their presence in the mountains.

"I'm afraid," Toby said, "that after this blizzard, we will have lost all sign of our quarry. We could spend many weeks searching in vain for the rebels. They're hidden in such a remote place that we might never find them."

Stalking Horse nodded solemnly. "It is better," he said, "that they find us."

Thus, rather than conceal themselves in the forest of scrub pine, they moved into the open beyond it, closer to timberline. Here the snow was not very deep, and they built their fire. A plume of smoke headed straight up into the sky and was plainly visible for miles in any given direction. What was more, the two men squatting beside the fire could be seen from almost anywhere in the surrounding mountains. After about two hours, as the thick smoke of the huge fire shifted, the alert Toby suddenly pointed toward a high ridge in the distance. There, outlined against a white background of snow, was a column of small figures, which moved slowly forward in single file. Even at this distance the pair, both of them endowed with keen eyesight, could make out the figures of young warriors.

So they had been discovered at last, probably by the men whom they were seeking! As the braves moved closer, they disappeared from sight. It was inevitable, Toby surmised, that they would eventually appear at the far end of the open field that stretched directly above timberline. The warriors could not know the identity of the two men squatting by the fire, but apparently they had no intention of finding out before taking action. They had decided to attack first and advance into the open only after killing or severely wounding the two men at the fire, or so Toby assumed. Consequently, he and Stalking Horse prepared a different reception for them than they anticipated.

Timing their move carefully, the pair waited until movement at the far end of the field told them the position of the braves. Waiting no longer, Stalking Horse shot an arrow high into the air. It came down not far from the moving, crouching Indians and stood with its point in the ground, the shaft trembling slightly above it. Prepared for what to do next, Toby stretched on the ground with his rifle on his shoulder, and peering down the barrel, he pulled the trigger.

The single shot echoed through the mountain vastness, and the braves stared in wonder, unable to believe the evidence before their eyes. The shaft of the arrow still protruded from the ground, but it looked as though it had been snapped in half, the upper portion having been sheared off by the bullet. Never had the warriors encountered such skill with the bow and arrow or uncanny accuracy with firearms.

Toby and Stalking Horse rose swiftly to their feet, then moved toward the Nez Percé. Nothing in the attitude of either suggested that they had displayed anything out of the ordinary in their marksmanship.

The young warriors slowly clambered to their feet, and not one of them showed any evidence of hostility, for the exhibition had greatly impressed them. They had no need to ask the identity of the pair who were approaching them. The white man had to be the governor of Idaho, a marksman second to none in the entire West—the son of the fabled Whip Holt. The Indian had to be the Cherokee blood-brother of Whip Holt.

As Toby and Stalking Horse slowly approached the Nez Percé braves, they displayed no outward concern for their safety, even though they were outnumbered by warriors six to one. But the Nez Percé, being careful students of human behavior, noted that the two men were alert, ready to raise and use their weapons instantly at the first sign of unfriendliness from the group.

The braves, having lost all appetite for combat, made no attempt to ready their weapons as the pair approached. In fact, the young Indians looked like mere youths as they stared in awe at the two legendary figures.

Halting only a few yards short of the braves in the front rank, Toby and Stalking Horse raised their left arms and held their hands palms upward in the customary sign of Indian greeting.

The Nez Percé returned the gesture.

The leader of the band, distinguished only by the bright colors of the feathers he wore in his scalp lock, stepped forward and found his voice with some difficulty. "What brings the great Cherokee and the son of Whip Holt, whose renown is as great as that of his father, to these mountains?"

Regarding it as a good omen that they had been recognized,

255

Toby decided to pull no punches. "We have spent many days," he said, "searching for those warriors who represent the Nez Percé nation when they go into combat. We wish to be taken to the headquarters of Running Bear and meet with him there."

The braves stirred uneasily as they exchanged sidelong glances, and at last their leader said, "Running Bear refuses to meet all strangers."

Stalking Horse drew himself up to his full height and folded his arms across his chest. "I have spent many summers in these mountains. I know every trail. I know the secret ponds and swift, flowing rivers in which the fish called trout swim, and I can find deer in tiny gorges where no one knows there are deer. As for my companion, he, too, knows these mountains as no other white man has ever known them. He knows them well enough that he could act as a guide and lead the Nez Percé through them. Is there a warrior among you who would dare to call Stalking Horse and Toby Holt strangers?"

The leader was deeply affected by the Cherokee's words and hung his head in shame. The others soon followed his example. Toby knew the moment had come to strike hard.

"We are no ordinary travelers in these mountains," he said. "It has been the will of the great spirits that rule over this land, as they rule over all lands, that our paths and the path of Running Bear have not yet crossed. But we are no strangers to Running Bear, just as he is no stranger to us. Take us to him so that he may prosper and so that all who follow after him may prosper as well."

The braves were badly shaken. They had received strict orders from Running Bear, but the words of two of the most famous men in the West made complete sense to them. Not only were they unwilling to earn the wrath of the governor and the Cherokee, but they were aware that something promising, something good, could arise out of their meeting with Running Bear. Therefore, they decided to face their own compatriot's anger rather than arouse the wrath of Stalking Horse and Toby.

"Come," the leader of the braves said. "We will take you to him."

The young Nez Percé were practical people, realists in most things, in spite of their tendency to listen to inflammatory idealism in political matters and to act accordingly. They knew that Toby Holt had repeatedly demonstrated his friendship for the nation in the past, just as his father had helped them from the early days when explorers had come to the Pacific Northwest. As for Stalking Horse, the mere fact that he was choosing to pay a visit to the Nez Percé was an honor that many lesser tribes would and should envy.

So, without further ado, they began their advance on foot deeper into the Bitterroot Range, followed by the two outsiders. It was ironic that even though Toby and Stalking Horse had been careful in their movements, they now moved at half the speed they had previously maintained.

For two days and two nights they pushed on into the mountains, pausing to rest only for short intervals and then continuing their journey. The sun shone by day, and the moon and stars provided ample light by night; consequently, they did not pause for any appreciable length of time. Toby and Stalking Horse were aware that their escorts were taking no risks with the weather at this time of year, remaining on the move as long as they could. Always hovering in the backs of their minds was the fear that they might be delayed by another blizzard that could cut them off completely from their goal or could make the farther reaches of the interior unattainable.

When they finally neared their destination, many of the Indians were exhausted, but these young men noted in awe that Toby and Stalking Horse seemed as fresh and energetic as they had when they had joined forces.

Toby knew there was no way he and his companion alone could have found the secret encampment. The Indians had established their headquarters in the recesses of the range in a connecting series of large caves, which opened onto the side of a mountain. Only by sheer luck would he and Stalking Horse have stumbled across this location.

There were no horses in the vicinity, of course, because the area was so inaccessible. No doubt the Indians, like Toby and Stalking Horse, kept their horses hidden somewhere down the mountain.

Sentries were stationed in twos and threes at the approaches to the cave entrance, and Toby's heart sank when he saw that at least half of these sentinels wore the distinctive war paint of the Shoshone. He had been unprepared for the fact that the Shoshone had joined the Nez Percé in their crusade against the settlers. This more than doubled the number of foes that he had to face. He knew now that it was even more crucial for him to reach an agreement of some sort with Running Bear, and equally important, he could not afford to lose face while doing it.

Maintaining one's dignity was all important when dealing with an Indian tribe, Toby had learned. The warriors would have no respect for a people whose leaders appeared weak or uncertain. He knew, too, that he would have to be prepared to back up his words with action, even if it meant threatening all-out war between the Indians and the army troops in Idaho.

The two newcomers were led into a cavernous outer chamber, where daylight, filtering in from outside, mingled with the lights of a dozen torches. At least thirty warriors were gathered in the cavern, Nez Percé and Shoshone alike, and a single glance at the elaborate feathers of the scalp locks was enough to tell Toby that these were the rebel leaders. Some of them were chewing on strips of smoked meat, and others were conferring in low tones, but all of them ceased their activities when they saw Toby and Stalking Horse.

The territory's governor and the Cherokee raised their left hands in the Indian sign of greeting and behaved as though nothing were out of the ordinary. The assembled rebel leaders stared with great interest at the pair and without any particular animosity, but neither did they make any attempt to welcome them.

After a few tense moments, Running Bear entered the chamber from an inner cavern. He was instantly identifiable to Toby and his companion, not so much because of any difference in his war paint or in the feathers that adorned his scalp lock, but because of his air of confident authority. He was obviously someone who had become accustomed to command and who took his authority for granted.

If Running Bear was angry that his braves had brought these outsiders to his camp, he did not show it. He actually seemed friendly as he greeted Toby and Stalking Horse, though there was a reserve in his manner, a coolness that indicated he was not for a moment forgetting his self-appointed mission to drive the white men from Idaho.

With regard for tradition, however, he made the visitors

welcome, bidding them to sit at a warming fire in the center of the cavern, beneath a hole in the ceiling that provided ample draft to draw out the smoke. While the newcomers warmed themselves, he lighted a pipe and offered it to them.

In the meantime, Toby was pleased to note, preparations were being made for the noontime meal. As the aromas of fresh meat, vegetables, and spices reached him, Toby realized that he was ravenous, not having had a substantial meal in many days.

When the meal was ready, the guests were served first, being handed steaming wooden bowls and large, slightly curved wooden spoons. Running Bear and the leaders were served next, the other warriors waiting their turns in the outer chambers.

Toby was struck by the fact that no attempt was made to divest him of his weapons. His rifle rested on the ground beside him, and his pistols dangled from his belt. He noticed, too, that Stalking Horse's quiver of arrows and longbow rested on the ground beside him.

During the meal, the Indians made no attempt to engage Toby or Stalking Horse in polite conversation, and Toby took this as a sign that they were far more advanced than the representatives of so-called civilized nations in this regard. Rather than force talk about inconsequentials, the Indians said nothing, knowing that their visitors had come to this remote place for a specific purpose and were awaiting the right moment to speak. In the meantime, they preferred silence, letting each individual dwell in the realm of his own thoughts.

One aspect of the situation caused Toby great concern. He counted at least three hundred warriors filing by to be given food. He reasoned that if half of their entire force was currently engaged in patrols attacking settlers, the total rebel army numbered at least six hundred and included warriors from the two principal nations represented in Idaho.

This was a much larger force than Toby had imagined the rebels were capable of amassing, and he knew it would require a major military effort to subdue such an opponent. These insurgents were too wise to take on United States Army troops in a pitched battle; thus, it would be necessary to root them out, small band by small band. This would be an almost impossible undertaking, since the Indians were thoroughly familiar with the terrain and were capable of disappearing completely from sight.

The need to reach an accommodation with the warriors was even more vital, more necessary than Toby had imagined. If he could not achieve an understanding with these braves, Idaho would not be guaranteed peace, and hundreds of settlers would die in the months and years ahead. And the more that innocent blood was shed, the more the people of the United States would demand retribution, and the more the Indian nations would ultimately suffer. It was for their good, as well as for the good of the American people, that Toby had come this far, and he hoped that he could persuade them to listen to what he had to say and to act accordingly.

After the meal was finished, pipes were lighted and smoked, and at last Running Bear took the initiative. Rising to his feet, the young leader made a long, rambling speech in which he welcomed Toby and Stalking Horse to the realm of the "new" Nez Percé and the "new" Shoshone. He dwelt at some length on the courage the visitors had shown by penetrating so far into the land of their people's enemy, and he praised both of them for their fortitude.

Running Bear paused and then went on to say that he

guessed the two men had come to offer new terms of peace. Peace was possible only on his terms, he said, which were that the settlers would vacate the entire territory of Idaho and turn these lands over intact to the two Indian nations.

Then it was Toby's turn to speak, and he knew better than to ridicule the terms demanded by Running Bear, impossible as they were. Instead, he traced the history of American relations with the Indians, beginning with the Lewis and Clark expedition during the administration of President Thomas Jefferson, early in the century. "Decade after decade," Toby said, "has been marred by suspicions and hostility, which have only led to still greater misunderstandings. I do not claim the Americans were right and the Indians were wrong, just as I do not believe the Indians or the Americans were always blameless. Both sides were at fault; both have shown impatience, immaturity, and an appalling lack of mutual understanding.

"But the steady spread of American civilization across the continent is inevitable," he continued, "and any attempt to prevent it will lead only to violence and destruction. The United States has, in recent years, begun to turn large tracts of land over to the Indians in the forms of reservations. Generosity has been shown to the Shoshone, who have been granted territory equal to that which they had been claiming. The Indians are free to live on these huge tracts of land as they see fit, governing themselves as they please, and there is ample room for hunting and fishing in the traditional ways of their ancestors. In return for this, the United States demands only peace.

"If the braves who follow Running Bear persist in their rebellion," Toby went on, "the United States will become increasingly exasperated and will assign more and more troops to silence them. Instead of having only two battalions and several independent companies of troops, the military governor will be given command of entire regiments, as many of them as are necessary to do the job.''

Toby looked at his silent listeners, and as his eyes swept over the cave, he concluded solemnly, ''I know my government, and I know its will. If you continue to reject the hand of American friendship, that hand will be withdrawn, and many soldiers with guns and even the large cannons that roar and send death and destruction will appear in its place. The war will continue until not one Nez Percé or Shoshone remains alive. Think about this before you persist in your rebellion!''

He was followed by Stalking Horse, who traced the history of his own people, the Cherokee, in their relations with the United States. No rebels had been more ferocious or more adamantly opposed to the peace treaty with America, but eventually the elders of the nation had decided there had been enough killing and that nothing could be gained by more bloodshed, and so they had made their peace. After that, the Cherokee moved to western North Carolina and to the Indian Territory on the Arkansas River, where they owned reservations larger by far than the lands they had previously occupied. They were hard-working, they built schools and joined Christian churches, and they had a constitution and a democratic government. Many lived on the reservation, but others had moved to Nashville or Memphis or Little Rock and were actively participating in the lives of those communities. There were no barriers to their advancement, and they were the equals of any other American citizens. The Nez Percé and the

Shoshone were advised to contemplate the example set by the Cherokee and to emulate them if they wished to live and to prosper.

Toby's words had made a deep impression on his listeners, and Stalking Horse's low-keyed address had driven home the lessons that the governor was trying to convey. No member of the audience rose afterward to protest. On the contrary, the young warriors looked at each other and slowly nodded. It was obvious they were on the brink of accepting Toby's unqualified offer of peace.

Running Bear, seeing the prospect of his campaign collapsing around him and of himself being reduced in stature and becoming just another warrior, leaped to his feet and began an impassioned retort. Calling on all of his skill as an orator, he played on the emotions of his followers, reminding them of past glories that the Nez Percé and the Shoshone had enjoyed—and paying scant regard to the truth.

Hearing the Indian leader, Toby knew he was exaggerating wildly, that neither the Nez Percé nor the Shoshone had ever enjoyed such standing in the world of North American Indian tribes as Running Bear was describing.

But if the rebel leader's listeners knew better and realized that neither nation had ever enjoyed the prestige and power that he delighted in describing, none of them called his bluff. In a climactic, sweeping statement, Running Bear flatly rejected Toby's offer. The pride and dignity of the Nez Percé and the Shoshone made it impossible for him and his followers to accept the offer Toby had made, he stated. The governor and his friend were advised to go back to Boise and begin to pack their belongings. The settlers would follow his example,

Running Bear hoped, and would leave the territory to the Indians, who rightfully owned it.

The warriors, eyes shining, shouted their agreement with him, and raising their fists, they shook them in the air. Running Bear had succeeded in arousing their emotions to the extent that their better judgment was swept away.

As Toby looked around, his heart sank. He knew that he was losing the debate. In the long run, the Indians, whom he admired and respected, would lose their lives, their freedom, and their reservations. If they followed the advice of Running Bear, they would become embroiled in a war far more vicious, far deadlier than anything they had ever imagined.

Speaking quietly, he made his final appeal directly to Running Bear, rather than to the rebel leader's followers. "I speak to you as a friend, rather than as the leader of those who will potentially be opposed to you. If you want to escape without bloodshed and with as many advantages as you can possibly win from the United States, you'll be wise to return your warriors to their reservations at once. If your warriors and mine engage in battle, the end would be disastrous for your people. True, your men are more familiar with the terrain and would initially have the advantage, but in the long run, they would be defeated. If two regiments were insufficient, the United States Army would send five, ten, or even fifty regiments to do the job. With each new increase in manpower, the generosity of the American government would diminish. They would offer less and less to make peace.

"Long after you and I and every brave in this cavern have gone to the next world, the mountains and the rivers and the snows of Idaho will remain. There will be forests that will be full of game; swift rivers that will be teeming with fish.

Nature will not change. But while we remain here, the Indians and the settlers must learn to share the bounties that Idaho offers."

When he finished his short address, Toby knew he had used the best arguments available to him and that if his listeners were going to be persuaded, they would be moved by his words sufficiently to accept his offer.

Running Bear, however, had the last word. "As long as I draw breath into my body," he said, "I will not surrender. If you and the people of America wish to have your way in these mountains, you must kill me first. But I offer you a way to prevent a battle and to save the lives of your soldiers and of your settlers. I issue you a challenge," he said. "Meet me in a fight to the death, here and now. If you win, if you kill me, my followers will do as you say and will let the settlers live. If I kill you, however, we will fight and we will win, and the United States will be driven out of the territory for all time!"

It was apparent from Running Bear's attitude that although he respected Toby's talents as a fighting man, he did not expect him or any white man to agree to his challenge.

But to the astonishment of Running Bear and his followers, Toby said quietly, "I accept."

Knowing him well, Stalking Horse realized the inevitability of his reply. A Holt could not have answered in any other way. All the same, the old Cherokee was dismayed. Toby had agreed to engage in a dangerous form of combat—a type of fighting to which he was not accustomed—with someone for whom such fighting was second nature. His courage was greater than his good sense, and he appeared to have invited his doom.

Aware that the eyes of the Nez Percé and Shoshone braves

seated in the huge, arenalike cave were upon him, Toby now stripped and donned the loincloth that would be his only attire in his fight to the death with Running Bear. Stalking Horse then anointed his friend's entire body with animal fat to make him a slippery, more elusive target.

The Cherokee was worried. "You have never been engaged in combat of this sort, Toby. Must you do this?"

Toby remained calm. "I have not forgotten," he replied, "the endless hours of instruction that I received from you in this type of fighting."

"You remember the many tricks that I taught in the use of your hands and arms?" Stalking Horse demanded sternly.

"I remember them," Toby replied.

"Do you remember, also, the many uses to which you can put your legs and feet?"

"I have forgotten none of them."

"Do you recall, also, the special ways in which you can utilize your head and eyes?"

Toby nodded solemnly.

Stalking Horse shook his head and spoke in an undertone so that none of the braves could hear him. "I can only hope now that your memory is accurate and that your reflexes are quick and strong. I don't approve of that which you do, but it is too late now to call a halt."

"Don't worry about me, please," Toby told him. "Take my word for it that all is going to turn out as it should. If I had any doubts, I would not have accepted the challenge."

Stalking Horse was not pacified. "You forget that you are no longer a single man and that you are responsible to others. You have a wife and son who will be alone in the world if ill should befall you in this combat. In addition, you are the military governor of the territory. If you are killed in this fight, it will be a signal to all the people of the Nez Percé, all the people of the Shoshone, all the people of every other tribe in every territory that lies in the Rocky Mountains and to the west of them. They will rise up in arms against the United States. You are taking a great risk by assuming the burden of this combat, Toby."

There was a faint gleam of amusement in Toby's eyes as he regarded the old Cherokee. "Stalking Horse," he said, "you persist in looking at the worst possible outcome. Do you think I am so neglectful of my wife and my son that I have forgotten them? Or do you think I've put aside my duties to the United States government and to President Grant? I assure you that I have not. When the sun sets today, the rebellion of the young braves will be ended for all time."

He extended his hand and accepted the knife that Stalking Horse handed him. It was no more than six inches in length but had an exceedingly sharp point and two razorlike edges that could inflict severe damage. Remembering what the Cherokee had taught him, however, Toby did not intend to go into the fight holding the knife. Instead, he dropped it into a sheath of leather that he wore on a simple belt, giving him the use of both hands to establish his fundamental superiority in the battle. This advantage, as his mentor had stressed to him frequently, was of paramount importance in this kind of combat.

The young warriors, unaware of the reasons for his behavior, concluded that he was boastfully showing off—that he was going into the fight unarmed to demonstrate his superiority over his opponent.

Running Bear, looking barrel-chested, compact, and powerful, dressed only in his loincloth, had also greased himself and was limbering his well-developed muscles as he gripped a knife in his right hand.

For an instant Toby wondered if going into the fight with his own knife sheathed was the right thing to do. He glanced at Stalking Horse, who merely inclined his head. This was the only assurance that Toby sought. If the Cherokee, who was so wise in every aspect of Indian warfare, approved of his strategy, then Toby knew he was doing the right thing and that all was well.

Toby noted that the ground in the cavern was rough and laden with rock, the very nature of which made it difficult for either combatant to engage in agile footwork. Every rock and every ragged surface could be felt on the soles of their feet.

Once the mammoth vats that had been used for cooking were cleared from the area of the fires and all the warriors were seated—the higher ranking braves closest to the place where the contest would be held—the two leaders could begin their fight.

Running Bear moved slowly into the open space, a dangerous light coming into his eyes when he saw Toby directly opposite him, also moving into position for the combat.

Toby braced himself as he cautiously inched forward. His opponent, although shorter, had long arms and a powerful torso. He also had the advantage of fifteen or twenty pounds in weight. What was more, Running Bear had no inhibitions to prevent him from snuffing out the life of his opponent if he possibly could.

The Indian initiated the fight by suddenly leaping high into the air and launching a kick at his opponent's middle. Toby demonstrated to his own satisfaction that his reflexes were sound. He sidestepped several inches, and the blow failed to touch him. In the meantime, Running Bear had lost his balance, and he stumbled and sprawled on the ground.

Toby instantly threw himself at the Nez Percé, landing with his knees on the warrior's shoulders and upper arms, immobilizing him. In the same gesture, Toby grasped him by the scalp lock and banged the back of his head hard on the ground several times. The Indian managed to get his knife hand free, but before he could retaliate, Toby stood again and moved out of reach. As Running Bear hauled himself to his feet and groggily tottered forward a few steps, it was obvious to the spectators that the governor had struck the first resounding blow of the combat.

Toby knew that the secret of success in a battle of this kind was to give one's foe no quarter, striking all the harder when he was down in the hope of ending the fight quickly as well as victoriously. Now it was his turn to leap into the air and to direct a hard kick of his right foot at his foe's chest.

His aim was true, and the power of his kick sent Running Bear staggering backward. The Indian again lost his balance and sat down hard on the ground. There he remained for some moments, breathing hard as he fought to regain his strength before the next onslaught. Expecting Toby to hurl himself forward again and to land on top of him, Running Bear was preparing to give him a far different reception than he probably anticipated.

But Toby found himself reading his foe's mind, and consequently he avoided the trap, dancing just beyond the reach of the Indian's knife hand and searching for an opportunity that would allow him to close in for a moment, strike a hard blow, and then retreat again before Running Bear could launch a counterattack.

Toby's thinking was sound and would have been effective had he been facing an opponent of ordinary strength. Running Bear, however, was endowed with a sense of purpose and a tenacity that made him a formidable opponent. As the governor attempted to move in, the rebel leader reached out with his free hand, caught Toby's ankle in his fingers, and in spite of the grease that made the leg extremely slippery, managed to hang on for several moments, finally bringing his opponent down on his back.

Toby tried to turn the situation around and gain the advantage by grasping the Indian's head as he fell. But his luck seemed to have deserted him, and his opponent remained free.

As Toby went down, landing full force on the hard ground, Running Bear rolled on top of him, his weight immobilizing Toby's arms. The Nez Percé's breath was hot on Toby's face, and Toby found himself looking into the wild eyes of a madman as Running Bear lifted the knife that he intended to plunge into his opponent's body.

With a supreme effort, Toby managed to squeeze his body a few inches to the right, and the blade landed harmlessly, burying itself in the ground between Toby's body and arm, which he now had free. Perspiration blurred Running Bear's vision, and he assumed that his blade had penetrated deep into the body of his foe. He was caught completely by surprise, therefore, when Toby lashed out with a fist that caught the Indian on the cheekbone, directly below his left eye.

Running Bear bellowed with pain and rage and made a great effort to pin down his foe's arms, but Toby refused to be pinned. He struck repeatedly with hard punches to his opponent's head and face that left their marks on the Indian. Although Running Bear had little to learn in the art of wrestling, he knew virtually nothing about boxing, and the use of fists bewildered him as much as it infuriated and frustrated him.

Toby had not expected to be superior in any phase of combat and was quick to make good use of his unexpected advantage. Flexing his aching, tired hands, he rose to his feet and hauled Running Bear to a standing position as well. Then, putting his entire weight behind each of his punches, he rained lefts and rights on the warrior, driving home blow after blow.

Running Bear took a beating that no one who witnessed it ever forgot. One eye was pasted shut, blood dripped from one nostril, and the opposite side of his mouth was badly cut as well. He stood stock still, almost numb, his arms hanging limply at his sides. Had the brave been a man of less courage and stamina, the fight would have ended then, but Running Bear continued to absorb the heavy punishment, somehow managing to stay on his feet and remain in the combat.

When even his ardent supporters had abandoned his cause as hopeless, he managed to plant his feet far apart to steady himself, raise his knife with a flourish, and make several vicious passes at his foe. Had any one of them struck home, the fight would have ended in victory for the Nez Percé.

It was a part of Toby Holt's heritage from his father that his mind functioned coolly and clearly in moments of great stress. He realized now that although he could attain certain victory by beating Running Bear to a pulp, he would lose all sympathy from the supporters of the Nez Percé leader in the process. They would claim that he had used an unfamiliar method of warfare, that of boxing, in order to achieve victory and had fought without honor by doing so.

It was ironic, Toby thought, that the onlookers would have cheered had Running Bear gained the upper hand by using a combat technique the governor did not know. But this was not the time to be concerned with injustices. Toby's one desire was to end the war between the United States and the young braves without further bloodshed.

Finally he decided that he would continue the pummeling but would add to it a bold and unorthodox course of action. This plan could cause him untold misery and place his own life in jeopardy, but if it worked, it could end the hostilities between whites and Indians once and for all.

Staying basically at arm's length from the rebel leader, who was still attempting to stab him, Toby moved closer long enough to unleash a flurry of hard punches to the head, face, and body while eluding his opponent's knife, rocking Running Bear on his feet. The crowd was beginning to mutter in protest by the time Toby judged that he had softened the Indian enough to take the risks necessary to carry out the next phase of his plan.

Jabbing at his foe with his left hand in order to keep the Indian rebel off balance, Toby suddenly reached out with his right hand and shoved the Nez Percé's broad shoulders with all his might. Running Bear staggered backward and fell, hitting his head on the ground with a sharp crack that reverberated through the cave. His head struck with such force that his eyes closed involuntarily, and he lost consciousness.

When the assemblage of warriors saw Toby reach for the knife in his belt, they drew in their breaths sharply, expecting the governor to kill their leader, as was his right and privilege under the rules of combat. To their astonishment, however, Toby removed his sheathed knife and handed it quietly to the nearest warrior.

Toby caught a glimpse of Stalking Horse's face and watched as the Cherokee's expression of incredulity and opposition changed to one of extreme relief as it dawned on him what Toby was doing.

"Running Bear, of the Nez Percé," the governor said loudly to the onlookers, "sleeps the long sleep of one who lost a wager and a gamble, but he has suffered enough." Looking at his own battered hands, Toby continued, "He will recover from the cuts and bruises he has suffered today, and his face and his body will heal. I agreed to fight him in a combat to the death, and having defeated him, it is my right to take his life. But I, the military governor of the territory of Idaho, am merciful, just as the government of the United States, which I have the high honor to represent, is merciful. I grant Running Bear his life in the hope that when he awakens and recovers his health and his strength, he will recognize the errors he has made and will become a loyal adherent of his nation's treaty with the government of the United States. Only if he persists in pursuing the error of his ways will it be necessary to intervene and to send him into exile for the rest of his days."

Toby said nothing to the young braves about their own future and made no suggestions to them regarding what he believed they should do. He expected them to find their own way out of the morass into which they had stumbled. He knew, furthermore, that they would be far more amenable to compromise if they made their own decisions.

The young braves looked at each other uneasily. The significance of Toby's words was not lost on them. Those who persisted in their opposition to the American government would be sent off somewhere in exile. They had no idea where or how Governor Holt would accomplish this feat, but his victory over their leader had been so complete that they did not doubt his ability to do whatever he pleased.

Toby had said and done all he could, and he was exhausted. Turning his back to his audience, he asked one of the braves where he might scrape off the animal fat and sweat from his face and body.

The Nez Percé signaled to two young warriors, who proceeded to lead Toby to a cavern behind the main cave. There they provided him with a stick used to scrape off dirt and grease. After cleaning himself as thoroughly as possible, Toby returned to the main room, where he stood near the fire as he donned his clothes.

After he was dressed, he announced to Stalking Horse, "My exertions have left me with a craving for fresh air. Let us leave this cave for a time."

Stalking Horse understood Toby's motives for wanting to leave. Embellishing on what Toby had said, the Cherokee exclaimed, "Your exertions will no doubt have also given you a great appetite that only fresh meat will satisfy. Let us go hunting for a time. I hope that our hosts will provide us with a guide who can show us some of the places where game may be found."

Six of the young braves promptly volunteered their services, and Toby and Stalking Horse went off with them, leaving the bulk of the Nez Percé and Shoshone in their encampment, free to determine their own destiny.

The hunters enjoyed extraordinarily good fortune. With

two shots of his rifle, Toby succeeded in bringing down a gigantic moose. The carcass was carved on the spot, and all six of the guides were pressed into service as bearers to help Toby and Stalking Horse as they returned to camp with the moose meat.

During their absence, those who had been left behind had not been idle, and as Toby had suspected, they had taken steps to ensure their own safe future. They told Toby that they had taken a vote on the matter, but he seemed indifferent to the results.

"I suggest we eat supper first, and later you can tell me about your vote."

Before the meat was prepared and the meal served, Running Bear awakened, and cold compresses were placed on his battered face and body. He was astonished to find himself still alive and went into a deep reverie for some time.

To enable the rebel leader to save face as much as possible, Toby avoided him and made no attempt to approach him or to engage him in conversation.

At last the meat was ready, and as he began to eat, Toby noted that several of the warriors were engaged in earnest conversation with Running Bear. The rebel leader did more listening than talking, but from time to time he nodded in agreement with whatever it was that his followers were saying to him.

When everyone had eaten his fill, a delegation composed of three Nez Percé braves and two Shoshone hesitantly approached the place where Toby was sitting beside the cooking fire. "We have reached a decision regarding our future, and we wish the governor of Idaho to know about it," their spokesman declared.

Toby turned to them, nodding pleasantly and acting as though the entire future of Idaho were not at stake.

"It has been determined," the spokesman said, "that we the warriors of the Nez Percé and of the Shoshone have rebelled against the council of our elders in error. We will accept the judgment of the council, and we will make our peace with the United States and its army."

Although Toby felt as though a great weight had been lifted from him, he took extreme care not to show it. "That is wise and sensible on your part," he simply said.

The braves of both nations nodded soberly.

"Those who do not agree with the council," the spokesman continued, "decided it would be foolhardy to try to wage war by themselves against a mighty power like the United States, and so they have bowed their heads and accepted the will of their brethren."

Before the brave could say anything more, Running Bear pushed forward through the crowd. His face and the upper portion of his body were battered and scraped, and he had several black and blue marks, but he was, nevertheless, looking far more fit than he had when Toby had knocked him out. "I made no attempt today," he said, "to influence the thinking of those who followed me here, deep into the wilderness. They have chosen their own paths, and they have decided wisely and well, but there is yet more to be concluded," he went on. "Twenty war parties are now abroad, scattered throughout the territory, and they will create grave troubles for settlers. They know nothing of what has transpired here; they know nothing about the decisions their brothers have reached.''

Toby caught his breath. Twenty war parties could do untold damage throughout Idaho.

''It is because of me that they are on the warpath,'' Running Bear declared. ''I led them to take up arms and defy the government of the United States and to do much damage to settlers' property. If I have learned but one thing this day, it is that the defeat I suffered when I fought Toby Holt awaits those of my followers who continue to defy America. It is up to me to undo the wrong that I have perpetrated. The warriors raised their fists against the United States because of me. It is for me to convince them to bury the tomahawk and to live in peace with their neighbors.''

Toby was uncertain whether the Indian leader was sincere, but a glance at Stalking Horse, who nodded slightly, told him that Running Bear meant every word.

Running Bear grasped Toby's wrist in a gesture of friendship, then was joined by twenty of his braves. Taking nothing with them but smoked meat and parched corn, they left the cave and began their descent to the base of the mountains, where they would find their horses and ride out to halt the depredations of the bands of warriors who were still at large.

No other act that Running Bear might have performed could have convinced Toby so effectively of his newfound maturity. He had sought power by placing himself at the head of a band of rebels; now he was disbanding his followers and, in so doing, was demonstrating that he was capable of assuming the even larger responsibility of becoming a leader of his entire nation.

Watching him as he went off on his self-appointed mission,

IDAHO!

Toby knew their paths were certain to cross again. Although he did not know the reasons, he felt that Running Bear would become one of the strongest forces for peace in all of Idaho and would become a valuable ally of the United States as well as a faithful representative of his own people.

X

Cindy Holt, in no way reconciled to the fate that was being decreed for her by her parents during her Christmas vacation home from college, was clearly irritated. She sat at the dinner table with her fists clenched, the color flaming in her cheeks, and her eyes blazing.

Eulalia Blake thought that anyone who had known Whip Holt would realize instantly that this was his daughter.

Speaking slowly and distinctly, Cindy struggled as she said, "I cannot, for the life of me, understand why I must endure the company of men in whom I have no interest and never will. It isn't fair to me—nor is it fair to them!"

General Lee Blake sighed gently and held his temper in check as he replied, "If you had your way, Cindy, you'd simply announce your engagement to Hank and have done with it. Is that what you're trying to say?"

"Exactly!" the girl retorted. "Hank and I *are* engaged, and I see no reason to hide that fact!"

Again the general sighed. "Through no fault of yours—and certainly not of mine, either—you've come up against a long-standing tradition of the military academy. As I explained to you and Hank before, it's been an unwritten rule that the betrothal of a cadet is never announced until he becomes a first-classman—a senior. So you and Hank have a year and a half to wait."

"But why should that be?" the girl persisted. "Hank and I made up our minds and came to an agreement, and you and Mama approved of it, so nothing stands in the way of an immediate announcement."

"It is also a tradition of the academy," Lee said, "for a cadet to be denied a wife, a horse, and a mustache. These rules are inviolable."

"Suppose that I were to get in touch with the Portland newspapers right now and give them the news of our engagement. What would happen to Hank? Do you mean to tell me he'd be discharged from the academy?"

Lee smiled slightly and looked at his wife in silent appeal. Then he said, "No, Cindy, I doubt very much if he would be discharged. However, the authorities there realize that he knows the rules, partly because he's my son and partly because he's already spent a year and a half there as an undergraduate. What would happen to him is a subtle thing that only takes place in the armed forces. Hank currently ranks second in his class academically and first in military affairs and in athletics. If he keeps up this record—or betters it, which he shows every promise of doing—he can virtually select his own assignment when he's commissioned. General Sherman has his eye on the boy, and I don't mind telling you that he has a beauty of an assignment in mind for Hank when he becomes a second lieutenant. But if Hank openly and flagrantly defies tradition—or if you do it for him—the army hierarchy will be forced to revise its opinion of him. For all practical purposes, Hank will drop to the very bottom of his class and will have the last choice of assignments. He'll carry the stigma with him as long as he remains in the army. As a good army wife, I don't think you want that for him—"

"Certainly not!" Cindy interjected.

"In which case, I can only advise you on the basis of my own experience to comply with military traditions whether you agree with them or not."

Eulalia was aware of the elements warring within her daughter and felt desperately sorry for her. At the same time, however, she knew from her own experience as an army wife that there was nothing she could do for her, no way that she could ease the burden.

Cindy abruptly gave up the fight. "All right, Papa," she said wearily, "you win. I'll do things your way."

Lee rebuked her gently. "Not my way, Cindy, the army's way."

His way and the army's were one and the same, she thought, but she knew better than to mention the obvious. Instead, she concentrated on the food before her and ate steadily, her eyes downcast.

"When is Lieutenant Hoskins coming to call?" Lee asked, referring casually to the cause of the dispute.

"He asked if he could drop in after supper tonight," Cindy said, "and I agreed. But under the rules as you've outlined them to me, I'm not allowed to tell him that Hank and I are engaged to be married. Am I right?"

"Not a word, if you please," Lee cautioned. "Young

Hoskins was graduated from the academy himself just this past June, so he's thoroughly familiar with the rules there.''

"I understand, Papa," Cindy said meekly, and continued to eat.

The sudden reversal of her daughter's attitude made Eulalia suspicious. All the fire had gone out of Cindy, and her mother couldn't help wondering if the girl had some diabolical scheme in mind to get her own way. On second thought, perhaps she was doing her daughter an injustice. Before condemning Cindy, she would wait and see what, if anything, the girl did to alter her situation.

Cindy remained meek and subdued for the rest of the meal, and subsequently, when they had adjourned to the sitting room for coffee and Second Lieutenant Eric Hoskins arrived, she greeted him with an appropriate smile and with a display of excellent manners.

The young officer was very conscious that he was in the home of a major general. Standing erect, shoulders thrown back, his uniform cap held rigid in the crook of his left arm, he shook hands with the general and then bowed from the waist to Eulalia. "Good evening, sir," he said correctly. "Good evening, ma'am."

Eulalia tried to make him more comfortable by offering him a cup of coffee. But when she served him, he sat on the edge of his chair to drink it, still very ill at ease.

Studying him, Cindy had to admit that he was handsome. In fact, she thought, he had probably been spoiled by too many girls because of his good looks. She knew he had graduated in the top third of his class at the academy and that he was commissioned in the cavalry, the choice service after the corps of engineers. She had no reason to dislike him.

On the other hand, she did not quite trust Eric Hoskins. She could not put her finger on the reason, but her instinct warned her to be very careful with him. That was probably nonsensical, she reflected. She was taking out her frustrations on him when he was completely innocent.

Watching him drink his coffee, she turned to her parents the moment he had finished it. "Would you excuse us, Mama, Papa," she asked politely, "if we go into the parlor?"

"By all means," Lee said, and Eulalia smiled her approval, although she was still uneasy about Cindy's abrupt compliance with the general's wishes.

Lieutenant Hoskins's talents for dissembling were not among his assets, and he looked highly relieved as he followed Cindy from the room. She led him to the formal parlor, which was generally used to receive distinguished guests, and there she perched on a divan, expecting him to take a chair opposite her. Instead, he surprised her by sitting down next to her.

Eric Hoskins began to relax, having escaped the intimidating presence of the commander of the Army of the West, and he became increasingly talkative, relating various incidents concerned with the activities of his troop.

Cindy had a hard time concentrating on what he was saying. Lieutenant Hoskins meant nothing to her, and the activities of his cavalry troop were even less significant. A random thought did cross her mind: She wondered whether, when she was married to Hank, their conversations would center on petty gossip about his military unit. She hoped not; she wouldn't be able to stand it.

Something the young man said caught her ear a moment too late to make any sense to her, and she asked him to repeat it. He did, telling her that his battalion, together with one or two others, might be sent out to reinforce the garrisons in Idaho in the near future.

"Really?" She made a valiant effort to look and sound interested. "My brother is in Idaho, you know."

"No, I didn't," he said. "Is he an army officer?"

Cindy shook her head. "No, he's the military governor," she replied casually.

His face turning a deep red, Eric Hoskins silently cursed himself for his stupidity. He had heard somewhere that Cindy was the daughter of the legendary Whip Holt and that her brother was the military governor of Idaho. These facts, combined with her being the stepdaughter of the army's senior officer between the Rocky Mountains and the Pacific Coast, made her a formidable figure. Unfortunately, he never thought of her in terms of her relationship to the famous; she just happened to be a beautiful girl who had great sex appeal, and it was hard to conceive of her in any other terms.

He inquired rather diffidently whether she had ever been to Idaho, and only after she assured him that she had not did he begin to regain his poise.

After discussing for some time what they knew of the territory, he was almost overcome by the urge to reach for Cindy and kiss her, but he refrained. If she protested, her stepfather might come into the room, and the mere thought of being interrupted by the major general, his supreme commander, so filled the young officer with fear that he was rendered helpless. Hoskins felt so gauche that he could not bring up the topic that had been the reason for his call that evening. Finally, however, after depleting every topic of conversation he and Cindy could think of, he blurted an invitation to accompany him to the New Year's Eve celebration that would be held for all officers and their ladies in the great hall of the Fort Vancouver complex.

Cindy's first instinct was to refuse the invitation, but remembering the heated conversation with her parents at supper, she knew her mother and stepfather would continue to hammer at her until she developed a social life with young men. It was far easier to accept and anticipate a dull evening, she reasoned, than undergo repeated unpleasantness at home.

When she accepted, Hoskins made no attempt to hide his elation.

As Cindy accompanied him to the front door, the young lieutenant lunged at her suddenly, took hold of her shoulders, and kissed her quickly but soundly. Then, before she could protest, he was gone.

She stood unmoving, lost in thought for a long while after he departed. Then, slowly raising a hand to her mouth and wiping the back of it across her lips, she went off to tell her parents what they would regard as good news, that she had accepted a date.

For days Cindy worried about how to explain to Hank that she had given in to parental pressure by accepting a social engagement for New Year's Eve with a young lieutenant of the cavalry. Then Hank solved the problem for her.

He wrote her at length, telling her about the weekend he

had spent with the sister of his roommate's girl, who was supposedly chaperoning Dave and Joyce. Alice, he said, was "a pleasant young lady," and he stressed that he had told her of his involvement with Cindy. He wisely made no mention of the preliminaries that had preceded that admission.

Feeling greatly relieved, Cindy replied with a long letter. She detailed the argument she had had with her parents and explained how she had finally made up her mind to pacify them by accepting an invitation from Lieutenant Hoskins for the New Year's Eve party. Eric, she stressed, was a complete gentleman as well as an officer, and she intended to tell him about her relationship with Hank before the evening came to an end.

Then, her conscience no longer bothering her, she went into Portland with her mother and bought a new dress for the New Year's Eve function. It was an off-the-shoulder gown of dull pink satin and was by far the most sophisticated dress she had ever owned. She wanted desperately to have her portrait painted in it, so that she could give it to Hank, but she decided instead to wear it for him when he came home on his one furlough during his four years at the academy, which would bring him to Fort Vancouver in another few months.

Her regular routines kept Cindy occupied until several days before Christmas, and she missed Hank more than ever. Then New Year's Eve came. General and Mrs. Blake were scheduled to head the receiving line at the party, and her parents, after pronouncing her beautiful, went off to the party, saying they would see her shortly. She sat down again at her dressing table and primped until Eric Hoskins arrived.

He looked trim and dashing in his dress blue uniform, and he surprised her by presenting her with a corsage of camelias.

In addition, he had provided them with a small, horse-drawn carriage to take them to the ball. Ordinarily, Cindy, being a Holt, went everywhere on horseback, but that night, in her evening gown, she appreciated her escort's thoughtfulness.

"You look just beautiful," he told her as she took his arm and, lifting her skirt, climbed into the carriage.

She had intended to tell him about her relationship with Hank immediately, but this was not the moment for it, and she resolved to await a more opportune time, later in the evening.

As considerate and attractive as Eric Hoskins was, Cindy dreaded their being classified as a couple when they appeared in public at the ball. The first ordeal she faced, after they arrived, was that of going through the receiving line. "Miss Holt and Mr. Hoskins," her stepfather's aide-de-camp called as they approached. Standing at the head of the line were her mother and stepfather, and Cindy greeted them appropriately, curtsying and murmuring, "Good evening, ma'am. Good evening, General." As the tips of her fingers, encased in long white gloves, touched their similarly clad hands, she could sense the pride they took in her, but she felt that she was showing off under false circumstances: Her escort was a stranger rather than Hank.

She dropped similar curtsies to the other major general stationed at Fort Vancouver and his wife, to the two brigadiers, and the eight or ten colonels who either commanded major units or held senior staff positions. She knew all of them, from helping her mother entertain, but this occasion was different, and she was on her best behavior. All the officers and their wives smiled at her and greeted her warmly, but she could not rid herself of the feeling that she was parading under false colors. If Hank had been behind her, she would have felt completely different, but now it was merely something that had to be done, and she was anxious to end it.

After they had successfully navigated the line, she breathed a sigh of relief, then put a gloved hand on Lieutenant Hoskins's arm and allowed him to lead her to the far side of the room, where a number of junior officers and their young ladies were congregated. Eric Hoskins handed Cindy her dance card with a flourish, and she noted that he had claimed every other dance, which was his right as her escort for the evening. The other names on the program, those of various first and second lieutenants, meant nothing to her and were undoubtedly his close colleagues. The one captain on the list, she felt certain, was his troop commander.

If Hank had been her escort, she felt certain he would have filled her card with the names of young officers who were her friends and with whom she felt at home. She could not rid herself of the feeling that the officers whom Hoskins had written in were simply eager to be dancing with the influential daughter of the general commanding the Army of the West.

Cindy made meaningless small talk with the young officers and their ladies until the last of the guests had gone through the receiving line. Then a long drumroll sounded, and the post's band, seated on a stand at one end of the hall, began to play the national anthem. Every officer present stood at attention, saluting the American flag on the bandstand, and the ladies, from Eulalia down to her daughter, quietly sang the words. Afterward the orchestra broke into the rhythmic tune of a Viennese waltz, which had become the most popular of dance tunes in the United States, as it was in Europe.

No couple dared to move onto the floor, however, until General and Mrs. Blake initiated the dancing.

Cindy forgot her discomfort as she watched her parents gliding effortlessly around the room. They made a handsome couple, and it was obvious that they were happy together, which pleased her enormously. After her father had been killed in the rockslide high in the mountains, Cindy had feared that her mother's days were numbered and that she would grieve herself to death, but when she and Lee Blake had found each other, they had taken a new lease on life together. She was delighted for them.

The spurs on Eric Hoskins's gleaming cavalry boots jangled as he clicked his heels, bowed, and asked Cindy for the privilege of dancing with her. He led her onto the floor, and she was pleasantly surprised to discover that he was a magnificent ballroom dancer. Cindy had always been exceptionally light and graceful on her feet, and the handsome young couple moved in perfect synchronization, dipping, swaying, and gliding in time to the pulse-lifting music.

Twirling, first to the right and then to the left, they cleared a space for themselves on the floor, the other couples abdicating to the obviously superior dancers.

Sustained applause broke out when the orchestra finished its number. Flushed and breathless, Cindy was horrified to discover that she and Eric Hoskins were alone on the dance floor. But Hoskins simply grinned, bowed to her, and led her away from the center of the ballroom.

Had Hank been her escort, she thought angrily, he never would have taken unfair advantage of her and shown off for the benefit of his superiors and colleagues.

Sitting at the long table that she and Hoskins shared with

his friends and their ladies, Cindy fanned herself while he went off to fetch them glasses of punch. Her fury, she discovered, was directed exclusively at him. He had tricked her by being such a superb dancer, calling the attention of the entire garrison to the fact that they made a wonderful team together.

He returned with her punch and, still grinning, sat down beside her. As Cindy's anger cooled, she realized that she was being unfair to Eric. It was hardly his fault that he was an accomplished dancer or that their talents happened to mesh so beautifully on the dance floor. She had no right to blame him, and rather than make herself miserable, she would be wise to relax and enjoy the evening. Like it or not, common sense dictated that she relegate Hank to the back of her mind for now.

She struggled through a long number with a first lieutenant from Eric's troop who was stiff and had difficulty in leading. Then it was time to dance once again with Eric.

The chemistry that had earlier made them appear as one on the dance floor was still at work. Eric deliberately worked in some complicated steps, but Cindy followed him with great ease, as though they had been dancing together for years.

The leader of the band picked up his tempo, and once again, other couples cleared the floor in order to give Cindy and Eric additional room in which to maneuver. Entering into the spirit of the occasion, Cindy found that she was enjoying herself and appreciated the challenge of following Eric's lead. No matter what he did, she followed him perfectly, and together they created a smooth and spectacular dance team.

"Thank you," she said enthusiastically when the music finally stopped. "You're good!"

He beamed at her and, speaking loudly to make himself heard above the applause that greeted them, replied, "You're wonderful!"

Parched after such exertion, Cindy quaffed two more cups of punch and basked in the admiration of her contemporaries. Unexpectedly she found herself enjoying the evening, and the thought crossed her mind that perhaps her parents were right after all. If she had refused the invitation on the grounds that she was engaged to marry Hank, she would have denied herself a pleasurable evening that did no harm to Hank or to her.

On the stroke of midnight, General Blake offered a toast to the new year, and everyone present drank a glass of champagne. Then they were served a supper of sliced turkey and smoked ham, together with potatoes and vegetables. After a dessert of brandied pears, the band started to play again.

"If it's all the same to you," Eric suggested, "perhaps we could sit this one out."

"What a good idea," Cindy said gratefully, pleased by his thoughtfulness. She was cool again and did not look forward to the prospect of becoming overheated on the dance floor so soon after eating.

When he suggested that she might enjoy a stroll on the balcony above, from which they would have a perfect view of the dancers, Cindy quickly agreed. Picking up her beaded handbag, she accompanied him up a flight of stairs to the balcony, which surrounded the hall.

As soon as they reached the top stair, Cindy began to fear that she had made a grave error. No lamps burned along the balcony; the entire area was dark. Paper decorations had been hung by the ball committee, obscuring the lights from the ballroom and hiding large sections of the balcony from the view of those on the main floor below.

To object now, Cindy realized, would be tantamount to an admission that she was afraid of him, and he had given her no cause for uneasiness. She would go along with him as though she found nothing unusual about the balcony and would handle developments as they might arise. With this resolution, she placed a hand lightly on his arm and began to walk with a deliberate, measured tread around the hall below them.

"What a surprise it was," he said, "to discover that we danced so well together! We must be one couple in a million."

"I think that's something of an exaggeration," Cindy replied with a light laugh. "It was all your doing, you know. All I had to do was to follow your lead. You're the dancer who deserved the applause."

"Not at all," he replied. "We've got to share whatever praise was due us. I've danced with a great many girls, and I've yet to find one who was anywhere near your equal." He halted behind a large pillar at one corner of the balcony.

"You're very kind to say so," Cindy replied, hoping she had not erred by allowing him to maneuver her into such a secluded location.

He placed one hand on the wall behind her shoulder and leaned against it casually—almost too casually—as he hemmed her in.

He was grinning at her, and so she smiled at him in return, hoping desperately that she was mistaken and that he was not intending to embarrass her by making any intimate gestures.

But her hopes were in vain. He leaned toward her, one hand dropping to her shoulder as he said huskily, "Together, you and I make a marvelous team."

She knew from the way he was closing in on her that within seconds he would be trying to kiss her and maybe do even more. She tried to move away, but he held on to her tightly. He was getting rough, dropping his hand to her breast, and at last she realized that this was a moment that called for definite action. She was glad that she had shown the foresight to prepare for just such an emergency.

Without taking her eyes from Eric's, Cindy fumbled in her handbag and then grew calmer as her fingers closed around the small, single-shot, pearl-handled pistol that she had bought for herself the day she and her mother had gone shopping in Portland. She did not resist as Eric continued to draw her close, but instead, she pressed the muzzle of her pistol against his chest. "If I were you," she told him, "I'd stop right now."

Feeling something hard pressing against his chest, he looked down and saw the pistol. "My God!" he cried in alarm.

"You have a clear choice, Lieutenant Hoskins," Cindy said, her voice cool and crisp. "You can either stop manhandling me instantly—in which case we'll return to the party downstairs and neither of us will ever refer to this incident again—or you can persist in trying to maul me. But you run a grave risk if you do, because I will pull the trigger of my pistol."

She spoke so quietly that he found it difficult to believe her.

"I am the daughter of Whip Holt, and believe me, I learned to shoot almost at the same time I learned to walk.

I'll have no hesitation in shooting you down if you force me to. As the stepdaughter of the commanding general, all I need to do is to claim that I was forced to protect my honor against you. No judge or jury within one hundred miles of Fort Vancouver would convict me.''

Eric gently disengaged himself, taking care not to upset her further. For an insane moment he toyed with the idea of taking the pistol from her, but he rapidly rejected the notion. She had a solid grip on it, and he knew from the expression in her eyes that she meant what she had said. He backed away until he stood several feet from her.

Cindy continued to keep the pistol trained on him. "I am *not* the sort of girl you can take to the balcony and steal some kisses from,'' she said.

"You've made that very plain to me,'' he murmured.

"Furthermore,'' she said, "I am engaged to a cadet currently at the military academy. In his absence, I am forced to protect myself.''

She needed no one to protect her, he thought, and smiled ruefully.

They walked the length of the balcony, with Cindy carefully but surreptitiously keeping the pistol pointed at the young officer. Had anyone encountered them, that person would have had difficulty telling that anything out of the ordinary was taking place. As they approached the staircase, Cindy put the safety catch on the gun with her thumb and dropped the weapon into her handbag.

"Never fear,'' she said. "I will mention nothing of this incident to my mother or to General Blake. Nor will you mention to a living soul that I told you I was engaged.''

Eric nodded and muttered his thanks, relieved beyond measure that he had not placed his career in jeopardy as he had his life.

Cindy put a gloved hand on his arm as they descended the stairs, and they were models of propriety as they made their way back to their table.

Catching a glimpse of her parents, who were beaming at her, Cindy grinned broadly and waved to them.

She knew now the strategy that she would employ in pacifying them in the future. Never would she object to spending time with a young officer, for she had learned the one certain way of protecting herself and keeping her honor secure for Hank. What her parents didn't know wouldn't hurt them.

The tensions that had attended the long journey into the deepest mountain recesses of Idaho had been exhausting, and Toby Holt and Stalking Horse were tired as well as dirty, cold, and hungry as they slowly made their way back to Boise. When they were no more than a full day's journey from the capital, they encountered a troop of cavalry assigned to patrol that area in lookout for the governor and his companion. The two weary travelers were immediately surrounded by the cavalrymen, and as they moved on that afternoon and the following morning, several other troops of cavalry on patrol appeared and joined their entourage.

So it happened that at noon, when Boise was busier than at any other time of day, Governor Holt returned with a full military escort as he made his way through the streets to his official residence. Old-timers in Boise could not help commenting that he and his Cherokee companion resembled two of the vanishing breed of mountain men and bore little resemblance to the dignitaries of current renown.

When the two travelers reached the governor's house, they found little White Elk and the even smaller Timothy Holt waiting for them at the entrance.

For some moments, the Indian boy, who was making a supreme effort to please Stalking Horse by hiding his emotions behind an unchanging mask, behaved with the aplomb of a veteran brave. Then his composure broke, and he hurled himself at the elderly Cherokee warrior. They hugged for a full minute and then went off into the house with White Elk smiling broadly and beaming at the man he considered to be his grandfather.

Tim Holt made no attempt to restrain his joy at seeing his father. Shouting, "Papa! Papa!" he threw himself at Toby, climbed onto the squatting man's shoulders, and when he was happily settled there, began to talk so rapidly that he made no sense at all.

Toby went in search of his wife, finding her in their quarters, where she chose to be reunited with him in private. Putting Tim down, Toby took Clarissa into his arms, and they kissed long, hard, and passionately. The concerns of their many days apart faded into insignificance now that they were reunited.

Before they had the chance to sit down and talk about what had happened during the weeks of their separation, Toby had important official business to transact. He sent for his secretary, and sitting in the parlor of his living quarters, he dictated telegrams to President Grant in Washington and to General Blake at Fort Vancouver. He was pleased to report, he wrote in each, that the uprising of young Nez Percé and Shoshone had been ended and that the territory was now at peace. There was no need for additional troops to be sent to Idaho, nor for any other military measures to be taken. He had just returned to Boise after making a reconnaissance deep into the interior, where he had met at length with Running Bear, the leader of the insurrection, whom he had persuaded to mend his ways and to obey the treaty that his elders observed. Running Bear had agreed, and both of the Indian nations of Idaho were now at peace with the United States.

Furthermore, the miners, drifters, and other riffraff who had come into the territory to cause trouble had been completely subdued. They had quickly learned that any lawlessness on their part would be dealt with severely by the United States Army troops in Idaho.

Therefore, Toby concluded in his telegram to the President, he had performed his mission successfully. He requested that he be relieved of his duties as military governor as soon as President Grant found it convenient to appoint a successor.

The telegrams were dispatched, and Toby accepted the drink that Clarissa had poured for him.

"You neglected to mention to either the President or to General Blake how you happened to persuade Running Bear to change his mind and give up his crusade against the United States, but you're not going to get off as easily with me. What happened?"

Speaking with great reluctance, Toby told her of Running Bear's challenge and its consequences.

Clarissa was shocked. "You could have been killed!" she cried. "Won't you ever learn to stop risking your life?"

Toby smiled sheepishly. "As it happens, everything worked out very well, and whatever risk I ran turned out to be negligible."

"As though you could have known that in advance," she replied with a snap.

"What about you?" he asked, hoping to turn her attention away from him. "Was everything quiet and peaceful here?"

"More or less." And then, with hesitation, she began to relate the story of the night that Otto Sinclair had appeared.

Outraged beyond measure, Toby threw question after question at her, but Clarissa, ignoring his burning impatience, answered him slowly, factually.

When he had heard her out, Toby suddenly burst into loud laughter. "You're a fine one to lecture me about taking risks!" he exclaimed. "If I understand you correctly, you were so angry that you went after Sinclair with a fireplace poker even though he was armed."

"Well . . . yes," Clarissa admitted. "That's more or less what happened."

"All I can say," he declared, "is that I'm glad we're going home to Oregon soon. If I need you to keep me from risking my life—and I do—then you've got to admit that you need me to protect you from taking foolish chances with yours."

Clarissa laughed as she threw her arms around her husband, hugging him tightly. They had reached a perfect understanding, and their reunion was complete.

Toby rode off to the governor's office, where his first act was to notify his military commanders to cancel all actions against the Nez Percé and the Shoshone. The hostilities had come to an end, he explained, and as soon as peace was firmly established on both sides, he intended to allow the Indians to visit Boise and the smaller communities of the territory whenever the need for such visits arose.

His final official task for the day was a lengthy conference with Rob Martin, and after they had finished their business, Rob said casually, "When you have the time, Toby, Kale and I want to discuss something of personal importance to both of us with you."

Something in Rob's tone made Toby curious enough not to want to delay the discussion, and he promptly invited the couple to supper that night, knowing that Clarissa would not object, even though this was his first night at home. Indeed she didn't, for she had already learned of Rob and Kale's engagement during Toby's absence. She suspected the purpose of their visit was to tell Toby.

That evening, while enjoying aperitifs in the family parlor of the governor's mansion before supper, Kale and Rob sat side by side on a divan holding hands. Their display of intimacy was so unusual that Toby couldn't help looking at Clarissa, who merely smiled.

Rob intercepted the glance. "Kale and I have some important news, which Clarissa already knows. We're going to be married."

Toby was genuinely delighted and extended his warmest congratulations to the couple. "When and where will the big event occur?" he asked.

"That brings up an interesting matter," Rob said. "Kale and I have talked it over, and nothing will make us happier than to have you officiate at our wedding."

Toby laughed. "I'm not certain that I have the power to marry you."

"Oh, but you do," Kale said. "We looked it up in the territorial constitution, and you have the power to perform marriage ceremonies."

"In that case," Toby replied, "I'll be delighted. But you'll have to have your wedding soon because I may not be military governor for very long. Strictly between us, I've tendered my resignation to President Grant, effective as soon as he can select a successor."

"Idaho will be losing the best leader it's ever had," Kale said, "but it suits us just fine to be married right away."

"It sure does," Rob added. "It saves me the need to tender a premature resignation. Whenever you leave office, I'll also leave."

"You sound," Clarissa said, "as though you've been making specific plans for your future."

Kale and Rob looked at each other. She smiled as he straightened his shoulders. "Indeed we have," she said.

"We had a number of choices," Rob said. "We could go to Montana and take up residence in the vicinity of our gold mine, Toby, or we could build a house in Washington near our lumbering interests, but neither prospect appealed to us, and in a way, they'd be as foolish as going to San Francisco simply because we once lived there."

"To put it bluntly," Kale said, "I was the most notorious courtesan in San Francisco, and we see no reason to begin our married life trying to overcome that severe a handicap."

"On the other hand," Rob said, picking up the narrative, "we know of no reason to avoid a town like Portland. My father still practices medicine there. My mother is very much admired as one of the members of the original wagon train to cross the continent, and I grew up there. So we've decided to brave any criticism and to make our future there."

"Anyone there who feels the urge to snub us because of my former profession is entitled to do so," Kale said, "but we'll say the devil with them. We'll quickly be able to separate our friends from those who want nothing to do with us.''

"Since we really can't escape from Kale's past," Rob said, "we've decided it would be futile—and foolish—to try to camouflage it. We'd be living in constant fear that we'd make a slip of some sort that would reveal the truth. This way, we have nothing to fear, and we can stand on our own feet with pride.''

"I think that's wonderful!" Clarissa said. "More power to both of you!"

"You have our support all the way," Toby declared. "We'll give a dinner party for you as soon as we get back to the ranch."

"We certainly will!" Clarissa added enthusiastically. "And we'll have every social leader in Portland there. Don't worry about your acceptance in Portland for a single moment, either of you. You're going to make out just fine."

Toby spent most of the following day catching up on the paperwork that had accumulated during his absence and conferring with members of the territorial legislature. He also received congratulatory telegrams from President Grant and General Blake. The long message from the President expressed regret at Toby's request to be relieved, but nevertheless thanked him for the months that he had spent in government service, stressing the valuable contribution he had made to the peace and security of the American West.

President Grant also indicated that he had a replacement as governor in mind and that he required a few weeks to confer with the subject himself and with Congressional leaders before nominating the man for the post. This was good news, which Toby was anxious to pass along to Clarissa, who would be pleased to learn that their sojourn in Idaho would end within weeks and they would be able to return to the ranch in Oregon.

Ulysses Grant paid Toby the greatest of compliments when he concluded the telegram by saying, "You are truly the son of Whip Holt."

A heavy snow began to fall in midafternoon, which cut down appreciably on the number of visitors who were calling on the governor's office. Toby was mildly surprised when one of his secretaries informed him, "Mr. Edward Blackstone is here to see you."

Edward, who managed to look dashing even in a fur hat, heavy boots, and short sheepskin coat, grinned amiably as he came into the office, shook hands with the governor, and stood near the fire blazing in the hearth to warm himself. "This is strictly a personal visit," he said, "so throw me out if you're busy."

"I always have time for you," Toby replied, making no secret of his admiration for the young Englishman. He indicated a chair, and Edward dropped into it, leaving his hat and coat to dry in front of the fire.

"I don't want to impose on you," Edward said, "so I'll come to the point of my visit at once. This noon I happened to dine at the inn with my cousin, Jim Randall, and with Pamela Drake. While we were eating, Rob Martin and Kale Salton came in and we asked them to join us. They told us that you're going to perform the marriage ceremony for them."

"Rob assures me that under the laws of Idaho, any ceremony I perform will be legal," Toby said with a laugh, "and as long as they're willing to take the chance, so am I."

"Pamela and Jim were very interested," Edward said. "They're betrothed, too, you know—"

"No, I didn't!" Toby said, interrupting him. "A great deal of wooing seems to have been going on while I was out of town."

"Apparently so," Edward said, grinning. "Be that as it may, they'd dearly love to have you marry them as well. Since I was coming to see you anyway, I volunteered to approach you on their behalf."

"I'll be glad to oblige them," Toby replied, "provided they intend to marry in the next few weeks. I don't want this information to go any farther, but I'm resigning as military governor, and I expect that my replacement will be named soon by the President."

"I'm very sorry to hear that, Toby," Edward replied. "Idaho would benefit from your direction in peacetime as well as wartime, you know."

"Thank you for saying so, Edward, but you must understand what a strain the governorship has put on my family. We're eager to get back to some semblance of normal family life. I hope my resignation won't become effective too soon for Pamela and Jim's wedding," Toby said.

"It can't be too soon to suit Jim and Pamela," Edward said, laughing. "The outdoor activities at his ranch are almost nonexistent in this kind of weather. So it's a perfect season to be married—and it's an even better season for a honeymoon."

"I guess so," Toby replied dryly, and then he fell silent, seemingly lost in thought.

Edward misinterpreted his silence. "Do you disapprove of their marriage?"

"On the contrary!" he said, shaking his head. "I approve heartily of it. If I didn't, I wouldn't consent to officiate for them."

"I'm glad to hear that."

"Quite so. What I was thinking was that I can't help but admire the courage that Jim Randall is showing. He's a brave man to be marrying a woman as strong-willed and independent-minded as Pamela."

Edward whooped with laughter. "I can see that you know her," he said.

"Let's say that I'm as well acquainted with her as I care to be," Toby replied. "Jim is very quiet and retiring, and at first glance it would appear that he's making a major error by marrying someone as aggressive and demanding as Pamela. On the other hand, I know his type, and I suspect that he's considerably stronger than he appears on the surface."

"I don't think there's much doubt of that," Edward said.

Toby nodded. "Once they've reached a balance and gotten accustomed to the compromises required in marriage, they should be very happy together. Besides, you're on hand to act as judge and jury if things get too rough between them."

Edward shook his head. "No, I don't plan to be in Boise. That's another reason I wanted to see you. I would like your reaction to an idea I have. I have an opportunity to make a trip of a lifetime, and I wondered what you'd think of it."

"I'll be glad to help in any way I can," Toby said.

"I've become acquainted with a fellow guest at the inn," Edward said, "a man who completed what sounds to me like a fantastic journey before the winter snows set in. He left

Saint Louis, Missouri, by paddle-wheeler steamer, and the ship took him more than two thousand miles up the Missouri River to its headquarters at Fort Benton in Montana. I have a very strong desire to make that same trip in reverse.''

"I can certainly understand why you'd want to," Toby said. "It sounds like quite an adventure.''

"Precisely,'' Edward said. "Besides, I've lived long enough here in the mountains that I have a good feel for this section of the United States. I'm still unmarried, I have the funds to do as I please, and I feel a great urge to satisfy my yearning for more knowledge about this country. As you know, Governor, I've been in love with America for a long time, and the idea of going down the Missouri River by boat through the Plains all the way to Saint Louis appeals to me enormously.''

"It sounds like a grand trip,'' Toby said. "I recommend it without qualification, provided that you travel on board a ship of the Harding Line. They're by far the best ships. They have extremely comfortable quarters, and I understand their meals are first-rate.''

"The Harding Line,'' Edward repeated thoughtfully. "I'll remember that. Thank you, Governor.''

"Not at all,'' Toby replied. "As a matter of fact, I envy you. You should definitely get your fill of adventure while you're able. But if you'll forgive me, I can't help wondering what will become of your cousin Millicent in all this. When Pamela marries Jim, she'll no doubt take charge at the ranch as mistress, and Millicent—well, she'll be left out in the cold. She has no interests in life other than her music—at least to my knowledge—and I'm afraid she may not be content without some purpose.''

"I've been concerned about Millicent for quite some time," Edward said, "and I've taken steps that will, I hope, keep her gainfully occupied, busy, and, consequently, happy."

"Good!" Toby said. "She's a lovely, talented person."

"Yes, but I'm afraid she's been tormented by a feeling of loneliness," Edward replied. "Not that she'd ever admit it. I wonder if you've seen the papers relative to the disposition of Dan Davenport's estate."

"Just today," Toby said. "I read a document to the effect that you and Jim Randall killed Davenport after he'd made the mistake of abducting Pamela and that you bought his gambling establishment through your attorneys. That surprised me somewhat, as I didn't think you were the type to engage in a gambling hall venture."

"I have no interest whatsoever in gambling halls," Edward replied a trifle primly. "Actually, I've had the interior of the place gutted, and a team of builders is at work, installing a new kitchen and redoing the rest of the interior."

"Oh?" Toby raised an eyebrow.

The young Englishman nodded. "I have an idea," he continued, "that Boise has grown large enough to support a first-rate restaurant—an eating establishment as good as the public can find in New York or in San Francisco. It occurred to me that Millicent is the perfect person to put in charge of such a place."

"I'm intrigued," Toby said.

"She's always enjoyed preparing food, and the meals she serves are always marvelous. The splendid Chinese cook she has working for her out at the ranch, Ah-Sing, is typical of the class of people she employs. She has no intention of taking him away from the ranch, of course, because she doesn't want to leave Pamela and Jim shorthanded, but I'm sure she'll find others equally talented."

"You sound as though you've managed to persuade her to take this venture seriously," Toby commented.

Edward shook his head. "It was unnecessary for me to talk her into anything. I merely mentioned the idea of operating a truly fine restaurant to her, and she took over from there. Frankly, she was badly upset when Rob Martin declared his intentions to marry Kale, and she's delighted for the opportunity to become involved in something. Indeed, I've never seen Millicent this enthusiastic over anything other than her flute. She's spending her days there, supervising the workmen, and in her spare time she's been interviewing cooks and waiters. She's utterly determined to make a success of the place."

"That's good to know," Toby said.

"Naturally," Edward said, "I haven't told her that I couldn't care less if the place is a financial success or a failure, as long as it keeps her occupied and happy. I'll be more than satisfied if she believes that she's doing a service for the community and for Idaho."

"This is mighty decent of you, Edward," Toby said.

The Englishman shrugged. "Not really," he replied. "I suddenly realized there's more in the old adage about blood being thicker than water than I knew. The place should open long before I leave on my voyage down the Missouri River this coming spring, and so all the bugs should be ironed out before I go."

"If we're still in Idaho," Toby said, "count on Clarissa and me to attend the opening. I think that we owe Millicent Randall that much."

XI

As Margie White made her way down the main street of Boise, men stared at her. At eighteen, she was a true beauty, with shoulder-length, blue-black hair, startling blue eyes, and a dusting of freckles across the bridge of her nose. Her modest, black woolen attire could not hide her ripe, full figure any more than it could conceal her vibrant, youthful exuberance.

That particular day, however, she was feeling anything but vibrant. In fact, she had never been so low. She had come to Boise a week earlier, all the way from Portsmouth, New Hampshire, in order to marry her childhood sweetheart, Bill Ferris, who had sent for her after earning a tidy sum in the gold fields. But Bill hadn't been anywhere in town when Margie arrived, and he had not shown up since that time. Only the day before she had learned that he had apparently forgotten her existence and had fallen head over heels in love with a dance-hall hostess, whom he had followed to Denver.

That, however, was only the beginning of her troubles. She had also run out of money the day before, and that very morning she had been forced to vacate the rooming house where she had taken quarters and had lived for the past week. In order to raise funds, she had sold all her clothes except those she was wearing. But that money had swiftly disappeared on rent and food, and she had not eaten anything in two days. She had not been trained for any profession, so it was impossible to find work in Boise. She was alone in the world; there was no one on whom she could call for help.

Before going out into the street that morning, she had counted her assets. She had only herself and her appeal to men, of which, young and innocent as she was, she could not help being aware. So at least she had *something* to offer, and she was reluctantly willing to sacrifice her virtue in order to live. She had heard of Madam Suzanne, the owner of the most prominent bordello in Boise, and she was on her way to see her now.

When Margie came to Madam Suzanne's house, where an oil lamp with a red-tinted shade burned in the front window of the parlor, she hesitated, standing indecisively on the street. She was being foolish, she told herself. The issue was already settled, and there was nothing more to be decided. Either she would become a prostitute or she would starve to death. There was no alternative. Taking a deep breath, she mounted the steps and rang the doorbell.

A serving maid in a black uniform answered her summons.

"I'd like to see Madam Suzanne, please," Margie said timidly.

The woman looked her up and down and then said curtly, "Follow me." A few moments later, Margie found herself sitting in the handsomely furnished parlor, where she assumed that the girls of the house greeted the customers. The furniture was plush and extremely comfortable, and she noticed there were several bottles of liquor and a number of glasses resting on a sideboard.

An overdressed woman with frizzy blond hair and wearing a heavy coat of cosmetics on her face entered the room. "You wanted to see me?" she demanded.

"Yes, ma'am." Margie struggled to her feet. "I—I'd like to come to work for you." The words seemed to stick to the roof of her mouth.

Suzanne's eyes narrowed. "Turn around," she commanded, and nodded slowly in seeming approval as the young woman pivoted. "Very well, you may sit down."

Margie felt so weak that she sank gratefully back into her chair.

"Have you had any experience in this type of work?" Suzanne asked.

There was no point in lying. "No, ma'am," she whispered.

"You've had experience with men, though?"

Margie shook her head miserably.

"You have a potential, I've got to say that for you," Suzanne told her grudgingly. "You don't look in the least like a harlot, and that's all to the good. If we can keep you looking fresh and innocent, you could be a very interesting addition to my establishment."

The young woman's heart pounded. "You'll—you'll take me on, then?"

"Not so fast," Suzanne replied. "We'll give you a little test first. Let me see. Go over to the Boise Inn and sit in the lobby just outside the dining room there. Pick up a man and either bring him back here or, if he's staying at the inn, he might prefer to take you to his room. Either way, you'll pay me half of what you earn. I should think twenty-five dollars would be a fair amount for you to charge, considering it's your first time."

Margie felt as though her head had been immersed in cold water. The woman was taking her at her word and had made a straightforward business offer to her. Suddenly she felt like fleeing.

But her stomach growled, reminding her that there were other, practical considerations in the world. "Please, Madam Suzanne," she said, "could I get an advance of one dollar from you, so I can get myself something to eat?"

The woman's hard eyes were fixed on her. Then she laughed. "If food is more important to you than men, you're never going to get very far in this business," she stated. "The girls on my staff learn my motto and learn it fast. If they want to eat, they work. If they don't care about earning money, they can starve for all I care. Have you got that straight? You get yourself a man over at the inn, and after he's paid you for your services, then you can eat to your heart's content. If you're lucky, maybe he'll even buy you a meal—*after* you've conducted your business with him." She rose to her feet, nodded stiffly, and withdrew from the room.

Margie knew she had no choice. She had been hired—on the

condition that she produce immediate results. Dragging herself to her feet, she walked the few short blocks to the Boise Inn. Her stomach felt so hollow that she was faint.

But she reached the inn without incident and slowly entered the lobby. Since she had never been here before, it took her several moments to learn the locations of various public rooms. Once she found the dining room, she started for it and then lowered herself onto a leather-covered settee just outside the entrance. Here she crossed her ankles, struck a pose, and forced herself to smile. It was the noon dinner hour, and various men sauntered in, singly, in pairs, and in threes to eat their midday meal. Several of them took note of Margie White's presence; one or two eyebrows were raised, but at least a dozen or more men passed her without responding to her inviting smile.

Edward Blackstone, having just come from the building he had bought for Millicent's new restaurant, was making his way to the dining room for dinner. He had dropped by the building to see how the workmen were doing in the remodeling. His mind was filled with thoughts of his cousin and how she would make out in her new vocation. Though he hadn't looked directly at Margie, he was vaguely aware of her smile.

She continued to gaze steadily at him, however, and now he took note of her. He realized she was exceptionally attractive—young, fresh, and innocent—and it struck him as odd that she should be soliciting like a prostitute. Something didn't quite fit.

Uncertain as to why he was bothering except to satisfy his sudden curiosity, he strolled toward her.

Somehow, Margie found her voice. "Hello," she said timidly.

The uncertainty of her greeting was like the tentative quality of her smile, and thus was even more intriguing. He was willing to bet that this woman could not be a harlot. "Good morning," he said. "Would you care to join me?"

She nodded, rose swiftly to her feet, and fell in beside him. In the dining room he found the head waiter, who conducted them to a table on the far side of the room away from the bar. There, once they were alone, they introduced themselves to each other.

"May I offer you a drink?" Edward asked politely.

Margie hesitated. She was not all that familiar with spirits and was especially afraid of drinking on an empty stomach. At worst she might become ill; at best she might lose control of herself at a time when she needed to keep her wits about her.

Conscious of her pause, Edward promptly amended his offer. "Perhaps you'd prefer something to eat," he suggested. Her swift nod, so rapid that she responded without even thinking, spoke its own story.

Looking at her carefully—her eyes and mouth—Edward decided that she was under great strain. Perhaps she was even hungrier than he had first thought.

He summoned the waiter and ordered the special of the day: oxtail soup. Several thick slices of bread and a slab of sweet butter were served along with it. Margie dropped all pretense as the food was placed before her. Caring nothing about manners, forgetting all about Suzanne's order to conduct business before she ate, Margie devoured the bread and butter and ate her soup rapidly.

Watching silently as he ate his own soup, Edward smiled to himself, convinced that his initial hunch had been right. This was no harlot but rather a decent young woman who happened to be famished. Saying nothing to her, he called their waiter over and ordered her a thick slice of roast beef, which, as always, the inn served in portions so large that one piece filled an entire plate. Accompanying the beef were a large baked potato with more butter and a salad of lettuce and tomatoes.

The meal was placed in front of her as she finished her soup. She proceeded wordlessly to consume it, too, eating quickly, not missing any crumbs.

Edward watched her carefully as he finished his own dinner. Her behavior fitted into a clear pattern for him: For some reason she had been in need of funds and therefore had decided to emulate the prostitutes of Boise.

A very tall, heavyset man, with his broad-brimmed hat tilted on the back of his head and a brace of pistols in his belt, stood in the entrance to the dining room, looking at the customers. He was especially interested in Margie and her companion, and ultimately he strolled toward them, his eyes fixed on the young woman.

Edward noted that Margie was bracing herself, although it was plain that she didn't know what was in store.

"Suzanne told me to look for you," he said. "She told me that she gave you specific orders and that if you broke them, she'd have to teach you a lesson. She said particularly that if you were eating here, I was to drag you back to her place, by the hair, if necessary."

Margie shrank from him.

"The lady is enjoying her meal," Edward said lightly. "I'm afraid you're interfering here."

The big man addressed the young Englishman for the first time. "If I was you, buster," he said, "I'd tend to my own business. In that way you'll avoid getting a busted nose and maybe a few cracked ribs in the bargain."

Edward smiled faintly, then summoned their waiter. "We'll be back in a few moments," he said, "to order dessert."

"Yes, Mr. Blackstone," the waiter murmured.

Edward pushed back his chair, and rose to his feet. "Shall we see this intruder outside?" he suggested. "I have a positive anathema to the creation of scenes in public places."

The young woman was badly frightened, but she appeared to have no choice. The giant was glowering at her, and Edward, her kind benefactor, stood waiting for her, one arm extended to her to take. She rose slowly and slipped a hand through the crook of his arm.

He smiled at her, patting her hand reassuringly. Then he started to walk briskly toward the rear exit, taking care not to go too swiftly, for Margie's sake, and with seemingly unconscious regard for the giant who loomed just behind them. The dining room opened onto the yard in the back of the inn. When they emerged into it, Edward carefully but quickly removed Margie's arm, stepped away from her, and turned to face Madam Suzanne's hoodlum.

"Put up your fists," he said, and at the same instant, he lashed out with his left, peppering the man's lips and nose repeatedly with short jabs. Then he drove a hard right into the giant's stomach. The blow was not long; in fact, it traveled no more than ten to fifteen inches, but it was delivered with such force that Edward's fist momentarily disappeared in the abundant flesh of the giant's midsection.

That was just the beginning. Edward continued to riddle his much larger opponent with lefts and rights, alternating jabs and long punches, upper cuts, and a variety of bewildering short blows.

The hoodlum was so busy trying to defend himself that he had no opportunity to counterattack. After driving him into a corner, Edward put all of his strength into each punch until his opponent could tolerate no more and fell to the ground.

Groaning, the man lay there, trying feebly but in vain to get back onto his feet.

Edward nudged him with his toe. "Get up," he said, "and go back to your employer. Tell her to leave Miss White alone in the future, and I'm telling you that if you ever annoy the lady again, this is just a small taste of what you'll get." He made a slight bow to Margie and offered her his arm again. "Shall we go back in?" he said. "The desserts here are quite good."

Margie had to admire his unblinking calm as he ordered them cups of coffee, along with slices of apple pie covered with cheddar cheese. He acted as though his fist fight had been an everyday occurrence and that its outcome had never been in doubt.

Suddenly, he leaned forward in his chair and looked hard at her. "Now, Margie White," he said in an unyielding voice, "I want you to tell me your story, all of it!"

She was so startled by his order, so stunned by his kindness and generosity, that the whole tale poured out of her. She told him how she had left her boardinghouse in Portsmouth,

New Hampshire, and had come out to Boise in order to be married, but that her fiancé had disappeared from town, and she had used up all of her money on rent and food. Then, only the day before, she discovered that he had become infatuated with a dance-hall hostess, whom he had followed to Denver. Faced with starvation, she had sought work from Madam Suzanne. "I guess you know the rest," she said dejectedly.

Edward's heart went out to her. This young, basically decent woman had been in trouble so deep that she had been unable to handle it. He waited until she finished eating her pie and drinking her coffee before he revealed what he had in mind.

"I need a little time," he said, "to decide exactly what's to be done with you. In the meantime, we've got to make sure you stay out of trouble. Come with me." He marched the bewildered Margie to the desk of the inn. "Give Miss White a room," he said, "and put the expense on my bill."

"Very well, Mr. Blackstone," the assistant manager said, and did not dare ogle the young woman for fear of offending the young Englishman whose temper was notoriously short.

"Put her meals—her dinner tonight and her breakfast tomorrow morning—on my bill, too, and I'll also pay for any incidental expenses that she might incur."

Margie was breathless. Her benefactor was being generous to her beyond belief, yet so far he had said nothing about what he wanted for himself in return.

"Go to your room," Edward ordered in a stern but fatherly tone, "and stay there. Avoid Madam Suzanne. And don't speak to any strangers. I'll see you before noon tomorrow."

He tipped his hat to her and walked away quickly, not bothering to glance back.

Margie thought she was dreaming, that none of the good things happening to her were real. She followed Edward's orders to the letter, spending the afternoon in her new, comfortably furnished room. That night, she went back down to the main dining room of the hotel, and looking at no one and speaking to no one other than her waiter, she demurely ate dinner. She ordered another enormous meal, but otherwise did and said nothing out of the ordinary and went straight back to her room after finishing it. She was tired, terribly exhausted, and she soon went off to sleep, with romantic visions of Edward floating through her mind.

The following morning, after retrieving the underwear she had carefully washed the night before, she dressed and again went down to the dining room, this time for breakfast. Her appetite had returned to normal; she ate a relatively small breakfast before going back to her room, which had already been made up by the hotel maid.

There, she spent the rest of the morning anxiously waiting Edward's arrival. Never had she known such generosity in any human being, but still she was sure that it would be necessary for her to repay him. In her limited view of the world, people—no matter how nice or generous they seemed—never gave something without expecting something in return. Edward Blackstone was a man, and therefore she would have to repay him the only way she could—by offering herself to him.

Shortly before noon a tap sounded at the door. Edward stood on the threshold, his hat in one hand.

He noted instantly that the strained look he had seen the

previous day in Margie's eyes and around her mouth was gone. In fact, she looked radiant. Although he had remembered her as being very pretty, he had to admit to himself that she was actually quite beautiful.

Margie, eyes shining, answered Edward's many questions in detail as they sat together on the divan. No, she had heard nothing further from Madam Suzanne, and she guessed that the beating administered to the woman's strong-arm man had been sufficiently severe that Suzanne had decided to give Margie White a wide berth from now on. Margie had seen no one and spoken to no one except her waiter at dinner last night and at breakfast again this morning.

"We'll have to go somewhere else for dinner this noon," Edward told her. "You must be growing tired of the inn."

"Never!" she replied. "You forget that I hadn't been eating decently for many days, and the luxury of having enough food has been more than enough for me."

He changed the subject abruptly. "Do you know Boston?"

"I can't say that I really know it," she replied. "I've made half a dozen trips there from Portsmouth, and I'm familiar with the general layout of the city, but that's all."

"What do you think of it?" he asked.

She pondered his question for a time. "It seems to be a wonderful place," she said at last. "It's a very large city and a very cultured city, yet at the same time, there's a nice, small-town atmosphere that makes me feel at home."

"You wouldn't mind living there, then?"

"No—I don't think so," she replied, not certain what he had in mind.

He took a card from his sealskin wallet and handed it over to her. "Take this to the address written on it and you'll be given a position as a receptionist. It's a very prestigious law firm with which I've done considerable business, and they'll give you a job on my say so. It won't pay you a fortune, but you'll earn enough to be able to live comfortably in Boston, to go to concerts and lectures there, and to eat occasionally in some of the town's better restaurants."

She looked blankly at him, then at the card.

"Of course you can accept it, and you will," he told her. "You'd do the same for me if our positions were reversed."

Margie remained silent for a long moment. Then, placing the card in her pocket, she slowly removed her jacket, which she placed on the divan beside her, and untied the bow at the neck of her white blouse.

"Here," Edward said in alarm. "What's this?"

Her eyes sought his, and when they met, she looked at him long and deeply. "The best I can do is to repay you in the only way that I can—the only way that's open to me—for your kindness."

"I won't hear of it," Edward said firmly.

"It was less than twenty-four hours ago," Margie said, "that I was prepared to offer myself to you for money. But you've given me so much more. This is the least I can give you in return."

Edward stared at her. It would be easy—all too easy—to take Margie up on her offer. She was a lovely girl—innocent, fresh, vibrant—qualities he had not seen in a woman in a long while. But he warned himself that he would be doing a disservice to her and to himself if they became sexually—and possibly romantically—involved. He was a man of the world who had lived in all parts of the globe and was familiar with dozens of ways of life. Margie was hardly more than a youngster, a small-town product of New England who, until she'd come to Boise, had never been anywhere and was inexperienced in the ways of the world. He was long accustomed to the power that his wealth exuded. She, however, had always lived modestly and knew nothing about money and its responsibility and power. Once they became involved with one another, their union would prove disastrous. They had too little in common, no matter how much they might end up being drawn to each other, and he had to promise himself to avoid entanglements, for both of their sakes. He had an exciting adventure ahead of him on the Missouri River, and he had already made up his mind that the best thing for Margie—and for him—would be for her to return to the East where she belonged.

"Under no circumstances could I allow myself to take advantage of you," Edward now said to her. "You're vulnerable because of your sense of gratitude, but you owe me nothing. If we were to have a relationship it could only be when you're standing on your own feet and I can approach you as an equal. Perhaps in a year or so when I return to the East we'll meet again. Then this experience will be behind you and forgotten. You'll have your feet on the ground, and you'll be making a new life for yourself. Until then, it's out of the question."

She couldn't believe what she was hearing. Edward Blackstone truly expected nothing from her in return for his generosity. She had never met anyone like this, and suddenly the thought of leaving him filled her with despair. She was sure that once she left Boise, she would never see him again, and her eyes brimming with tears, she leaned toward him, her lips trembling.

Edward looked at her, and the room began to spin. Forgetting his resolve, he took her in his arms. Margie was warm and alive, as he knew she would be, and she responded to his kiss with a fervor so great that it took his breath away.

But he could not and would not be a cad. He now forced his arms to his sides and leaned back on the divan. Both of them were breathing hard.

"We'll go to dinner now," he said at last. "It's high time."

In the next two days, Edward Blackstone's involvement with Margie became even deeper. In addition to paying her rent at the inn and buying her meals, he found it only natural to buy her a new wardrobe, toilet articles, and luggage. The couple kept very much to themselves, and with the exception of the afternoon they had gone shopping, they spent their time at the Boise Inn. By now, they were having their meals served in Margie's room, where they would be spared the inquisitive stares of the other hotel guests and would be able to talk freely and in private.

Margie told Edward more of her life story, how her parents had both died a year earlier in a fire that had burned their house to the ground. She had been left very little money and had lived in a boardinghouse in Portsmouth, biding her time until her fiancé sent for her to come West.

"I had no one else," she told Edward quietly, "and I'd have no one now if it weren't for you."

Again she gave him a look that was filled with longing, and Edward found he had to tear himself away from her before he lost control and took her to bed. She was so young and lovely, so innocent and unself-conscious, that he had all he could do to return to his own suite.

There was no question in either of their minds that Margie was falling in love with him. As for the way he felt toward her, he was uncertain. All he knew was that he was going to make his trip down the Missouri, just as she was going to travel east.

At last the day came when she was scheduled to leave. They ate a farewell dinner at the inn, and when he presented her with a small bouquet of flowers, his gift almost backfired. Margie's eyes filled with tears, and she was so deeply affected that she could not speak for several seconds. Thereafter, she was overly gay to compensate for the aching void that she felt inside.

They collected her new luggage, then slowly walked the short distance to the stagecoach depot. There, various people were engaged in farewell conversations, but Edward found that all at once he had nothing to say. He realized now just how much he regretted having to put Margie on the stagecoach, how he would miss her when she was gone. Any attempts he made to rationalize why they had to part—that she was young, unsophisticated, and naive, that they had too little in common—only succeeded in compounding the misery that he so unexpectedly felt.

Margie was conscious of his inner conflict, as she had been all along, but she kept silent. Her own position was clear. She loved him, and she felt certain that she would never again care for anyone else as much.

What made Edward feel slightly better was the belief that eventually she would get over the way she felt for him and that in time she would regain her equilibrium. Edward knew that he would, too. He had to. He had too much yet to do, too much yet to see.

The stagecoach approached from the direction of the stables, and when it pulled to a halt, the driver busied himself lashing the luggage to the roof.

Edward and Margie stood facing each other. The moment they had dreaded was upon them. It was too late for words, which would have been unnecessary and a waste. With one accord they melted into an embrace, and into their final kiss they put all the unrequited longing that they felt. At last, they drew apart.

"Good-bye, my love," Margie whispered.

"God bless you, Margie," he replied.

She stared into his eyes for a long moment, then turned abruptly toward the stagecoach. He helped her as she climbed into it, and a moment later she sat at the window, forcing a smile as she looked out at him. He stood in the dust of the grounds outside the depot, looking up at her. Perhaps he was insane to send her away, but he had to obey his instincts of what was best for them regardless of how those feelings clashed with their desires.

A moment later the stagecoach began to pull out from the depot. Margie could no longer see Edward standing outside the building, his hat still clutched in his hand. Her tears streaked her face and blurred her vision.

At last, Edward turned away when the stagecoach dwindled in size as it vanished down the road. Jamming his hat onto his head, he walked the short distance back to the inn. Scarcely realizing what he was doing, he walked through the lobby and stared at the settee where he had first seen Margie.

His pain was very great, but he knew he had to bear it, for her sake and for his own.

He went into the bar and ordered a drink for himself. When the bartender gave it to him, he clutched it in one hand and then raised it into the air. "Blackstone," he murmured, "here's to you, you damn fool!"

Toby Holt's replacement as governor had not arrived by the time Millicent's new restaurant had opened. Therefore, he and Clarissa were able to attend the opening night festivities and were given a large table. Joining them were Lieutenant Governor Rob Martin and his bride, Kale, who had been married several days earlier by Governor Holt in a simple civil ceremony.

Seated at another table were newlyweds Jim and Pamela Randall, who also had been joined in wedlock by Governor Holt. With them was Edward Blackstone, the sponsor of the establishment, looking dashing and self-assured as always. No one seeing him tonight would ever know of his recent interlude with Margie White and the fact that for a brief time he had not been quite so sure of whom—or what—he wanted.

The cousins had managed to persuade Millicent to call the restaurant "Millicent's," which she had finally, reluctantly agreed to do. Tastefully but modestly attired in a black gown with white collar and cuffs, she seemed to be everywhere at once on opening night, hurrying between the kitchen and the dining room, generally making certain that service was smooth and prompt, and that all went well in the kitchen. Toby and Clarissa took note of her activities, reflecting that Edward was completely right: Millicent was in her element. Her shyness was forgotten, and she was genuinely concerned over the welfare of her guests. She approved of every dish before it left the kitchen, and she circulated through the dining room constantly to make certain that the guests were satisfied and that they were enjoying what they had ordered.

The restaurant was a success from the night it first opened its doors. It instantly became the most popular dining establishment in Boise, and its renown for first-rate food spread quickly throughout the West to cities as far as Denver and San Francisco. Out-of-town visitors clamored for tables, as did the local citizens who could afford to pay Millicent's relatively high prices. It was the boast of the proud proprietress that no one ever left the restaurant hungry, and she went to extraordinary lengths to ensure that her high standards were consistently maintained.

When the new governor finally arrived in Boise, Edward Blackstone attended a farewell dinner for Toby at Millicent's, and during the course of the evening, he observed quietly to the guest of honor, "I'm definitely going ahead with my plans to travel down the Missouri by boat. I've written to the Harding Line at Fort Benton. I didn't want to make any moves until I was sure that Millicent would be all right here, and she's successful beyond my imagination and her own dreams." He didn't add that he also prayed daily for Margie's well-being and success.

Not everyone in Boise was pleased by Millicent Randall's good fortune, however. Suffering the greatest disappointment was Suzanne, the blond bordello owner whose attempt to expand her business by hiring Kale Salton had failed miserably, and who had experienced defeat a second time when Edward

Blackstone had taken Margie White away from her and had beaten up her hired man.

It seemed that the damned Englishman was constantly meddling in her affairs. Even when Suzanne had entered a bid for Davenport's building as soon as she had learned of the owner's death—it being her intention to transform the place into a brothel that would have been much larger than her present establishment—she had been outbid by Edward Blackstone.

Determined not to let these defeats get her down, Suzanne had wired a reliable contact in San Francisco to hire three new women for her Boise establishment. The madam made it clear that these women had to be real stunners, far more attractive than any of the current women in her bordello.

When the women finally arrived in Boise—causing quite a stir at the stagecoach depot—Suzanne faced the problem of advertising her new wares. She soon hit on a simple scheme, however. She would take advantage of Millicent's restaurant by going there for dinner, accompanied by Carmen, the most attractive and expensive of her new employees. She believed Carmen could fill the gap that she had wanted Kale to occupy, and explaining the situation to her new employee, she suggested that Carmen make no secret of her availability when they went to the restaurant.

Now, having taken the precaution of reserving a prominent table, Suzanne dressed for the evening and then went to the sumptuously furnished chamber that Kale had briefly occupied. There she sat in an easy chair and watched Carmen primp for her initial appearance in Boise.

Watching Carmen brushing her long, auburn hair, Suzanne realized that she was enjoying good fortune. She had found a star for her stable who was easily as stunning as Kale and who in the long run would probably prove more reliable. Based on the income she expected Carmen to generate, in addition to what the other two newcomers would earn, Suzanne would be able to double what she made, provided that she found suitable facilities for such an expanded business. Her need for a large, well-located place like Davenport's— as she still thought of Millicent's establishment—was more urgent than ever, and in one way or another, she would have to do something about it.

Carmen added kohl to the rims around her eyes, put on an extra coat of lip rouge, and affixed a red velvet flower to her hair. "How do I look?" she asked as she turned.

"Stand up, please," Suzanne said and walked around her, examining her critically. Admiring the snug, smooth fit of the girl's skirt, she couldn't resist stroking her buttocks and then circled to the front of her. It was apparent at a quick glance that Carmen wore no brassiere, but her appearance was somehow lacking in drama, in daring.

Suzanne stood, lost in thought for several moments. Then she reached for a tiny black velvet patch on the dressing table and, with it, a small container of glue. Then she opened another button on Carmen's blouse and deliberately began to toy with the girl's breasts. Smiling in satisfaction when the nipples hardened, she affixed a beauty patch to Carmen's skin above her cleavage, calling attention to it. "I've engaged us a table close to the entrance," she said, "so it should be quite chilly whenever anyone comes in or out. That will help your breasts to stay firm, and that's all to the good."

Carmen nodded. Obviously she was working for a woman who knew her business.

Suzanne wound a long silk scarf around the other woman's head and neck, then helped her into a fur coat. "Unfortunately," she said, "we don't have an elegant carriage to drive to the restaurant, but we have only a very short way to walk."

They made their way to Millicent's, which was crowded in spite of the cold, and were given their table at once.

Carmen removed her scarf and coat, each movement deliberate and calculated to draw attention to herself. Suzanne was pleased to note that every eye in the place was riveted on the girl. The auburn-haired beauty was a natural actress, and her performance was letter-perfect. Carmen dared to order a gin and bitters, and while waiting for it, she caused a fresh stir in the restaurant by lighting a long, thin Havana cigar, which she puffed nonchalantly but with obvious familiarity. Any man in the place looking at her knew at a glance that she was erotically experienced in the ways of the world. The demand for her services was certain to begin that very night.

The two women ordered their dinner, and as they ate leisurely, with Carmen deliberately posing between bites, those watching her noted that she was totally unself-conscious about appearing in public seminude and that she was exuding an aura of intense sexuality.

The more Suzanne observed the effect her new employee had on the men in the room, the more vitally important it became for her to gain possession of this building. She would leave the new kitchens where they were and would continue to serve meals to clients, but the upstairs rooms would be converted to elegant suites for Carmen and the other two new arrivals, with the other women all housed in attractive rooms on the third floor. Handled correctly, Suzanne saw the business earning a large fortune for her.

Finishing her oxtail soup, Suzanne quietly beckoned to Millicent Randall, who stood nearby holding a sheaf of menus. Millicent went to the table, and when Suzanne offered her a seat, she took it, trying not to show her natural distaste for the young trollop and her brazen, overdressed, older companion.

"My dear," Suzanne said warmly, "you have a truly wonderful place here. It has been furnished exquisitely, and the food lives up to every bit of praise you've been getting."

"Thank you so much," Millicent replied correctly. "I'm glad that you're enjoying it."

"What impresses me most," Suzanne went on, "is the tremendous effort that a success such as you're enjoying entails. You must keep busy for eighteen hours out of every twenty-four!"

"Something like that," Millicent admitted, and quietly adjusted her skirts, which were touching the skirt that Carmen was wearing. It was plain that she had no use for the woman and wanted to put as much distance as possible between them.

Carmen was conscious of the insult, but long accustomed to what "good" women thought of her, she paid no attention to it.

Suzanne was aware of the gesture, too, and smiled to herself. This was one time when the righteous were not going to triumph, she thought, not if she had anything to do with it. "I wonder," Suzanne said, "if I could interest you in selling the restaurant?"

Millicent was so startled she could only stare at the woman.

"I'm willing to make you a generous offer," Suzanne said, "enough to pay for the improvements that your cousin Edward made, plus the cost of all your new equipment—and then some. In fact, you could retire and live on the income from the capital for the rest of your days."

Millicent tried in vain to conceal her incredulity. "You'd continue to operate a restaurant here?"

"Well, yes, in a manner of speaking." Suzanne hedged. "I certainly would find employment for all your kitchen help, and for a number of your waiters as well. Actually, I'd operate the restaurant in conjunction with a rather specialized hotel that I have in mind."

Millicent needed no explanation of the type of hotel the woman meant. "I'm terribly sorry," she said, "but I'm afraid I have no interest in any deal, at least at present. My cousin was kind enough to set me up in business at a considerable expense, and I'm delighted to find that I have a natural knack for the restaurant business. Our initial success has whetted my appetite for more, and I daresay I'll be in this business for a long time to come, operating out of my present quarters. Thank you for your interest, and I wish you the best of good fortune in finding some other place to establish your—hotel." She smiled impersonally and, gathering her skirts, left the table.

"Snooty bitch," Carmen said. "I need another gin."

"Of course," Suzanne said, stroking the other woman's thigh beneath the tabletop. "Never you fear, though. She can refuse me all she likes, and it doesn't matter. I've got to have this building, and believe me, I shall have it! This place is going to be mine, and if I've got to trample on Millicent Randall in order to get it, that's just too bad—for her!"

*   *   *

Two regiments of regular army troops were ferried across the Columbia River from Fort Vancouver, as was the post band. Scores of people lined the road that led into downtown Portland, and the closer one traveled to the center of town, the thicker the crowds became. Toby Holt and Rob Martin, the reluctant heroes of the occasion, were mounted on their respective horses and rode on opposite sides of the open carriage. They were en route to the Portland City Hall, where General Lee Blake, acting as the deputy for President Grant, would award them with citations thanking them for their services to the United States.

In the carriage rode their wives and children. Clarissa Holt wore an off-the-face hat that enabled the crowd to see her smile clearly. She tried in vain to tamp down Tim, who bounced up and down in time to the music provided by the army post band and waved uninhibited greetings to the cheering crowd. Kale, who was hatless, held the wide-eyed Cathy in her arms. Unlike Clarissa, Kale was sober-faced.

The band ended a number, the crowd grew quiet for a few moments, and as the carriage rattled on the cobblestones, it was possible to converse briefly. "I feel like an interloper, an impostor," Kale said to Clarissa. "This is a most uncomfortable experience."

Clarissa shook her head. "You're wrong to feel that way," she said firmly. "Rob is regarded as a hero and is being rewarded accordingly by President Grant. So you—as his wife—are expected to share in the glory with him."

"I can't," Kale replied. "I still feel strange as Rob's wife.

I have no idea whether the people of Oregon accept me as Mrs. Rob Martin.''

"If they disliked you," Clarissa said emphatically, "you'd know it fast enough, believe me!"

The band struck up another tune, making further conversation impossible, and Clarissa saw that her words had been without effect. Although Kale forced herself occasionally to smile at the crowd, she was noticeably tense and sat with the fingers of her left hand tightly clenched, while she gripped Cathy hard with her right.

Rob, waving his broad-brimmed hat to the throngs, looked down at his wife and smiled warmly at her. Kale tried to respond in kind, but her return smile was wan and forced.

Toby couldn't help wondering why there was all the fuss. He had done his duty as he had seen it, and he had been fortunate that it had paid off. Peace in Idaho and throughout the Pacific Northwest was now assured. Those who really deserved the acclaim, he thought, were the settlers, who endured many hardships as they eked out a living on the land they had chosen.

Toby looked down at his wife in the carriage beside him and said something to her.

Clarissa saw his lips move, but the music was too loud for her to hear what he was saying. That was unimportant, however, because she saw the look in his eyes, and that was all that mattered. She knew she had his total love.

Tim was growing wilder, dancing up and down on the carriage seat as he became increasingly excited, and Clarissa knew she was going to have to do something more to quell his enthusiasm. Obviously, his father knew it, too, because

Toby suddenly reached down, plucked up Tim, and held him fast in one strong arm.

The crowds were three and four deep as the procession drew near to the heart of the business district, where the ceremonies would be conducted. At the same moment, Toby and Clarissa caught sight of a huge banner strung across the road, high overhead:

WELCOME   HOME,   CLARISSA   AND   TOBY

Kale saw the sign, too, and all at once she ached all over. That greeting was a spontaneous gesture of affection toward the Holts, and she knew how proud Clarissa must feel, and how secure she must be in the knowledge that she shared the popularity of her husband.

All at once, another sign loomed ahead. It read:

WELCOME   TO   PORTLAND,   KALE   AND   ROB

Kale found it difficult to believe the evidence before her own eyes. The people of Portland were extending a welcome to her as an individual, not just as Rob's wife, to become part of their community, of their lives. She had paid lip service to Rob's contention that people cared only about what she was, not what she had been. Now, suddenly and unexpectedly, his statement had come true. She was being welcomed to Oregon, her past safely behind her, and she felt a warmth suffuse her.

Blinking back the tears that came to her eyes, Kale looked ahead and, seeing the reviewing stand in the distance, recognized Rob's parents, who were waiting to honor her as well as him. Her heart filled with joy and gratitude, she looked up at her husband and exchanged a smile of complete bliss with him. As he had indicated to her repeatedly, all was going to be right in their world.

STAGECOACH STATION 13:

CARSON CITY

by Hank Mitchum

Frank Gannon's dark mood matched the weather. The stage-coach he was riding east from Placerville, California, to the Washoe region of Nevada had left the springtime of May 1864 behind. Overnight, the climb into the Sierra Nevada had brought back winter. Late snowdrifts blanketed the towering granite peaks. Dropping away from Echo Summit, with Lake Tahoe to the north and Carson Valley dead ahead, the snow cover was raveling out to ragged drifts. Overhead, swollen clouds hung heavy in the sky. Sharp wind gusts raked the trees, whipped at the stagecoach, and forced Gannon and the driver, who sat beside him atop the vehicle, to pull their hat brims low and to settle deeper into their windbreakers.

The driver, a solidly built and whiskered man named Barney Powers, had taken over the reins at the last station and had been wanting to talk ever since. But he had respected Gannon's obvious desire for silence and kept his horses working in their harness as the big Concord coach rolled smoothly over the twists and turns of the mountain road. Finally, Powers blurted out the question that was eating at him. "Is it true, Frank? Are you really bein' called onto the carpet? Word's travelin' all along the line 'bout a telegram orderin' you back to Carson City. To a meetin' with old Ben Holladay!"

Gannon glanced quickly at his driver and then forward again at the horses and the road winding before them through dark ranks of timber. "I suppose bad news moves quickest," he commented dryly. "Don't worry about it, Barney. It's my problem. It goes with the job."

"But it ain't fair," the driver protested angrily. "Holladay's goin' to lay it on you for everything that's gone wrong with this division. The truth is we're all of us at fault. Hell, you've been the finest boss any of us ever worked for. And here we've gone and let you down!"

"That's nonsense," Gannon said firmly, shifting his six-foot frame on the wooden seat.

"Then why are things in such a mess?"

"Not because anyone's laid down on the job," Gannon insisted. "Drivers, guards, station tenders—there's not a man in this division but would put his neck on the line for the good of the Overland. I don't need to name the ones that already have. But these past months have put us up against a situation different from any we've faced before."

"Yeah . . ." Powers said, his voice trailing away while both men thought of recent events. During the last week, another shipment of silver bullion had been stolen by outlaws, and in another incident, two company men had been killed at Eagle Point Station and all the stage-line horses stolen from the corral.

"The fact remains," Gannon went on, "Holladay promoted me and put me in charge of this final stretch west of Carson City. He's going to want to know why things haven't been ironed out. It's his right—and he can't be blamed for not being interested in excuses."

Silence once again fell between the two men. As the morning wore on the road gradually dropped out of the higher reaches of the hills. Low clouds continued to scuttle before the push of crosscurrents, but the coach was protected by the mountains. Frank Gannon knew every mile of the Kingsbury grade, every pass and switchback. Before his promotion to division agent, he had driven plenty of stages over it himself. Only a few years earlier, this heavily traveled route between California and the Comstock region of Nevada had been a tortuous thoroughfare of wheel ruts worn into barren rock. Thousands of travelers had crossed it, along with tons of freighted supplies for Nevada's burgeoning silver camps and millions of dollars in Washoe silver. The toll road had been macadamized for its entire length at a reputed cost of more than fifty thousand dollars. The paving job had smoothed out some of the most arduous places and shaved a little off the twenty-four-hour run for Ben Holladay's Overland Mail and Express Company stage line.

Still, the trip could be a tough haul for both vehicles and team horses, to say nothing of the passengers, who had to endure to exhaustion the constant sway and jostling as they sat on the crowded coach seats or clung to places on the roof, with only the briefest of stops at the scattered stage stations.

The coach on which Frank Gannon rode had left Placerville the previous evening at dusk. It had been a bone-chilling night and a bleak and sunless morning, but without any real incident. Gannon had had plenty of time during the trip to think about the telegram in his pocket and about the meeting that awaited him with his employer. As noon approached, the stagecoach came through a shallow pass, and suddenly Carson Valley opened before it under weak shafts of sunlight spearing through broken fields of clouds. The toll road leveled off. Just where it joined the ancient emigrant route, a cluster of buildings marked one of the Overland's principal stations.

It was a peaceful scene. Smoke rose from the chimney of the main house, and a couple of stock tenders stood ready to unhook the tired stage horses and replace them with fresh teams. Barney Powers yelled to spur his horses into a faster pace, bringing his coach in with grand style. As they rolled nearer he looked at Gannon and said, "Well—so far, so good. We're out of the hills, practically into civilization. Ain't likely now we'd run into trouble."

"We'll hope so." Gannon was not inclined to take anything for granted.

The station came alive as they rolled in. Stock tenders waved and yelled a greeting, and the stationmaster came out onto the porch to watch them arrive. Powers brought his horses up with a flourish that set the big Concord coach rocking on its thoroughbraces; then he stayed aboard while the lathered horses were being unhitched. Frank Gannon stepped down from the high front wheel and swung the iron step into position. He opened the door of the coach for his weary and half-frozen passengers, who climbed stiffly but gratefully from their places.

Of the eight people in the stage, all but one were men. They were the usual mixed bag, including a couple whom Gannon knew personally—a mine superintendent from the Comstock and a law clerk returning to his post at the Nevada territorial capital in Carson City.

It was the woman who had caught Gannon's attention. It was only natural that she would, since she was alone in a coach full of male strangers. Throughout the dark night Gannon had wondered how she was, wrapped in the robes and blankets the stage line provided and with men sleeping or talking around her. The fact that she was uncommonly pretty—blue-eyed under a wing of auburn hair that showed beneath the edge of the hat she wore for traveling—had made him take particular notice of her the moment he first saw her waiting to board the stage at Placerville.

He took her hand to help her down and was surprised by her strong, sure grip. Her step was light in spite of the cramp and chill of hours on a crowded coach seat. "You can see we're down off the mountains," he told her. "The rest of the way will be level going. I hope you haven't had too bad a time of it."

The answering look she gave him was direct, making him suddenly conscious of his two-days' stubble of beard. There was a distinct reserve in her voice as she said, "I'm fine, thank you. Famished, at the moment."

Gannon nodded toward the station. "Here's the place to take care of that. A good, hot meal will be welcome for all of us."

"I've never made this trip," she remarked. "How much longer is it to Carson City?"

"There'll be one more stop, at Genoa. We should hit Carson City well before dark." She thanked him with a smile and a nod. It was the thought of her alone in a strange place that bothered Gannon enough to venture a personal question. "Will you be meeting someone?"

He had thought it would be harmless enough to ask, but perhaps it had been a mistake. As though resenting his curiosity, she withdrew behind rather cool formality and her answer was brief. "Yes, I am. My husband."

"I see."

As he stood aside so she could move toward the station building, he had a rueful sensation of having been put in his place.

A voice from inside the coach commented, "That's a handsome young lady. Married, unfortunately."

The last person to step down from the coach was a tall, spare, and grizzled man in a canvas windbreaker, slightly stooped but with a hint of strength in the set of his jaw and with intelligence in the eyes that peered from beneath a gray thicket of brow.

Gannon nodded. "She just now told me she'd be meeting her husband at Carson City."

"Then you got as much out of her as I've managed in all the time since we left Placerville. I guess she's pretty enough to be choosy about who she talks to and how much she says. I did get her name, at least. It's Kirby—Laura Kirby, I believe she said. I never learned anything at all about her husband."

Since Gannon considered this to be no business of either of them, he thought it time to change the subject. "I don't remember that we introduced ourselves. I'm Frank Gannon," he said.

The other man nodded. "I already know who you are—division agent for the Overland. My name's Fox. Linus Fox," he said, offering his strong but bony hand.

Gannon indicated the front of the other man's coat. "Did I see a sheriff's star under there?"

Linus Fox pulled aside the front of the canvas jacket, revealing the metal star pinned to the front of the coat he wore underneath. "I carry the badge over at San Andreas," he explained, "north of Placerville. I guess by rights I really should take it off while I'm outside my own bailiwick—the gun, too." He touched the revolver in its well-worn holster, which he carried openly on his right leg.

"Fact is," Sheriff Fox went on, "I'm here on business. Got extradition papers on a prisoner in the pen at Carson City. Soon as I have your Nevada governor's John Hancock, I can collect my man and take him back to California to hang for murder. I was wanting to ask you if there'll be any problem taking him on the stage."

"Not so long as you keep him under control," Gannon replied.

"Don't worry. I intend to handle this fellow with real caution. I understand he's something of a wild man when he's crossed. A couple years ago, before my time, he tried to hold up a store and went berserk. Put three bullets into the owner when the man argued with him. He was tried and convicted but killed a guard and got away 'fore they could hang him. Nothing more was seen or heard of him after that, until a story in a newspaper said he'd been arrested and convicted here in Nevada—for stage robbery."

Gannon looked up sharply. "Stage robbery? What's the man's name?"

"Bart Kramer. You know about him?" Fox asked, curious about Gannon's reaction to the name.

"I should. I helped put him in prison. There's been a gang operating in these mountains. They've given us nothing but trouble on this stretch of the Overland, west of Carson City. With a hundred miles of toll road to cover, there's nothing much the stage line, or the local law, has been able to do." Gannon shook his head ruefully.

"Just once," he went on, "we've laid hands on a member of the gang. During a raid on one of our treasure coaches, we were able to drive them off—and this Kramer had his horse shot out from under him. We nabbed him before he could get away. The sheriff tried everything he could think of to get some information out of him—who the gang was, where they operated out of, anything. The fellow was too tough, couldn't be made to open his mouth." Gannon kicked at a rock in the road and brushed a shock of brown hair from his forehead.

"Finally there was nothing to do but try him on the evidence. We had only the one count against him. I testified at the trial. He was convicted, and the judge gave him a full twenty years, but made it clear there could probably be a shorter sentence if Kramer would only decide to open up and inform on the rest of his gang."

"But no luck?" Sheriff Fox asked.

"It's been over a month and he hasn't opened his mouth— either from sheer stubbornness or his own strange notions of honor. Given enough time, we'd thought he might still soften up and decide to talk." With a sharp look at the lawman from California, he added, "But now you show up, wanting to take him out of our hands and *hang* him—close his mouth forever."

A sudden coldness settled between the two men. The lawman considered Gannon for a moment, then said, "Yes, I can see you might object to that. I'm sorry. But according to the law, murder has to take precedence over other crimes. Soon as these extradition papers are signed I'll be taking Bart Kramer back to California. If possible, I'd like to do my job without raising any hard feelings. But I intend to do it!"

They stared at each other. "I suppose you're only doing your job," Gannon said flatly.

"I hope we can manage to be civil about it, at least." From an inner pocket Sheriff Fox produced a leather cigar case, opened it, and offered it to the other man. Gannon hesitated, then accepted one of the cigars with a nod.

"Thanks," he said. "I'll save it for after dinner." They followed the rest of the passengers into the station.

When Gannon lit up his cigar an hour later, the stagecoach was rolling once again, behind fresh and rested teams. He got the cigar burning smoothly, and the wind of their passage carried the smoke across his shoulder. He found himself thinking of Laura Kirby, recalling the hesitant smile she had given him as he helped her back into the coach. Perhaps she had wanted to make amends for her earlier brusqueness, he thought. At least he chose to take it that way. A Virginian by birth, Frank Gannon still retained a Southerner's idealistic attitude toward women, in spite of the time he had spent on the frontier. He tended to think of them as something apart and very special. And though Laura Kirby traveled alone in a rough country, and with great self-reliance, there was something—perhaps in her very directness—he found attractive about her.

But with Carson City only hours away, Gannon told himself he had better start thinking about his approaching meeting with Ben Holladay.

Word of his employer's coming had been wired from Salt Lake City to Placerville. Though no purpose for the summons had been mentioned, Gannon had no doubt why he was being called back. He already had decided there was nothing to do but to be completely open and frank about the problems besetting his stretch of the Overland on the border between Nevada and California. After all, Holladay, back in his eastern office, had an uncanny way of seeming to know everything anyhow. Gannon was grateful for his promotion. He had done his best, and it was for Holladay to decide whether he should continue in the job.

The new teams of horses had settled to a familiar, mile-eating gait. The road was level, running north along the old Emigrant Road with the sage flats of Carson Valley wheeling past on the right and sparsely timbered foothills lifting dramatically above them on the left. As Gannon gazed at the scenery, a wink of reflected sunlight caught the corner of his eye.

Instantly alert, he peered closely in the direction of the flash but saw nothing except rocks and trees. But he knew that momentary flash could only have been reflected from metal. Instinctively Gannon leaned forward, groping for the rifle underneath the seat. Even as his hands closed on the weapon he heard the unmistakable report of a gunshot. Its echoes were still bouncing along the hills as he straightened with the rifle in his hands, looking for a target.

He glimpsed a faint wisp of powder smoke, but it was instantly lost in the screen of scrub timber and the forward motion of the coach. A sound from the driver next to him made Gannon turn in alarm. Barney Powers was beginning to slide off the seat into the boot, his head hanging loosely to one side, the reins slipping from his grasp. Gannon caught a glimpse of blood but knew there was no time to learn where or how badly Powers was hurt. He let go of his rifle and grabbed for the leather reins, barely managing to trap them before they were lost.

Making sure the stagecoach did not race out of control must be his only concern. All he could do for Barney Powers was to ram an elbow against the man and try to keep his limp body from sliding farther off the seat. Genoa lay ahead. There the wounded man could be tended to. At the moment Gannon had to get the stage and its passengers to safety.

He heard more shooting—hand guns, this time—and glimpsed a line of horsemen racing down a gully toward the road. From one of the coach windows below him, a gun suddenly opened up. Gannon yelled at the startled horses, shaking the lines to straighten them out. Instantly the horses lunged into their harness, and the stage gave a lurch as it picked up speed, leaving the attackers behind.

One persistent thought forced its way into Frank's mind as he drove the team for all it was worth: If he had not caught that wink of sunlight on a rifle barrel and hastily reached into the boot for his own weapon, he would probably have taken the bullet that had passed above his bent shoulders and struck Barney Powers instead.

The unknown enemies of the Overland Stage might have discovered that the division agent was riding this particular coach into Carson City. Gannon shuddered involuntarily at his next thought: That bullet could actually have been meant for him!

Explosive danger, gripping romance and adventure await the men and women of Carson City. Don't miss STAGECOACH STATION 13: CARSON CITY, on sale wherever Bantam paperbacks are sold.

Please turn the page for news of other STAGECOACH adventures you'll enjoy.

FROM THE
CREATORS OF WAGONS WEST

STAGECOACH

"The Stagecoach *series is great frontier entertainment. Hank Mitchum really makes the West come alive in each story." —Dana Fuller Ross, author of WAGONS WEST*

Look for these Stagecoach adventures wherever Bantam paperbacks are sold:

STATION ONE: DODGE CITY (23954-6 * $2.50)
The massive Concord stage thundered across the empty lawless miles of the Great Plains bound for the Wickedest Town in the West—Dodge City. It was a wide-open cattle town always itching for a fight, and a big one was about to start. For Burl Channing was on this stage, a Federal marshall hell-bent on a mission of personal vengeance to bring a vicious murderer to justice. The man he seeks is Frank Killian, a cunning gambler with a killer's finely-honed edge. Frightened of one man ,and betrayed by the other, Emily Barker, a beautiful young widow is suddenly caught up in their struggle—a battle that will soon explode in front of the legendary Long Branch Saloon in one of Dodge City's deadliest gunfights.

STATION TWO: LAREDO (24014-5 * $2.50)
At high noon the dusty border pueblo of Laredo would be charged with excitement! The wily curly wolf of an outlaw, Bart Campion—a legend along the Rio Grande—had finally been caught and was about to be hung for murder. Spectators from all over the rugged spine of Texas and beyond filled the

Laredo-bound stages to bursting, including vulnerable eighteen-year-old Molly Bishop desperate to have Bart reveal the answer to the question that has shadowed her entire life before he dies. For help she turns to the strong young rancher Owen Pryor who has his own dark score from the past to settle with Bart and his gang. And he will get his chance because Bart's longriders are also headed for Laredo—sworn to spring Bart free and turn the streets of Laredo to blood.

STATION THREE: CHEYENNE (24015-3 * $2.50)
The magnificent Wells Fargo stage speeds along the perilous trail from Billings, Montana, to Cheyenne, Wyoming, carrying a secret cargo of gold. Riding on board is the beautiful, strong-willed Caroline Wells, a young woman who will risk the dangers of marauding Indians, treacherous frontier and the darkest corners of Cheyenne to bring her runaway brother back home. She finds help in the proud, rugged rancher Kyle Warner. Kyle has a debt to pay to the man who once saved his life—and a score to settle with a band of bloodthirsty, revenge-seeking highwaymen who are planning a vicious showdown on the back streets of Cheyenne.

STATION FOUR: TOMBSTONE (24009-9 * $2.50)
It was The Town Too Tough to Die, Tombstone, the biggest and wildest site in the Arizona Territory. Up to now Wyatt Earp had ruled the town, walking the hard line of law and order. But many feared Earp's ruthless ways and the guns of his brothers and the notorious Doc Holliday who were in his control. There were even those who suspected Earp of breaking the law himself. That's why investigator Dan Stockard was secretly sent for, to stop the robbers who were terrorizing the treasure coaches from the Tombstone mines—even if the trail led right to the Earps. Stockard soon discovered that at any moment you could find yourself rubbing elbows with your deadliest enemy in Tombstone. His only ally is the beautiful Nellie Cashman, the one woman brave enough to stand up to the Earps. Yet time was against Stockard, for soon all of Tombstone would explode in the streets near the O.K. Corral in the West's most famous gunfight.

STATION FIVE: VIRGINIA CITY (24016-1 * $2.50)
Grant Jordan, ex-Rebel, spent the years after the war as a sometime buffalo hunter and full-time loner. Until he rescued Gwen Quinn from the Indians attacking her stage near

Virginia City, Montana. She was determined to carry vital supplies to her father's hard-rock mine through hostile Indian country. Jordan couldn't let Gwen travel unprotected, just as he couldn't stop himself from risking his life to stop an ambitious army captain from executing a brutal massacre against Crow Indians Jordan knew to be peaceful. Suddenly, Jordan was racing with Gwen along a torturous mountain road with both the cavalry and the Indians chasing them and nothing but an unstoppable Concord mudwagon, their stubborn courage, and their growing love to get them through.

STATION SIX: SANTA FE (23314-9 * $2.50)
When he led the westbound stage out of Kansas, Clay Reiner, chief field agent of the Hanlon Stage Line, had no idea how severely this trip would test his skills as a troubleshooter. During the grueling four and a half day run to Santa Fe, Reiner must lead the passengers through savage mountain weather, Indian warriors, and scavenger outlaws. However, one of the passengers is being stalked by a menace that is even deadlier because it comes from an unexpected source. Beth Hanlon, the stage owner's spirited daughter, has been rushing home to be reunited with her father and her fiancé, Frank Colby. When Colby unexpectedly rides out to join her on the stage Beth has no idea that he is a wanted man—on the run from the vicious murder he has committed to cover up his embezzlement from her father's company. Colby's desperate escape plans threaten Beth and every man, woman, and child on the Santa Fe Stage—unless Clay Reiner can expose his secret and bring him to justice.

STATION SEVEN: SEATTLE (23428-5 * $2.50)
To the far frontiers of the Pacific Northwest fled the dreamers, like Kate Harrow. She was willing to lead a stage full of women on the hazardous journey through the Rockies, to challenge the hairpin mountain trails and the raging swollen rivers for the chance to make a new start in the rugged coastal mining camp of Seattle. But the greatest danger came from the Indian Red Feather and his band of renegade braves, and there was only one man worth a damn in Indian country, only one man who could safely escort Kate's stage: Scott Winslow, former U.S. Deputy Marshal. Unknown to Kate, however, Winslow's skills were endangered by his relentless vengeance hunt for a brutal killer. Yet even after their stage joins forces with a wagon team of settlers, Kate and Scott cannot escape the

stalking treachery of Red Feather. For the renegade chief has a secret partner, a member of the wagon party whom the Indians call Crooked Face: a man who plans to betray his own people, and has sworn that all those who hoped to find new lives in Seattle will find only savage death along the trail.

STATION EIGHT: FORT YUMA (23593-1 * $2.50)

They struck as swiftly as deadly desert snakes. Ernie Bodine's gang ambushed his army escort and suddenly the outlaw leader had cheated the law of his date at Fort Yuma prison. Bounty hunter Luke Faraday caught Bodine once—and is now more determined than ever to bring the killers to justice, especially when Bodine brutally kidnaps a beautiful young woman. Stage passenger Lorene Martin wants to help Faraday track the gang and free their hostage . . . but with a renegade band of Apaches raging through the Southwest Territory, Lorene and Faraday face savagery down every trail.

STATION NINE: SONORA (23723-3 * $2.50)

When gold fever raged through the California boom town there was usually enough money riding the stages to tempt an angel—and the Sonora Kid was no angel. Hidden beneath his black silk hood he waged an unstoppable one-man war of violence and robbery against the gringos he despised. Aboard the Sonora stage Marcia Cortland would not let even the fear of the Kid sway her from continuing her cross-country search for her brother, who mysteriously disappeared in the gold-diggings. As her hunt becomes more desperate, Marcia accepts the help of young prospector Dan Prentiss. Trapped in a wilderness of treachery, they must test the strength of their courage against the avenging madman who hopes to bring Sonora to its knees.

STATION TEN: ABILENE (23858-2 * $2.50)

"Hell is in session!" was a cry that rang through Abilene's untamed streets. Notorious as a wild end-of-the-trail town, Abilene reeked of gambling, drinking, and fighting—and at any time, day or night, cowboys full of whiskey courage could set off shock waves of sudden death. In desperation the town's leaders brought in a new marshal: the legendary gunfighter "Wild Bill" Hickok. He was a hard man who brought a hard law to Abilene . . . the law of his lightning-quick guns. Yet Hickok stirred up his own deadly controversy. Some thought him too bloody, and others sought the new marshal out as a target to prove their manhood. Crusading Eastern reporter Elliot Carson and struggling divorcee Conni Witherspoon are new to Abilene's dangers, but are soon swept up in the raging turmoil of a town ready to explode.

STATION ELEVEN: DEADWOOD (23998-8 * $2.50)
Out of the Black Hills of the Dakota Territory the raw mining town of Deadwood exploded. During the bustling summer of 1876 a brave and colorful troupe of theatrical performers arrives by stage to cash in on the boom town wealth. Suddenly, they are swept into the deadly drama about to be played out on the streets of Deadwood—side by side with the legendary Calamity Jane and Wild Bill Hickok. As ruthless gambling-hall owner Johnny Varnes plots to take control of this rough, teeming town, he finds his schemes obstructed by two tough opponents, stage owner Tom Murdock and Wild Bill. Varnes' simple—and vicious—solution is to remove both adversaries with a bullet. Trapped in the middle of the battle is the beautiful actress Ellen Dorsey, whose growing love for Murdock and compassion for the victims of Varnes' brutality leads her to an act of heroism that could prove to be the difference between life and death in deadwood.

STATION TWELVE: TUCSON (24126-5 * $2.50)
They shared a father but little else besides a burning hatred for each other. Jonathan and Cooper Dundee, half-brothers locked in a stubborn struggle to control the Dundee ranch and transport empire. With brutal cunning, Jonathan launched a ruthless plan to sell out the rest of his family for his own gain. But then his secret partners got impatient, and set loose a bloody double cross that moved events beyond his control, a shocking betrayal that endangered all the Dundees—as well as the fiery Regan O'Rourke, already torn by her mixed feelings for both Jonathan and Cooper. Suddenly a seething family rivalry boiled over into a wave of terror, kidnapping and murder that threatened the entire Arizona territory.

★ WAGONS WEST ★

A series of unforgettable books that trace the lives of a dauntless band of pioneering men, women, and children as they brave the hazards of an untamed land in their trek across America. This legendary caravan of people forge a new link in the wilderness. They are Americans from the North and the South, alongside immigrants, Blacks, and Indians, who wage fierce daily battles for survival on this uncompromising journey—each to their private destinies as they fulfill their greatest dreams.

☐	24408	**INDEPENDENCE! #1**	$3.95
☐	24651	**NEBRASKA! #2**	$3.95
☐	24229	**WYOMING! #3**	$3.95
☐	24088	**OREGON! #4**	$3.95
☐	26070	**TEXAS! #5**	$4.50
☐	24655	**CALIFORNIA! #6**	$3.95
☐	24694	**COLORADO! #7**	$3.95
☐	26069	**NEVADA! #8**	$4.50
☐	25010	**WASHINGTON! #9**	$3.95
☐	22925	**MONTANA! #10**	$3.95
☐	23572	**DAKOTA! #11**	$3.95
☐	23921	**UTAH! #12**	$3.95
☐	26071	**IDAHO! #13**	$4.50
☐	24584	**MISSOURI! #14**	$3.95
☐	24976	**MISSISSIPPI! #15**	$3.95
☐	25247	**LOUISIANA! #16**	$3.95

Prices and availability subject to change without notice.

Buy them at your local bookstore or use this handy coupon: